This Shared Dream

KATHLEEN ANN GOONAN

A TOM DOHERTY ASSOCIATES BOOK
NEW YORK

This is a work of fiction. All of the characters, organizations, and events portrayed in this novel are either products of the author's imagination or are used fictitiously.

THIS SHARED DREAM

Copyright © 2011 by Kathleen Ann Goonan

Edited by David Hartwell

All rights reserved.

A Tor Book
Published by Tom Doherty Associates
175 Fifth Avenue
New York, NY 10010

www.tor-forge.com

Tor® is a registered trademark of Macmillan Publishing Group, LLC.

ISBN 978-0-7653-5210-1

Our books may be purchased in bulk for promotional, educational, or business use. Please contact your local bookseller or the Macmillan Corporate and Premium Sales Department at 1-800-221-7945, extension 5442, or by e-mail at MacmillanSpecialMarkets@macmillan.com.

First Edition: July 2011
First Mass Market Edition: October 2016

Printed in the United States of America

0 9 8 7 6 5 4 3 2 1

For Joseph, with love:
these years are not enough.

ACKNOWLEDGMENTS

Thomas E. Goonan, my father, generously contributed a small portion of his self-written and edited memoirs to *In War Times*. In *This Shared Dream*, Sam Dance's "notebook entry" about the Squounch Club is my father's work, as are other "notebook entries" herein. Thank you, Dad, for all the music, and for your enormous contribution to my life in literature. You and Mom made books my world from the very beginning.

The Serendipity Book Store at Pickett Shopping Center in Fairfax, Virginia, was opened, operated, and owned by Steve and Danni Aloi, a wonderful community-oriented couple, in the late 1960s. It was a popular, wide-ranging bookstore filled with anything you could possibly want, or we would order it immediately. I met the Alois around 1966, and worked in the main store and at all the branches until that dream ended when the original store was destroyed in a tornado on April 1, 1973. The other branches did not remain open for much longer after that.

Many thanks to Steve Aloi, and to the memory of Danni.

Salutations, as well, to those with whom I worked there. You know who you are.

The only remaining book vestige of the Serendipity Crew, that I know of, is Mike Nally's Hole in the Wall Books in Falls Church, Virginia.

Diane "Danni" Aloi passed away on July 4, 2003.

The Serendipity Book Store in this novel is nostalgically named after the original.

The original Halcyon House, after which I have

named the Dances' house, was the name of my friend Marilyn Bott's family home on Staten Island.

Thanks to Ann Wobil for her help with the African chapters, and for countless other, more important acts of dedication and kindness. Thanks to Sage Walker and Steve Brown for reading countless early iterations. And finally, many thanks to David Hartwell and Stacy Hague-Hill for seeing this novel through all its changes.

Eliani Hadntz

TIMESTREAM ONE

[*July 1890, North of St. Petersburg, Russia*]

Y EARS AFTERWARD, Eliani realized that the meadow and the small country dacha belonged to her St. Petersburg grandmother.

The dacha was directly on the shore of a clear, cold lake. On this summer morning, Eliani, five years old, in her second-story bedroom, struggled to button her dress. She was eager to join her mother, Rosa, who was framed by the dormer window and limned by sunlight as she stood below on the weathered dock.

Hands on her hips, Rosa gazed outward, her cotton skirt fluttering in the slight breeze. She turned, saw Eliani, and waved. "Come down!"

As Eliani grew, so did her awareness of her mother's uniqueness. Rosa Hadntz was a medical doctor in an age when very few women were, and was therefore, quite naturally, a feminist. She was also a poet, and a pacifist.

But now, Rosa Hadntz was just her mother, out by the lake.

Eliani gave up on the rest of her buttons. She ran down the stairs, through the house, ignoring the maid's shouted *Slow down!* and pounded onto the dock.

"Be careful of that rotten board," her mother said. She looked back at the house and sighed. "The old house used to be so beautiful. Not so . . . shabby. When I was a little girl, visiting my cousins, it was paradise. White crystal and linen and laughter."

Eliani, used to the looming streets of Vienna, breathed the spice of fir trees and the scent of fresh, clean water. Beyond the meadow, where blue cornflowers swept through tall grass, lay a mysterious, sun-dappled forest, riven by the arrow-straight road that they followed from

train station to carriage house in her grandmother's tarantass, pulled by four black horses.

She saw nothing but vast, open, intense paradise. Below, golden, wave-scalloped sand shimmered through water clear as glass. "Can we swim?"

Rosa smiled down at Eliani, her eyes shadowed by wings of loose, shining black hair. "It's cold," she warned. "And you don't know how. It's easy, though."

To Eliani's surprise, her mother began unbuttoning the long row of buttons on her dress. She shrugged it off, along with the complicated cotton undergarment she wore, stooping, finally, to unlace her low black boots and kick them off. Then she stood on the dock, naked.

Eliani was astonished. Her mother's quintessential space was a dressing room, draped with clothing, which she donned with care and precision. Eliani had, once or twice, glimpsed her mother naked—but never like this! Never boldly, out in the sunlight, framed by forest and green hills.

"Well?" Rosa threw back her head and laughed, not just to her daughter, but also to the lake, the forest, the intense, blue sky. She dashed to the end of the dock, dove in, and surfaced, shrieking and breathless. "Come on, then!"

Eliani undid her just-fastened buttons quickly. The air and the sunlight felt good on her bare skin. She stood on the edge of the dock, hesitated, then jumped. She plummeted down, shocked by the cold, then saw, through the water, her mother's pale, blurred body move toward her. Her mother caught and boosted her to the surface. "Move your arms," Rosa said calmly as Eliani spluttered and coughed and felt a peculiar tang in her nose. "Kick your legs. That's swimming. Good. I'm right here."

Eliani no longer felt the cold, only the cool, unfettered liquid, a new, silken atmosphere. The sun, in contrast, was hot on her back. It was delicious. Her mother's deft hands turned her over so that she squinted at the brilliance and glimpsed a ring of pointed firs surrounding

the circle of blue sky. "Take a deep breath. The air in your lungs is lighter than water. Relax. You'll float."

Her father's violin music suddenly pierced the air, and seemed a part of the forest, the lake, and the house, where he practiced every morning in the parlor.

Eliani looked up at the blue summer sky, cloudless and intense. She took a deep breath, and floated.

Timestream Two

∾

1991

Jill

THE CRACK-UP

[*March 21, Washington, D.C.*]

THE WORST thing was that Jill Dance couldn't talk about what had happened when she was seventeen. Not with anyone.

Their mother had vanished, history had flipped to a new path, her brother and sister had no memory of the years Jill had stolen from them, and the tragedy was entirely her fault. She had been reckless and impulsive, like any teenager, but the consequences had been so shattering that words, explanations, and many memories had been swept from her and her family with the force of a hurricane scouring away homes, historical artifacts, even entire lives. Hurricane Jill.

She had kept it inside until she was forty-one, a doctoral student in political science at Georgetown.

The tall, wavy-glassed windows in the old classroom stood open. A cool, page-riffling breeze, the distant cries of children, and the first sunlight in weeks encouraged students to think of little else. Certainly, no one but Jill was paying attention to their professor, a Soviet expat.

A slow and measured speaker, Koslov framed his English precisely. His pause after "In this case . . ." seemed to last forever.

Jill said, "I disagree."

"On what grounds?" Koslov responded, his normally placid expression roused to interest. One of the undergrads sighed loud. Koslov, a seasoned debater in his seventies, was Jill's doctoral adviser, and they often got into long, obscure disagreements.

Jill stood, and leaned forward, palms pressed against the desk. "After the Soviets took Berlin—"

"Would you mind repeating that?" Koslov's eyes narrowed. He pushed his shaggy gray hair from his forehead and waited, hands on his stocky hips.

"I . . ." She paused. Everyone was looking at her with great interest.

Wait a minute. The Soviets had *not* taken Berlin. The Allies had not handed East Germany to Stalin on a silver platter. Instead, Patton, ignoring orders, forged through Germany and took Berlin before the Soviets could get there, which dramatically changed postwar politics and territories.

She said, "I mean, after Patton argued with Eisenhower about taking Berlin and finally obeyed Eisenhower's orders—" *That* was right, wasn't it? Yes. That was what had happened, *here* . . . or was it *there, before*?

Damn.

She stopped speaking. Somewhere, a bell rang.

Relieved, she stuffed her Q, an all-purpose computer and communicator, into her pack and hurried toward the door, tired and wondering what the hell had gotten into her. It was the last class of her last day at Georgetown—a makeup class, actually, to satisfy her doctoral requirements, one that she would have ordinarily taken when working on her master's degree. She worked part-time at the World Bank, and the full-time job she had taken a hiatus from awaited her, with near-doubled PhD salary. She also worked part-time in her bookstore, Serendipity, and took care of her five-year-old son, Stevie. She didn't have time for this, or much of anything else either.

Koslov boxed her in by the door as the other students rushed out behind him. "Jill?"

"I have to get to an appointment." She tried to get past him. He stepped sideways, blocking her exit.

"Please." Lev Koslov, tie askew, as usual, and his brown suit rumpled, moved in a perpetual haze of acrid cigarette smoke. He favored a Russian brand with a wolf on the package, and did not care if the ashes fell on the floor, on his suit, or on a student's desk as he strutted

past, waving his arms and expounding. With a reputation for being blazingly intelligent, he had little patience with idiocy. Several students, all much younger than Jill, glanced back in surprise as they left, having expected, no doubt, a more barbed approach to her outburst. Like other professors at Georgetown, he frequented her nearby bookshop, Serendipity, so she was not at all intimidated by him.

However, she did not want to discuss her lapse.

He fished his classbook from his jacket pocket. "This is not the first time that you have mentioned such . . . ideas." The book-sized screen lit with print when he touched it. He found what he was looking for and handed it to Jill. "Last week's test."

"I already checked my grade."

"Yes, I gave you an A. As usual. It was the extra-credit question, which you did not need for the grade, as it turned out. I didn't take off for your answer."

She read, "'Since the assassination of John F. Kennedy . . .' Oh." She gave the reader back to him. Kennedy had not been assassinated. Not *here*. He was an international statesman, a celebrity, the father of the space program, as well as the father of several children born to women not married to him. "I'm sorry. I think . . ." She tried to imagine how to gloss over her idiotic outburst, and failed. Either she could say she was going crazy, which she didn't think would cut much slack with Dr. Koslov, or . . .

"I'm writing an alternate history," she said.

"A what?"

"An alternate history. I used to write comic books when I was in high school, and . . ." Damn. Worse and worse. She still had to defend her dissertation before this man. "Well, I must have been thinking about it when I wrote this." She smiled briefly, and, she hoped, disarmingly.

"Mmm." Koslov's long look, from deep-set pale blue eyes beneath tangled gray eyebrows, was one of keen

appraisal. "And in this alternate history, what happened after Kennedy died? I seem to remember that Franklin Roosevelt died too, in his fourth term, before the war was over, instead of completing two years of his fifth term and negotiating the settlement with the Soviet Union that made them relinquish Poland, Hungary, and Romania. What did that difference lead to, in your alternate history? I'm just asking in theoretical terms."

"I'm sorry, but I have to leave." Angry to hear herself apologize for the third time in five minutes, she pushed past him into the now-empty hall and hurried down the stairs.

Jill unlocked her bike, adjusted her helmet, and coasted off campus, disturbed and distracted. Lost in thought, she turned left onto M Street from Wisconsin Avenue instead of right, as she had intended. She passed a rare diesel-powered Metrobus and coughed in the cloud of exhaust. Mostly, the streets swarmed with tiny electric cars, and the new fleet of smaller electric and alternate-fuel Metrobusses. As charging kiosks became more plentiful, it was easy to use a prepurchased pass or a credit card to pick up a car, bike, or scooter, and drop it off at another kiosk, but Jill preferred her own custom-built bike.

But riding through the city was sometimes unpleasant, especially when she was tired. Stress removed some filter, so that the landscape of the city appeared as it was *before,* when the city, and time, and everyone's history, was, sometimes subtly, and sometimes starkly, *other.* She saw the old streets, before a particular overpass was built, before a block was razed for offices. She saw houses, for seconds at a time, which were no longer there. Of course, everyone did, to a certain extent; cities were in constant flux.

Except that Jill saw some houses, she was sure, that

never had been here, in *this* history. Instead, she saw a District of Columbia that was different than the one she lived in now. Different in its past, and therefore changed in those textural details, great and small, that belonged to her previous historical reality.

She saw houses of people who no longer seemed to exist, whom she could never find, even with Q. For instance, she sometimes saw the house of Bridget Donnally, she of the long nose, pale face, and superior attitude who regularly made pronouncements such as, "Dance, if you don't do your best, you won't get anywhere."

Bridget's house, which Jill had often visited, was in a neighborhood that had never existed in this world. For a year or two, Jill had done a lot of research, trying to reconcile the discrepancies, but there was no evolution of land use from residential to commercial. There was only stark difference. The old plat in City Hall showed the Donnally home site as the location of a small hotel for the past hundred and fifty years, in a commercial area presently quasi-bohemian. In Jill's childhood, the same corner held a welcoming old-fashioned single-family house surrounded by oaks and spilling over with Bridget's siblings, also nonexistent in this world, on a block of houses built to order, in a time when that was the norm.

Bridget had always called Jill by her last name. Even in sixth grade, Jill found this odd, coming from another sixth-grader. Jill had been surprised and somewhat gratified to see normally dauntless Bridget immobilized down in the creek bed one day when they were gathering sand to enhance their cardboard Egyptian school project because she suddenly noticed the snake Jill had leapt over without even thinking about it.

"It's just a rat snake. It won't hurt you." Jill grasped it behind its head to show Bridget, but Bridget trembled, all color drained from her face, and insisted that Jill lead her back upstream and uphill to the safe, snakeless

sidewalk. This chink in Bridget's intellectual detachment was Jill's first deep awareness of the difference between persona and hidden emotional triggers.

Bridget was real as real could be. But there was no trace of her or her six siblings on any records Jill found. No one by the name of Donnally had ever attended Jill's school.

So, the hard question she asked herself constantly, was: *Did I kill them all? Did they never exist?*

Did the potential nuclear holocaust that hung over the world back then actually happen? Did Vietnam worsen and consume the United States, as it did in my alternate past? Or are they all happily living, somewhen, each with their own six children, in that world in which Kennedy actually did die in Dallas in 1963, twenty years ago?

The mere fact of Kennedy's living had unfurled a new history. The history she lived in shared many aspects with the one she remembered. But not all. It was keeping the details in place, some to one history, and some to another that was so damned hard.

She cut down a cool, leafy avenue, reflecting that she'd been a fool to go into political science, given this very large problem. But then, history had become like a puzzle to her, one without a solution, only different resolutions, or a kaleidoscope. If you moved one piece, turned the tube one click, the whole picture might change. She wanted to think she was studying the pivots of history, the real world-changers, but she had discovered that every major historian had her own opinion of what such pivots might be.

Jill remembered, as clearly as if looking down one of those lost streets, that Sam Dance, her father, had marveled at the swift miniaturization of computer components, the internationalization of communications satellites and the like, once Kennedy and Khrushchev achieved their historical 1965 alliance. The great scientific and technological minds of the entire world were

free to work together, and they had enabled the sudden emergence of Q in 1983.

She knew that, along with her, Sam could look down the other road of the sixties that they had also lived through, the one with massive Soviet crackdowns, the American assassinations, the Vietnam War, with its ten million Asian and sixty thousand American casualties, and attendant, deadly international student riots.

She also knew that no one else in the milieu in which she lived now—she had taken to calling it a timestream, which elicited the sensation of precarious fluidity that sometimes overwhelmed her—could do that. If they existed, she had not heard from them. She was enveloped by a world that seemed more peaceful, more cooperative, more focused on communication and education, and less focused on aggression. She hoped this was just the beginning of a huge change in human history, which was almost entirely a history of wars.

But her father had vanished. Perhaps, when Sam had disappeared, five years earlier, he had just taken another road, one newly opened. Perhaps he had found an avenue to Bette, Jill's mother, who had vanished in November 1963. She too went on a trip, as far as Jill's brother and sister knew, and never returned. Kind of like going to the corner store for cigarettes, leaving your family to gradually realize that you might be gone for good. But perhaps Bette Dance, née Elegante, had not had much choice.

Jill had to think so. It was wrenching to think that your mother would willingly abandon you. But she had a more precise idea of what had really happened, and all of that was because of the Infinite Game Board.

She downshifted, with a smooth *click* of her gear-changer, to climb a small rise.

She'd had no warning that her father was leaving. Why hadn't he spoken about what had happened? Why hadn't she asked? It always seemed like there would be time for that later, when she would somehow be able to

formulate questions about the enormity that had occurred, or even venture to mention it. Maybe he had felt
the same way.

A horn blared to her left. Jill, startled from her reverie,
veered out of the driver's way and became aware of her
surroundings.

She was on a busy street and not anywhere near Serendipity Books, across from where Key Bridge traffic flowed
onto M Street. Instead, she was only about a mile from
her old family home, Halcyon House, which was in a
completely different Washington neighborhood.

Damn! She wiped sweat from her forehead as she
braked for a red light. Traffic whizzed past in front of
her. She was falling into these fugues more and more often, and was screwing everything up. Elmore was expecting her to take over in their bookstore after her class
today so that he could work on one of his important
cases. He didn't actually work in the store any longer,
but she'd implored him to open this morning when
Jane called in sick, so she could attend this last class.
No doubt he'd been calling her frantically, but she had
not heard her phone over the roar of traffic, the roar of
her own thoughts.

All his cases were important—much more important
than what she was doing, it seemed. Elmore had been
complaining for three years that she was doing too
much. Translation: Suspend your doctoral work so that
I don't have to take care of Stevie. Or at least, if you're
going to go to school, get a useful degree. In law.

His complaints were wearing her down, but he'd get
over it. He'd have to. She loved Elmore. Loved her bookstore, in a town house they'd bought for a song, which
was actually a fortune to them when they'd first married.
They'd finished the gutting that time, neglect, and a leaky
roof had begun, then built it into their dream: a home
upstairs, a bookstore downstairs.

Now, they had moved to a finer address, one with

more cachet, one that would impress the partners in Elmore's law firm. New dreams.

Just not, exactly, hers.

But she could not actually say what her dream might be anymore.

Sometimes, when she perched on a stool behind the counter, studying as customers browsed, she might look up and see a different store, one filled with counterculture freaks. Young men with long hair and beards. Young women wearing brightly colored skirts, Mexican huaraches, or bell-bottom jeans. And then, on her shelves, other titles wavered: *Steal This Book, The Whole Earth Catalog, Howl.* Instead of the classical music her customers preferred, she heard lively, lovely, humane rock 'n' roll with lyrics decrying war.

Jill knew she was insane to long for that world, that history. It was like wanting to revert to dysfunctional, emotionally stunting, but comfortingly familiar family behaviors, wanting to slip back into patterns of pain instead of living the new, happy life years of therapy had wrought. Yes, she thought, the ancient human familiarity with war, the straight lines in which one must march, the submersion of one's own will to that of national intent, were all *so* much better than peace. The new, spreading peace sprang from positions of strength, not from appeasement. People chose peace because, strange and simple as it might sound, people now knew better. With more education, with greater understanding of the costs of war, and of what the results of various actions might be, people worked to find solutions less expensive than war.

This different world had wars, of course. Obscure, distant, small wars.

The problem still was that her small, obscure war was another person's holocaust. Any war was. But what was the solution?

In Jill's opinion, education was the solution.

Radical peace groups distributed classbooks imbued with Q all over the world. Each classbook contained all languages and adapted to the one it heard when the first person picked it up. Q constantly assessed and challenged each user, meshing with individual learning styles. Anecdotal stories about a child walking through a field or a slum, picking one up, and having it talk to her, show her pictures, shapes, games, anything that would get her moving her fingers and thereby her mind, abounded. Jill had heard rumors that an international children's pidgin, like Esperanto, was evolving, but from the bottom up, instead of being foisted on adults, so that it actually worked.

Before the age of eight, the manipulation of concrete, physical objects was necessary to lay down neural pathways, but once those were in place, learning could become more abstract. Classbooks taught everything, from reading to calculus and beyond. The content was so broad that every age, from preschoolers to adults, could benefit from it. Enhanced communication was changing everything rapidly, facilitating the integration of information previously isolated. It was like atomic fission, generating enormous energy, except that this energy was intellectual, artistic, and completely of the human mind. Naturally, many people and organizations were against internationally distributed classbooks, and even free-access classbooks, on various grounds, and destroyed them whenever possible. But Q was everywhere; classbooks were unstoppable. Those who wanted one could get one.

Across the circle from Jill, the light changed. She should turn around and go back to the store, but that seemed too difficult. She should call Elmore, but didn't feel up to an interrogation or scolding at the moment. Desperately thirsty, she looked around for a place to buy a bottle of water, but traffic compelled her onward, through the intersection. Had she eaten breakfast? She couldn't remember. Her legs shook as she pedaled, and then there were

only nine more blocks, eight. *I can make it, I know I can . . .*

She flung her bike on the overgrown front lawn when she reached the old house, pushed her way through the towering bushes that hid the sidewalk. Bleeding from brambles, she gained the rickety steps of the front porch. Her leg went through a rotten board. She yanked it out, leaving a deep gash she barely noticed, and stomped onto the porch, with its mold-greened, cobwebbed wicker chairs, and an antique, rain-ravaged rocker. Hands trembling, she went through her keys. Town house, bookstore, apartment upstairs from the bookstore, car, storage shed, a friend's house when cat-sitting, Elmore's office, storage shed—where was the key to *this* house, the house of her childhood? Had time swallowed that too?

She flung the keys into the empty clay pot that once held her father's geraniums and grabbed the heavy wooden rocking chair by both of its furled arms. Lifting it chest-high with astonishing ease, she smashed it through the picture window, where scenes of her other life were obscured by closed, wooden venetian blinds.

She did not feel the gashes the broken glass made on her arm, her chest, as her momentum carried her through the window, onto the dusty old carpet of her childhood, taking the venetian blinds down with her with a crash.

Brian
[*March 21*]

BRIAN DANCE, Jill's younger brother, was in his air-conditioned office trailer going over the plans for a new office building with Phil Fenster, the District Fire Marshal.

Fenster advertised the burden of his responsibilities, as well as his self-vaunted experience in the field, with a worn expression of "I've seen it all," which had deep-

ened this afternoon into a definite scowl. His suit was rumpled, his tie stained with food, and he had even asked Brian permission to smoke a cigarette, which Brian granted.

When Brian had seen him that morning, the suit had been impeccable, as if newly stripped from a dry-cleaning bag. After being called away for an emergency meeting, Fenster had returned in a far worse mood than when he'd left.

Brian said, for the second time, "We can do this with fewer sprinklers."

Dance and Associates, Brian's engineering and construction company, was picking up quite a few new, prestigious jobs lately. With prestige came more scrutiny, sometimes flowing from the friends of those who had not gotten the contracts. Fenster was not immune to such influences.

In a belligerent tone, Fenster said, "You need every one of these sprinklers. Maybe more." It was a threat. He had the power to make Brian's clients pay much more than necessary for their building, thereby undercutting Brian's bidding credibility.

"Look at our test results."

Fenster waved his hand. "Young man—"

At thirty-nine, Brian was indeed younger than Fenster, but quite well seasoned. He'd benefited tremendously from his father's guidance, and also from his father's large footprint and reputation as the best fire protection engineer and systems designer nationwide for some years before he vanished. Keeping his expression impassive with difficulty, Brian braced for the inevitable. It came, right on cue.

"Why are you arguing? Your father developed these codes."

"We didn't have Tensano then." *That's good. Voice calm, reasonable.* "This is a completely new material. It's been extensively tested. Did you get the files I sent you?

We did our own tests too, as usual. I have all that information there. Ignition time, burn time, all that. As you can see, if you'll take the time, we have worked with the architect to use it extensively—"

"It doesn't matter."

"It does matter. Keeping costs down is what fire protection is supposed to do. Reducing costs means that fire protection will become more widespread."

"Until there is a code upgrade, we go with the code we have." Fenster stood. His sour expression belied his outstretched hand: *Don't tell me what my job is, young man.*

Brian stood as well, and shook Fenster's hand. "You're the boss."

"Damn straight."

After Fenster shut the flimsy door, shaking the trailer, Brian leaned back in his chair and put his hands behind his head. That was a wash. Even though he'd kept an even keel this time, he'd lost his temper with Fenster before. That episode kept coming back to bite him. He'd have to think of another approach. It was a delicate matter. In D.C., where many of his jobs were, they used his father's reputation and work to keep him in check.

If Sam were here—

Brian smiled. If his father were here, he would be quite excited about Tensano and its fire-retardant properties. The difference was that he'd have been able to schmooze Fenster into thinking that less sprinklers was his idea.

Brian shared his father's unusual height, but was more filled out, his short, sandy hair curly rather than straight and dark. Unlike his father, he was prone to bad-tempered outbursts. He liked to think he was improving on that count.

Time to wrap it up for the day. He wanted, badly, to take a swig from the bottle he used to keep in the bottom drawer of his desk.

But the bottle wasn't there, now. Couldn't be. That

was all there was to it. A drink now and then wouldn't
send him into a tailspin, but no sense keeping it handy.
In his opinion, alcohol was a harmless sedative, one that
opened his mind to musical dreaming, during which he
doodled on his electric guitar, at home, and in all-day
Sunday jam sessions at various hole-in-the-wall blues
and jazz clubs in D.C.

Several years ago, Cindy, his wife, had pointed out
that with two children to raise he needed less dreaming
and more focus—as well as more money than a musician
made—and gave him an ultimatum. Stop drinking, get
in gear, expand your company, grow up. Or live alone.

After Brian had met Cindy in the Peace Corps in
Africa, they managed to get posted together on the little
island of Tonga in the Pacific. There, they built houses
together and taught. Well, Cindy had done both; Brian
was quickly bounced from teaching and put into building,
full-time. Cindy could wield power tools, carry lumber,
and drive a nail into a roof she was shingling with two
strong blows. She could also keep kids in line while
teaching them something at the same time. Almost as tall
as Brian, Cindy moved with enviable grace in body and
in mind. She was just about perfect—except for her mad-
dening ability to almost always be right, and her insistence that he lay off strong liquor.

They'd been married for fourteen years. Together, they
juggled her teaching job, his company, and their kids—
Zoe, thirteen, and Bitsy, four.

Zoe had wild blond hair, a lovely complexion that
tanned easily in summer, and was immersed in music no
one else could hear. She obsessively carried a notebook
of blank music staffs in which she inscribed her compo-
sitions. Just as obsessive was her need to keep a set of
broad, music-nibbed markers with her, in an array of
hues, for her notes all had colors.

She didn't talk much.

Zoe had taken over their piano when three, but it was
in storage while they lived in a cramped apartment. Just

before Brian's business had scored a marvelous array of projects that took full advantage of his design, contracting, and fire-protection strengths, he and Cindy had found their dream home, a beaux arts gem in the District—sound, but in need of extensive renovation. They figured it would take a year, sold their house to finance the work, and took the first apartment they could find. As soon as they gutted the house, Brian was flooded with accepted bids, the fruit of reputation-building years. It didn't hurt that he'd assumed the name of his father's firm, Dance and Associates. Sam had taken him to his jobs when Brian was a teenager, and walked him through all aspects of fire protection, which drew from many engineering and scientific disciplines. When Brian finally got going he had a tremendous head start in skill, practical knowledge, and contacts. He took every new job that came down the pike—a prestigious, challenging office building, or a mundane kitchen remodeling.

Cindy was increasingly anxious to get into their house, and Brian was hardly ever home. Zoe was without her beloved piano and refused to use the electric model they'd bought for her. At least she had her violin, but neighbors' complaints strictly proscribed her playing hours.

Luckily, Bitsy was forthright, uncomplicated, and happy as a lark no matter where she was. After the difficulties they'd had with Zoe, who'd been diagnosed variously with Asperger's syndrome (soon discarded), a very high IQ (true, but so what), and OCD (no, just extremely particular about every little thing), Bitsy was somewhat of a relief.

Cindy and Brian were far too compulsive to pull their crew off paying projects to renovate their beaux arts find. Paying projects could vanish overnight, leaving them high and dry and penniless. They were stuck in the apartment.

Cindy worked for the city. She had begun a project called Free D.C. Montessori, and convinced the D.C. City Council that she could get property owners to donate

space for Montessori classrooms in return for tax rebates. She had pioneered Pan-Pacific Montessori for the Peace Corps. She had also set up workshops where local people manufactured precise, beautiful Montessori materials fashioned of renewable bamboo, print shops where the artist-created matching cards that ran the gamut of the natural and man-made worlds were made, and created scholarship programs to help train teachers. Just a week earlier, Brian and the kids had watched her on the local cable channel, talking to the D.C. City Council, which wanted to replace the rather expensive Montessori bells with cheap electric pianos.

Every well-equipped Montessori classroom had two sets of twelve bells—two identical-sounding diatonic scales, representing the twelve tones from middle C to high C on the piano. Each bell looked like a six-inch-tall lamp, with a rectangular wooden base, a stem, and a wooden finial holding a hemispheric metal bell perfectly tuned to one note. When gently struck with a small, round mallet, it filled the air with a pure, resonant tone. The bases of one set, the control, were painted white and black, to correspond to piano keys beginning with middle C, and were labeled by note. The bases of the matching set were plain varnished wood. They were not labeled.

Cindy set up the bells at the meeting, the labeled set on one side of the room, the unlabeled set on the other. She then had a three-year-old ring one labeled bell, to which he had to find the match. The boy crossed the room, which took about thirty seconds. During that time, he had to hold the sound of the first bell in his mind. He rang one unlabeled bell, rejected it, rechecked the original, and, after testing four more, found the matching bell. She challenged the board members to do so. The three that tried failed.

"You couldn't remember the tone for as long as it took to cross the room," said Cindy. "You missed your sensitive period, obviously. Children who work with these bells often develop perfect pitch."

"What good would that be?" asked one member.

"We'll just have to find out in fifteen years when we have a whole lot of young adults with perfect pitch walking around in D.C."

They all laughed, and gave Cindy what she wanted.

As had Brian. He stopped drinking hard liquor. The alternatives Cindy presented were disagreeable, and he now had to admit that she had been right. He could still be manic, depressed, disagreeable, irascible, and spin out lovely, effervescent skeins of music without the aid of strong drink.

He could still and ever more sharply after discarding his trusty nightcap dream that his plane, struck by Vietcong missiles, plummeted ablaze through jungle canopy, and wake screaming just before the crash.

He had never been in a plane crash. He had never been to Vietnam. Hardly anyone in the U.S. had. Kennedy, in December 1963, had refused to Americanize the war. Yet, the nightmare persisted, real enough for Cindy to regularly shake him awake.

He could still desperately, and ever more sharply, miss his father, and still wonder if he had somehow precipitated his disappearance, though that made no sense. His father had left home years after their mother, Bette, had vanished, presumably in search of her, though he had told no one that he was leaving or when he would be back.

Perhaps Sam had not known.

If only, Brian sometimes thought, he hadn't lost his temper with Jill that time they'd tried to track Dad down in Germany. But there were more if-onlies that he couldn't quite pin down, lurking in nightmare and shadows, and even within bright spring days like this. Was his father waiting, somewhere, somehow imprisoned by forces within or without him, for his children to find him, to bring him home? Had he been injured, was he languishing somewhere, brain damaged? Brian sighed, and grabbed his jacket from a hook next to the door.

When Brian stepped out onto his plywood porch, a gust of wind flapped the tie he'd worn for Fenster, much good it had done. As he strode to his black pickup, obstinately and almost proudly powered by gasoline, Brian loosened the tie with one hand. He climbed into the truck, whipped off his tie, and tossed it onto the seat, where it fell across an empty barbecue potato chip bag, empty foam coffee cups, a camera, a hammer, and a pipe wrench, all of which rested on three or four dismembered *Washington Post*s. He turned up the news on the radio and was headed up D Street when his phone rang.

Brian turned down the radio, which was telling him about the election campaign. The story, heavy on history, referenced the 1978 election, when Richard Nixon challenged Robert Kennedy after Robert's first term, and lost. The two Kennedy brothers, Jack and Bobby, had hogged the presidency for sixteen consecutive years.

"Brian?"

"Hi, honey. What's up?"

"It's Jill." Cindy's voice, calm yet firm in almost all circumstances, was unusually sharp. "Elmore just had her committed to St. Elizabeth's."

"*What?*" Brian was silent for a moment. "That sounds like him, doesn't it? What happened?"

"Not much, really. Instead of riding her bike to the bookstore after class, she rode over to your old house."

"Halcyon House?" That's what they'd always called it. The house was close to their apartment, and they'd considered living there instead. But, though Brian never said so, Cindy understood that, for him, it would be like living in a very disquieting past, the past that had caused him to drink to excess.

Cindy continued. "Yes. Her keys were on the porch by the front door, but she broke the front window with a chair. She got cut on the glass, pretty badly. A neighbor called an ambulance."

"When?"

"Around one."

"Huh. Fast work, even for Elmore. So, she should have just gone to the emergency room, and now she's in the nuthouse, courtesy of her own husband."

"I just can't figure out why you don't like Elmore." Cindy's default mode, humor, often shaded into sarcasm. "What do you want to do?"

"Are the kids home?"

"I can take them to Delia's."

"I'll swing by and pick you up. Did you call Megan?" Megan was their sister, the youngest of three.

"I tried, but I don't think she has her phone on."

"See you soon."

Brian sighed as he closed his phone. He'd seen this coming. He just hadn't had any idea of what to do about it.

Megan

MEGAN GETS RILED

[March 21, Northern Virginia Suburbs]

MEGAN THOROUGHLY enjoyed riding the Metro. She loved surrendering to motion; motion without attention. It gave her two extra hours a day to read.

She read, with great enjoyment, things that few people enjoyed reading: scientific papers. Her field was memory research. Unlike her sister Jill, who had taken years to finally buckle down and finish her doctorate, Megan had gotten on the fast track while still in high school.

Why memory? Because that was all that there was.

Everything that you think is happening now already happened. You're processing something that happened a few seconds ago. Our reactions are slow. We live among wavelengths. We are wavelengths. Wavelength is all there is. All right, I know I just said that memory is all there is, but now we're getting down to the physics of it. All the

bits and parts of us, the fabulous multiplicity of us, is
what I want to know about.

Try using those lines at a cocktail party. She usually
just said, "I'm in research." When pressed, she said,
"Scientific."

Thoughts flowed randomly, which she found stimulating, as the Metro car glided next to, over, and below
traffic. She liked the physics of sound, the change in pressure as they went into a tunnel. She liked how quiet everyone was. She liked to look at the clothes people were
wearing and think about their lives. The woman sitting
across from her, reading the latest literary best seller, carried a canvas bag that proclaimed WETA; black high heels
were crammed in the top of the bag. She had exchanged
them for purple running shoes, because walking, and
sometimes running, were a part of using public trans-
portation. Megan was fortunate. Her job did not require much dressing up.

She usually kept her Q-phone—most people just called
them phones—off while she was on the Metro. It was
her thinking time.

She couldn't imagine life without Q. It was a portable, always-accessible brain. After JFK and Khrushchev
negotiated détente, much to the dismay of hard-liners
everywhere, who still tried to stir up trouble, much scientific information was rapidly declassified. Satellites now
provided access to public information. Q—short for
"quantum"—was a new form of communication built on
ever-changing but always-there particles. They flashed in
and out of existence rapidly, a form of energy capable of
holding and transmitting vast amounts of information.

Megan had heard rumors, generally from slightly
drunk physicists at parties or out-and-out geeks, that an
early variation of Q—a very strong, consciousness-
changing form—was embedded in the cereal-box space
toys they'd all played with as children. Whenever she
tried to track down more information about that esoteric
conspiracy-type twist, she found nothing.

She'd gotten hold of Bette's war records—it was no secret that she had been in Europe, in the Women's Army Corp, but exactly what she had been doing was not clear. The huge stack of paper from the Army was mostly black with redactions. The CIA did not admit that Bette had been an agent. Out of the bits and pieces of information that Megan had acquired privately, from old letters, or remembered snatches of conversation she'd been too young to understand, she'd put together a rather surprising tale: her mother, Bette Elegante Dance, and father, Sam Dance, had helped develop Q—a more radical form of it than was now used for daily communication. Megan called it Strong Q—a form of Q that promoted neuroplasticity. Strong Q could rewire brains, accelerate learning in adults to preschool speed, and mess with the very stuff of memory. Strong Q explored and used the quantum-physics basis of mind and consciousness to its own advantage, as if it had a personality, an agenda. It was really kind of frightening, so it was no wonder that this deep basis of the Q that everyone—well, most everyone—knew and used and loved was not public knowledge.

Megan had very little idea of how this had come about, though she had tried very hard to get to the bottom of it. Oh, there were standard histories of Q's development, but strange physics shrouded its depths—the physics that people had heard of, mostly related to Einstein, but about which even those who had worked on the theories disagreed. Through dogged research, Megan had found papers authored by Rutherford and Hadntz, and Meitner and Hadntz—except that no one seemed to know who the mysterious Dr. Hadntz might be. One rumor had it that she had died in a concentration camp during WWII.

Presently, the great leap in communications fostered by Q was explained by the Synergistic school of thought, and various esoteric mathematics, new ways of looking at phenomenon; but when you got right down to it, as

Megan had tried, one encountered a maze of human thought that rivaled that of early quantum physicists—in fact, it was based on those stunning, early twentieth-century revelations by Curie, Einstein, Dirac, Born, Heisenberg, Meitner, Planck, Schrödinger, and many others. But the legend that drunken physicists shared at parties was that Q had something to do with the basis of human consciousness itself.

Which brought Megan back to memory research. The questions *What is memory? What is consciousness?* seemed pedestrian, even meaningless, to most people, but, to Megan, they burned more brightly than magnesium.

Classbooks using Q were embedded with an altruistic baseline able to evaluate the intent of the user. Q could not be used for injurious purposes. It made decisions drawn from a wide philosophical, biological, and moral database. It was able to discuss decisions and argue with users, and was a vast, consensus-based network.

Q readily passed the Turing test. This pleased some, frightened some, and angered many.

It delighted Megan.

When questioned, Q declined to answer questions about its own development. Megan assumed that it had decided to lie. For altruistic reasons. She assumed that Q was engaged in a constant hacker war in its nether reaches. Despite this, the world had accepted Q as a necessity, like electricity. Electricity could be dangerous and deadly, but tamed by engineers, it made modern life possible.

If Megan tried to talk to Brian and Jill about their parents' possible role, they shrugged it all off—Jill, most vehemently, and Brian because how could his little sister know more than him? At least, that's how it seemed to Megan. But there was a lot that Brian just plain wouldn't talk about. Just like most people. At least he didn't drink all the time anymore.

Megan had decided that it might be best to keep her thoughts to herself unless she could prove them beyond a doubt. And the only reason she wanted to prove them was to find her parents. If they were even findable.

But why would they stay away from their family if they had a choice? That was the heartbreaking question she had to face and try to answer, if her theory was true. If they were alive, where were they? Couldn't they at least leave a clue? What might they be afraid of?

As a parent, she realized that her child, and protecting her child from assault or injury, was her most primal underlying concern.

So, if her theory about their mother was correct, what were she, Jill, and Brian being protected from?

Abbie, her five-year-old, would be home with Jim by now after a day at Montessori school. Jim was a political commentator, and worked at home. Megan was thirty-six. Jim was fifty. His curly black hair was graying at the temples, and his beard was almost white. Of medium height, and a bit too heavy, his blue eyes twinkled through old-fashioned round glasses. Once-divorced, he was tickled to have another chance. He was astonishingly kind, adored Abbie and Megan, and had the wicked sense of humor Megan was so used to in her family, though he usually kept it sheathed except when writing. They lived in a forty-year-old suburban neighborhood, Tall Oaks, nestled beneath a canopy of deep-breathing trees.

Megan might be too involved with her pursuit of information; she might appear to be completely absent-minded, and sometimes even cold, to her brother and sister, but she was busy. She tried to connect to people. Really, she did. Jill was much more outgoing. Megan preferred to sit back and observe.

She transferred to a local bus, which soon trundled through her neighborhood.

Every few blocks, a grandiose monstrosity hulked over the modest split-levels and ranch homes that had

housed a generation of postwar children. Less-kempt yards, here and there, contrasted with smooth, glowing green lawns. The tall-grass yards were often those of people who bought there when the houses were new, although one young man maintained that he had a right to have a meadow, rather than a lawn. In true Tall Oaks spirit—different than more restrictive outer suburbs where 1984 was reality—no one had challenged that right.

When she passed the tall-grass homes, Megan missed her parents. Halcyon House, her childhood home, was empty now, enveloped in the wild evolution of her father's famously inclusive one-acre flower garden, and ever-smaller areas of grass irregularly mowed by a succession of local kids. Megan mostly missed her dad. She had lost her mother in 1963. Mom went somewhere and never came back.

That was probably why memory interested her so much. She didn't so much want to look at a photograph of her mother—which were strangely few—as feel the touch of her hand, smell her hair, hug her legs, as Abbie hugged hers, and be drawn into her tight embrace. Take the drug that would reactivate experience.

She wanted her childhood back.

All that was long, long gone.

New leaves shimmered in late-afternoon sunlight, and kids on bikes shouted and waved to one another. The bus passed Rathbone Place. Jim occasionally expressed thanks that they didn't live on such an ominously named street. Megan mentally said hello to her closet doors, which were somewhere on that street. She had seen an ad in the community newsletter asking for original cupboard and closet doors. The little row houses built for commuters had transmuted into fifties chic. The Rathbone folks had probably bid on her unrepentant never-renovated house in the first place. She and Jim had outbid a couple of other buyers to snag it.

Because she felt oddly happy in small, confined places, she had removed the doors from the upper closet in her study when they had moved in, and stored them in the attic until she saw the ad for AUTHENTIC ORIGINAL TALL OAKS HOUSE PARTS, and those plain closet doors brought her a hundred bucks. A few pillows, a lamp, and books— all things from her parents' old house downtown— furnished her tiny Megan loft.

In fact, thought Megan, she was oddly, but blessedly, happy with just about everything in her life. Everything was in order, unsurprising. She liked it that way. The only thing not perfect, right now, was the state of her research. She might well lose her funding if she didn't come up with the more focused chimera she had pursued all of these years: *What is the neurobiological foundation of empathy?* and *Can it be dependably, pharmacologically or otherwise, replicated?* Memory, including the phenomenon of false memory, and the ability of humans to create stories and share them, was a vital part of her theory, and her colleagues took these astounding abilities for granted. Memory was not sexy; no one threw money her way, money with which to hire, set up research, and enable experiments. This did cast some darkness on her life. It seemed so damned important. The spread of true empathy, disseminated via carefully thought-out vectors, might well unravel the world as everyone knew it. Such a change would be as momentous as the other great watersheds of human history: the invention of printing; the development of science. Perhaps, Megan often thought, she was just not very good at convincing others that she was on the track of something important.

At other times, she thought that maybe she was too good. Maybe she was on the track of something that many people feared: a power shift from the few to the many.

Revolution, pure and simple, and all the blue sky and heartache that revolution might bring.

From deep in her purse, her phone emitted a muffled beep. A message.

Instead of going home when she got off the bus, Megan called Jim, spoke with him briefly, and then headed down the service road bounding a creek that ran into a small, marshy lake. This was where she always went to think.

But first she rummaged deep in her bag, where she kept her pack of cigarettes. Yes, she had stopped smoking when pregnant with Abbie. Yes, she never smoked at home, and in fact, hardly smoked at all. She did, though, buy a fresh pack of Chesterfields every month and give the old, usually unopened pack to the first bum she saw when she came out of the drugstore.

She ripped open the cellophane, took out a cigarette, and had it match-lit in record time. Clamping it between her teeth, she hoisted her bags, headed down the wide gravel path, and took deep, mind-sharpening drags as she moved with long strides into the preplantation, Revolutionary War–vintage forest. Braddock's famous road was just a mile away, and she liked this living vestige of the past, wise and restful, her refuge.

Two boys poked at something in the creek with sticks. Hundred-year-old oaks towered overhead. Geese honked, harsh voices rising in eternal goose argument. A bike swished past.

It was hard to believe. Jill, committed.

Then again, sometimes Jill let fly with odd comments that revealed she was in what could be charitably described as another reality.

Megan trudged along. Her shoes got muddy. Her briefcase and purse weighed heavily on one shoulder. She turned things over in her mind as the road dwindled to a path and the smell of thawed earth grew stronger. She stored her spent cigarette butt in a little metal pillbox and lit another.

Brian was at St. Elizabeth's now, and said they had Jill on lithium. Why were they using such a big hammer?

In Megan's opinion, Jill's life was much too demanding. She was completing her dissertation and working at the World Bank and in her bookstore, as well, to pay for what Megan thought of as Elmore's Folly. What she really needed was a vacation from her life. Elmore's insistence on his showy Folly had forced Jill to leave her full-time job at the Bank, predicated on the promise that when she finished her languishing doctorate, her pay would double. Jill's schedule had been manageable before she went back to Georgetown. The Bank paid for Jill's doctoral work, but Elmore was incensed about the temporary loss of income, saying that she could go back to school—not poli-sci, but law school, which assured one of an income—as soon as he made partner. Everything in life was supposed to sync with his internal schedule of How His Life Would Move Ahead, presumably trailing Perfect Spouse and Child in his wake to display when necessary. At least, that's how Megan saw it. She knew that Elmore and Jill had ferocious arguments about whether or not to sell the bookstore property, which had appreciated tremendously in value, to pay for the Folly—either that, or transform the store into living space. Jill would simply not let go of her store, even though, as Elmore often pointed out at family gatherings, it didn't do a whole lot more than break even and took up too much of their time.

Their new home was certainly a fine town house, on one of the best streets in Georgetown, although, to twist the knife, Elmore often mentioned that the bookstore, with its commanding view of Key Bridge and Rosslyn, would have been *the* perfect place from which to trump everyone who was anyone. D.C.'s hottest designer, who had categorically excluded Jill's garage sale finds, decorated Elmore's soulless triumph. After a battle, Jill had angrily stored her own things at Halcyon House.

Add to all that Jill's concern about five-year-old Stevie, whom everyone thought was more than just childishly dotty, particularly since he'd begun insisting that his name was not Stevie, but Whens.

Megan lit her third cigarette and the gnats fled. The budding greenness of the forest enveloped her. She turned down a little-used path lined by starry spring wildflowers. Two kids in a rowboat struggled with oars far out on the lake.

Megan dumped her bags, sat on a rock next to the water, and stretched her legs out in front of her. She and Brian and Jill should really do something about the old house downtown. It would free up a lot of money. Their parents had left a mysterious trust, held by a secret trustee that even Elmore, who considered himself a legal wizard, could not track down. The taxes were paid on time; checks were sent to Jill, the oldest, for bare-bones maintenance, and all three children got a small monthly stipend. Since neither parent had been declared dead, Megan knew that Elmore frequently raged that various time limits were up and that they needed to sell the property and divide up the money, but none of the Dance kids wanted that. Elmore's latest feint was to attack the very legality of the trust, but, since no papers were available, he was having a difficult time doing so. The property had not been in the best location when their parents bought it, but now, it was worth a bundle, and their tax bill reflected this. Halcyon House, bordered by a park much like this one, was bound on one side by a strong, fresh-running stream. Just try to find another house like that downtown. But the old mansion had fanciful turrets and odd roof junctures that made leaks hard to find, and was monstrously huge. Elmore thought it a wasteful hobby that the sentimental Dance brood needed to cash in on.

The emotional turmoil Elmore seemed bent on maintaining might have something to do with Stevie giving himself a new name. A new identity called *Anyone but*

me! Elmore's wearing bid for partnership, which seemed to have permanently warped his once easygoing personality, might last years. Jill had jumped hand-in-hand with Elmore into the maelstrom, so it wasn't as if she hadn't known what might happen.

But maybe Jill's deepest problem was that she missed their father.

Megan did too; fiercely. Megan, Brian, and Jill had gone to Germany, his last known destination, but they had not found him. Jill's screaming fit, a month into the search, convinced Megan and Brian that it was time to quit. Brian had hired a private detective, who showed up one day at Brian's house looking frightened and returned the retainer. He refused to say why, just cited family problems that kept him from traveling.

So now they were left with this double hole in their family. The Vanished Parents.

Dad had not gone to look for Mom in '63, even though her body was never found. He had held no funeral. It seemed very strange to Megan, now that she was grown. You'd think he would have done both, but he did show them the letter from the State Department that said Bette Elegante Dance was missing, presumed dead. Megan had been too young to question Dad as she should have during those years before he too left. Or died, somewhere, undocumented, maybe even under a different name. Megan was now positive that her dad had known all along that Bette was still alive, and was furious that he had withheld that information.

Obviously, the Dance lines of communication were not as clear as they ought to have been. Megan was sure that Jill knew something she was not talking about— something about why both parents were gone. But, if so, why not tell her and Brian?

Megan stood, rehoisted her bags, and headed out of the woods. She passed through an empty ball field and emerged from the woods many blocks from home—if the meandering streets of the Tall Oaks could be said to

contain blocks. Regaining the sidewalk, she continued to muse, admiring the gardens of her neighbors in spite of her worry. Crocuses, yellow forsythia. Lovely front porch, with those wicker chairs. Jill always enjoyed this walk, and exclaimed about everything she saw, along with Whens. *Stevie,* Megan told herself firmly.

Megan suspected that Jill's hardcore medications were the result of Elmore's fears, which he'd no doubt communicated strongly to the doctor. These were drugs for schizophrenia, and, perhaps, from Elmore's point of view, that was Jill. Schizophrenic. Seeing things, hearing voices, needing to be controlled.

Megan walked faster. Her role was suddenly clear. She would have to meet the doctor, have a talk with him. Jill probably didn't need drugs at all. Not her Jill! She needed something. But not drugs. Megan knew a lot about pharmacology—not that M.D.s were inclined to listen to anyone else. She'd give them all a talking to, raise hell. As she walked, she got more and more fired up.

She called Jim and asked him to pick her up at the corner. "Take Abbie to Beth's. I know; tell her that I love her and that I want to see her. But I think we need to get over to the hospital."

Jill

A FEW GHOSTS

[*March 25, St. Elizabeth's Hospital*]

THERE WAS lithium, benzodiazepines, and God only knew what else. Something clamped shut deep inside Jill.

The dayroom at St. Elizabeth's was full of people who would not look at her and that was fine. She didn't want to look at them either. She noticed that the hallways were narrow and dirty but that did not bother her. It didn't bother her when Elmore told her that he was filing for

divorce because he couldn't afford the expense of an insane wife who couldn't even take care of their son. She did think, silently, that it was vastly inappropriate of him to bring it up at this particular time, but then, his emotional compass had swung to some bizarre new bearing lately. It was remotely pleasing not to have to worry about that anymore. It didn't bother her when Brian came and begged her to say something, nor did it cheer her when she heard her sister Megan, who had a doctorate in molecular biology, raging at the doctor in a slightly hoarse voice, so Jill knew she was smoking again and that, like everything else, it was her fault.

She started talking after her mother and father came to visit her, because their visit perked her up considerably. But when she told Brian he just looked alarmed, particularly when she went into detail about the visit. So she did not mention the other two visitors at all.

Jill saw her parents, Sam and Bette Dance, when she opened her eyes one night, soon after she was admitted. Dimmed lights revealed a clock on the wall that said 2:17 A.M.

Footsteps passed the open door. The rattling wheels of a cart grew loud and then soft; an impassive female voice paged Dr. Hogart for the third time.

Sam and Bette leaned over her, looking worried. Jill was not surprised. It seemed to her as if they had just been gone for a while. Of course they would visit her in the hospital.

She wakened more fully, and realized that she was not dreaming. She tried to speak, urgently, but couldn't. Something that sounded like *bllg* came out. She felt as if she were pinned underwater.

Bette wore a minimalist blue evening dress that revealed fit arms and shoulders. The pendant hanging from a chain around her neck was a simple design, and glinted like her short, silvery hair in the dim light.

Sam, in a completely uncustomary suit and tie, took her hands. "Jill, I'm sorry."

Bette bent down and hugged her, pressed her cheek against Jill's. "You're not crazy, Jill." Her voice was strong and fierce. "We came as soon as we heard. We were at a party at McMillan's, and got on the Underground, and—"

"Shhh," said Sam. "Someone might hear you. And we shouldn't talk about anything sensitive."

A sensitive party? wondered Jill. She felt a distant impulse to giggle. She later realized that their unconventional way of getting from a fashionable party in London to a hospital room in the United States, probably from a different timestream, when there were people who might be able to trace them through that action, was what Sam meant by sensitive.

"I don't care," said Bette, although she lowered her voice. "This is my girl they've got here." She turned and lifted the IV bag, squinted. "What is this crap?" She shut off the IV.

Sam said, "Bette! You're not a doctor."

"Well, this one should lose her license."

"Maybe Jill needs fluids."

"Not if the fluid is full of this much lithium and all kinds of other junk. No wonder she can't talk! It's a wonder her heart is still beating!"

Jill struggled to speak once again, but could not. Tears of frustration welled from her eyes and trickled down to her ears. Part of her wanted to laugh—I have tears in my ears from lying in my bed at night thinking of you. She couldn't move, couldn't get up, couldn't hug them. Where have you been? Stay here!

"Listen carefully, Jill," said Sam. "Until we knew about particle physics, we didn't know this was possible. But it's dangerous."

What is this? Jill tried to ask. What is it?

Bette picked up her chart, which was clipped to the end of the bed. "Sam, this is 1991. Wink didn't tell us

that!" She blinked. "So much time . . . just gone . . . we've got to leave!"

Sam kept talking to Jill, his voice low and urgent. "Now we know that it is possible, but we don't know all that much about it. It's difficult to . . . move around. There are other forces at work. Other people who want to know what's going on, and we keep finding things out—"

What *things*?

"We have to go, Sam. Now."

As Bette yanked on his arm, Sam said, "Read my notebooks, Jill. If you still have the house you still have them." He looked very old, and very tired. "I love you."

Bette bent down, gathered Jill up with strong arms, and crushed her face to Jill's, so that her muffled voice was close to Jill's ear. "I love you so! And I'm so, so sorry. We'll be back."

"Bette, you can't promise that." Jill heard anguish in Sam's voice.

"I promise, Jill," she said in a firm voice. "I promise that we'll be back." She kissed Jill.

"We really do have to go," said Sam. He gave Jill a long hug, a short kiss, and held both of her hands for a moment while gazing at her *as if to remember,* Jill thought. And she looked on them as if it were her last look, gathering their dear faces into herself.

Bette and Sam stood facing Jill, arms around one another's waists, and looked at her for seconds that, for Jill, were stripped of everything except their shared gaze. Then Bette pulled Sam from the room. Jill heard Bette's heels and Sam's heavier tread recede down the hall.

Come back, she shouted, with the voice in her head that didn't make it to her lungs, her vocal cords, the voice that was so submerged she couldn't even open her mouth.

But the intensity of her interior cry finally forced her mouth open. She sobbed: deep, hoarse, alien sounds that took all the air in her lungs. She could not stop. She didn't want to.

A nurse came in. She turned off a beeping sound, frowned, and said, "Don't you dare touch your IV line again or I'll tie down your hands." She opened the line and left.

She remembered then that she'd had another visitor, earlier, before Mom and Dad. She had no idea what time he had been there, of course. He had looked vaguely familiar to her semi-dreaming, drugged mind.

He sat in the chair in the corner. His short beard was grayish, perhaps, but most of his face was shaded with a fedora with the brim snapped down over his left eye, so that she could see only the right one, appraising and somewhat sympathetic. Shadows obscured any details of what looked vaguely like a government-issued uniform. His ankle rested on his right knee as he sprawled back in his chair, so one muddy, well-used boot was visible in the sliver of light from the doorway.

She went over it in her mind after he got up and left, which was as soon as she tried to sit up. A loud, medical beep signaled that she had pulled something loose.

He had a long stride. One, two—and he was out the door.

"Hey," she heard from down the hall. "Who are you?" Then someone—presumably that same nurse—paged security. "Dr. Yellow to third floor east, please."

As Jill sank back onto the bed, she realized that, despite the drugs, her heart was beating very fast. She rather thought she had seen him earlier that same evening, after they had done the evening bustle to get her battened down for the night, and dimmed the lights. Or maybe it had been some other time . . . so hard to remember . . .

She closed her eyes and tried to memorize him, but he rapidly became entangled with a long-ago cartoon of Popeye and Brutus fighting, and then she was back in limbo, and then Mom and Dad showed up.

When the third man came, she screamed.

I was born in 1950, Jill wrote in her imaginary journal. *The War was over, at least on paper. Germany had been divided in a series of ad hoc agreements.*

She started over again, in her head. She could not write a real journal because she did not want anyone else to read it.

She was lying in her hospital bed, one ear on a pillow. She pulled another pillow over her head to block out the television sounds. She went over and over them again, each time from the beginning, to set them in her mind. She continued.

I was born five years after the end of the War, and its shadow lingered. I knew it had been a terrible War and an exciting War and that its end released the world in a burst of great light. I gathered that we were now living in a wonderful time, The Future, where an image of superimposed ellipses illustrated the font of all being, The Atom, and that all would be good, henceforth and evermore, because the War had been fought, the War had been won, and the War was over.

But the War was still there.

The War was in the chairs, rounded and tucked in the lines of the thirties, the years when War was accreting like leaves in a headlong stream, lodged against implacable economic and political rocks. The War was in the black-and-white photographs of my father in uniform on my parents' dresser. It was on the bookshelves and in the acrid pages of old newspaper clippings I found in trunks, in the books I found and read at my paternal grandparents' house—books like Boots and her Buddies, *or* Nina and Skeezix, *illustrated by pictures of German and Japanese spies with narrow, ominous mustaches, wearing spectacles that blanked out their eyes, war propaganda for kids. It was in movies, where black-and-white spies played out their games on mysterious trains and in narrow dark streets*

that seemed the epitome of Europe, where the ominous two-toned siren of the Gestapo signaled deportation and death.

Walter Cronkite narrated The Twentieth Century *on television. Tiny puffs of smoke emerged from rolling valleys; troops marched; the Prudential Company's impressive logo, the Rock of Gibraltar, announced its sponsorship, and my father watched, always leaning against a doorway, never sitting down, gleaning information about what he had been through. Winston Churchill's great tomes proclaimed themselves boldly on the Danish Modern bookshelf he built in his basement workshop:* The Gathering Storm, Their Finest Hour, The Hinge of Fate. *By day, Danny and I writhed like movie soldiers through hibiscus bushes and hid behind sandboxes in our backyards, carrying machine guns and avoiding Germans. At night, when a tiny bedside light illuminated the fine, old well-polished bedstead with carefully turned down, smooth sheets at the house of my maternal grandparents, the War was in the shadows, sharp and deep, and on the lace-covered dresser where a picture of the two sons who had died in the war, Keith and Jerry, forever smiled, boys in overalls, holding between them a string of striped bass.*

She went over it again and again, etching it into her mind, so she would not forget. They wanted to sweep everything from her with these drugs, but that was wrong. She had to remember.

She had to remember *everything*.

No one else did. But that was her fault too. No one else could.

Things were better now, she supposed, than they would have been otherwise, as if histories were shifting toward the more positive end of an unseen spectrum. The Palestinians had not been moved wholesale from their land, and had been paid well for the huge tracts where Euro-

pean Jews could settle in what was now Palestine-Israel. But she could also remember a war in 1967, when Israel took great swaths of land with weapons the U.S. had given them. Now, in this timestream, there were still disagreements, but the Middle East was not a festering powder keg.

The African Union, formed in 1964, elected and sent delegates to a Pan-African Congress, which seemed forever mired in bickering. This was not surprising, because the African population contained many more cultures and languages than Europe, but much progress had been made, progress being defined as decreasing territorial, cultural, and religious disputes, healing the injustices and exploitation caused by colonialism, and increasing health care and education. But that legacy was so strong that much of Africa was still mired in deadly civil wars, large-scale ethnic murders (the term "ethnic *cleansing*" disgusted Jill), disease, and subjugation of women and children.

Germany had not been divided, post-war, and the Soviet Union had not sucked the life out of countries around its border in rough approximation of Hitler's original plan for Germany's use of those same countries.

In the United States, in the wake of victory, Roosevelt had been able to pass a strong civil rights bill in 1946.

But—why? How had this happened?

How was it that she could remember a far different world? Why did she think that she had had a hand in creating *this* world?

It was easy to take their point of view: She was crazy.

The problem was that she knew she was not.

The roots of this timestream lay in whatever her mother, Bette Elegante, and her father, Sam Dance, had done during the 1940s, and she did not know what it was.

She only knew that whatever they had done had birthed, somehow, this slightly different, slightly better

world, which slid a new history into her past. Had this world existed parallel with that other world, in which Roosevelt died in his fourth term, Truman had ordered the bomb dropped on Hiroshima, Germany was divided, and John F. Kennedy was murdered? Or had she, with one, decisive, wild action, wrenched that old history onto a new track, one that neatly provided a past for everyone, except her, that was perfectly consistent?

Or was she, really, delusional? Maybe her mother had been a perfectly normal WAC, rather than a spy; her father a perfectly ordinary ordnance engineer, rather than someone who knew more than he could say.

If so, why did that old past insist on itself, cling to her, aggravate her, heap upon her such real sorrow and such real responsibility?

If her parents really were alive, somewhere or somewhen, why did they not help her?

It had something to do with the war. She knew nothing of her mother's life during the war.

She returned to her journal. From the top, now.

I was born in 1950 . . .

Jill

WELCOME TO THE FUN HOUSE

[*April 5, St. Elizabeth's Hospital*]

"YOU'RE ALWAYS angry," said Jill to Elmore.

She had been in St. Elizabeth's for a couple of weeks. She and Elmore were eating lunch in the cafeteria.

"That's right." He was sitting, right now, but sideways to the table, as if poised to jump and run. Elmore hardly ever sat down when he came, no matter where they were. He even stood in their joint therapy sessions, leading Jill

to note that he seemed crazy too. She hoped that the therapist noticed.

Elmore shoveled potato salad into his mouth. His thin, pale face was set off by the perfect, expensive cut of his thin, pale hair. He took a bite of his hot dog. "Everything is falling apart."

"And it's my fault." Jill said this not as an accusation, but as if it were a fact. She believed it to be true.

"You got it." He wiped his hands on his napkin and threw it on the table. "I can't handle all of this. Taking care of Stevie. Running the house. Scheduling employees at the bookshop, which we don't need to keep. A lot of extra work for nothing. I paid the store's insurance—it was almost overdue—and the utility bills, but I didn't order anything. There are already too many books there. And God only knows how much the employees are stealing."

"Right. Naturally, I hired a bunch of thieves."

"You're such a bleeding heart. Jane is a slacker— always late—"

"She's taking care of her father."

"Doesn't matter. If we're not open on time, we lose customers. I fired her."

"What?"

He shrugged.

"You used to be a bleeding heart."

He glared at her. His glasses were gray, like his eyes. His shirt and suit were immaculate, as usual, and tailored in Hong Kong. His face was no longer the face of the young man that she'd married—expressive, committed, kind. This face gave nothing away that the enemy could use—in court, in the office. Or, thought Jill, to his wife or his child.

"Why do you keep saying that?" He sounded genuinely irritated.

"Our newspaper—" she began, but stopped, remembering that she'd shown him one of his old editorials a

few months ago and he'd just said, "I wrote this? I never believed this crap."

Now, Elmore said, "It's no wonder that Stevie is confused. You talk about things that never happened."

"I need to see him. He needs to see me."

"No. You only encourage him. Miss Sally—you remember his teacher's name, don't you?—says that now he'll only answer to the name 'Whens.' *Whens?* What kind of a name is that, Jill, for chrissakes? Is that what you call him?"

"I have the same problem as Miss Sally. He won't answer to anything but Whens."

"You could call me Winnie," said Stevie-Whens, while helping his mother fold clothes. He picked out his own small jeans, shirts, and underwear and folded them with great concentration, his yellow fluff of hair illuminated by winter sunlight coming through the window, his glasses sliding down his nose.

"Don't you have enough names?"

"Well, this would be like calling me Whens, except that people wouldn't think it was so strange. Abbie calls me Whennie now, and it almost sounds like Winnie anyway. Winnie is a real name, like Winnie-the-Pooh."

"Stevie is a real name too."

"It's a real name, but it's not my real name."

"I just don't understand this Whens stuff."

His surprised eyes were magnified by his glasses. "You don't remember? You named me."

"I named you Stephen Dance-Wentworth."

"No, you were sleeping and I was sleeping with you because of a bad dream and I woke up because you were crying and yelling. So I tried to wake you up and you did wake up and you hugged me and said, 'You are my Whens. You are all my Whens.' Then you fell asleep and you weren't crying. I like it. It just makes so much sense. You're always saying When-You're-Older. When-You're-Bigger. Even though I'm almost five. I'm really just a lot of Whens."

She laughed. "I never did that. You're making it up."

"No, I'm not," he said, smoothing a striped T-shirt like a fussy store clerk. "And you know it."

She didn't say anything. She did know it.

"Jill? I've got to get back to work. Here's a napkin. Stop crying. Wipe your face. Jeez. I bet you can't even find your way back to your own room." Then he was gone.

Eventually, an orderly helped her stand, took her back to her room, and gave her a pill.

"So why am I better than Hitler, again?"

It was May first. Jill was with her assigned therapist, Nancy.

Nancy's sleek brown hair curved obediently around her face in a precise oval, and fell forward and back, each hair in perfect unison with the rest, as she bowed her head, looked at her watch, then raised her head and looked at Jill again. Jill found the precise movements of her hair fascinating.

"Jill? Hello? We have five minutes."

"I'm glad that you don't believe me." Of course, Jill had only told Nancy anything because she knew she wouldn't be believed. She hadn't told anyone about the man she'd scared off by screaming.

His face, as he'd observed her, was deeply shadowed, but his SS uniform, Gestapo-gray, and the death's head clearly affixed to the cap just above the visor, were unmistakable.

Her scream had at least brought the doctor, in minutes, and a big adjustment in her meds. She wasn't at all sure if he had been real, or just a dream. It certainly wasn't like her to scream. That bothered her almost as much as the memory of the man. She definitely wanted to put that embarrassing, scary moment behind her.

No, she wasn't going to talk about that clear sign of deep insanity. They would just say she'd read too many books about the war, and she really did want to go home.

Nancy sighed. "Let's look at the facts, Jill. You do have many symptoms of post-traumatic stress disorder. Some people are able to hide extremely horrific events from themselves. This disorder doesn't always stem from war. Originally, it was called 'railroad spine.' Victims of early train crashes reported strange psychological and physiological symptoms for years. Victims of sexual abuse, people who've been in some kind of accident—there can be many causes. People have the ability to tamp these events deep down into their subconscious, but the memory of them can emerge in sudden, startling ways. Or, they know that these things have happened—like a car wreck—and seem to resume normal life, but are psychologically damaged. You seem to fit some of the diagnosis criteria. The problem is, no one but you believes that another timestream"—Nancy smiled briefly—"existed before this one. Think about all the questions you have to answer, all the things you have to explain, in order to make that true. What happened to all those other lives, those people in the other timestream?"

"My point exactly."

"You talked about Painting Woman, once."

"What?"

"You used to draw. Paint."

"No. I never have." Not in this world. It was dangerous: What she drew came true. Suddenly, she agreed with everyone: She must have been absolutely nuts to mention this. It was nobody's business but her own, as the old tune went.

"It might be a good idea to try it out again. It might help unite these disparate parts of your personality."

"Fix my railroad spine."

"Do you want to get better?"

"Of course," she said, belatedly remembering that this woman had to sign off on her release. "I could try doing some art stuff. Sure. Take a drawing course or something."

"From what I understood, you are rather beyond that."

Damn. What had they given her, Sodium Pentothal?

Nancy changed the subject abruptly. She often did. "I'm glad you're using makeup again."

"My sister Megan put it on. I'm going back to work pretty soon. Whenever I'm ready, they told me. I still need to defend my dissertation." Jill laughed. "Megan seemed to think that makeup would get me in the right frame of mind. Maybe it does. A mask."

"You'll be working at the World Bank, right?"

"Mmm-hmm. In charge of an international school project. You know what happens without me. Things fall apart." Her mouth trembled and she grabbed a Kleenex.

"Just remember, Jill. You are just the manager of some people who work at the World Bank. You are not in charge of the entire world and all of time. And—let me ask you a question. You still haven't told your brother and sister exactly why you're here, right?"

"My husband committed me."

"Don't be obstinate. I know your husband committed you. But underlying all of this—your guilt, your disturbance, your actions—is one belief. You need to tell them what that is."

"I don't see how I can."

Nancy looked at her deadpan with cool blue eyes. "What if it's true? Mightn't they suspect? Don't they deserve to know? Shouldn't you apologize?"

Jill got up to leave.

"Thirty seconds. Answer my question. Don't they?"

Jill said, her hand splayed over her chest, "My heart is pounding very hard." Then she fled down the hall.

She ran to one of the dayrooms, where catatonics shuffled about, two old men played checkers, and a young woman sang, quite beautifully, "The Yellow Rose of Texas" over and over and over again, accompanying herself on a well-worn piano. She did this every day, while Jill watched the *Golden Arrow of Breath* relaxation tape from the tape library, which she had memorized, finding

she enjoyed this form of self-hypnosis and neurolinguistic programming.

Jill sprawled on a couch, closed her eyes, and tried to remember whether or not she had told the therapist about the Infinite Game Board, but she couldn't. If she had, she hoped that Nancy had not made a note of it.

She didn't think that Brian and Megan remembered the Game Board at all. It had been swept from them like the childhood toy they'd all thought it was, at first, found in the huge, old attic on a rainy day, with a strange surface that changed constantly. They had found a few games that worked.

Found? She snorted aloud, but of course, no one in the dayroom noticed. Most likely, the game had tailored itself to their level. It was Q, in another, earlier incarnation: potent, seductive, and revelatory. She knew that now. They had hidden it from their parents, naturally, since it was so much fun, but after a while it gave them visions of future histories—holocausts, flames, wars—that made them, literally, ill. Eventually, Jill had sequestered it for herself, and told Brian and Megan that it was lost. Her ideas for her ten-minutes-of-fame comic book, *Gypsy Myra*, which featured a tall, fierce woman with long, black, curly hair, who wore long gypsy skirts, played gypsy violin, and told the future, sprang from the board. She hadn't the faintest idea how it worked. And finally, the board had shown her the scenario she had first made into an underground comic book in 1968, after King and Robert Kennedy were murdered. The board, and Gypsy Myra, showed her that her brother might die in Vietnam. It showed her how—where—to change that history, how to hitchhike into time. The board had led her to Dallas, five years in the past of that timeline. Somehow her father had followed her, rescued her, and they emerged . . .

Here. Back in 1968, but a 1968 in which Jack Kennedy had not died, nor his brother Robert, nor Martin Luther King Jr.

A 1968 in which Brian and Megan accepted that their mother had disappeared in 1963, rather than living with them in Halcyon House, working on her doctorate in education, and opening a Montessori school in a large back room of the house.

Her memories of that time, were, not surprisingly, vague, shifting, like dreams that, when you wake up and try to recall the specifics, evaporate.

She wanted, desperately, to remember what had happened. She wanted, now, to know how it had happened. What about the Game Board had precipitated a shift in history? That was what her political science studies were all about, at heart. She had hoped they would fill that gap, give her and Brian and Megan, Bette and Sam, without the hard work of *remembering* . . .

She wiped away tears and stared at the ceiling, surprised, realizing that before now she had not wanted to remember. It had been too enormous to comprehend. She had wanted to push all that aside, to get on with what people did as they grew up.

So she went to college, got married, started a business, had a baby, pursued her ferocious interest in international politics.

And all that got her was exhausted and crazy. Just goes to show you.

But she was no longer exhausted. Not today. She sat up.

Was she crazy? By all normal measures, yes. Except that she knew that she wasn't.

So she had to try to figure out, after all these years, what had happened, and why. What was memory, anyway? What was time; what was that elusive subject, history, which she'd studied so long and hard? Megan was working on a memory drug. Maybe there was a reason. Maybe Megan remembered more about the past than she would admit to. Or not as much as she would like to.

And Brian—well, he'd worked hard at blotting everything out. Kind of like her, she supposed, only she used work, while he used alcohol.

The trees outside were fat and green. The streets, she knew, were hot and packed with traffic; the sky was full of smog; evenings released refreshing thunderstorms.

It was spring in Washington, which she always found glorious. The city would heal her, if she would just get out into it.

It was time to leave this place.

Elmore allowed her discharge mainly, Jill thought, because their insurance had run out and he was tired of paying the au pair he'd hired to take care of Stevie. She hadn't seen Stevie in a month. Children were not allowed at the hospital.

Elmore went on a tirade as they drove through Washington, but his words were a bit like the trees and houses, things that passed with whooshing sounds and were gone. It was actually kind of funny. Phrases like "Sick of this," "You're acting like a child," "I told you [fill in the blank]" had no meaning anymore. She interrupted his running narrative of her faults.

"You used to be different."

"What?" He actually turned and looked at her. "She speaks. Okay. I'm trying to listen. But don't you realize that's what you've been saying about everything this past month? Everything used to be different." He sighed. "I shouldn't have let them talk me into committing you, but you were . . . combative. Hysterical."

"I was?"

He shook his head as the light turned green, and moved the car forward another block. "See? You don't remember. They told me that it was likely that you would experience more . . . cognitive breaks . . . As time went on."

"Cognitive breaks," she said thoughtfully.

"Yes. You may be schizophrenic."

"Hence, lithium?"

"You have to understand, I didn't know what to do. I still don't know what to do."

"It's not right."

"I know, but—"

"I mean, it's not right that if I argue with you, you can label it as being combative and say that it's bad. It's inconvenient, I know. It takes up your valuable time." She stirred, restless, feeling as if she would like to jump out of the car.

And run home.

Maybe that was the best thing to do. Just because her last attempt had failed didn't mean she shouldn't try again, and succeed. Before that, she hadn't even known what she wanted.

She said, "What about Stevie?"

"What do you mean?"

"You talked about a divorce at the hospital. In fact, it sounded to me as if you'd started proceedings. Did you send me any papers? I don't remember. Do I need a lawyer?"

"Jill, we can talk about this later."

"Where's Stevie?"

"At preschool."

"I want to see him."

"He'll be home around three."

"I want to see him now. Take me there."

"I don't want you to cause a scene."

"I just want to see my son." She was surprised to hear that her voice was firm and strong. Inside, she was trembling, on the verge of tears. She watched Elmore as he pressed his lips together. In a second he would say "No," as if she were Stevie's age.

"Elmore. Listen to me. I'm sorry this happened. I understand how unhappy you are with me."

"It's not—"

"No, wait. Let me finish. I think you're right about a divorce. I will keep Stevie. I will—"

"No."

She continued to talk, slowly, firmly. "You can see him whenever you like. Stevie and I will live at Halcyon House."

"With what money?"

She laughed. "Well, they actually do want me at the World Bank, although I know that amazes you. And I'll have the money from selling our bookstore and town house."

"I don't want to sell them."

"I thought you did. But fine. We'll get everything appraised and you can pay me my half."

"I can't afford that."

"You can make payments. Oh, but we don't have to talk about it now. I know you're a little disturbed. There's Stevie's school." She thought a moment. "Maybe you're right. Let's not bother the class. Let's go home. I'll see him soon." She turned her face to the open window, hoping that the wind would dry the sweat of her effort from her face before Elmore noticed it.

Jill

HOME AGAIN

[May 4]

A COUPLE of weeks after Jill's release from St. Elizabeth's and many unpleasant legal machinations, Jill stood on the city sidewalk facing her childhood home.

It was a Saturday morning. The clear, clean creek, to her left, roared from the culvert swift and full. Brilliant yellow forsythia ranged through the landscape, bending beneath the breeze, dotting its way down the bank through Sam's old rock garden, past Bette's place of solace, a small roofed pavilion. The air was clean and cool, probably the last breath of coolness before summer hit—which, according to the weather report, would be around noon, when the temperature would soar and humidity move in.

Whens clutched her right hand. Manfred, who was mostly Saint Bernard, sat next to them. Elmore was only

too happy to get rid of Manfred, since she shed on his ten-thousand-dollar custom-made couch, and could clear his priceless porcelain from the coffee table with an affable wag of her powerful tail.

Whens asked, "Mommy, is this the house?"

"Yes. It's the house Uncle Brian and Aunt Megan and I grew up in. Grandma and Grandpa's house." It seemed funny to say this to Stevie. To *Whens*; she'd finally fully succumbed to calling him Whens. He had never met her parents; they had disappeared years before he was born.

"But Gram and Gramps live in Annandale."

"They're your daddy's mother and father. This is where my parents lived—Grandma and Grandpa Dance."

Steady on, she thought, staring at the house with eyes as wide as Whens', seeing it for what it truly was: an old, neglected wreck of a gargantuan, yet stately Victorian mansion, complete with a ballroom on the second floor. Sam's gardens engulfed the house like a sea, waves of varyingly high foliage topped with hollyhocks yellow and violet, lower eddies of mostly spent tulips frothing white and magenta; spears of pink lilies and a whole patch of orange, self-seeding bachelor buttons that had helped themselves to ever-widening territories. Vines ran riot over the porch. A climbing yellow rose blocked the windows of the north front room, obviously delighted with its house-sized trellis. Oak limbs the size of elephant legs overhung the roof. They would require surgery, preferably before the next strong breeze. The house needed a serious infusion of cash.

Halcyon House was principally green, although that was debatable, what with the paint peeling so badly. The stained-glass trim above the windows on Jill's old tower room shone yellow, red, and blue. The window was open, just a bit; rain would have gotten onto the hardwood floor.

That was the least of her problems.

Whens tugged on her hand. "Let's go in."

She smiled. "Okay."

The sidewalk leading up to the porch was frost-heaved. She remembered roller-skating here, dashing streetward but making sure not to let her skates catch on the bump. It had been five years since she had been inside—save for the episode that had landed her in St. E's, which she did not remember—and apprehension seized her: What would be different? What would be the same?

And could she bear it?

She glanced down at Whens. She had to bear it.

"There's a hole."

She lifted him over the rotten wooden step. She held him on her hip as she slipped the house key from the pocket of her jeans and unlocked the door. She pushed it open, and the musty smell of pent-up years rushed out.

"It's dark."

Jill said, "Let's open the blinds."

Megan had had the front window repaired. Though Jill didn't remember bursting through it, she had a scar on her chest from one of the shards. She was lucky not to have cut her throat.

"I'll do it, Mommy." Whens pulled on the cord with all his might, hand-over-hand like a seaman raising sail.

The wooden slats clacked. Sunlight brightened the multicolored spines of several thousand books on their built-in shelves. Jill unlocked the tall, wavy windows on each side of the repaired plate glass and raised them. Fresh air washed through the room.

Whens looked around. "It's pretty. Like a storybook."

"Yes," she said, transported. In Whens' voice she heard Megan's, when she was five, skinny and antic, always laughing or dancing. Whens, despite his similar voice, was serious, almost grave, with a sense of humor too grown-up by far, and she wished for a moment that he might imbibe some of Megan's cheerful spirit here. But even Megan was serious, now.

Megan must have dusted the eclectic mix of furniture, and washed the gilded-frame mirror over the fireplace, for everything was splendidly clean. On both sides of the fireplace, shelves overflowed with an irregular tapestry of books. Old friends, some her mother's: international policy, the brain, DNA, and ancient Chinese poetry.

Her father's books were more concrete. World War II. Physics. Engineering. Watson and Crick and obscure journals. But after . . . after . . .

She sighed. Say it. After Mom Left.

After Bette vanished, Sam read more novels, almost as if questing after information about the physical world was completely useless. He devoured fiction, she recalled, lying on the couch and smoking, day and night, when he wasn't working.

"Mommy."

"What?"

"I'm thirsty."

Jill returned to the present. "Ha! Look at this." She rushed toward the kitchen, pulling Whens behind her. Manfred padded along, turning her head from one side to the other, inhaling and sorting the huge house. "No problem! We've got everything here. Electricity! Garbage pickup! I've started the *Washington Post*! And—ta-daa"—she turned on the tap triumphantly—"water!"

Whens, unmoved, gazed at his mother and then at the sink, pondering. "We usually have water, don't we?"

Jill smiled. "I know you take all of that for granted, sweetie, but it doesn't happen by magic."

A large, round oak table, painted white, anchored the kitchen. Glass-fronted cabinets, framed by dark walnut, reached to the ceiling, showing off their early-sixties contents. Green, yellow, and red Fiestaware, a Tupperware Popsicle-maker, Bette's well-used electric coffee percolator. The backsplash was tiled with pale green tiles.

Whens frowned. "I don't want water. I want a Slinger."

"No Slingers. Too much sugar."

She tried to ignore the doubleness she had come here to confront, the two lives, stretching out behind her, seemingly parallel and yet not, with that paradoxical break, its Möbius-like twist that baffled her ideas of continuity, linearity, cause and effect. Had she not gone to Dallas, what might be different here, now?

It was a good bet that Brian would have died in Vietnam. Headstrong and patriotic, he had joined the Navy, in that life, in that world, that she had run from. Had that world been completely obliterated? Did it go on, somewhere, elsewhen?

That was the timestream where her mother lived, and ran her school, *there*, down the broad hallway that led to the back of the house, in a huge, high-ceilinged room filled with manipulative materials whose scientific provenance was completely evident. The binomial cube, a physical, manipulative cube-puzzle showing the mass of each of the products; the little baskets holding the Exercises of Practical Life—shoe and silver polishing, table scrubbing, the contents to be laid out and used sequentially, accomplishing some purpose, some change in the environment, then put away and shelved by busy children.

Jill helped out in the school during summers. She saw herself, sitting next to one of the children, watching them think about how to make a hexagon out of isosceles triangles, or which letter to pick out of a box of letters in order to write "s-u-n."

Memories of her family flocked around, and the present faded. She saw Brian building an Erector Set Ferris wheel on the kitchen table. Her mother frowned over a crossword puzzle while, behind her on the stove, rice burned.

Jill took a deep breath with her eyes shut, willing the memories, the visions, to be gone when she opened her

eyes, so she could concentrate on her son—although, admittedly, getting a plastic tumbler from the cabinet next to the large porcelain sink, rinsing it, and filling it up did not take up much of her mind.

"It's not cold," he said, after taking a sip.

"I don't think we have ice yet." Her heart was beating hard—a paroxysmal problem, she had learned, for which she now took pills—and she felt like crying.

"Mommy, what's wrong?"

"Oh, I'm just sad."

"Why?"

"I miss my mom and dad."

"I miss *my* daddy."

"You little rascal!" She laughed and sprang toward him, ignoring her pounding heart.

He shrieked and fled, running through the dining room, spattering water everywhere, and then through the family room, before she scooped him up, drenching them both with the water left in his glass. "Don't try to pull that on me. You see your father almost every day."

"But I want to see him all the time."

"He has to work."

"Yes," said Whens, as if talking to himself. "He has to work. Okay."

Jill put him down. "Look, isn't this a wonderful backyard? I think the first thing I'll do is cut the grass. Then we'll go get a swing set."

"A swing set!" Previously, they'd had to walk to the park for such a luxury.

"With a slide."

The lawn mower was in the shed. The boy that cut the grass used it, so it worked, and there was almost a gallon of gas in the gas can next to it. Through the years, grasscutters had ignored the perimeter of the lawn. Opportunistic plants had advanced with enthusiasm, some of them small trees now, so that the lawn was a much smaller place than when Jill had grown up here.

Jill bent over the oil-encrusted mower to fill it with gas. Drops of sweat fell from her forehead and sizzled on the hot metal. It immediately stalled in the knee-high grass, and Jill's shoulder soon ached from pulling the starting cord. Whens played in the creek where she could see him, and the roar of the mower isolated her in thought.

Yesterday, she had successfully defended her dissertation. Koslov, to her surprise, did not even hint at the gaffe she'd made the day of her breakdown. She had kept her two histories quite straight, never letting one pollute the other, and the other professors were polite, though not at all soft. Jill's dissertation was titled *Postwar Russia and Germany: Strategies That Led to the Postwar Russian-German Manufacturing Powerhouse.* She received summa cum laude and suspected that someone had twisted Koslov's arm to make it unanimous.

And so, she had invited her Georgetown crew, including Koslov, the World Bank crowd, and all the neighbors to her Fourth of July party. Since her release from the hospital, it seemed as if she had revved into high gear. A manic phase, her therapist warned her. *You have to tell your brother and sister what's bothering you. It's like a pea under your mattress. It's distorting your life.* Unspoken subtext: It's so ridiculous that once you talk about it all that energy will dissipate.

Yes, she thought, going up one straight row, then turning and making a square of the uncut grass in the middle, it's true.

She had to tell Brian and Megan.

Right.

Bette

[*May 5*]

A TAP on her shoulder startled Bette awake. "End of the line, ma'am."

The train conductor moved on amid the bustle of passengers retrieving luggage from overhead racks before she could ask him where here was. She unwound from her curled-up sleeping position, neck aching and hair, she was sure, a mess. An unfamiliar black patent-leather purse, wedged just below the window, yielded a brush, which Bette ran through her hair, not taking the time in the general hubbub to further survey the purse's contents. The hair left in the hairbrush was golden blond, not brilliant white, as it had been at one time ... when? Where? She had been a lot older, obviously, but that was all she could infer. If she ceased worrying about it, the information would return soon. She hoped.

But where was Sam? Wasn't he supposed to be here, with her? They had set out together, from ...

She couldn't recall. It would come back, she was sure, but how long would that take? She examined the flow of travelers moving past her seat toward the door, looking for clues. Aside from a few businessmen, many passengers wore blue jeans, although the train was quite spiffy—even luxurious. During the 1940s, when women wore uniforms such as hers, no one save farmers wore jeans, and certainly not on trains. One man wore a fedora, slanted over his eyes, but he was the only one. A Women's Army Corp hat lay on the empty seat next to her; she put it on, took it off, then put it on again, reflecting that perhaps, at last, she had gone completely mad. She didn't even know what year it was. A bad sign.

Well, it happens to the best of us, she thought, as she searched under her seat. Her uncle Hank, a once-brilliant

Harvard professor, ended his days collecting antique pocket handkerchiefs and picking out the embroidery, as if to free every handkerchief in the world from the subjugation of permanent ownership.

She stood and smoothed her skirt. Everyone had left the car. She saw no suitcase that might be hers.

But this is a bit worse than Uncle Hank's situation, thought Bette, clanking down onto the metal conductor's step with the help of his steadying hand. Uncle Hank's madness didn't cause him to career through the cosmos—at least, not that she knew of. The hot, damp, familiar swelter told her the season, and the sign above the gate ahead of her proclaimed that she was at Union Station, Washington, D.C.

That was rather a relief, atop her previous relief that everyone on the train spoke English; she would not have relished being in Russia or in Germany in various years, and this was even better; she was quite familiar with—

But no, she thought, as she stepped inside, firmly ignoring curious glances from those around her. *This* Union Station was glorious: glitteringly gold-leafed and beaux arts, yet very up-to-date, she supposed, since many people stood at what looked like Q kiosks, studying and touching screens. During the many years she had passed through the station, in the forties, fifties, and sixties of what she referred to, in her own mind, as World Prime, with other, always slightly differing iterations slotted into different file cabinets in her mind, the polished marble she now trod had been scuffed and dull, toward the end, with ceilings and corridors boarded over with plywood. Now, gleaming shops unreeled down corridors. Gargantuan statues overlooked the human ants below.

Because she was wearing her Army uniform, circa 1945, passersby stared at her curiously, perhaps not even recognizing the provenance. Or maybe she had entered a world where a war was presently taking place, and the

U.S. had been taken over by the Soviet Union, or China, and she wore an enemy's uniform—

Oh, stop it, Bette, she thought. The people passing purposefully through or window-shopping appeared neither cowed nor deprived. Everything was fine.

After reading a plaque commemorating the inauguration of the American Maglev System, AMS for short, and noting that its network spanned the country, she spotted a café in the north corner of the station and headed toward it thankfully.

She settled into a booth where she could observe the lobby over a mahogany partition, set her WAC hat on the table, unbuttoned her tailored jacket, and straightened the knot of her tan tie.

She ordered a double espresso and a dozen raw oysters, but did not relinquish the menu to the waitress, as the back of the menu had information about the renovation and the startling, thrilling fact that Dance and Associates had been a part of the architectural team for the renovation. Presumably, they had done the fire protection work.

Obviously, she was in a nexus.

Although Hadntz seemed to be able to negotiate timestreams, Bette could not hold many of them in her mind at the same time. Timestreams were physically real consciousness-consensuses and, until Hadntz had invented her tool for knowing about other timestreams, they had been invisible to humanity, like bacterium before the invention of the microscope, and other galaxies before the invention of the telescope. Hadntz's Device theoretically gave humans access to other timestreams, and, because they were consensus realities, it also gave humans the power to change other timestreams.

Theoretically, of course, thought Bette, sipping scalding-hot espresso through a sugar cube.

It made her quite ill, physically, to move from one timestream to another. Maybe she had slept that off in

the train. A memory teased her—a long, long tunnel—then vanished like silvery fish in a dark lake.

Insertion of oneself into another timestream changed it. The long-term physical effects of timestream jumps were unknown, and Bette felt lucky she had not ended up drooling in front of a television set in an old folks' facility, or in Bedlam a couple hundred years ago.

Sam's signal was music: bebop, in particular, a distant music he heard and then was able to follow, although he did not like to and did not want to.

Jill. Yes. Now Bette was remembering. The splinters—yes, really it was an appropriate word, considering—were coming together again, forming a complete, if distorted vision. When had that visit been? Where had she and Sam come from? Another timestream? This one? That had been a very brief visit, wrought with great difficulty. She remembered that much.

Now, she hoped, she was back in that same timestream, just a bit farther on. She hoped that Jill was no longer in the hospital. And no longer in—

Danger. Yes. Some dark threat. What? What?

The waitress slid a plate holding a dozen pale oysters in front of her. Their fresh, briny scent was tantalizing. One thing that she had learned in her life was that it was best to eat when food was available, because she had gone through many times, during the war, when it was not. Bette swallowed three oysters quickly, and considered motive, trying to hit on the key that would unlock the mystery of her presence *here*.

Hadntz had recently enhanced her invention with a genetic alteration that increased mirror neurons in the brain, which thereby increased empathy. She claimed that once male team aggression, a trait that evolved in agrarian prehistory to protect property, and the predisposition to consign outgroups to a subhuman status—which made it easier to kill and torture others—were modified, conditions for all life on earth would improve immensely.

Why did Hadntz, Bette, Sam, Wink, and by now, uncountable others, think that such modifications were morally acceptable?

The answer went back to the War. And, actually, not just the wars of the twentieth century, which had been the crucible for its tandem development with the atomic bomb, a project that Hadntz had left early on, but all wars. Anyone who had experienced polio knew for a fact that modifying humans with a vaccine was better than allowing polio to occur. Anyone who had experienced war knew that there should be a better alternative. A positive alternative, not just appeasement, which Churchill had likened to feeding a crocodile, hoping that one would be eaten last, when Chamberlain had appeased Hitler in 1938 by signing the Munich Agreement, ceding to Hitler the Sudetenland. Appeasement had not worked; Hitler continued his aggression. Living in a dictatorship, or a religious tyranny like the women accused of witchcraft, though perhaps peaceful on the surface, was not an alternative to war either. No—cessation of war could only occur in a human atmosphere of communication, universal suffrage, and universal literacy agenda-free education. Many studies—at least in some timestreams, Bette thought, looking around and wondering if this was one—had proven that the empowerment of girls and women, through education that led to jobs, was key in creating the strong economies that would short-circuit war-inducing poverty.

Neural pathways laid down early in life were potent, but alterable. Enhanced brain plasticity, an explosion of neural growth, was one important effect of being exposed to the Device, so that late-life learning could take place. Continued expansion of intellectual frontiers and wisdom were major factors contributing to a better world.

Bette's larger mission was to make sure the Device, and its offshoots, were used to optimal positive effect.

Sam, Jill, Megan, and Brian were intimately involved in the evolution and distribution of the Device, like it or not. Was she here because of love and longing for her children, or was there some sharp, underlying purpose, such as specific protection of them?

And where was Sam? They had started out from somewhere—somewhen, together . . .

She was quite uneasy, now that she was becoming more oriented. Something must have happened to him along the way.

She opened her black patent-leather purse and inspected the contents without taking them out, in case someone might be watching.

Seven passports. A handful of documents representing the political outcomes of various wars, strategies, and time-lines. Four were in a hidden compartment: One for the United German Republic, in a timeline in which Germany had not been divided, post-war. A *Reisepass* for Deutsche Demokratische Republik, East Germany, with a compass inscribing a circle on the cover: "We, the East Germans who have survived the war, must in penance work for the Soviet State as a Nation of Engineers." Next, a dark green passport with a stylized eagle and five-pointed star on the cover, from the Bundesrepublik Deutschland, West Germany, propped up and occupied after the war by the United States. Another for a single, recently reunited Germany—not, she hoped, of this time-line. She hoped she had arrived in the timeline in which Germany had never been split.

Sam had filled her in on the history of their children's world after he left them and then finally found her in Mönchengladbach, Germany, in a slightly different time-line. These documents gave her political legitimacy in several offshoots of their own World Prime. Wink had left that world in WWII. Or they had left him.

Let's see. One passport for a Russia divested of satellite nations. Another for the Union of Soviet Socialist Republics sucking surrounding countries dry. One for the

United States. Also a Washington, D.C., driver's license for 1960, a piece of cardboard with no photograph. Most were in different names.

Egad.

She snapped her purse shut. She and Sam had tried to aim for Jill with arrowing intensity, because of the threat she could not now remember. John F. Kennedy had lived to do who knew what, but that single event was accompanied by an entire fabric of past, as well as present.

The waitress leaned over her. "Another espresso?"

"Just regular. Do you happen to have a newspaper?" She hoped that she wasn't making a terrible gaffe; she saw others here and there reading from handheld tablets that she assumed were some kind of Q, which she lacked right now.

"I saw one behind the bar." She returned with a disorganized *Washington Post* and a mug of coffee.

It was May 5, 1991. The Metro section led with a pleasant article about a rapidly dropping murder rate; Style interviewed a hot movie director. Buried deep in the A section was a long piece about a new war in Africa. Plenty of jobs for Q processors of many persuasions. Finally, Bette found the rumpled front page: National and International News.

Above the fold: The temperature would soar into the eighties this afternoon, and Robert Kennedy, with the help of his brother Jack, was running for a second term . . . She leaned back and allowed rare relief, just for a moment. So she *was* in the timeline Jill had wrought; the one she had so unwillingly left—she again checked today's date—almost thirty years earlier.

Or at least one that was similar. She no longer thought of time as linear. Instead, it built on itself, it switched tracks; it jumped, it split, it flowed in currents that looped and intertwined. It grew, like a garden, seeded with differing events, philosophies, art, music. It turned back upon itself. Ultimately, one ran out of similes and models. Time was more strange, and more malleable,

than she could grasp, just like consciousness itself. Whole lifetimes had flown past, hers, and those of her children, and here she was, young again, wartime-young, as if some threat from those times had reappeared. But who, how, what?

Sam, or Wink, had proposed at one time that they were the conscious components of a Q-like analogue of the M-9 Fire Director, the radical, top-secret weapon using shortwave radar that Sam and Wink had worked on in the Army. The fire director was able to follow a moving target, anticipate its future path, and calculate missile speed and direction. It had changed the course of WWII.

The "missiles" of avarice, greed, ignorance, poverty, and ill health were still among them, and still required eradication, from what she could glean from the *Post*. Perhaps their particular model of the M-9, the core personalities of Bette, Hadntz, Wink, Jill, and even, perhaps, Brian and Megan, had been called forth by some circumstances and were being assembled into a new, advanced version of the M-9, ready to calculate the trajectories of disease, ignorance, poverty, disaster, and fire the appropriate missile to explode them before they hit their target. Maybe that's why she was wearing a war uniform, eh? She was Bette-of-the-war again.

She opened her purse. She hoped that Past Bette, or whoever had booted her into this timeline with so many disparate passports, as if they had little control over where she would end up, had given her some folding cash.

In the bottom of the purse she found sundry change and felt a moment's panic. If she had a lot of money for the 1940s, when a cup of coffee cost about a dime, she might not be able to pay the unbelievable seventeen-dollar bill that lay on the table.

But in a green alligator-skin wallet she found five hundred dollar bills, and a sheaf of smaller bills. Relief. In the other compartment, she found an assortment of marks, rubles, something called euros, and a plastic card that said American Express. She did have a vague mem-

ory of something called a credit card, in a year future to her Army self: 1959. Sears and Roebuck, the only credit card she and Sam had owned. Good. She did have a sort of working memory. Physical artifacts triggered memories. She definitely needed a few more flashes of illumination.

Happily, she also had a pack of Chesterfields and got one out, noticed there was no ashtray on the table, and then felt the disapproving looks of the people in the table next to her, and then the SMOKE FREE signs all over the damned place. She put it away.

She left nineteen dollars on the table and stepped out into the vast atrium, heading for the light-streaming rectangles of the front doors.

She stepped into the bright sunlight of early May: red and yellow tulips arrayed in front of the Capitol, newly leaved trees, a lovely Washington day. Though hot. Pulling out another cigarette, she lit it, and wanted to stroll, relax, let memories unfold. She couldn't, though. She was uneasy, and her instincts were well honed and reliable.

Mini cars, tiny as in England during the war, and packs of bicycles coursed down broad avenues. A Free Montessori School in a shop front replaced the florist she recalled. Wonderful!

Then a sign for a Metro stop reminded her of the Underground, and it all came back.

She and Sam had been at a party in London—in another timestream, of course, but one more analogous in time, to this present.

Wink had surprised them, moving through tuxedoed and ball-gowned guests with his natural social ease, despite the fact that he wore an Army uniform, circa 1944.

Like the one that she now wore.

"I thought you were dead!" Sam said, as Wink grabbed them and pulled them in his wake, parting the crowd on their way out.

"Glad to see you too," Wink replied, grinning over his shoulder. "Let's move."

Bette had no idea how long the tunnel trip beneath the Atlantic lasted. She recalled that Wink said something about "leaving a marker," which meant their physical presence in this timeline, which would guide them back without his help. They came up out of the Metro—a Metro with this logo—and visited Jill.

They had then returned to England, to lure away some unknown enemy of Jill's—signified to Wink as perhaps his roaring tornado or the whistling of a buzz bomb. But timelines had snarled, as wires or strings, left to their own devices in dark drawers, gleefully tied themselves in knots. She and Sam were together, and then separated, in one of the 1944s—"Where it all began," Wink had said, in the moment before the blast, as if at that point there was some single sturdy thread with which they could pull themselves, dragging their heavy histories, hand over hand, to safety.

She did not recall seeing Wink again after that flashing moment in the pub. She only remembered Sam's muscular grasp, pulling her from the toppling doorway, running to the Underground, shoving her back on the train with shouted directions to *here*, which she had somehow remembered, with her trained spy-brain, all the tortuous leaps and changes until she was back beneath the Atlantic, and he had reentered the smoke-filled maze of rubble to find Wink.

What a mess. Was this snarl deliberate sabotage? Definitely a possibility. Maybe someone had followed them from Jill's hospital room. That had, actually, been Wink's hope.

But who?

She stopped walking and looked around. She had apparently walked several blocks while musing, and was in a familiar spot.

Al's Grocery. Yes, she had definitely been here before.

The kids used to ride their bikes here to pick up milk or bread for her, or trade in pop bottles on their way home from school and get candy bars (Brian and Megan) or comic books (Jill). She knew Al the grocer. Or, she had known him.

Wispy shadows of branches moved gently across the sidewalk. Al's front door was propped open with a crate that held bouquets of iris, purple sheaves with yellow hearts, five dollars each.

She pushed her hands into her pockets, felt the small, familiar pistol she always carried, and remembered more. She and Sam were working together—yes! Still! She would never think of Sam as being gone! They were distributing the Device among the timestreams in various ways, using different mediums and different methods, always hoping to create that critical point where they could safely rejoin the lives of their children. Their work was not easy. It was war work, dangerous and risky. It required a lot of preparation and calculation. It did not always work. It hardly ever went as they expected.

Sam had found her, ten years earlier. He had left their grown children with no plan, no notice, depressed and discouraged because she had been unable to contact him for so long, and found her—or she had found *him*, perhaps—in Mönchengladbach, where they had once met during the War, in the remnants of that *Biergarten*. Place mattered deeply to the human mind. It had called both of them—she in her red dress, he wrapped in desolate loneliness.

Where was Sam? She needed to get back to him—help him—

She was suddenly aware of someone observing her, as a target. It was a very familiar sensation, for a spy. She was certainly easy to spot. Had someone been on the train with her, loitered outside the oyster bar? That short man, wearing a—homburg? how curious!—crossing a block behind her against the light?

Her environs sharpened, snapped into her mind with the certainty of a well-drawn map.

She entered the grocery store. Her low military heels clipped sharply on wide floorboards. An elderly black man, wearing a blood-smeared white apron and mopping the floor, looked up with recognition and nodded, concealing the surprise he must have felt on seeing Bette in uniform, and looking so young and fit. Al had changed; he was heavier, and his hair was grizzled with gray. She nodded at him, glanced behind herself and back to him in mute appeal for help, and ducked behind the butcher counter at the rear of the store, removing her shoes. She slipped through a door into the storage room.

The bells rang again. She heard three running steps, a man's shout, the clang of an overturned bucket, and a splash. A heavy thud, shouted curses, and Al's, "Sorry, mister— Hey, no call for that kind of language—"

Shoes in hand, she ran down a dark hallway and left by the screen door in the back, darting through a maze of back alleys until delivery trucks gave way to backyards and then backyards merged into a small wood mazed with narrow, forking pathways. The ground was cool beneath her feet; she yanked open the buttons on her jacket as she ran toward the one place of safety, the one place she probably should not go.

A narrow verge of bluebells ran down to a creek, and bowed beneath a gust of spring wind as she passed them. She stumbled down to the creek, wincing as her feet landed on sharp rocks, and waded toward a viaduct tunnel. Traffic rumbled overhead. She splashed through the head-high concrete pipe toward the hazy circle of light at the end, cursing Hadntz and her Device and the whole mess of "nexes" and "splintering" and other aberrations of human consciousness and its previous, comfortable ordering of the phenomenon of time. About to emerge into the circle of light, she looked up, stepped on a slippery rock, and fell to her knees.

She remained in the cool, clean creek stream, inside

the dark tunnel, and her heart melted. There was no other word for it.

A little boy squatted at the creek's edge, about ten yards from her, poking something with a stout stick. He was a towhead, like her own kids had been. He looked up with Sam's eyes, over glasses that had slipped down his nose, and smiled at her. She smiled back and put one finger to her lips. Up the hill, in the backyard of their beloved, dilapidated mansion, her daughter Jill, unmistakable in her determined gait, pushed a lawn mower, her mouth moving, frowning, muttering to herself, immersed, Bette suddenly knew, in her own past madness, her hospitalization, which Bette's own actions had visited upon her. Even from this distance, Jill looked older. She was no longer thin as a stick, but mature and rounded. She moved like an older woman with a few aches and pains, rather than the limber tomboy she had once been.

Bette almost rushed up the hill to gather Jill to her, hug her, and dance with joy. But she could not. She could not reveal her presence to her children until she knew more.

The dark tunnel contracted. Bette, who had learned and left behind countless maps, had no maps for this, none at all. It had been so, so long since she had seen Jill. Her chest spasmed in sobs. She tried to hold them in, but they echoed through the tunnel like the cries of a wounded animal. Jill could not hear over the lawn mower, anyway.

Hugging herself, ignoring the tears running down her face, Bette retreated inside the viaduct to wait until dark. The boy seemed to forget her, and dropped to his knees to grab a wriggling creature. But then he looked straight at her, smiled brilliantly, and gently put the creature back into the creek.

Suddenly, Bette knew why she was here.

Jill

THE NEXT day, after she got Whens off to school, Jill went up to her tower room.

She had not been here in several years. All the big-leaved tropical plants she had cared for had died slow deaths. Webs festooned the corners, spangled with desiccated victims.

She struggled with the sash of one tall window until it finally gave way and opened. Two men, one white and one black, jogged past. The black man, who had a beard and moved in a slow, easy lope, gazed at the house a long time, then saw her, and waved.

She waved back and dropped into a chair covered with old clothes. During most of the sixties, when this was her retreat, her lair, her art studio, her mother had run a Montessori school in the back room downstairs and was absent every few months on what she and Sam told them were "education seminars." Brian and Megan had not lived through those same years.

How could one possibly atone for such an act? She couldn't return those lost years.

Everyone's memory was unique, anyway, she told herself, but that didn't help much. Neither did "Maybe things are better for everyone than they would have been otherwise," or "Everyone has regrets," her therapist's favorite. Sitting back in her chair, she thought about the world at large: Yes, it was demonstrably better. It was a game of averages. Kind of like quantum mechanics. Taken as a whole, events were predictable. But singly, quanta—packages of light—were not.

Jill absently picked up a piece of cloth from the pile on which she sat and ran it through her fingers, feeling its texture: thin, but striped with a slightly more dense

She was surprised to see Brian drive up in his unrepentant gas-guzzling truck as she climbed the stairs to the porch. She ran back down and met him on the sidewalk.

"Howdy, stranger," she said, and hugged him. "Come on inside."

Brian stepped into the foyer. "Hi, Manfred." He patted Manfred as he looked around. "Wow. You've really cleaned it up."

"Yeah. And the whole house looks as good as this." They both laughed. "Want something to drink?"

"Some iced tea would be good."

Of course she had some. All of them were iced tea fiends, even in winter. The tea had to be loose, preferably purchased from a certain teashop in Georgetown, perfectly steeped, with only lemon.

"Do you remember when you spit out your iced tea at Hogate's because it had sugar in it?" she asked, setting their glasses on the table.

"Ugh, yes." He frowned. "An awful surprise to spring on somebody." He looked at his glass with suspicion. "Why did you have to remind me?"

They sat with their elbows on the kitchen table, sipping tea. The windows were open, and a breeze ruffled the curtains. "It's kind of nice here," Brian said.

"How's business?"

"Oh, going great guns. We just landed a new contract."

"And the kids?"

"Fine."

"You're all going to have to come over for dinner. Maybe this Sunday afternoon?"

"I'll ask Cindy. Sounds good to me." He was quiet for a moment. Then he said, "Jill, I'm kind of worried about you and Stevie living here alone."

"Call him Stevie and see what happens."

"That's another thing."

She shrugged. "We're fine. Especially with Manfred."

"Daniel Kandell," said the other man, holding out his hand. "Did I see you up in the turret window?"

"That was me."

Daniel took Jill's hand, grasped it quickly, and released it. "You're moving in?"

"Moving back in. It's my family's house."

As he looked across the street, hands on his hips, she studied him.

He was a large man, about five-eleven, and in better shape than Will. His legs and shoulders were not those of a bodybuilding fanatic, but looked solid and strong. Smile creases radiated from the corners of his brown eyes, but right now his expression was serious, appraising, as if he were collecting information, engaging in reverie, and coming to interesting conclusions simultaneously, nodding as he thought. He kept his hair short and his beard, with barely discernable gray, professional looking, had no odd stylistic spaces or weirdly shaped patches. She couldn't tell how old he was. Forty-five? Fifty?

He realized she was looking at him, and smiled at her so quickly that she wondered if she had imagined the seriousness of his expression as he'd examined the house. "How old is it?"

"Built in the early nineteen hundreds. It, um, needs a little work."

He laughed. "I hope you're independently wealthy."

Will began jogging in place. "I'm stiffening up. I'll either have to call an ambulance or get going."

"Nice to meet you." The two men waved and continued their run; Jill saw Daniel look over at the house once again.

She took leave of Emmie and crossed back to her house, thinking, *Why are those pants still here? And the house; my brother and sister?*

What part of that life is gone, and what remains?

* * *

and met the boy's mother as she came out of her front door, carrying the child.

The neighbor's house was a well-maintained American Foursquare, with dusty-yellow brick and delphinium-blue trim. They shook hands and the woman said, "Emmie Weatherton. I'm sorry. Terence, you're too heavy to carry." She set the boy down. "The kids have said for years that ghosts live there." She laughed. "I'm glad to see a real person in the house again." Terence tried to hide behind his mother.

They shook hands. "Jill Dance. I grew up here."

"I work at the Library of Congress, so I'm usually not home during the day." Emmie's fine-featured face was ebony, and she was tall and thin. "My au pair is here, though." She gestured toward a white woman who waved from inside the window. "Her name is Jenny. Terence, say hi to Jill. Shake hands."

Jill squatted down. "Terence? My name is Jill."

He regarded her with suspicion. Jill said, "I have a little boy named Whens. He should be home soon. Maybe you can come over and play. We have a new swing set in the backyard."

"I have a sandbox. With lots of Spacies. They live in tunnels on Mars."

"Sounds perfect!" Jill rose. She and Emmie smiled at each other. "Drop by some time for coffee," said Jill.

A breeze fluttered the leaves of the huge oaks in Emmie's front yard. The two joggers Jill had seen earlier rounded the corner again, looking as if they were definitely on their last lap. Emmie saw them and waved them into the yard. "Are you two trying to kill yourselves? Let me introduce you to our new neighbor, Jill—"

"Dance." Jill held out her hand.

"Will Jacobson," said the pink-faced man, mopping his face and hands with the tail of his T-shirt before shaking hands with Jill. His pale hair was plastered to his head by sweat. "I live two streets over, next door to Dan."

ribbing. She had made bell-bottom pants out of this fabric in—

1967.

She held up the pants. Apparently, she had been impossibly skinny. Though she was thin now, she could not possibly wear them.

She closed her eyes and let the spring-scented breeze play across her face. Warming asphalt, cool scent of water from the creek, fresh-cut grass.

The Summer of Love, they had called it. Walking the streets of Georgetown, you caught the sweet scent of marijuana and hashish wafting from upstairs apartments, could duck into hole-in-the-wall head shops, walls aglow with black-light posters. There had been a frontier of the unknown then, like a new horizon, a time when everyone thought that the future would be very, very different.

Well, it certainly was.

Besides, those years had never happened. Not here. There had been no Summer of Love, no Vietnam War, no student protests.

But where were those years?

Her mother had a clapping exercise that she did with the children to show them how the parts of language functioned. "Clap!" (Lots of clapping.) "Stop clapping." Silence. "Where has the clapping gone?"

Those were the verbs, symbolized by a red circle.

Nouns, however, symbolized by a black triangle, did not vanish. They filled the room: floor, table, chair.

Those years had vanished, like verbs.

But, then, why were these pants here? Huh. Some of the nouns were left. Sturdy old things. She tossed the pants aside and returned to the window.

A little boy playing in the yard across the street looked up at her and screamed, "A ghost! Mommy!" He ran crying inside his house.

Jill, grinning, hurried downstairs, ran across the street,

"She's just a big creampuff."

"Yeah, but she sounds like a raging boar and can push people over with one paw."

"Do you have a gun?"

"With a kid in the house? They are illegal. And, as you know, this is a very safe neighborhood. What are you really worried about, Brian?"

He stood up, loosened his tie, rubbed his hair so that it stood up. He looked out the kitchen window and she let him look. He had to say it himself. He took down one of their mother's old, and little used, cookbooks from a nook and flipped through it.

Finally he turned to her and said, "Why don't you move in with us? I've talked about it with Cindy and she thinks it's a great idea."

"Sure, she does." Jill grinned. "You've got plenty of room. I could sleep on the coffee table. And I could help with the kids?"

"No, it's not that."

"So?"

"You're just too fragile."

"Fragile?" She jumped up and lifted the heavy wooden kitchen chair over her head. "Want to step outside, buster?" *Say it*, she thought, *say it*.

"You know what I mean."

"No, I don't."

"Crazy!" He finally yelled. "Crazy!"

She set the chair down and plopped back into it. "That's progress. Sure. I know you and Megan think that I'm nuts and want to keep an eye on me." She took a sip of tea. "If you're that worried, there are a few extra floors you guys could use here."

"That's not it, Jill. This is the worst place you could possibly live. You're just dwelling on the past—in the past."

"I'm sure I am," she said soberly, thinking, *several pasts*, actually. "But what's wrong with that?"

"You can go back to work if you want?"

"I'm not just mooning around the house twenty-four hours a day, if that's what you mean, and going mad, mad, completely mad. I've been moving in. I'm going back to the Bank in a few days, full-time; I've been working part-time. I'm managing the store again, and I'll work there two evenings a week and maybe Saturday mornings, depending on whether Elmore has Whens."

"Don't you think that's a little too *much* work?"

"You're clearly one of those people who are never pleased. How much do you work, Mr. Take-It-Easy? Eighty hours a week?"

"Oh, only about sixty."

"That means it must be at least seventy, and look at what a nervous wreck you are. Besides, we're letting this valuable house go to rack and ruin. I have to get it back in shape. Dad might come back . . ."

"And that's another thing! You wouldn't let us look for him when we could, not for nearly long enough."

"That's not true. You could have stayed there. I was just . . . too . . . I don't know." *Too sad. Too responsible.*

"Too what, Jill? You just plain flipped out, back in Germany. Kind of like you did last month."

"Good grief, Brian, that's a very rude way to talk to a fragile woman. You didn't do much better. If you recall."

"It's not funny. Now we all have kids, jobs—it would be much more difficult. If—well, we just need to know what happened to them. I think it's driving us all crazy."

She thought, *Yup, that's probably true.* A horn honked outside. "That's the van."

"Lucky you. Saved by the horn," he muttered, and followed her to the front door and outside, knocking aside the head-high hydrangea blossoms bowed across the bottom of the stairs.

Whens leaped from the open van door. "Uncle Brian!"

Brian picked him up and swung him around. "Your pack is bigger than you are! How do you like your new house?"

Whens responded by climbing onto Manfred's back. "Giddyup, doggie."

Jill glared at him. "Get off her back right now!"

"She said that she wanted to pretend that she was a horse."

"I doubt it. Sit!" Manfred sat down. Whens slid from her back. "Listen, after dinner, Daddy is going to pick you up."

Brian said, "Got to get back to work. See you soon, Stevie."

"My name is WHENS!"

As Brian drove off, Whens frowned. "I don't want to go to Daddy's. I hate that lady."

He screwed his face into such a fierce scowl that Jill had to choke back laughter. "What lady?"

"The Lavender Lady. She's there all the time."

Jill thought carefully, unsurprised, trying to decide what to say. Her name was Tracy, and she really did wear a dense fog of what was probably incredibly expensive perfume. Of course, she was a lawyer who worked at Elmore's dream firm, and much more aligned to Elmore's worldview. Jill felt an odd rush of relief. Jill cared deeply about Elmore, but the last few months had burned away the gloss of misplaced optimism that had sustained her for so many years. Maybe Tracy could help him come to terms with himself better than she had. "How do you feel about that?"

"*You* need to be there. Not her. She won't let me into the room at night. She locks the door."

Whens was used to running to their bedroom at the least glimpse of his many nighttime monsters.

"And?"

"And I don't like it! I get scared."

"Did you tell Daddy?"

"I banged on the door! I cried and screamed! They wouldn't open the door. I heard her laughing! I went back and cried and cried into my pillow. I made it very, very wet." His face grew solemn. "I knew that when

Daddy looked at the pillow, he'd know how sad I was. But by morning it was all dried out." He slumped to the ground, leaned against his pack, and sighed. "I should have poured a glass of water on it."

Jill succeeded at not laughing. "I'm sorry, sweetie. It upsets me that you're afraid at night. I will give you a phone, and you call me any time you wake up."

He shrugged.

"Let's go sit on the porch. Watch out for the hole in the step. Your father and I are not going to live together anymore."

Whens did not sit. He threw his pack onto the porch and kicked it. "You and Daddy have to live together."

Jill sat in a rocking chair. "No, we don't. I don't want to, and he doesn't want to. It's not your fault."

"I'll make you!"

She hugged him tight. He squirmed, then relaxed. Then he began to cry.

After he was finished and had blown his nose, she said, "Let's go look around in the attic."

"Why?"

"Just to look around. At some of our old things. It's fun."

They went inside.

"Mommy, what's wrong?"

She caught her breath. Closed her eyes.

She had just seen Brian in the living room, telling their parents that he had enlisted in the Navy so that he could fly fighter jets. It had been a terrible scene. It was like she was there again, with all of the rending emotions of not wanting her idiot—but deeply loved—brother going to Vietnam.

What was memory? Was this memory? Fantasy? Dream?

Here, whatever here was, that hadn't happened.

"What's wrong?"

"I was just thinking about something that happened a

long time ago. Megan poured a glass of water from the stairs onto Brian's head. Boy, was he mad. You must have reminded me of it. The attic?"

Whens took the bait. He ran up the stairs. "Come on!"

Jill

A VERY LONG DAY

[*May 7*]

THE FOLLOWING Tuesday, Jill's alarm went off at five and she sat bolt upright, thinking, *When is it going to snow?*

Then the oriole trilled on the gnarled oak branch, which was as thick as the trunk of most trees, outside her window, and sweet spring air, cleansed of traffic smells, ebbed and flowed with dawn's breeze. It was spring, she was in Washington, and it wouldn't snow for a good long while.

Her dream dispersed, she rolled out of bed and hurried to Whens' room.

It was Megan's old room. Jill would have been happier to have Whens sleep with her, in her large, high-ceilinged bedroom, at least until they were both more used to living in such a large house, where one could rattle off anywhere.

Which he had. His bed was rumpled, but empty.

She didn't have all day. "Stephen!" she yelled, but got no reply.

She checked, the screen was in the window, good. He had not climbed out onto the roof, as Megan used to do. Angry and concerned at the same time, she ran down the stairs. "We have to hurry," she hollered. "It's my first full day back at work."

Unfortunately, he was not calmly eating cereal at the kitchen table, as she had hoped. The basement door was

closed, which somewhat abated her fear of finding his lifeless body at the foot of the long open-stringer stairway, which Megan had always refused to descend, thinking she would slip through between the steps. Whens was generally fearless.

She glanced out the window over the sink and glimpsed his wraithy figure in the backyard jungle, just for a second. Bare feet in gray dawn on dew-wet grass before he slipped behind a tree on his way down to the creek. Who else might be there, waiting in the culvert to grab a little boy?

Tearing down the steps, she called out to him. The overgrown garden tore at her arms and face. Bushes had become small trees, and as she ran, her heart pounding even though she knew, really, that Whens was safe, she wondered: Why had her mother not come back to her? Why had she left them? How could she have left them? It seemed utterly impossible to her mother's brain as she found Whens, squatting next to the small creek, his long T-shirt soaked along the bottom, pecking pebbles into a pool.

She made herself take a breath. "Please don't come down here unless I'm outside. I already told you."

He turned his blond-tufted head and stared at her, but didn't say anything. He turned his attention back to pebble-pecking. Then he stood, hoisted a big rock with both hands and smashed it down hard so that it splashed them both.

"Come on, we have to get dressed."

"I'm looking for a pink rock."

She grabbed him around the waist, hoisted him onto her hip, and strode toward the house. "I have to go to work, and you have to go to school and then spend three days with Daddy."

"No!" He flailed his arms and kicked. "That Lavender Lady hugs me and squishes me and her perfume makes me sneeze."

Jill set him down on the steps. "Her name is Tracy,

honey. I don't think she should lock you out of Daddy's room. I'll talk to Daddy about it tonight, okay? But he might not change his mind. If you're afraid at night, you call me on the phone. There's not anything to be afraid of there."

"There might be ghosts there too," he said darkly. "Bad ghosts."

"Get moving! The van will be here in five minutes."

Bette
[*May 7*]

IN HER little garret at the very top of Halcyon House, Bette opened her eyes and stretched. God, but she was stiff!

She sat up in her nest of sheet and blanket and looked out the small window right next to her.

It really was a lovely view. Thirty-five feet below was the roof of the grotto Sam had built for them, and the rushing creek. She was at treetop-level, and the oak leaves fluttering in the crisp morning breeze partially veiled the window, which was good. In the woods behind the yard, spring-green treetops glittered, catching the early sunlight. Her grandson, wearing a long white T-shirt, thumped down the dewy back stairs and ran down the broad stone stairway to the creek.

Kneeling, he reached into the water, and stood, examining something in his hand. Dropping it, he commenced picking up stones and tossing them into the water.

Bette heard Jill, several floors down and therefore very faint, yelling "Stephen!"—her voice distant and irritated. *Is that how I used to sound?* Bette wondered.

Whens/Stevie/Stephen glanced over his shoulder: He'd heard, all right, but was not making a move. He squatted in the tall grass as his mother rushed down the steps, looked around, spotted him, and stormed down to the creek. Bette saw her hands on her hips, her arm stretched

out with one finger pointed in imperious demand, then finally Jill swept him up and carried him, kicking and screaming, into the house. She'd heard something about "work." Good.

Pulling on a T-shirt she'd found in a ravaged box in the attic the night before, Bette moved two narrow wood strips to the left and pushed open what appeared, on the outside, to be broad paneling at the back of a closet. Pivots at the top and the bottom of the wood allowed it to swivel. She sat on the side of the bed and slipped into some battered old Keds from the same attic box.

Parting the ancient clothes hanging on the rack, and stifling a sneeze, she stepped into a tiny bedroom filled with piled-up hatboxes, old furniture, and knickknacks. The room's wallpaper was faded rose, with small bouquets of white posies marching in strict order from top to bottom. The bedroom was beneath the eaves. Bette imagined it had been built for a maid, for the small bathroom, now accessible from both her side and the bedroom, held a toilet and a sink. Having filled the tank the night before, she peed, but did not flush; she'd wait till Jill and Stevie had left.

The final step to getting out was to unlock the pivot bookshelf.

The wall opened into the attic. Laden with old *Reader's Digests* and *National Geographics*, it nevertheless swiveled easily and quietly. She closed it and shot two large bolts into their holes, then twisted them tight; they didn't look any different than the other bolt heads that formed what looked like an ad hoc bookshelf slapped together on one side of the attic. Sam had installed it in the sixties.

She stood for a moment, torn. She needed to find Sam, to rescue *him* if he were in some sort of trouble. But he knew enough about navigation by now that he ought to be safe. He would find his way here, somehow. That is, if he remembered. The lump of dread returned to her chest. He had become more frail lately.

As had she. But he was worse. Timestreaming took a toll.

Jill and Stevie knew a lot less about what might be going on than Sam did. And Wink had insisted on some sort of danger. To Jill. Perhaps she had landed in the hospital because of her former contact with the Game Board.

Or maybe those who knew about it were in pursuit of the Device, but didn't know quite enough about it. Yet.

She moved gingerly across the attic so as not to push over precariously balanced piles of stuff, and got to the front of the house. She looked down on the yard and the street through a dingy window.

After fifteen minutes, Jill, in a business suit, put Stevie into a van and waved good-bye. She walked down the sidewalk and turned the corner, heading, Bette presumed, toward the bus stop. She ached, simply ached, to hold her daughter within her arms, to hug her so very close. But right now, it was wiser to remain hidden. Wait for the enemy to show him- or herself. Then move.

And then there was the simple, yet immense problem of her children, especially Jill, absorbing and processing the changes in which they had played an integral part.

The human mind was an odd amalgam of past and present, and hers, a bit of it, contained some of several futures. No one *learned* just by being told something. Only experience, motion, emotion, changed the brain physically so that learning, which was a change in neural pathways, took place.

After all she and her family had been through, she did not want to short-circuit that process. Through the Infinite Game Board, through the Device's infusion into the physical objects in the attic, and, most probably, their growing, vulnerable brains, the neural foundation for such deep learning had been laid down. It would take some kind of catalyzing experience to bring it to fruition, to make all the hard work, angst, and anger they must have suffered worth it by moving them forward into the

next phase. She could not just walk up to the door and say: *Hi, I'm here to explain.* They could not truly change until they were immersed in an event, in decision. Currently, there was no simulation-learning experience one could use to log hours on mastering timestreaming. But she was certain that her children had experienced such flashes, and Jill had actually done it. No wonder she landed in the nuthouse.

The larger problem was simply the presence, here, of dangerous individuals or organizations who would stop at nothing to get at the secrets of the Device, the driver of Q, a potential means of controlling the world. Optimally, so many humans would be synched into the consensus mind of Q that sociopaths would be overruled—perhaps even healed. Until that tipping point occurred, whoever was after Jill, whoever was following her, did not need any more ammunition or clues. Bette had to seek them out and destroy them in secret, from her war center here in the attic of Halcyon House. She had to force them to reveal themselves.

If Stevie ran out in front of a bus, though, she knew that she would break her own neck to get down there and save him.

Throughout the night, Bette had slowly recovered from the awful disorientation that segues from one time to the other always brought. She recalled her life lived here now. If she somehow returned to her original WWII self, she would not remember those years, though. Maybe in glimmers, here and there, or in dreams, but the life she could look back on, from here, would not occur if she returned with a memory of it. Her entire life had become permeable, a collection of nexes, during which she moved from stream to stream, not with the ease of Hadntz by any means. She too was just a student, not yet a teacher.

With each move through the timestreams, she brought more information back to what she thought of as her "central" life, but there was really no center any longer.

A lot of her "life," which she thought of as a collection, possibly infinite, of clear bubbles that sometimes touched another bubble, or was enmeshed in a foam, was not informed by other parts of her life. It was not like knowing what would happen in some linear future, and investing in the right stock, railroad, or mountaintop. Instead, she had a sense of ascension, of improving the lot of humanity, of curing the disease of war, bit by bit, as knowledge and information accumulated. She had found that it was better not to know what the future held, anyway. After all, if she had actually believed that she, a ten-year-old girl, could really change to the near-sightless, crippled, ancient-faced (but still cheerful) grandmother she had known, would she have really wanted to grow up at all?

She and Sam, and, later, just Sam, had planned for many possibilities. This house was a perfect instrument for them, part of their plan.

She ventured down narrow attic stairs to the rarely used third floor and glanced into the bathroom at the end of the hall. Hmmm. Grimy, no soap or shampoo in sight, no toilet paper, no towels.

But wait—there was an old linen closet mid-hallway. Yes, inside, were perfectly flattened sheets from, probably, the 1940s, a pile of thin, rough towels, washrags, and cakes of Ivory soap, "So Pure It Floats." And a half-used bottle of Estée Lauder shampoo, but so old that it was petrified.

The second floor—gah, what a mess! But lived in. Jill and Stevie used the bathroom at the end of the hall. Luckily, a lot of half-used shampoo bottles were on Jill's bathroom windowsill. She grabbed shampoo and a razor. In her own old dressing room, another small bedroom lined with clothes racks, drawers, a vanity, and some mirrors, she found what she was looking for. She took some slacks, a few nice blouses, some underwear—evidently no one had decided to clean out this room. She felt a pang. Of course. They always hoped she'd come back.

She took her first look in the mirror with some shock. Hey, what a beauty. Wide, blue eyes stared back, framed by a youngster's twenty-six-year-old face, fine as porcelain. Unkempt brilliant golden hair cascaded to her shoulders, catching highlights from the sun coming in the window. Not a wrinkle, not a mar.

She found it amusing that she was not at all pleased. Her real face, which showed that hard-won maturity, every iota of pain and love and joy etched in skin patterns, was much more pleasing. She had always worn every scar as a badge, as evidence that she had survived, and grown, and regarded her face as being much the same. Shedding her clothes, she found she rather liked the look of the rest of her body—long, strong legs, good for running; the fine, rounded breasts, with attraction power that had always so amused her. All that was much better than her nearly seventy-year-old body, even though Sam told her she looked more like she was still fifty.

Grabbing her clothes, she hurried upstairs and took a quick bath after scrubbing the tub. Evidence of use, yes, but who the heck would notice. When she was finished, she stood for a moment in the long hallway, dressed, but barefoot, and then descended to the first floor, her heart more flooded with sadness with every descending step.

The house was like her own body, entwined with her emotions, as if it pumped neurochemicals through her blood and into her brain.

It was like a dream.

Most everything was the same, until she got to the kitchen. None of her spattered cookbooks on the quarter-circle shelves. No *Dell Crossword Puzzles* magazines scattered across the big table.

Mom had indeed been erased, here.

Battling tears, she went over to the sink to look out at the view she'd gazed at so often while washing dishes, thinking it would soothe her. The woods were closer; the huge stone grill and wood-burning oven Sam had built were just big green kudzu-covered lumps.

Then she refocused on the windowsill. Smiled. Plucked up one of the many Spacies arranged in a moon-colony tableau on the wide surface. They were overhung by philodendron leaves, which assumed the mien of gigantic jungle plants, a tropicalized moonscape, or perhaps another planet altogether.

She held the one she'd always called Bootstrap Jack, a standard-issue blond guy astronaut, who had been standing, perpetually heroic, next to a Chinese woman seated somewhat pensively on a half-used spool of white thread with a needle stuck into it.

The Spacies had not been here when she left. They were here because she *had* left. Bootstrap Jack reassured her, gazing blankly and dedicatedly outward toward the New Frontier, toward The Future, reminding her that she had actually made a difference. She sank into a kitchen chair, because everything came back with such a wallop.

Timestream One

∾

1963

Bette

DALLAS IN 3/3/ TIME

[*November 22, 1963*]

ON NOVEMBER 22, 1963, Bette was in Dallas, Texas. She wore a suit she'd bought in downtown D.C., hem exactly at the center of her knees. White gloves. Pillbox hat. A suit worthy of an ambassador's party or a Junior League soiree.

Grasping her briefcase handle with her left hand, she followed the railroad track, which was on a rise above Kennedy's motorcade route through Dealey Plaza, and bordered by a parking lot.

Spotting the pickup truck she knew would be there, she put everything out of her mind: that she was about to try to change history—one history, at least—to save, not the world, not the country, but her daughter Jill. And that she was enraged with not only Eliani Hadntz, but herself.

She stepped from the tracks and walked on the grassy verge so as not to alert the men by crunching cinders or gravel beneath her low-heeled shoes. Approaching from the back, she reached into her holster with her right hand and drew her silenced Luger. At the same time, she crouched, setting her briefcase on one end to partially disguise her action—from any viewers on that side, at least, but everyone seemed intent on the approaching motorcade, just rounding the Elm Street curve below the Texas School Book Depository.

Anson and Mac, standing in the bed of a pickup, raised their rifles as the motorcade approached. They were all part of the international espionage community. People were known by reputation, or by code names. The best were not known at all.

Bette remembered Mac the instant he sensed her presence and turned; the instant she shot him. She had made

a drop to him in Prague in 1943. When Mac collapsed, Anson Konrad swung around and smiled ironically, in recognition, and without surprise, as he too died. She'd come out of nowhere, but someone was bound to, some-day, somewhere. People in their line of work rarely died in their beds, after all. She probably wouldn't either.

She'd met Anson Konrad in Copenhagen during the war, before he had been remade into an American. His oldest son, a member of the Hitler Youth, had died in the Battle of Berlin. His German wife and only other child, a boy, had been given an American small-town past by the OSS in exchange for secrets.

In Copenhagen in 1943, Konrad had been blond. He died bald. Bette reholstered her gun, rose, grabbed her briefcase, and hurried down the low hill to Elm Street.

Sirens drowned out the crowd's cheers as two images rose before her, superimposed: Kennedy splayed back in the speeding Lincoln as Jacqueline crawled onto the trunk of the open limo. And then the ghostly overlay of cheering crowds, the waving President, and safe passage beneath the overpass as the President headed toward the Trade Mart, where he was to give a speech.

The second vision strengthened to reality. Bette stopped for a moment, astonished, and a quick tremor ran through her, a cold snap of the spine.

Her vision darkened. A period of time passed, but she had no idea how much. Sight returned gradually. Her arms ached; she embraced a lamppost as tightly as if it were a lover. Trucks and cars flowed smoothly down the motorcade route. Gingerly, she let go, reeled, and grabbed the lamppost again. The crowd dispersed, hav-ing glimpsed the President, and headed back to work. But one man, prone on the sidewalk across Elm Street, an umbrella lying next to him, was drawing a crowd.

At the same time, a familiar figure hurried, limping, toward the underpass. She almost called out "Wink!" but bit her tongue. Wink had been stationed down among the crowd to take care of the Umbrella Man—

so-called because he was armed with an umbrella that fired poisoned darts to pick off Kennedy should the other snipers fail.

By the time she reached the underpass, Wink had vanished. In fact, in those few moments, many things had changed. Here, now, she was one of just a few people out for their lunch break. No crowds. No assassination. No attempted assassination, apparently.

The Texas School Book Depository was a block east, square and anonymous looking. The sky was blue and bright. She smelled exhaust. No pickup truck, no dead men, were in sight.

Where had it all gone?

She staggered a few steps in her low heels. A bum ambled past, giving her a glance of commiseration. Keeping her balance with great concentration, she vomited behind one of the pillars of the underpass and wiped her mouth with a hank of weeds she yanked from the ground. Then she straightened, walked to the Texas School Book Depository and went inside.

She did get a few looks as she found her way to the elevator. After all, this was a warehouse; she wore a fancy dress suit and smelled like vomit. She took the elevator to the sixth floor; stepped out.

Piles of lumber, boxes of nails, and open toolboxes filled the open space. She prowled through the room, checking behind each pile of lumber, peering into corners. No Jill, no Sam. Which, of course, was good. They were not lying there dead.

Then, on the floor near one of the windows, she spied the small Army pack Jill had bought at Sonny's Surplus on M Street.

In her haste to grab it, Bette stumbled over an open toolbox and cut her knee on its edge as she fell.

She lay on the floor for a second, surprised. Her coordination was excellent; she generally moved in perfect tune with her surroundings, a part of her mind constantly gauging and adjusting, helping her run or drive through

the most irregular kinds of places, sometimes while shooting at people. Maybe she had suffered a concussion? She did have a headache, which worsened by the second.

She gazed straight ahead and saw the gray metal of the toolbox, a hammer's wooden handle. She carefully got to her feet. Blood seeped through her ripped nylon stocking and ran down her leg. She ignored it, caught up the pack, unzipped it.

A copy of *Gypsy Myra,* Jill's comic. A pair of ragged jeans, a T-shirt, some underwear.

And the Infinite Game Board.

She held it in both hands for a moment, watching images skitter across the flat surface, seemingly random, so fleeting that they were almost subliminal, tempting the user to touch them. She understood that they were possibilities, rendered visual, an interface between the mysterious quantum realm, which rooted and infused everything, including human consciousness, and the "slower" level of reality that humans believed was absolute and immutable, because that was what their senses told them. It was indeed a phenomenon that humans could only attempt to define, yet Hadntz's Device drew its energy from that level, sorting, sifting, linking with untold numbers of conscious minds, conscious lives, to bring forth something new. Rough analogies might be radio, sorting coded signals from the atmosphere and turning them back into spoken words or music, patterns. Hadntz had hoped to somehow access the best in humans and distribute that; lock, transmit, and then unlock those signals of altruism and peace, transmit them, move them into historic reality.

But obviously, something was missing. Perhaps, Bette thought, altruism did not exist. Or if it did, it was in tiny, rare amounts, and needed some kind of massive magnification in order to overwhelm all that was evil and take hold, result in decision, resolve, action.

The board was the offspring of Sam's, Wink's, and

Hadntz's efforts, during the war, to bring a new world to fruition. And her efforts too, of course. How often she and Sam had wanted to throw the resulting H-3, H-6, H-23, and various self-manifesting incarnations of the Hadntz Device into the ocean, into a volcano, blast it into space.

They should have tried harder.

Her dizziness returned as the images grew stronger, more insistent. She sank down to a pile of lumber, pulled off her hat, loosened her bobby-pinned hair, and ran her fingers through it, desperately needing a drink of water. The board pulsed in her hands.

"*Damn* it!" She flung it like a Frisbee across the room, where it clattered to the floor. Vision wavered again. Another nexus? She couldn't stand another!

There seemed to be as many ways to switch timestreams as there were people. Bette and Sam had known for years that Hadntz moved through times with conscious intent and control. She called the nodes where one could traverse the timestreams easily "nexes." Wink, who had navigated them, always described them in a different way, but timestreams in general were like constant jazz improvisations by humans who were changing and learning instant by instant. She'd asked him how he recognized a nexus. He looked puzzled, then said, "It's kind of like getting close to a traffic jam. The traffic gets dense. Cars slow down. Or . . . maybe it's like seeing a twister up ahead. Ever see one of those? Or—the end of a rainbow? Some anomaly, a shimmer in the fabric of reality, if you want to get fancy, an off-note that gives rise to a whole new way of playing a tune. Hell, Bette, I don't know. I just know I have to head in that direction." When she raised her eyebrows, he shrugged and said, "I helped start all this. I have to do what I have to do."

"And that is?"

"Help. Help you and Sam and your kids. We're all in this together."

"Hadntz's vision? What about all that? Ending war forever?"

"There's that too."

Yes, she thought. *There's that too. Maybe. Isn't it pretty to think so.*

Getting to her feet, she retrieved the board, shoved it back inside the dusty pack, and ground her teeth during the interminable elevator descent.

She was in a parking lot. No one was around. In front of her was a Buick Skylark convertible, top down, in the shade.

She had slung her bag, briefcase, and Jill's pack across the vast, plastic turquoise seat, slid in, hotwired it, and nosed out onto the street before she saw that the car she had stolen was not a Buick. A metal insignia above the radio claimed the car was a Durant, a car she'd never heard of. Stylistically, though, it was identical to a 1962 Buick Skylark. She'd owned one.

A newspaper on the front seat claimed that it was November 22, 1963. Above the fold, a smiling Richard Nixon shook hands with Nikita Khrushchev.

"Damn, damn, *damn*!" Now something *else* had happened. She'd been whipped around—probably by touching the Game Board—into an entirely new timestream.

She concentrated on staying exactly at the speed limit until she reached the outskirts of the city. Then she floored the gas pedal. The Durant leaped from thirty to eighty in ten seconds. Not bad. In Texas, her speed was the norm. The newspaper whipped into the sky.

She drove away from Dallas without her usual haste—that would have been 110 mph, for her, on this straight road—to avoid police questioning, and to try and think.

The vehicle she had used to get here, bringing Wink and Sam with her, resembled an airplane, and had grown from Hadntz's Device, as had the Game Board in Jill's pack.

Bette did not know who might be in this timestream, what they might surmise, or how they might punish her,

and her family, for what she had done. She almost laughed. Causing Nixon to be president, if that was what she had helped foster, was crime enough!

By now, Bette had moved from feeling drunk to merely feeling disconnected. She tried to think she might be dreaming, but knew, her heart heavy, that she was not.

She tried to focus. Part of her mind registered the fact that the speedometer of the big Durant had crept up to ninety. Yet, it seemed to take a full day to pass a weathered farmhouse. Her vision lingered on and analyzed every sun-bleached board, every remaining streak or chip of white paint. Maybe it was some kind of new brain state, due to a too-swift negotiation of timestreams: the *whens*. A hypnotic locus. Whatever it was, she felt as if she had been hit on the head. Punched in the stomach. In her spy career, she had experienced both events. Her visual abilities were acute, near photographic, so the small differences between this world and her last glared. Sun Oil gas stations rather than Sunoco; a billboard advertising the previously nonexistent Trans-America Rail Company, with windowed star roofs and fine cuisine, like the Union Pacific Streamliner cars she recalled.

A lone, low structure loomed ahead, the color of sunscoured bone. Big Mike's Hideaway. At the last second, she wrenched the steering wheel, slid into the dirt parking lot in a cloud of dust, and pulled up next to a telephone booth in the parking lot.

She sat still for a moment, head down, eyes closed. It had to be done.

Stepping out of the Durant, she pushed open the phone booth door and picked up the receiver. Dialed zero.

The operator answered. "May I help you?"

Bette couldn't speak. She saw her faint reflection in the glass of the door, royally snarled hair and haggard face belying the composed, sophisticated suit.

"Would you like to make a call?"

"I—" a whisper. She cleared her throat. "Person-to-person, Sam Dance, Washington, D.C., National 5-7333."

She heard clicking and whirring. "No such number. Are you sure?"

She repeated the number, but the results were the same.

"Try information for Samuel Dance." She gave the address.

"No one by that name."

Bette dropped the receiver and pushed herself from the booth. She staggered to the open door of the Durant but did not get in. She leaned back against the side of the car and looked at the sky but did not see it.

"Ma'am?"

She looked down and saw a bearded face shadowed by a brown cowboy hat, blue eyes narrowed in concern. "Ma'am? You all right? Need some water? Or somethin'?"

"A cigarette, if you have one."

He straightened and fished one from his shirt pocket. She did not see the brand. She put it between her lips and he lit it for her. She took a deep drag.

Gone. All gone. Was it possible?

"Bad news?" He glanced at the dangling receiver, reached into the booth, put it back on the hook.

"Yes," she managed. "Thank you. I'm all right now."

He looked doubtful, so she thanked him again, tossed the butt on the gravel, got in the car, and pulled onto the empty highway.

The answer was definitely yes. Bad news.

They were gone.

Her beloved family may have survived, in another trajectory, but she might never see them again. Perhaps that was the price: her own exile in time.

She steeled herself, and rejected that possibility. She was jumping to conclusions.

She had brought Sam and Wink here, in the timestream-jumping—no, say it, timestream-*causing* plane—that had grown, from a portion of the Hadntz Device in the Nazi Messerschmitt caves near Oberammergau. In doing so, she had saved Jill. She hoped.

But maybe she had simply eliminated all of them, forever. Maybe she had caused a new timestream that did not include the Dance family at all.

She was adrift, in neither world. Not, it seemed, in the new world that she, Jill, Sam, Wink, and Hadntz had hoped to usher in by foiling the Kennedy assassination, the one they had left in 1968, in a panic, following their daughter. The year was 1963, but not the 1963 she and her family had lived through. In this world, Nixon, not Kennedy, was President on November 22, 1963.

Hadntz had given Jill some sort of path from 1970, World Prime, she decided to call it, to a 1963 slightly different from the one she had lived through seven years ago. It all had something to do with that damned socalled Game Board in Jill's pack, now in the backseat. That was what the kids had called it, back when they'd first found it, back when the Hadntz Device she and Sam had hidden in the attic had manifested in the fun toy for kids which was now in Jill's pack, having done its damage.

She halted her mental rant. It would do no good.

Holding the wheel with her left hand, she teased a Camel from the owner's pack of cigarettes, which was wedged in the ashtray, punched in the cigarette lighter, took a drag, and then loosened the blue scarf covering her hair. She watched it fly out the window and hang behind her, from the side mirror, for an absurdly long ninety-mile-an-hour speck of time dilation, flowing in slow, beautiful wind-driven billows.

She wrenched her attention away from that. So. New worlds would fly—had flown—out of Pandora's box. She was in a new timestream she herself had helped create. One couldn't think about it too much; it was impossible to trace the trajectories.

Sam was probably lost to her as well. Everything, everyone she loved.

It seemed like a very bad deal. She had made a devil's bargain with Hadntz—with her *ideas*—and had lost.

But no, no. There was another way to look at it, which was, *This is not finished yet*. For instance, there was the matter of Wink, limping away. Injured, but alive, in the 1963 in which Kennedy was President, and had *lived*, before the Device had swirled her around to this present Nixon-land when she picked it up in the Texas Book Depository.

Both of which, in the shifting landscape of timestreams, were probably infinitely small threads, never to be found again, judging how easily, how wildly, she had careened into *this* thread.

The land rolled slightly, dun colored beneath its wash of green shrubs and occasional trees. Jill would have seen this on her way into Dallas, if she'd come during the day.

But Bette didn't even want to know too much about that, about any of those details.

Because knowing Othertime changed Othertime. It was as simple as that. What you saw or knew was changed by the weight of your new knowing. And then all that was left was the simple hard bones of action, nouns: curved skeletons others might come across, unable to deduce the flesh, the action, the living verb of being that had grown and housed those bones. Just as the action that went into preparing to sew a dress left only the dress.

This noun was a whole new timestream.

And she, perhaps, was now one of those skeletons. At least, in her deep being, she felt like one, scoured of everything that mattered. She had thought a lot about timestreams in the past few years. Sam preferred Hadntz's metaphor of timestreams as gardens, wisely managed by the new, improved humans to come as a result of the Device.

Bette's metaphor was that a timestream was like a human body, previously diseased and morally damaged by violence and war. Change the concentration of some hormone, add or subtract vitamins, repress disease-causing genes, give that body the right education, and a

still-recognizable but slightly different human timestream would result, one where humans might make wiser decisions.

But reality was now well beyond metaphor for Bette. This was worse than war. Simply deep, unending pain. Devil's bargain was definitely a viable addition to the list.

Bette turned onto the thin line in the dust that led to a lone windsock, brilliant red against high blue just-past-noon. Had Kennedy, with all his flaws as well as all his good instincts, been saved, somewhen? If so, why?

For love of a thin, tall girl, Jill. That was all. It all came down to the personal, in the end—what a surprise. And what would she do now, that girl? For Bette had to assume that her family still lived, somewhere, in some time, or she would go mad. What would her other children, Brian and Megan, whom she loved as fully, as deeply, do? In 1963, they were still very young, and they would not have a mother. What would Sam do? Would another Bette be there, another mother, who would see them grow up? Bette added irrational, intense jealousy to her list of deadly sins.

She'd given up much in the war, for her war's cause, but it had been miraculously restored by Sam, with Sam. She had sworn to him that she would leave the CIA as well, but she'd been drawn back into the tangled weave of history by something that had started a long, long time ago, and Sam had been hooked too. By daring to have a family, they had created three valuable hostages— Jill, Brian, and Megan—whose existence would force her to do anything to keep them safe. And what did the CIA, or other, more shadowy parties, want? Information about the Device, which they, and many others, knew or suspected existed.

Oh, she'd had her rosy visions, all right. Advanced understanding of the neurology of learning, and of brain plasticity—neurogenesis—in children and in adults, would help every child to know the thrill of accessing

written culture, art, music, and science, and enable them to contribute to more growth. It would help adults learn new skills, new knowledge: it might even help some gain wisdom. It would unite the two cultures, those of science and literature. Each scientific and literary discipline had its own code, or codes. More people would be able to decipher more codes, and cross-reference them. Humans would go to Mars, and beyond. She expected vast, accelerated change and improvement in all spheres. There might even be equality of rights and enforcement of them for all, food for all, universal and excellent education. Not just in the United States, but in the entire world.

Would that be worth division from her family, their division from her, which would be like death?

She couldn't think like that. The power of human thought, linked by new technologies, would grow more quickly, fertilized from all directions, and perhaps there would be a nexus.

A nexus, or maybe a choice of nexes, where she could catch up with them, would appear, perhaps proliferate. She might be able to walk right back into their lives. Up the walk, onto the porch of Halcyon House in downtown Washington, through the screen door, and into the heart of the house, the kitchen. Into the arms of Sam Dance, who would give her one hell of a kiss.

Yes.

It was important to have dreams, vision, a model for what she wanted to happen.

Her thoughts were not very focused as she got out of the car and slammed the door. She had no idea what she should do.

Leonard, a man who looked like an old Texas cowhand but was not, rose from his rocking chair to meet her. He didn't speak, just nodded, and his nod was short.

He opened the car door, and after she got out, grabbed her bag and her briefcase. His mouth quirked a bit when

he retrieved Jill's backpack, but Bette was not sure it counted as a smile.

She set the briefcase on the trunk and opened it. At least it was the same, as far as she could tell. Various weapons. Lots of cash, several passports. And—there, in plastic bags beneath some papers, were Spacies.

Spacies were small plastic figures dressed as astronauts, space workers, and other characters who might play a role in a future, fictional space program. They were a little bigger than the ubiquitous green Army men Brian hoarded—more detailed, life-colored, and bright. They glimmered with the seductive lure of The Future. The Future had begun a long time ago, perhaps during the Enlightenment, but had lately picked up serious speed. Her kids watched *The Jetsons*. Disney's Atomic Genie towered over the globe like a huge mushroom cloud, and was then tamed back into the magic lamp by wise humans.

This was one genie that couldn't be stopped. Or tamed, apparently.

Spacies had been manifested by the Device. The Hadntz Device H-26, or H-27? Contact with Spacies would modify the genetic predisposition for unthinking rage and violence and render them subject to consideration of appropriate actions. Touching Spacies also stimulated controlled neurogenesis, and might result in undreamed of artistic and intellectual abilities in children as well as adults. So perhaps Spacies, or something like them, or something that might grow from them, were the mitigating factor, that which would add the missing ingredients of empathy, altruism, and hope, to humanity's grim history.

Bette touched the helmet of the African-American astronaut, a woman—caressed it, really, though it was just a brush with her fingertips—thinking, *This is what I must do now. Ensure that future.* That had been the plan. Had she—had the Device—known this was going

to happen? Anger and joy, like electric shocks, shot through her. Was she part of some damned *plan,* some kind of predetermined process? Or was she a free-willed participant in the continuing twists and turns of an evolution toward light?

She let joy—choice, power, responsibility—win. Anger, now, was useless; deadening. She did have a choice. She did have agency. She would continue the fight.

She asked Leonard, "Did—did Jill and Sam come back here? Wink?" Memories of Sam and Wink, fast buddies during the war, in England, France, and Germany, rushed into her mind. Young, brilliant, committed, reckless. Lovers of jazz. Pranksters, jokers. Marvelous men.

"You could say they did. You could also say they didn't."

"Fuck you, Leonard."

"Everything go okay?"

"I guess you could say so. You could also say it didn't."

His pale gray eyes had seen it all and more. They sat deep in his wizened, too-tanned face like the eyes of a hawk. "It was your call."

"Doesn't seem like it, right now." She looked around at scrub and high clouds, at this new-changed world, now moving, like a sideswiped billiard ball on a new trajectory. Right or not right, this was what she had, and where she was. She had to go forward. Sideways. Wherever necessary, however difficult, in this quest.

They walked toward her small plane, grown from a piece of the Hadntz Device, which made her desperately sick whenever she flew it and traversed the timestreams, two tiny figures in a vast, grass-covered field. She carried a briefcase, a purse, and, in the pack and in her mind, all that remained for her of hope and love, dream and possibility.

Timestream Two

~

1963

Eliani Hadntz
[*November 22*]

THE HUMAN brain was distantly capable of understanding that the possibility existed for what Eliani Hadntz now called Q, for kinetic knowledge of Q and the ability to actually use and manipulate it via "thought." Scientists had nosed around it for years, like tiny fish nibbling on a huge kernel of corn drifting through their waters. Nibble and dart, nibble and dart. Physicists, biologists, biochemists, neurologists, even novelists; even theologians and philosophers. Nicking off little bits, swallowing them. A dangerous idea. Too radical, too like Augustine's God, simply That Which Was Outside the Boundaries of Thought. The Unknown. So the idea had never been devoured; digested. It remained ever-drifting, an object of fascination, a type of hunger, a cipher for a hunger never satisfied, sought through the substitutes of war, money, worship, science, gardening, needlepoint, car racing, and sports: something ultimate.

And so the infinite tunneling pathways of Q remained undiscovered, unexplored, unexploited.

Until now. She had not created them, merely intuited their existence, studied and defined them, as electricity, atomic fission, and DNA had been illuminated and used by humans, and created her Device. Her alternative to war's solution to war, which always resulted in more war. An alternative that might bring peace.

And suddenly, now reached backward, forward, sideways, around all corners, to encompass Everything. The singing strings of which the universe was composed could be known, and used. Humans could learn how to play their own music of time at last.

At least they would at some point in this process, which might be a long one. Or which might happen in just one or two generations: an evolutionary leap.

That was, roughly, what Dr. Eliani Hadntz was thinking on this particular afternoon, November 22, 1963, in this new timestream.

She perched on a stool in a dingy bar in Dallas, wearing jeans and a plaid shirt, a red bandana knotted around her neck, drinking a cold long-neck Bud while pool balls cracked off one another behind her. She was watching John F. Kennedy's speech at the Dallas Trade Mart, the speech he had intended to make the afternoon of November 22, 1963, on a small black-and-white TV that sat on the bar. She was the only one in the bar who seemed interested in the President's speech. She'd paid the bartender a dollar to change the channel.

She had to meet with Bette at some point. Hadntz was not sure where Bette was right now, but she was in extreme danger. Bette was resourceful. She would know what to do in any circumstance, yet Hadntz was uneasy. The exceedingly complex, vast computational power of Q had shown that World Prime had been headed toward some very heavy storms, which included global environmental disaster, increased proliferation of nuclear weapons and the will to use them, financial disasters of great magnitude, and widespread, willful ignorance of scientific education. Consciously controlled evolution would ensue on this new path, where the Dance family, except for Bette, resided now. But whose consciousness, whose idea of goodness? Hadntz was not the first person to think deeply about how to bring about the greatest good for the greatest number of people, plants, animals, and the living membranes of air and water in which they lived, but she was the first who had ever attempted to try to affect such change using the tools of mathematics, physics, and the biological sciences.

Others who knew about the existence of the Device were few, but powerful, and most definitely not altruistic. Would Q, at this point, even allow itself to be used for a negative purpose? It might still be fragile enough to be vulnerable. And certainly Sam, Megan, Jill, and

Brian Dance were fragile, though Sam and Jill were the only ones who knew about the Device. And Wink—Alan Winklemeyer—knew. His timestream had diverged from World Prime within a day after the Device's true activation, in the presence of Sam and Wink, in the observation plane that flew with the *Enola Gay*. Wink was a curious man. Rather a playboy, he had never married, and found himself, with the rest of their Army compatriots, in Sam's company during their reunions—though he and Sam were the only ones who realized the intersection of timestreams, that nexes, and knew how it had come about. Since then, he had gained some skill in traversing timestreams, as had Hadntz long ago. But where was he now?

Ah, where were they all? Dead and gone; ashes. Her renowned father, lecturer in physics in Vienna, who had enabled her physics doctorate; her mother, Rosa, with a medical degree from Switzerland, the only place she could get one in Europe at the time, but could not practice, nor own property, in Vienna. Freud, in whose salons Hadntz had participated; Lise Meitner, whom she had met at the German front in Lviv, Poland, 1915, where she was doctoring and Meitner was taking X-rays and avoiding developing poison gas at the Kaiser Wilhelm Institute. Her former fiancé, who died in her arms in that same hospital, gassed, who had married another woman because he had not wanted to marry a woman doctor . . . so very, very many, gone in this war-torn century. Rosa had died in a concentration camp at the end of the war, captured in a hospital in Budapest, while Eliani had been elsewhere in Europe, developing her Device, which might save millions of future children from the same fate: the most terrible choice she had ever made, for surely, she could have saved her mother. Yet, her mother would have understood her choice completely, for she had fiercely reared her daughter to make such choices, to be in a position to be able to actually make changes. Big changes.

Hadntz dashed away tears with a bar napkin. She had neither time nor tolerance for self-pity. She had made hard choices. No one would ever know their depth, or their cost.

She had recruited Bette during Kristallnacht, in Vienna, and Bette had worked her own relationship with Dulles and the OSS to enable secret development of the Device, which kept it out of the hands of any government. Bette, and Sam, had paid the price too, of their own free will. Their only mistake had been in thinking they could protect their children.

She, Hadntz, could seemingly live "forever," whatever that meant, fragmented among timestreams, continuing her work. In other timestreams, which repeatedly branched, she was an internationally lauded scientist. But she was repeatedly and strongly drawn to this timestream, just one step removed from that of her birth. If hunger for a long life had ever mattered to her, that hunger was long extinguished—except for her desire to help humanity change for the better. After her husband had died, and after all the atrocities she had witnessed, during two world wars that lay bare the darkest corners of humanity's appetite for atrocity, her own life seemed unimportant to her, just one life among billions. But on a larger scale, regarding her work, it mattered tremendously. She still envisioned an egalitarian world, free of all that was worst in human nature. An Africa, Middle East, Asia, and South America free from the legacy of colonization, artificial nations, corruption. That world was based on universal, science-based education, which Dr. Montessori had so brilliantly pioneered, and which continued to evolve as its tenets were confirmed by FMRI and other tools. The path was not easy, but her training in the biological as well as physical sciences was an unusual combination, giving her a uniquely wide view of the physicality of consciousness, and of the brain's astounding plasticity, in which she placed all her faith. Change for the better could and would sweep across the world,

perhaps in a very short time, much as the printed word had washed away the Dark Ages. But *this* change would spring from human biology itself.

Focusing once again on a small, black-and-white Kennedy, Eliani Hadntz allowed herself a rare second of satisfaction: surely there were a lot of pissed-off people in Washington right now.

Familiar heartache eclipsed her satisfaction. At least, this sadness confirmed, for her, that she was still human. This event, for those who could straddle the timestreams—and this event would, in itself, help spread that capacity—spectacularly confirmed the existence of the Device, which she, Bette, Sam, and Wink had kept secret from most of the intelligence community. They would relentlessly pursue Bette and her family for the notes, the knowledge. For the Device itself.

Bette would have to vanish.

Hadntz motioned to the bartender to turn up the volume as Kennedy wound up his speech:

"Finally, it should be clear by now that a nation can be no stronger abroad than she is at home. Only an America that practices what it preaches about equal rights and social justice will be respected by those whose choice affects our future. Only an America that has fully educated its citizens is fully capable of tackling the complex problems and perceiving the hidden dangers of the world in which we live. And only an America which is growing and prospering economically can sustain the worldwide defenses of freedom, while demonstrating to all concerned the opportunities of our system and society."

Equal rights. Social justice. Education. Economics. Those were the high points, and she fully agreed. Who wouldn't? The main question was whether or not Kennedy had the clout to carry through on his vision.

At least now he had a chance to try.

Hadntz slid off the barstool, slapped a dollar on the counter, and headed for the door. She had to keep watch over the Dance family now. They were her responsibility.

It was time to get back to work.

She knew by now: The War, and her work on the Device, would never end.

Bette
[*December 1963, Battle Creek, Michigan*]

THE MAN behind the mahogany desk at General Mills in Battle Creek, Michigan, responded to the secretary on his intercom: "Who?"

"Mrs. Bette Elegante."

"I don't recall the name. Do I have an appointment with her?"

"Yes, sir."

"What is the nature of the appointment?"

"She says that it is national interest."

"Tell her she has five minutes."

The woman who entered his spacious office on that winter day wore a subdued black business suit. Her blond hair was perfectly coiffed in a flip. High heels showed off rather spectacular legs.

He rose and held out his hand. "Hello. Fred Alexander."

She shook his hand firmly and quickly. "My name is Bette Elegante, and I would like to propose a business arrangement. My firm has developed a line of inexpensive, exciting toys for cereal boxes."

"We already have arrangements with—"

She had already set her briefcase on his desk. She opened it and took out a plastic case, the lid of which displayed a picture of a large American flag planted on what appeared to be the moon.

He leaned forward. "All right, as long as you're here, what do you have?"

She opened the box, removed one small figure, and set it on his desk. It reminded him of the green plastic soldiers his boys played with, but it was a bit larger, and brightly colored. "This is an astronaut."

"A what?"

"That is what we will be calling people who go into space. Look. The helmet comes off."

"Isn't that . . . a girl? Is she . . . colored?"

"Oh, yes. We will have girls, boys, black, white, and in between."

"Well, I don't know . . ."

"This is a space capsule. See how the door opens?" She popped one of the tiny figures inside. "And this is a launchpad. You operate it with a rubber band—like so." A tiny rocket, with the capsule snapped onto the top, flew across the room. She walked over, stooped with fascinating grace, and picked it up. "The capsule separates from the rocket as soon as it gets into space. Oh, here are some cards—you get one in each box of cereal—that give facts. Like, 'Where does space start, anyway?' "

"I don't know."

"Sixty-two miles, or one hundred kilometers, above the Earth." She handed him the rocket and space capsule. "Just pop that off—that's right. Kind of fun, isn't it? Kids will love it. Their parents will have to buy a lot of cereal to complete the set—which we plan will continually grow in size." She opened another small plastic box. "Here are some components of the planned moon colony. President Kennedy mentioned one in his last speech."

"Yes, yes." He pointed. "What's that there?"

After fifteen minutes of examining the toys and putting them through their paces, he had assembled, with Bette's help, a moon colony complete with twenty different astronauts and scientists. Finally he looked up. "And how many different toys?"

"Fifty."

"That's a lot of cereal."

"Exactly."

"I'm interested. What do I do?"

Bette took a contract from her briefcase. "Sign here."

"I'll have our lawyers look this over."

"Of course. You can get in touch with me at our office. Here's the number."

"This is an exclusive, correct?"

"Of course. It's all in the contract."

It was late afternoon when Bette walked out into downtown Battle Creek, and the sky was darkening. An icy wind blew a curtain of snow down Main Street. The sidewalks and street were narrow corridors bounded by mountains of plowed-up snow.

Another step completed. She had appointments with the other big cereal manufacturers, and had slightly varying lines of toys for each of the big cereal manufacturers—different colors, different designs. She'd hired a woman, back in Virginia, to answer the phone number she'd given and take messages.

Her black Mercury Comet station wagon was parked on the next block, and she managed to keep her composure until she flung her briefcase into the backseat and slid into the front seat. She slammed the door and leaned her forehead against the steering wheel.

Bette had at least realized why Hadntz did not seem to age in a normal way. She ping-ponged around in time. Whatever that meant. Whatever time was. Bette had experienced that, now, and it was simply sad, and wrenching.

She wondered where—or, to put it differently, *when*, Hadntz was now. Certainly, she would meet Hadntz again, and she didn't know what the good doctor's intentions would be, at that point. They were ever changing, based on a much wider palette of possibilities than Bette's.

Bette's intentions, on the other hand, were absolutely clear. The essential agents in Hadntz's Device, which

fostered altruism, were also in the cereal toys she had just sold to General Mills. These agents were transmittable, through touch, and through the very air. They formed networks, which would grow. Their molecular design came from another timeline, one in which engineering had accomplished molecular replication. Should one be cut in two, each would regenerate a complete figure. This practically guaranteed worldwide distribution in a short period of time. She had no idea how long it would take to generate any real results. It could be decades. It was just another prototype spawned by the Device, another vector.

Bette was doing the only thing she knew to do, at this point—continuing the evolution of humanity through distribution of the Device, in the form of a very attractive children's toy, to be used when they were going through their very precise intervals of sensitivity to various stimuli, their brains categorizing, organizing, linking.

She had made it back from time-fractured Dallas to her family's timestream, fighting with the plane's programming all the way. She stashed her timestreaming plane, which she supposed broke the time barrier, rather than the sound barrier, in a barn in Woodbridge, Virginia, which was on a thirty-acre property with a long stretch of flat ground: an airstrip. She bought the property instantly, meeting the owner's asking price without haggling, and gave the county property tax assessors a way to access an account she set up, explaining that she would probably be overseas for several years.

It had taken her two weeks to recover, in an old motel on Route 460 near Pearisburg, in southwest Virginia, which had a view of a mountain called Angel's Rest. She climbed Angel's Rest twice that week, feeling as far from angelic as possible, since she had recently killed two men. They were not the first she had killed in her long career as a spy, but she had decided that they were the last.

Now, she could play out her plan. She had plenty of

financial resources. Money dropped into the lap of spies, as it had hers, throughout the forties, fifties, and sixties. She had carried hers with her, in the form of diamonds, across timestreams, and much of it was now in Switzerland. Within weeks, she would be able to produce millions of the space dolls for cereal companies, all of them imbued with Hadntz material, which would radiate and link with one another, continuing that mysterious, ever-evolving brain-changing process Hadntz had created. Money from the cereal companies would go back into the shipping process, which would be mostly automatic. Any excess would go to the development of teacher-training centers in remote regions of the world. Someday there might be a generation that removed the obscene profit war brought to so many people, who might be able to throw a rod into the civilization-crushing gears of war.

She had not been able to come to terms with her personal situation, though. At first, she had been jubilant, euphoric. Sam. Jill. Brian. Megan. They were *here*. She had made her way back.

She was afraid to contact them, badly frightened by finding herself in a world where they did not exist. She didn't want that to happen again. That was not the main problem, though.

She was now a very obvious target to those who had passed, with memories intact, from the Kennedy assassination timeline to this. She'd thoroughly blown her cover. The CIA knew where she lived, though she'd been officially out of the game for years. They also might know their long-held suspicions were true: that Bette knew about the legendary, shadowy device they'd been after since the end of the war, certain it would give the nation, or whoever held it, even more power than the atomic bomb. How had this all started?

On November 8, 1938, Bette Elegante was in the Staatsoper, the Vienna State Opera House, in a particular seat,

as instructed. At least, the strange note she had received contained a very strong hint to be here.

She disliked Vienna. Yes, it was a beautiful and cultured city, with narrow, winding streets bounded by neatly kept shops. The Ringstrasse, a broad avenue encompassing the inner city, was cosmopolitan and seemingly inviting.

But the huge swastika flags draped from balconies and in parks revolted her. Germany had annexed Austria in March, threatening to send in troops if the Austrian chancellor did not agree to the takeover. He had welcomed the Fascists, with open arms and a celebration, and the city was now a muted shadow of its former self.

Bette still did not know why she was here. So she was annoyed with herself when the jasmine-perfumed woman who had been sitting next to her the entire time said, "Come," as the orchestra swelled for a finale, which Bette was pleased to escape.

The woman did not speak as Bette followed her through the opulent gallery and into the smoke-filled night, and grabbed her arm and pulled her back as a mob of people ran past wielding sticks and clubs.

"What's going on?" asked Bette, in German.

The woman didn't reply, just nodded at Bette to follow the mob at a safe distance, and set off.

She was about five feet three inches tall, and wore a tight, fashionable red dress beneath an ocelot coat that flared out behind her as she strode along. A broad-brimmed red hat swept aslant her face, preventing Bette from reading the expression in her eyes, but enhancing the intensity of her red lipstick.

"Who are you?" asked Bette, in German.

"My name is Eliani Hadntz." She spoke in strongly accented, oddly stilted English.

"Who sent you?"

"No one. *I* asked for *you*."

"Again."

"The code name you so quaintly ask for is Amarin Konisky."

"I don't make the rules."

"Perhaps someday you will. In the meantime, you should learn to trust your judgment. I am not any part of your organization. I got that password through subterfuge."

"Why?" asked Bette, and stopped walking.

Hadntz wheeled around to face her. "By the end of this night, I might tell you."

"Fine." They resumed walking. This woman was not exactly a spy. She wanted to strike some kind of deal, for reasons unknown to Bette. Okay. That was her job: to gather information.

Hadntz took her arm and steered her down a side street, staying half a block behind the shouting men. The leader pointed to a shop front, and those behind him rushed forward, smashed the window, and swarmed inside. Books flew out the window. One shadowed man sprinkled gasoline on them from a large can and tossed a match; the books caught fire with a *vroomp!*, followed by hoarse shouts of approval.

Part of the crowd circled a man who reached into a flour sack and withdrew something. The circle broke with applause, and the man with the bag threw a rope over the bookseller's sign and hoisted a collection of rags so that it swung above the street. It vaguely resembled a human being, as it had a rag-stuffed sphere where the head should be. A large sign hung below the sphere: MARIA MONTESSORI. The effigy, once lit, flamed up and further illuminated the mob.

"Maria Montessori?" asked Bette. "I don't understand."

"You visited one of her many schools in Vienna, as I suggested?"

"That note was from you?"

"Yes. Did you?"

"I did."

"And what was your impression?"

As she watched the terrible blaze in the alley grow stronger, and devour the chairs and shelves shoved out of the shop through the broken window, Bette said to Hadntz, "I was surprised that such young children were reading, writing, and doing mathematics. But who is Montessori?"

Hadntz said, "An educator. She has given us a stunning revelation of human possibilities. We know very little about our own potential as humans. What you saw the children doing should not seem amazing, because it is very normal. What else could we be doing, if we were not wasting our time with the other nonsense, like wars, that being human seems to require? It appears that the developing child passes through discrete stages, during which she focuses deeply on learning about one facet of the environment, then moves on. Perhaps the whole of humanity is going through a larger stage of learning about our environment, as a whole, as one organism. For thousands of years, we have been learning about conflict. Perhaps we are ready to move to the next stage."

Tendrils of Eliani Hadntz's hair, black and curly and wild, surrounded her strong-featured face, half-shadowed by a streetlight. Her eyes, too, were black, and Hadntz's gaze was commanding, yet calm. Her low tones had an impact that wakened something in Bette, showed her a tantalizing glimpse of a path both radical and revolutionary, one she had never before considered.

They walked through darkened, narrow streets lined with stone and brick buildings, through which roamed many more packs of riotous men, some in suits, some in Nazi uniform. Bette passed one side street, then backed up to get a better look.

A group of men, shouting *Juden!* had backed one man against the brick wall of a town house. The beleaguered man raised his fist. One assailant darted from the

crowd, grabbed both of his arms, and held him against the wall. Another moved in and battered the victim's face and abdomen. His groans, and the dull thud of the punches, sounded clearly, along with the jeers that followed each blow.

Bette ran down the alley, the clip of her heels like shots from a pistol. Hadntz followed, shouting, "No!"

Bette edged along the building, working her way in front of the jeering men. She pulled her revolver from her purse, widened her stance, and held it with both hands on his assailant. "Stop!" Bette cocked her revolver, which sounded a deep, threatening metallic snick. "Leave! Now!"

The attacker got in one last punch to the man's kidney, glared at Bette, turned, and walked away. One of his cohorts spat on the man's face. Bette kept her gun trained on them until they turned the corner, then slipped it into her coat pocket.

The shop owner's white shirt shone, slick with blood, as he slumped to the pavement and vomited.

A woman, her face pale, opened the door, glanced at Bette and Hadntz, and helped the man to his feet. "Thank you. I—didn't know what to do." Her voice was hoarse. Tears started from her eyes, and she let them flow. Her teeth chattered. Hadntz picked up the man's ruined jacket from the street and wrapped it around the woman.

The man spat out a tooth. "Do you believe me now?" he asked his wife. He put one hand on his nose.

Hadntz said, "Please. I am a doctor." She examined his nose, put one arm on the small of his back to steady him, and pushed on his abdomen here and there. "Your nose is not broken. You may have internal injuries, though."

"Dr. Isaak will come," said the woman.

"There's no time for that. You must leave this minute," said Hadntz. "Before they return. Take only what is absolutely necessary." She gave him a small card. "Please get in touch with me if you have difficulty. Go to this address, show the woman there this card, and she will

shelter you, get him medical care, and help you with the necessary documents."

"We have visas," said his wife. "For the whole family." She sighed. "My grandfather started this store. I didn't want to leave. It's not right." She helped her husband into the stairway. Bette heard her shoot the bolt.

Hadntz said, "You took a great chance."

"Not really. They were obviously a bunch of cowards. Ten against one. I was sure they would run."

"And you do look like Hitler's own avenging Aryan goddess, with your blond hair. That probably confused them." They moved quickly down the now-dark street, the *click* of their heels mingling with the distant *pop-pop* of random gunfire and the high notes of glass as shards hit the pavement.

A German officer ran from around a corner a hundred feet from them and stopped when he saw them, holding his pistol aloft. "Halt!" he shouted. He lowered his pistol and took aim at them from a hundred feet away. One of the men from the mob Bette had run off stood behind him, pointing and shouting.

Bette drew her pistol from her coat pocket and shot the officer in the leg. He collapsed onto the cobblestones, screaming. The other man disappeared into the alley.

Bette grabbed Hadntz's arm and pulled her across the street, down another alley, a map springing instantly to mind. A storage shed, full of old junk not worth locking up, was around a corner—this one!—she pushed open the door and dragged Hadntz in behind her; shut the door and waited as they crouched in what might have been a stall. Distant running footsteps of men who may have been looking for them or randomly hunting for new victims. After a few minutes, Bette said, "Let's go."

When, after twenty minutes of an angling course they emerged from a network of tiny streets onto a boulevard, Bette said, "I think we're safe."

Smoke billowed down the street, and looters dashed

from shop to shop in anarchic disarray, boots pounding on bricks, shouting with rough voices and wielding bats, hammers, and crowbars. They moved through the chaos in their theater finery, unmolested, almost as if they were invisible.

"You are a cool one," said Hadntz.

"Reflex. Training. I haven't seen anything quite this bad before," said Bette. "Just a lot of threats and intimidation and firings. Not any direct violence."

"This is Goering's test. He's been planning it for some time. All over Germany and Austria, a few men are to deliberately begin the attacks. As you see, others are not reluctant to join in."

"It's a test? Do I understand correctly?"

"To see how the public reacts to the outright, public humiliation of Jews and the destruction and theft of their businesses. Obviously, Goering will be pleased with the results of his test, at least here. Already, of course, Jews have been thrown out of academic positions and jobs in Germany, but many here hoped that Vienna might remain safe."

"How do you know this about Goering?"

"You need to ask yourself why you did not know why it was going to happen tonight. Your intelligence network is useless."

A blast of heat and noise met them as they rounded a corner.

Across a square, a synagogue door stood open. The synagogue's arched roof collapsed, timbers groaning, and the flames licked overhanging trees. The stained-glass windows of the still-standing walls were lit from within; two were broken, and conflagration surged outward, blackening what remained of the building. Outside, a band of children cheered at the collapse and hurled rocks at the remaining windows.

"Do you want to know why people do such things?" asked Hadntz.

"I'm not sure I want to," said Bette.

"You need to know. Because you, or I, or anyone, could do such things. This way of seeing other groups is what human history is built on. A seemingly endless round of hideous barbarity. I believe it has something to do with brain chemistry."

"Brain *chemistry*? What do you mean by that?"

"We are simply exquisitely imprintable."

"Imprintable?" Just then a German soldier approached. "Papers." He held out his hand.

Bette, thankful that her gun was now in her pocket, took them from her purse.

He perused them. "Berlin!" He looked up, smiling. "My mother lives there."

Using her flawless Berlin accent, Bette chatted with him about the Berlin neighborhood where his mother lived. When Hadntz produced her papers, he frowned, then looked at her with suspicion. "A professor?" He shook his head and handed them back.

To Bette, he said, "You are staying at the Imperial? You must return to your hotel immediately. It is not safe to be out this night." He pointed. "Ringstrasse is that way. When you get there, turn left."

He glared at Hadntz. "And you, Doktor Doktor Hadntz. Go back to Hungary."

As they walked toward Ringstrasse, Bette said, "Doktor Doktor?"

"Germans give you the titular benefit of all of your doctorates. They like titles."

"No intellectuals wanted here."

Hadntz snorted. "I grew up in Vienna, unlike that German soldier. I went to school here. He, and all of these Germans, are a foreign army occupying my country."

They walked quickly, and finally caught sight of the Imperial, one of Vienna's finest hotels, blazing not with fire but with light. Several black sedans idled in front of the hotel. The doorman admitted them, nodding at Bette.

In the posh lobby, two men chatted over brandy. "That is Himmler, head of—"

"The SS," Bette finished. "He checked in three days ago. He prefers beer with his caviar. I attended a party he gave last night."

"And you heard nothing of their plans? What a waste of time."

Bette's room was on the third floor. After looking up and down the empty hallway, Bette unlocked her door. The wall sconce was dim, and served only to keep them from tripping over furniture as the two women crossed to the French doors and looked out over the city, where orange tongues of fire flared, block after block, in wanton destruction that was a complete contrast to the safe, luxurious refuge room from which they watched.

"Dulles certainly knows how to spend money," Hadntz said after a moment, turning to survey the shadowed, but obviously elegant, room.

"I'm an heiress from Berlin."

Hadntz opened the French doors, stepped onto the narrow balcony, and stood in silence, gripping the railing. Bette saw tears, and anger, in her dark eyes, caught in the light from the sconce when she turned.

"You are young," she said. "But I think you'll do."

"I always have," said Bette. Now it was her turn to use an ironic tone.

Hadntz stepped back inside, closed and locked the doors, and drew the drapes. "Turn on the lights." She removed her hat and put it on a mahogany side table next to an art deco lamp, and then undid her hair. She sat on the teal-colored silk couch and began to unbuckle one of her high heels. Her hair fell across her face like a veil as she spoke. "There are many things that I must tell you, Miss Elegante. I will be here all night." She shrugged off her coat and crossed her stockinged feet on the coffee table in front of her. "We will need dinner, and several of their best bottles of wine."

Bette picked up the phone and ordered grilled fish for

both of them, a pot of coffee, and specified the wines, two German, and two French. She also ordered a bottle of Scotch and four packs of Fatima cigarettes.

All of those were useful, that night, while Dr. Eliani Hadntz educated Bette about neurochemistry, quantum physics, research into human violence, and genetics.

Bette realized, much later, that some of the information that Dr. Hadntz had used to develop the device she claimed would end war, had come from other, future, timestreams.

But at this point, Hadntz was still working on her device. It was not ready. She simply wanted to prepare Bette.

Eliani Hadntz had a quiet, yet forceful and convincing manner. She drew diagrams on hotel stationery, and Bette soon called for a ream of paper. If Bette did not understand, Hadntz moved back, step by step, until she arrived at a common point of departure. Bette's education had been eclectic, beginning at a state school in Michigan, continuing at Duke, and finishing at Cambridge. She had usually been the only woman in the largely technical and scientific classes she had taken, and had some background in the areas feeding into Hadntz's many-threaded device, but much that the woman talked about was completely new to Bette, and she suspected that it was known only by highly specialized chemists, physicists, and biologists—and that, moreover, few of them knew what the others knew. Hadntz also gave Bette stunning news: Lise Meitner, a physicist who had lately fled Nazi Germany in fear of her life, had just confirmed the possibility of atomic fission: an atomic bomb was possible.

Hadntz had a different chain reaction, one of empathy and altruism, in mind. And she had hard physical plans to create the initial device, which would then replicate and go on to change the baseline of humans from one of constant war to one of constant peace, productivity, and intellectual expansion.

She left, just before dawn, taking all the papers with

her. She told Bette that, for her own safety, but, much more importantly, for the sake of the Device, that she would probably not have much direct contact with her in the future. But she planned to make use of Bette, who agreed to be on call. Hadntz was setting up a network, trying to think about all possibilities that might arise, including her own death.

Bette stood on her private balcony at the Imperial, bundled against the cold in her opera coat, drinking bitter coffee. Smoke from burnt Jewish homes, businesses, and synagogues blotted out the sunrise. Its acrid smell, and a small whirlwind of burnt debris swirling down Ringstrasse, presaged a deeper, more universal destruction, a flame that might spread from the sickness in Germany, which had now overtaken Austria, and engulf the world. Bette knew it. Everyone knew it. Yet all the world's leaders wanted to deny its imminence. Churchill, alone and ridiculed, had been sounding the alarm.

Bette brooded, realizing the truth of Hadntz's predictions, which seemed like unavoidable consequences, given what she knew, and far from mystical. Yet somehow, Hadntz reminded Bette of the figure of Blind Justice: one weight pan freighted with the awful density of humanity's murderous history, the other with her brilliant, probably impossible, Device.

After her night of coffee, cigarettes, whiskey, and extreme ideas rendered as scientifically achievable, two opposing ideas thrust themselves forward.

One was the convoluted hate-riven atrocity titled *Mein Kampf*, through which she had slogged, trying to get a clue about what drove Hitler's murky thought process. It had filled her mind with a Frankensteinian monster much more horrible than Shelley's original vision.

The other was a poem by the Irish mystic, AE:

Out of a timeless world
Shadows fall upon time,
From a brightness older than Earth:

A shadow the soul may climb.
I climb by the timeless stair
To a brightness older than time.

If Hadntz's Device was actually created, and if it worked, then beyond the destroyed city she surveyed from the balcony she could almost glimpse, in the ideas Hadntz put forth with such certainty, a timeless stair, shimmering beyond sight, which just might surmount these deep and fearful shadows. Hers was a stair built to the highest standards of what humanity might possibly achieve, designed by a strange architect who had imbibed of a mixture of astounding knowledge, to synergistic effect.

Exhaustion blotted out Bette's image, so that all she saw now, looking down on the Ringstrasse, were shards of shattered glass dull beneath a heavy sky, reflecting emptiness: The ruins of civilization as she, and many others, knew it.

At the end of September 1946, Bette took a train to Berga, a small town in occupied East Germany. That was the day she decided to go home.

She wore a Party uniform—a well-worn skirt, a white blouse, and a jacket with Party insignia. She had a good number of forged papers with her in a flat leather bag worn over her shoulder. Bureaucracies loved documentation.

It had been a long war. She had shepherded the development of Hadntz's Device throughout. She had been a superlative spy.

She had fallen in love with Sam Dance.

She had set love aside, because, although countries had surrendered and treaties had been signed, the war continued. There was no shooting, not right now, not with atomic bombs on the table. But the war went on. She had been working as a double agent in the Soviet Union for a year. Today, she was collecting evidence for

German prisoner-of-war atrocities that were coming up for trial.

Hours later, in a cemetery filled with dead prisoners of war, she leaned against a linden tree and sank to the ground.

She had been on a similar grassy hillside, covered with wildflowers, a few days ago, where she had walked past the new grave of a cousin on her mother's side. The cousin had been a Russian tank commander in the war, and then the Soviets shot her for some reason or other; it never mattered what for or why to them. Because Bette was a spy, she had to pretend that she had no idea who the new grave was for. She had, by now, spent almost ten years in Europe, the last few months in the bitter atmosphere of Stalingrad.

And then, there was Eliani Hadntz. Bette had ignored several of her attempts at communicating, just as she had ignored queries from her superiors about Hadntz, the Device, and Sam.

As she sat there, looking out across the bucolic-looking village where so many horrors had taken place, she thought about Hadntz's Device and all her crazy claims for the way it would change humanity for the better.

Oh, yes, Dance and his buddy Wink had had some success with it, in their little shop in Gladbach. So much success—what was it, a burst of light or energy or something?—that Bette had actually entertained some hope for the past year.

Silly of her, eh?

She burst out laughing, then cried, then laughed some more until she gasped for breath. How absurd to think that a mere invention, no matter how complex, could change such overwhelming evil. Brutality welled from the ground from here to the Middle East; the very soil was made of human bones. She had probably walked over the unmarked graves of millions of dead since she had arrived. What made Eliani Hadntz think that she could change anything?

The vast history of this millennium-long crush of humanity on the landmass of Europe was, suddenly, deeply overwhelming. She thought of Sam, and, surprising herself, veered into a mood that was alien to her. Sam, or her own surviving brothers, could have been buried here, right here where she sat. The Americans brought here had landed in Le Havre only a few weeks earlier. They had no idea that all the territory Germany claimed was full of death camps, or that they might end up in one of them.

How could anything but more violence and revenge, come from this? What would unwind in the future—if not here, then elsewhere in the world, forever? Could anything ever change? The same extremes of human behavior manifested in the Third Reich now ran through the Soviet Union, an unending plague.

She shook a handkerchief from her pocket, blew her nose and mopped at her face. Then she lit a cigarette, stood, and brushed off her skirt. It was late afternoon. She had intended to stay the night in this wretched town, but she just couldn't stand to be here a minute more. Not in East Germany, not in Leningrad, not in France. Not in Europe at all.

She had to get home.

In 1964, in her second timeline, Bette lifted her head from the steering wheel. Stars glittered in the frigid sky over Battle Creek.

She depressed the clutch, ignited the engine, shifted into first gear, and eased onto the street.

She drove toward her small, bleak apartment, one of many small, bleak apartments in which she had left no trace during her long career in intelligence. She would gaze at the black-and-white pictures of her children, which were like chips of gold that she had hidden in the lining of her briefcase. Then she would fall asleep.

Bette

BETTE WAS startled back to the Halcyon House kitchen in May 1991, by a footstep on the porch.

Still holding Bootstrap Jack, whose prototype had stood on the desk of the General Mills executive so long ago, she slipped over to the open door to the attic steps, then heard the slap of mail falling through the front door flap onto the foyer floor.

Just the mailman.

Hurrying up the narrow back stairs, she reached the third floor, gathered her dirty clothes from the bathroom floor, and returned to the attic. Back inside the refuge of the pink bedroom, she turned yet another bookshelf on pivots to reveal a small room containing a bank of electronics. She sat down and flipped the main switch. The ancient computer, from the early 1980s, flickered on. The radio amplifier did not work. She removed the lid and replaced two tubes with new ones from a supply drawer, and it lit up. She turned on the microphone that was in the library and got a green light. The kitchen and living room were live as well. They had not bugged their children's rooms. A reel-to-reel tape recorder sat on the floor.

On the computer screen was a radar sweep, of sorts. A line swept around and around, deforming at a certain point. Somewhere in Georgetown was as accurate as she could get. Not good enough. She needed more sophisticated equipment, and she was reasonably sure that it existed in this timestream. All the other technological markers were here. She'd have to learn more about how things worked here to find the best way to do it. Opening the top of an old Victrola, she removed two thousand dollars, then reconsidered and added another thousand, in large and small bills, then closed up the electronics room.

Inside the closet of the pink bedroom, she put the money into a leather purse from the attic, which also held a stashed pistol, ammunition, and a birth certificate for one Jane Smith from Arkansas, with which to get a current ID. Opening yet another pivot door in the closet, she descended a hidden staircase that opened in the basement. The doorway was concealed by a built-in shelf. She shut the shelf, full of cobwebbed cleaning supplies, and let herself out the basement door.

She hoped she'd returned before Jill got back from work.

Emerging from the viaduct, wearing new gardening galoshes to trudge through the stream, she bushwhacked through the enjungled backyard, passing her long-ago grotto refuge, and gained the mowed lawn, hidden from the street by vast growths of roses, well-seeded perennials, and tall, fragrant peonies.

She'd made friends with Manfred before leaving that morning. The big dog loped toward Bette. Bette put down her heavy shopping bags and cooed at her, scratched behind her ears while Manfred wagged her tail.

Bette climbed the secret stairway, depositing her booty in her little bedroom.

She'd quickly bought a lot of up-to-date, anonymous-looking, moderately expensive mix and match skirts, slacks, blouses, a few dresses, a business jacket, underwear, hiking boots, high heels, running shoes, and casual shoes, which she placed in the little closet, mixed in with the older clothes. She now had a D.C. driver's license and a passport in her purse. On Fourteenth Street, she'd purchased a few knives, a throwing star, and ammo for her gun.

And now, dessert.

She opened her tech purchase—a marvelous Q module, and all that went with it—a Q-phone, a larger screen, and a plethora of programs. She'd acted like a complete idiot in the store, which regarding this version of Q, she

was, and the salesman had worked with her for two hours, selling the capabilities and applications, showing her how it worked.

Bette sat on her little bed, cross-legged, thrilled. Even a bit teary.

This was not the culmination of what Hadntz, she, and Sam had worked on for years. She knew that all war had not yet vanished. But this was a huge step forward. Everyone had these. Well, almost everyone she had seen today, whipping them out to take calls or to get information. She wondered how other places in the world fared.

She went into her radio room and turned on the living room microphone, wearing headphones. As Bette played with her Q, she heard the front door open. Jill said, "Manfred! Down!"

The microphones worked. She turned them off; she had no desire to eavesdrop on her family, except to hear the magic of their voices.

She returned to her little bed, leaned against a pile of pillows, and began exploring the capabilities of her Q, quickly reaching a place where she could eavesdrop on local Q conversations, before then turning to other matters. In a few hours, she uncovered the problem: She was here because one imperfect Device, given to Sam by a German named Perler, in World Prime, was here, somewhere in Georgetown. It was dangerous; near-functional because it fed upon Q's advances and updated itself sporadically, imperfectly, yet, over the decades, with increasing strength. She was able to triangulate to some extent, but these tools were not powerful enough to locate the imperfect Device precisely. And, for the same reason, whoever was in possession of the Device could not find the later evolutions of the Device, the H-5, the H- . . . oh, she didn't really know the number of evolutions any longer, because there had been so many that it had become a smooth continuum, like the growth of a child to an adult. Yet, despite the power of Q, this imperfect, early

THIS SHARED DREAM | 137

incarnation held disruptive power, which, combined with, say, the Game Board, would become much more powerful.

She had to find it.

Jill

A PHONE CALL

[*May 7*]

THAT EVENING, Jill indeed missed Whens, but she was also blessedly alone—which was, in her opinion, much different than loneliness. Aloneness had charged potential. She could think.

After talking with Elmore about Whens' aversion to his new girlfriend—or at least, newly revealed, as Jill suspected that she was not exactly new—Jill felt better. Somewhat surprisingly, to herself at least, she viewed Tracy as a positive development, if only for her own selfish reasons. An Elmore caught up in a new relationship was an Elmore with less time to make her life more difficult than it had to be regarding Whens.

Home after a long day in the chilly, air-conditioned Bank, she turned on the radio and unpacked the salad she'd picked up on the way home. She'd thrown open all the windows, admitting the ambrosia of spring air, laden as it was with creek dampness, the fragrance of hidden roses, even the smell of wet asphalt.

Her colleagues had welcomed her back coolly, but she didn't care. They were probably jealous of all her time off. She'd dealt with paperwork having to do with a loan to Kenya, met with her long-suffering assistants, and treated them to lunch.

Otherwise, it was as if she'd never left, although she was quite pleased with her hefty raise. The only bothersome part of work was the Ohio guy, Bill, who apparently believed he was the living incarnation of some

Norse god. Even though, supposedly, his family had lived in the Midwest for generations. Jill gathered that he was deeply aggrieved about many things, which he managed to convey through intimate asides that seemed calculated to elicit a response from her. She always left his vicinity as soon as possible and took care not to put herself in situations that included him. She didn't like the guy at all, case closed—except that, unfortunately, he seemed to fancy her. She wasn't at the stage of filing a complaint, but if his behavior continued, she might.

Oh, well. Much to do.

She cleared a place at the kitchen table, dished out the salad she'd picked up, poured a glass of pinot grigio, and sat down with her notebook. As she ate, she jotted down her forthcoming tasks and attendant concerns.

Her main job, right now, was to gather information for an upcoming meeting regarding the Bank's international preschool buildings, called Children's Houses. She'd fostered the project for many years. These modular buildings, in distribution at last after years of waiting, had a backload of orders and loan applications. They were autotelic—self-teaching, projecting holographic children that demonstrated the use of materials. Refinements would inevitably continue, because the process was open source and on Q, and could be vetted and edited by thousands of qualified engineers and educators.

Now—this was the exciting part. She lifted her pencil, breathed in the rain-fresh air, and relished the moment.

Now she could finally devote more time to an ongoing, parallel school project, Q-Schools. During the past five years, soliciting input from worldwide experts in education, architecture, microeconomics, molecular engineering, and epidemiology, she had kept tabs on the development of a prototype school pod, a tough little embryo that could grow in almost any terrain. Each school was self-healing and imbued with Q. She was still pondering all kinds of ramifications.

Q-Schools were not like Children's Houses.

Local municipalities had to request Children's Houses, oversee construction, and comply with local code requirements. Communities requesting Children's Houses were in agreement about the need for more schools, but did not have the means to finance them. The Bank's role, under several mandates, including the promotion of gender equality and economic empowerment in areas of need, was to provide financing for targeted projects such as these schools. Jill's long-term dream was that a higher level of worldwide education might empower those who might be able to, eventually, be clearheaded about war.

But perhaps deeper changes had to take place in humans before war could be eliminated. Neurobiological changes. That was what Megan claimed, that was her true work: figuring out what those changes might be, and how to nudge them along biochemically.

"Yes," Brian had said, just a few days ago, in his smart-alecky way, holding up her vitamins. "This pill for weight loss. This little yellow one—memory. And this big clear one, folks—this pill is for world peace and international cooperation on all good things." Megan had fumed out of the room.

"And what do you think about this Q-School plan, Manfred?" she asked. "Yes?"

Manfred beat her tail against the floor.

"Good girl."

Q-Schools would grow from nanotech seeds. They would be much, much cheaper than even Children's Houses.

Q-Schools would, of course, be linked to Q. Q would assess need and place the schools, based on statistics and studies of gender inequality, general poverty, availability of education, and the likelihood that the people in the area of need would probably not even know of the existence of the prefab Children's Houses, much less have the municipal organization to request them. Most rural, poor communities would welcome such schools. Shoot,

even affluent communities would want them, but they weren't Jill's concern.

Forgetting her salad, Jill jotted down means of informing the populace about Q-Schools—dropping classbooks, even old-fashioned flyers, ways to prepare communities. Optimal time frames. Material for those who could read, recordings and videos for those who could not. Often, small children had little to do, and families conscripted older children, who might otherwise be contributing to the family income, to care for them. Q-Schools were naturally attractive. Once parents knew they were safe, they would allow their children to use them, obviating the need for parental or older-child supervision. Kind of like day care, but with education thrown in. That might be a good angle—freeing up those older children for income production—although, of course, they too, needed to be in school. . . . At any rate, Q's baseline altruistic algorithms would optimize each school according to local needs. The agricultural or other work in which their parents were engaged would be the focus of pedagogic materials. If their local environment was embedded in the environment, children learned to read and write easily. Their crops and their biological processes, the local flora and fauna, were real, concrete, and then they were pictures, represented by words holding strong meaning to those children. Children could write stories about what was actually happening around them. Once they realized how reading and writing empowered them, there was no turning back. Jill had seen this in her mother's school.

Jill was certainly aware that some communities and cultures would not welcome Q-Schools, even though their curriculum was value-free. All preschoolers had the same urge to learn, to master their physical environment. Learning how to count, how to manipulate objects comparatively, even mastering putting one's thoughts in writing, were not cultural acts—except that some cultures valued such acts, and some denied them to certain members.

Jill, and many other people, firmly believed that denial of the basic tools of reading and writing was a form of child abuse. Censorship, as well as denying literacy, was one of the main tools of repressive regimes. The list of those who had denied literacy to certain people was long, and included the Catholic Church during the Spanish Inquisition; Southern states that had prohibited literacy for slaves by law; fundamentalist religious groups, equally distributed among Jewish, Christian, and Islamic sects; and every other society that limited literacy for one reason or another.

A recent United Nations Convention on the Rights of the Child had produced a document that recognized the child's right to an education. Primary education was to be, ideally, compulsory and freely available to all.

This was impossible in many locations. But the Q-Schools would give those places, those children, the opportunity to go to school and become active agents in the international community.

A nanotech school set down by Q in a place in which girls and women might be persecuted for literacy could be problematic—and dangerous—for the girls and women in that community who insisted on attending them. Perhaps, thought Jill, the men in control in such places, and the women who abetted them, needed education just as much as the girls and women disbarred from participating in society. She leaned back and laughed. *A quick shot of tolerance, please! Really, Jill, you're too much*. Why did she, much less the huge group of people around the world, think they had the right to foist education on anyone?

The history of education was fraught with such battles.

At any rate, such schools would fall under a UN mandate. There were fuzzy plans in the works to send Peacekeepers to areas denying their children access to the schools. They would safeguard the rights of those children, much as Johnson had sent the National Guard

to Mississippi in Jill's first, lost timestream to safeguard the right of black children to attend school.

She had not developed the seed plan, only sparked it, though over the years she had helped shape development and facilitated contact between interested parties. The seed was the result of international cooperation, and had been the subject of heated discussion in many United Nations committees. Public opinion deemed the schools too controversial to use, presently.

She had a copy of present, constantly updated plans. Though the Q-Schools were controversial, she had invited a speaker to her forthcoming meeting just to put the idea into people's minds.

"This Q-School, Manfred? Here in my notebook? It's just a seed. Just a gleam in the eye of a planning committee." She closed her notebook, and pushed it aside.

Next, she had to find her father's notebooks in the attic and start reading them. She'd tried, soon after he left, but it was too painful, and she had put them aside. It was another way of avoiding the past, she realized now. Her therapist likened it to war veterans refusing to talk about their war experiences, or even, sometimes, acknowledge them. In the worst cases, those memories could erupt suddenly, landing the victim precisely where she'd landed.

The notebooks might hold some clues about what had happened. Maybe not. But Sam had told her to read them, when she saw him in the hospital. Had she seen him in the hospital?

Yes. She had. She laughed. The therapist thought she should tell Megan and Brian this gigantic thing she'd done, yet Brian had gone around the bend on just hearing she'd seen Mom and Dad.

She finished her glass of wine, poured another, and relished the cool condensation beneath her fingers as she sipped. She glanced at the closed notebook, full of important tasks.

Maybe she should wait until she had more time, until

things were settled. She had to get the house in shape for the party. The party was important to her. It would be the official threshold into her new life.

She reopened the notebook, added more to her list.

Tomorrow she would call the bookstore accountant and get back on track with her business. She had to get the store checkbook back from Elmore, who would surrender it gladly. She needed to schedule meetings with salesmen. She could do those during lunch hours, have them meet her at a restaurant near the Bank.

Once she got caught up, everything would run smoothly. Then she'd have time to read the notebooks.

She realized that she'd forgotten her salad and pulled it toward her.

She wondered, as she stabbed radicchio leaves and enjoyed the tang of vinegar, if she was doing the right thing in staying silent, but spent only a second on the answer, which was, how in the world would she know? She might do more harm than good if she told Megan and Brian what she'd done. Their lives might fall apart too.

Finished with her dinner, she opened the back door, carrying her glass of wine, and stepped onto the porch landing, high above the yard, and into the evening, always an enchanted time. Lightning bugs flickered in the dusk. Whens' swing set, all bright paint and as many rings and trapezes and seesaws that could be squeezed onto one play structure, his holy grail of motion, gleamed against a backdrop of misty woods.

To her left, their land dropped swiftly to the fast-running creek spilling from the viaduct. Kudzu completely enveloped her father's outdoor kitchen, and a tangle of climbing roses and woody vines obscured the tile-roofed stone grotto Sam had built for Bette down by the creek. Jill slapped a mosquito, and recalled her mother sitting down there, laughing with her father about how her cigarette smoke kept the bugs at bay.

It was more than a memory, though. It was as if Bette's laughter rose from behind the veil of vegetation; as

if her brother and sister, still kids, were running down the hill yelling at each other. It was almost as if she smelled cigarette smoke, and maybe she did, from across the street or something.

Jill descended the stairs with resolution. Memories would definitely splay across her vision—brilliant, lovely memories, intense, and overwhelming—but she just had to live with them and let them go. She was here now, and they were part of being here. She had to come to grips with it all, although now, as Venus appeared and the cicadas took up their rhythmic whirr, she suddenly felt frail and rent.

She made it to the bottom of the stairs and a few steps into the wet grass, with Manfred on her heels, when the house phone, still on the kitchen wall where the old phone had been, rang.

She set the wineglass in the grass—of course it spilled—and ran up the stairs, only because it might be Whens, rattled anew about crushing hugs and perfume. But she was too late. The answering machine clicked on.

"We need the Device," a muffled male voice hissed. "Now."

She picked up the phone in time to hear the *click* as the caller hung up. "Hello?"

Silence.

In her attic garret, Bette stubbed out her cigarette and tried to trace the call, but failed. She turned out the light and lay back in her bed, aching, simply aching, for Sam.

Megan and Brian

THE WALKING MAN

[May 10]

IT WAS about eight o'clock on a Friday evening.

Megan sat at the dining room table, where the *Washington Post* was spread out, reading the funnies and avoiding the dishes. Sometimes she got through the funnies and the op-ed page before the dishes got the better of her. It was rather Jillish of her, she had to admit. Megan was always the neat, orderly sibling, sweeping, dusting, mopping, and complaining about her older sister's physical, philosophical, and emotional messes. But dishes . . . they were another matter altogether.

It was Jim's turn to put Abbie to bed. Sloshing sounds and bits of song emanated from the upstairs bathroom.

Megan looked up from the funnies when Bingo, their golden retriever, ran to the door, barking. Brian's truck was out front. She was surprised. Brian lived downtown, and they generally didn't get together more than once a month.

Megan jumped up and ran to open the door for him. "It is *so* nice that you've come to help me clean up." She grabbed a Pyrex dish that had macaroni and cheese burned onto it, stacked that with other dirty dishes, and carried her pile into the kitchen.

Brian shrugged and began rinsing plates and handing them to Megan, who slotted them into the dishwasher. "Have you talked to Jill lately?"

"Just yesterday. Why?"

"Whens has been calling Bitsy lately, talking about a ghost."

"And?"

"It seems strange."

Megan snorted. "Whens, if you haven't noticed, is strange. So, what kind of ghost?"

"What do you mean?"

"Casper, for instance, was friendly, white, and floaty. 'Kind to every living creature.' Seems to me that if there is a ghost, it must have some specifics."

"Yeah. Maybe even neurochemistry." Brian rubbed his forehead with his wrist and grabbed another plate.

"You think that a real person is in the house? Besides them?"

"It's so big that ten street people could be living there undetected. I guess I'm just nervous about Jill living in that big house alone."

"She's not alone. She has Whens and she has Manfred."

"Right. She refuses to keep a gun."

Megan glanced at Brian. "Spare me your NRA idiocy, please. Aren't guns illegal in the District? Do you keep guns in your house, with two children?"

"No, of course not. I keep mine in the work trailer, locked up. But I think she needs some kind of protection. There are some bad neighborhoods just a couple of streets over. She's just like Mom and Dad, though. She ignores all that. I'll bet she doesn't even lock her doors at night. She always has been kind of . . . I don't know, unaware that bad things can happen."

"Brian, downtown is a lot safer now than when we were growing up, and nothing happened to us then. Not a damned thing."

"Yeah. I suppose."

"Well, what do you want to do?"

"I'm thinking—just wanted to run this by you— maybe Cindy and the kids and I could move in. We're renovating that house in Northwest to move into, but it's going really slow because I have so much business, and the apartment is driving us nuts."

"It's fine with me. I wondered why you didn't move in there in the first place."

THIS SHARED DREAM | 147

"It was so . . . closed up. I don't know. It wasn't inviting to us."

"Maybe Cindy thought it might revive your drinking habit?"

"Maybe. The mind of woman is often difficult to discern."

"Just about everything was difficult for you to discern a few years ago."

"I agree," he said mildly, rather disappointing Megan. Sometimes she missed the old, fiery Brian.

"You playing guitar much?"

He shrugged. "I sit in somewhere every few weeks. When you guys come out with your power sleep drug, let me know."

"You'd probably just use it to take on three more jobs. Delegate! Why can't Cindy do that? I'll bet she'd do a fine job."

"Oh, she would. But in case you haven't noticed, she has a more-than-full-time job already, and she wouldn't give that up for anything. You're right, though. I haven't found anyone who knows enough to pay attention to all the things I care about. You can take a lot of shortcuts in construction, and I never do."

"You're just obsessive," said Megan. "There are drugs."

"I hope you're taking those particular drugs." Brian bent over the macaroni and cheese pan and scrubbed hard. "Why did you let this burn? Oh, of course, *you* wouldn't. It was Jim. You have him on double duty tonight? Cooking *and* bedtime? What a slave driver."

"I'll be on all weekend. He has a Sunday night deadline. Just let it soak."

Brian wiped his hands on his pants, leaned against the counter, and folded his arms. "I guess it's not really that Jill's alone. It's that she isn't . . . herself."

Megan nodded. "I've thought that too. But I'm not sure why. Actually, that's a kind of psychosis. Thinking that someone has been taken over by someone else.

That's what those mass psychosis movies in the fifties were about."

Nestled within the field of memory studies was the new theory of false memory formation. She had been reading more about this, thinking that perhaps Jill was a victim. "Maybe stress has caused her to make things up that she believes are real."

"Can people do that?"

"They can and do, all the time."

"Jill said she saw Mom and Dad while she was in the hospital."

"She was on some really heavy drugs. I think she misses them even more than we do. Especially Mom."

"So you don't think she really could have."

"Do you . . . think she *might* have?"

"Mom was never found. I mean, not her . . . we never had a funeral or anything."

"No, there was never a body."

"And Dad—well, same for him." Brian put soap in the dishwasher and turned it on. "I mean, it could be one of these false memories you're talking about, or a hallucination, or—"

"Or she could have really seen them. Why didn't you mention this before?"

"Well, I guess—I just got mad at Jill when she said that. I know that sounds—"

"Just like you. What else did she say?"

"After that, she just shut up. I asked her about it last week, and she looked at me like I was the crazy one." He looked around the now-clean kitchen. "Man, you're lucky I came by. You're so slow—"

"'Meticulous' is the word. But don't try to change the subject."

"No, 'slow' is the word. It would have taken you all night. I've got to go home and do it all again."

"Oh, poor thing. I'm glad to hear that you do something around the house."

"It's that or death." Brian grabbed a large glass, opened the refrigerator, got some iced tea, and followed Megan into the living room. Jim, upstairs, said to Abbie, "Okay. But just one more."

Brian sat down and took a long drink of tea. "We should have tried harder to find Dad. I think that's part of the problem. Everything feels unfinished."

Megan lounged back on the couch and put her feet up on the coffee table.

"Maybe one of us should go now," said Brian.

"To Germany? You mean Jill."

"Well, she's the obvious one."

Megan laughed. "Great idea. A nice trip to Germany to find our vanished father right after she gets out of the booby hatch. You do remember that she went nuts the last time, right?"

"She has less responsibilities than we do," Brian protested.

"Yeah. Just a five-year-old, a dog, a bookstore to manage, a full-time job, and a lot of legal shit to keep up with."

"Well, there's that . . ."

"What was your plan? Keep Whens at your house and bundle her onto a plane with a map?"

"Something like that," he admitted. "She's been strange ever since she came back from New Orleans twenty years ago. Remember? She was supposed to interview for college and wrecked the car."

"She and Dad would never talk about that either. Maybe we should ask Jill about seeing Mom and Dad in the hospital again."

"Isn't she kind of . . . fragile? I mean, I don't want to be the one who lands her back in the loony bin."

"Seeing them again is what we all want to happen. I dream about them all the time. I'm sure she imagined it, but if we ask, it might get her talking about things we need to talk about."

They heard the barely audible click of a door closing. Jim, wearing shorts and a T-shirt, tiptoed down the stairs. "She's out at last. Iced tea, Brian? Didn't your sister offer you a beer?"

Megan sent Jim a look that said, loud and clear: *Brian! Shouldn't! Drink!*

Jim ignored it. In his oft-expressed opinion, Brian was a grown-up. Megan wasn't sure.

Brian said, "Well . . . it is Friday."

"Indeed." They heard the *whoosh* of bottle tops being removed with a church key, and two *clicks* as they hit the counter. Jim brought Megan a bottle of San Pellegrino water without asking. Her aversion to drinking alcohol often led to mild needling in her family, but this time, Brian let it pass without even mentioning how much more expensive her fancy water was than his beer.

"You know," said Megan, "my memories of those times are kind of hazy."

"We were young."

"Sure, but . . . remember Mom, in Hawaii? How—glowing—energized, she was? She loved us. How could she just . . . leave us? Something happened. She was kidnapped, or something. And how . . ."

"Abbie?" said Jim, turning around in his chair. Abbie was standing at the top of the stairs.

"I need cereal," she said.

"You need to go back to bed."

Instead, she came downstairs and went into the kitchen.

"No. You already had some milk."

She walked into the kitchen, opened a low cupboard, and took out cereal boxes, which she set on the floor.

"Abbie. Put those away and get back to bed."

She pulled a baggie of small figures from the depths of the cupboard, held them to her chest, and hurried up the stairs. She slammed her bedroom door.

"She just wanted the Spacies," said Megan.

"They're still pretty popular. Remember when we first got them?"

"Yeah. They were so cool. Girl astronauts. Before we even went to space. I guess kids all over the world had them. I brought a few of the old ones from the house for Abbie to play with. Maybe I should have put them in the safe-deposit box—I bet they're going to be collectors' items."

"Yeah. Did you ever notice that they heal up when the dog chews them or kids decide to crush them with an asteroid? Kind of spring back, like the plastic swells, or something. I've heard that if you could cut the damn things in half they'd grow two, but the new ones don't do that. I think it made the cereal manufacturers mad."

"Oh, Brian, you're so naïve. They're an early form of nanotechnology. Molecular replication. The government decided they were dangerous and insisted that they be taken off the market—not that anyone in any government lab has been able to crack the code and disable them, or use it for anything else. Whoever really developed them was way ahead of their time."

"Really," said Jim. "My investigative reporter's ears are burning. Aren't there notes? Formulae?"

"So proprietary that no one's ever laid hands on them—lots of shell organizations, dead ends. It is pretty interesting." She laughed. "I mean, you can see why they were banned. What if they took over the world? Literally? Our homes and busses piled high with Spacies—"

"Well," said Brian, "I took a few of them too, for Bitsy. She plans to live in the moon colony."

Megan grimaced. "I'd hate that."

"It takes a certain personality. Didn't one of them go batshit not long ago?"

"Ha! NASA didn't ask us to help. We can do anything with drugs. Just about. Did I tell you? We're working on a memory drug."

"What's that?"

"Just what it sounds like. It enhances the formation and retrieval of memories."

"Like for when you're studying?"

"Probably, eventually. Right now we're concentrating on the geriatric market, which is about staying oriented."

"But what if you want to forget?"

"Well, then it could be torture. Too much memory could be very painful. Forgetting is often therapeutic. Who's that?" Megan turned and knelt on the couch, peered out the window. It was getting dark, and the interior of the room reflected back at them. Megan cupped her hands against the window so she could see better.

"Just some man taking a walk. Calm down, sweetie," said Jim.

Megan lowered the shade. "We have to keep this closed in the evening. People can look right into our house."

"Like you do," teased Jim. He told Brian, "She always cranes her neck to look into people's living rooms after dark. She'll say, 'Oh, I didn't know the Fabers liked to read—look at all those books. Let's go closer. Maybe I can see the titles.' She'd trample the flowerbeds if I didn't hold on to her."

"Seriously. I've been feeling watched," said Megan.

"What?" asked Jim, frowning. "Really?"

"Yeah. I've seen that man before."

Jim said, "I've noticed him. Yeah, he seems odd. It's the fedora, I think. Who wears them anymore? Or maybe the beard? Plaid shorts. Leather shoes, wingtips or something, and black socks. Old-fashioned aviator sunglasses. When it's cool, he wears green khakis and boots. Carries that walking stick. Aloof guy. I guess I've never gotten close enough to say hi."

Megan bit her bottom lip. "I wonder what his name is. Doesn't he have a job? He must live around here somewhere. People don't just wander through subdivisions. They might go on a walk in the evening after work, but they don't have time to do that in the daytime."

"Maybe he had a heart attack," said Jim. "Maybe his doctor told him to walk. I really do see him a lot. At least once a day. And I'm at home most of the time."

"Well, if I were spying around, I'd at least have a dog with me. People believe in you when you're walking a dog." Megan crossed her arms and hunched forward.

"Why don't you call the clothing police?" asked Brian. "Report him."

"Don't make fun of me. I'm not kidding," said Megan.

"I'm not either. Hello, police? I have something suspicious to report. Strange man. Walking on the sidewalk. Plaid shorts. A fedora, for chrissakes! And here's the kicker, officer—no dog."

Abbie came to the head of the stairs again. "I'm scared."

Jim sighed and turned around in his chair. "Of what, honey?"

"Falling."

"When did you fall?"

"In my dreams. I'm in a high, high tower, and I always fall off, and I think I might die!" She burst into tears.

Her father ran up the stairs and grabbed her. "It's okay, I'm here." He shut the bedroom door behind them.

"She has these falling dreams," said Megan. "I guess they seem pretty real."

"Yeah," said Brian. "They can. Especially to kids."

"You know," said Megan, "I have this recurring dream. Or, maybe not a recurring dream. But dreams where I feel as if I'm going to the same place, a place I've been before. And when I go there, it's not . . . thin, like dreams, but dense, like it's full of potential, full of things that I need to discover."

"I have that kind of dream too," said Brian. "It's like I need to find out something and I'm searching, and looking, and walking, the whole time I'm there."

Megan nodded. "There are riots in my dreams. Fires, angry mobs shouting, National Guardsmen. God knows why; I've never— What?"

"I have them too. Riots. Lots of fires, and yelling . . ."

"Huh. Maybe we were both in a riot. At some point. When we were real little."

"Mine are later. I'm maybe fifteen. You're thirteen."

"I'm there too?"

"Of course. We're in the old house. Dad tells us not to go out . . ."

"Yeah. And you go out anyway."

"Right."

They stared at each other for a moment. Finally Megan said, "What else?"

Brian closed his eyes. "They're because someone died."

"Martin. Luther. King." Megan felt sick to her stomach.

Brian said, "This is very, very strange. Because, yes. It's him. Sometimes I see him on TV and I think, this is amazing, what a bad dream I had, because here, he is, alive, and an ambassador, and will be the head of the UN, and I keep thinking that he should be dead."

"Shit," said Megan.

"Now, now, Mom," said Jim, coming down the stairs. "No need to swear. I think she's asleep at last." Then he looked at their faces. "What?"

"I don't know," said Brian. "It's about Martin Luther King."

"Oh, yeah. Right," said Jim. He sat down and picked up his beer. "It was in the *Post* today. He's perfect for the head of the UN."

"No," said Megan. She stood abruptly, pulled her hair back with one hand while her other went to the small of her back, and paced back and forth in the small living room. "It's like—we're having the same dream, Brian. King was . . . assassinated. Right? *Right?*"

"Honey, you're shaking." Jim got up, put his arm around her waist. "Come on, sit down on the couch with me. That's right. You're just wound so tight. You do too much. Want a drink of water? Something stronger?"

She shook her head. She stared at Brian. "Well?"

"Right," he said, nodding his head slowly.

"Where?"

"In . . . Memphis?"

"Look," said Jim, "will somebody please tell me what's going on?"

"I don't know," said Megan. Her eyes filled with tears. "Suddenly I have no fucking idea what is going on."

Brian

A DAY AT HALCYON HOUSE

[*May 18*]

BRIAN TRUDGED up the narrow, dusty steps to the Halcyon House attic. It was Saturday morning.

Jill had only been living in the house for a few weeks. Brian was still considering moving in, and Cindy had volunteered to help with repairs, somehow much easier to contemplate than making rushed, wrong choices on their beaux arts beauty. At least, so Cindy claimed. They'd spend the morning and afternoon with Jill, planning the work. It was, of course, Brian's house too, but he still had mixed feelings about living here again. The minuscule apartment, though, was unbearable.

Bitsy, Abbie, and Whens were running around shriek-ing with the sheer joy of being together, to magnified ef-fect: When together, they seemed more like six or ten children than merely three. Zoe was in the second-floor ballroom, with its lovely herringbone parquet floor. The floor sagged, and Brian had at first declared it off-limits. He'd locked the door, and Zoe had just looked at him, her hazel eyes impassive, and then sat leaning against the door, as if that room was the dearest in the universe, and opened the notebook in which she wrote music. He de-cided that the worst thing that could happen was that she might get beaned by a chunk of falling plaster, un-locked the door, and handed her the key. He heard her

lock it after she went inside: No screaming children for her, thank you.

She was the only one of the cousins who might have memories of Grandpa Sam. She had been two when Sam left. Zoe was actually one reason that Brian had resisted moving back here. When it became certain that Sam would not come back, Zoe had run through the house like a whirlwind, screaming, crying, angry, ungrabbable as a monkey, screaming, "Grampa! Grampa! Grampa!" as she looked in every corner, every closet, until she was hysterical. Then, she wouldn't talk for a week. For another year, she drew black arcs that she said were burnt rainbows.

Sam had adored her, carried her everywhere, became a very convenient babysitter, propping her on the couch as an infant while he played a rich variety of jazz records to "get it into her brain," read Bette's Chinese poetry to her, let her noodle on the piano, and played the saxophone for her. She had particularly loved "Somewhere Over the Rainbow."

Cindy and Brian had made a big effort to help her, to gradually reintroduce her to the house, to keep pictures of Sam on the walls, until finally she could visit the house without sadness—and sometimes, even with joy, walking the overgrown gardens and identifying the flowers she had "helped" him plant.

No need to reawaken all that by moving in, though.

The kids' din receded as Brian climbed.

Brian could tell by the faint light spilling down the stairs that someone had left the attic door open again. That sucked any summer coolness, or winter heat, from the three downstairs stories like a chimney. He heard his mother's voice, scolding them for doing this. Their father was often the culprit. He always seemed to be in another world.

It would have been useful, Brian thought, if one of them had spoken German when they went to Germany to try and find their father.

* * *

As it was, Megan spoke it quite badly, Jill's fluid French helped a lot, and of course a lot of Germans spoke fine English.

Jill, who was six months pregnant, had made a map of where Sam had been during the war, and drew up an itinerary. Their last stop, after a fruitless search lasting several weeks, was Berlin.

As they were walking down a street, Jill said, "Look. A *Deutsche Post*. I've got some postcards from Dad. They say—"

"What postcards?" asked Brian. "I didn't know we ever got postcards from him."

"They all just say he's fine." Jill turned into the *Deutsche Post*, which was empty, and went up to the man at the counter and pulled the postcards from her purse.

"Let me see those," said Brian.

Jill ignored him, and showed them to the official. "Do you know where this was sent from?"

He looked at them one after the other, then laughed. "They are some kind of hoax. There is no East Berlin. Or West, for that matter. There is just, you know, Berlin. And of course, Berlin is in Germany, not the Soviet Union. What an idea!"

All of the postcards were postmarked "East Berlin, USSR." "How about the neighborhood?" Jill turned the postcard over and tapped the picture. "Do you recognize it? How about this café?"

He shook his head. "Berlin is large. Walk around. Ask people. Try the War Museum. This neighborhood might have been destroyed in the war. Just about everything was."

After they emerged from the post office, Brian said, "Let me see those."

"Let's find a place to sit down," Megan said.

They found a café with outside seating. Brian ordered a stein of beer. Megan and Jill rolled their eyes at each other. "What?" snapped Brian.

"That's your third beer this morning," Megan pointed out.

"I'm in Germany." Brian spread the postcards out on the table. "I've never seen these before, Jill," he said. His voice had an edge of accusation.

"I didn't hide them from you. I told you both about them."

"You didn't *show* them to us," said Brian.

"I don't think you mentioned the postmark," said Megan.

"Maybe he . . . made them up," said Jill. "So he couldn't be tracked."

"'Dear Jill,'" Brian read. "'Your mother and I are fine. Please don't worry. Love, Dad.' No, Jill, I don't think you mentioned that he was with Mom."

"Maybe they're really not from him at all," suggested Megan.

"Who the *hell* would be sending them, then?" asked Brian. "And why? Couldn't we have discussed these things *before* we came all this way?"

"Can we not look at this in a positive way?" said Jill. Her cheeks were getting red. "We're here now, and here are the postcards."

"They just fucking don't make sense." Brian flung the postcards out over the iron railing, into the street.

Megan and Jill rushed after them. Jill held up her hand to stop traffic while Megan picked them up. They huffed back to Brian.

"Look at this," screamed Jill. "It fell in a puddle. You can't even read it anymore!" She flung it on the table and bent over it, sobbing, holding the other wet postcards in her hands. "This is all we have!"

"Brian, what is wrong with you?" Megan yelled. Everyone in the café was looking at the Americans with great interest.

"What's wrong with *me*?" He pushed his chair away from the table. It fell over backward. He stalked out of

the café. He booked a flight home. Soon afterward, he joined the Peace Corps.

And then Cindy had straightened him out.

He hadn't remembered that incident until just now. He had to admit, he'd been at least mildly inebriated most of the time he was over there. Jill had given birth several months later, and he could understand why she'd never brought it up, at least to him—she'd probably forgotten it too, what with not sleeping for a year or so afterward.

East Berlin? Was he imagining that too? His own memories were pretty mixed up.

Brian reached the top of the stairs.

The attic was illuminated like a cathedral. Dancing dust glowed in modulated sun coming through the windows at each end of the enormous room, leaving the center in shadow. Brian immediately broke out in a sweat.

The tops of trees, and the streets and houses far below, were suitably blurred by the dirt on the tiny windowpanes, as if the neighborhood existed in some other age so far away that all detail had faded. Mysterious heaps of stuff—much of it left by previous owners—emanated style-embedded memory. An eight-foot-high mahogany headboard, stern in its right angles, vied with the oak headboard tilted against it, carved with fluid, musical flowers, leaves, and a woman's face wreathed with long, flowing hair, a fairy creature observing humans from her forest redoubt. The floorboards were several inches thick.

Brian found the chain that turned on the two rows of lightbulbs that his father had installed years ago. Their light was discouragingly sparse. He rested his hands on his hips and tried to decide where to start. He was looking for something quite specific.

He and his sisters had given different forms to the contents over the years. It was a malleable medium. Megan's month-long attempt to organize it one summer,

sweating gallons and emerging in the evenings streaked with dirt and coughing, had fallen to the forces of entropy. Her avenues, lanes, and paths became obscured as her brother and sister tossed objects this way and that in search of something or other—a croquet set in a once fine, now cracked black leather case that they would set up on the flat front lawn and that became a neighborhood attraction on summer evenings. Fragile bagpipe records; Jill's favorite strategy for a rainy afternoon was to put one on the living room record player and turn it up loud. Within minutes Bette would appear in the doorway, a pained look on her face, and suggest that they go to the Uptown on Connecticut for a movie, her treat. Megan, Brian recalled, actually liked them, and danced along in her own interpretation of a Scottish reel—which lent a touch of authenticity to the purely avaricious intent of Jill and Brian. Yes, there were many useful objects in the attic, and it was a source of endless wealth. There was always a new quadrant to explore, a new source of object wonder.

But today, Brian's search was not fueled by serendipity. He was looking for his dad's nickel-plated saxophone. Something—he did not know what—had put it into his mind. Maybe just being back in the house.

The area under the eaves was most promising. He pulled his flashlight from his pocket and cast its beam over dark mountains of nearly a century's worth of junk, and moved into the suburbs, the most recent deposits.

As he roved, he recalled the life they had made up for the fictional family they imagined had lived in the house at one time. They were Russian. Some of their silk dresses hung on a dowel near the front of the house. They never exactly fit the girls, but that hadn't mattered. For Brian, there was a moth-eaten tail coat and a water-damaged silk top hat. They'd had a lot of fun up here.

He stepped on a board that rocked beneath his foot and was a bit surprised. He moved back carefully, think-

ing that it must be something on top of the board, but no; it was the board itself.

He caught one end with his fingertips and pulled it up. There was indeed a hollow place beneath—an imperfect hiding place, given that he had found it just by accident. But it was empty.

He reached around inside it and came up with a little bobble of stuff, kind of like gum. Yuck. He was about to toss it back in when he decided to be a good guy and throw it in the garbage later. That's what he'd tell his kids to do. He wrapped it in a nearby shred of paper, stuck it in his pocket, and replaced the board.

The mere fact of the space tugged at his mind with insistent gravity. This was important. But why? And then he became irritated that he could not remember.

He had drunk quite a bit the year that they had given up on finding his father. When he began blacking out, after he and Cindy left the Peace Corps and moved back to Washington, he realized the magnitude of his problem—particularly when Cindy gave him the ultimatum. This mystery made him flat-out mad at himself. There were missing pieces. This was one of them.

Maybe Jill would know what had been in the vacant space.

There was no point in lingering on it right now. He'd pass out from heat exhaustion, not alcohol, if he didn't find what he wanted soon.

He headed for the northwest corner of the house, where his mother had cleared out a space for more current storage. It took some poking, but after another fifteen minutes he scored not only his dad's saxophone, but a trombone as well.

As he made his way back to the door, carrying his finds, he noticed an open cardboard box that contained composition books. Setting down the instruments, he turned on the flashlight on the box. IN WAR TIMES was written on the cover on the flap, in his father's neat engineer's print.

There were five such boxes. He sat on a rolled-up carpet, and plucked the first composition book from the top.

He brushed grime from the cover. Written on it was "Notebook #11." So there was an order. Glancing inside, he saw that it was about Sam's time in Germany.

He'd had no idea that his father had kept a war diary. It was fascinating. And, apparently, abandoned.

If they had known about this before they went to Germany . . .

He wanted to read more.

Downstairs, he would be inundated with kids and chores. If he read just a bit up here, infernolike as it was, he could have a few moments of privacy with his father.

He settled back and began to read.

As Brian did so, he felt as if he assumed the personalities of Sam, his father, and his buddy Wink. His awareness of the hot, dusty attic faded: He was in Germany, in a little town called Mönchengladbach, just a bit east of the Rhine, in March 1945, several months before Germany surrendered on May 8.

Brian absorbed it all: the long, dark wait in Britain as the Invasion was planned and Company C assembled jeeps, guns, radar equipment, and . . . something else, it seemed. Something secret.

He fell into the world of Sam and Wink, into the chaotic end of the Third Reich, through which the two men were ordered to travel.

It was April 1945. Their assignment was to go to the town of Merkers and present their passes to the CO, where they would get more information about their assignment. It was about thirty miles south, in the mountains, on the other side of the Ruhr.

"Has this area been liberated?" Sam asked Hap, their CO.

"More or less." He spoke against the dull, thudding background of shelling along the Rhine, where occupying forces moved steadily northeast. "Here's a map."

It was a German road map of the area, printed in 1936, illustrated with a colored drawing. A happy Aryan family motored through fields of wildflowers; in the background were mountains toward which the road wound.

Sam and Wink left immediately, and within five miles were stuck behind a tank battalion. "We won't get through this town till tomorrow morning," a sergeant told them when they wanted to get past.

Sam got out the map. "Think we can get around this way?"

The sergeant shrugged. "Your guess is as good as mine. But watch out. There aren't many resisters, but the ones who are still fighting are about thirteen years old and in control of mortars. Call themselves Werewolves. Savage little shits. They shot at us in a village this morning. So we called for air support and held back while they pulverized the place. Whole goddamned town had to suffer because of these zealot kids. Hitler's done a great job with them. Just get 'em when they're young, that's all you gotta do."

Sam and Wink returned to a well-marked crossroads and took the road to Erkelenz. One of the marvels of Germany was that the road signs were intact, and that nobody even thought to turn them around. "They must have thought they would never be invaded," said Wink.

"They love us," said Sam.

"They love food and cigarettes and not being forced to die for Hitler."

So, generally, their map worked. If they were lost, Germans willingly and correctly redirected them. They found such behavior just this side of unbelievable. No self-respecting boy in the U.S. could resist sending someone down the wrong road—particularly an enemy, which they were, because Germany was still at war.

It was easy to blunder into a battle or run into diehard SS patrols, so they were hyperalert. After being shot at by snipers, they looked down the road onto which they

were to turn and saw billowing black smoke. "Alternate route," said Wink, who was presently navigating. It was growing dark, and they decided to stop as soon as they saw a likely place.

Suddenly they passed a sign, and entered a town. Wink halted at sight of a white flag hung from the top window of an intact building.

Another white flag emerged from the cellar.

"What say we take the surrender?" asked Wink.

Before Sam could tell Wink not on your life, rifles flew through a shattered window and landed in the street. The front door opened, and out marched a file of Wehrmacht, their hands in the air.

"Damn," breathed Wink. "Think it's a trick?"

"We surrender," one of them shouted in English. "We are unarmed." And then from all around, Germans emerged from cellars, all of them surrendering, putting themselves at the mercy of the American conquerors.

The soldiers invited them into their cellar for brandy as night fell. First Sam gathered the rifles and relieved the soldiers of sidearms and grenades and secured them in the jeep's footlocker, removing chocolates, coffee, a string of bologna and a crate of sustaining Bordeaux to make room. Wink handed him an American flag. "Think this will keep us from being shelled tonight?"

Sam went upstairs to hang it from a window. The house was intact and neatly decorated. In the front bedroom, he had finished securing the flag and turned from the window when heard a bloodcurdling scream. He took out his gun and opened the closet door, revealing a little girl who continued to shriek.

Her mother emerged from behind a rack of clothing, thrust the girl behind her, and screamed invective at Sam until the German soldier ran up the stairs and calmed her down. "She thinks you are going to rape her. I told her that you are not Russian, but American."

"Ask her if she can help us with dinner," said Sam.

They had plates of fried bologna and potatoes, carried downstairs by the little girl.

The German soldiers had a fire going, and seemed quite comfortable in their outpost. "We are very relieved to see you," said the commander. "We've been waiting for you for several days. We were afraid the Red Army would come first."

"Yes," said another. "We hear that the German POWs are well taken care of by the Americans."

"Better than they take care of American soldiers," said Wink bitterly, referring to the soldiers fighting in December and January, during the Battle of the Bulge, without proper boots, socks, food, or clothing. Sam silenced him with a sharp elbow.

The following dawn, as they were getting directions on how next to proceed, two American jeeps rolled in.

"They've surrendered," said Sam, when the first jeep stopped next to theirs, but the soldiers rushed past them to "secure the town." One of them returned with an SS knife, which the others admired profusely. "Yeah, hands off," said the soldier as he stowed it in his pocket.

And then children emerged from houses bearing flowers. All the civilians came out to stand on their doorsteps, and waved as Sam and Wink brought up the rear of the procession, behind two Shermans.

"It's so easy. And it was so hard."

"You would have thought they'd fight to the death."

"They're finished and they know it. They're just trying to get on our good side."

By noon, they had made good progress, passing through Jülich and heading toward Krauthausen, a tiny town close to the Ruhr River. "Let's see," said Sam, who was trying to make sense of their latest intelligence. "I think that there's a pontoon bridge a little bit east of here where we can cross the Rhur. Try that left fork."

In late afternoon, they turned onto a twisting lane that

clung to the side of a mountain. Trees on one side had been crushed down by tanks to afford a track around bomb craters.

Merkers was a small, ugly town on a plateau. Grim barracks and fences surrounded the entrance to a salt mine. Two cog railroad freight cars lay sideways, blasted off the track.

The guard looked at them suspiciously and left to check on their orders. He returned and waved them through with a bored expression.

Inside the fence, two GIs with machine guns lounged against a gray concrete wall on either side of a metal door. Wind roared in the pine trees above them, and brought the sharp, clean scent of snow.

They stepped into a rusted cage elevator, which moved slowly, with the ominous creak of poorly maintained machinery. "This is fun," said Wink. "I like small, closed, deep places out of which it is impossible to escape if something goes wrong. Like the generator poops out."

"It's not closed," said Sam.

"Gee, you're right. We could reach out and scrape our hands against that stone shaft." He looked up through the cage. "We'll actually be able to see that rusty cable snap. And here we are! Two thousand feet underground."

They stepped out into a damp, vast tunnel, where Vs of light from bare bulbs on the walls extended into the distance. Posted on one side was the required HEIL HIT-LER sign, except that someone had painted out HEIL and replaced it with FUCK. Beneath it, several men worked in a makeshift office, a space sectioned off by wooden crates. After a moment, one of the men looked up and came over.

"I'm Levi. I guess you're the guys we've been waiting for. Dance and—"

"Winklemeyer."

"Right. We've got a big transfer job. Need help on the logistics."

Sam looked around. "Well, what is it?" He was think-

ing, the ultimate Wonder-Weapon. The manufacturing process, blueprints, mechanical drawings, impenetrable scientific papers.

"Gold."

"Nah," said Wink. "What is it?"

"Gold," said Levi. "Come this way."

They followed him to a small side gallery. Two more guards stood next to a dynamited hole. Levi stepped through the hole into a place where the lighting was not very strong. "Here." He yanked open one of a vast army of canvas bags, so many that they stretched far away out of the range of the lights.

Sam reached in and felt a cool, smooth surface. With both hands, he lifted out a small block of gold. It was heavy. "Must be what? Fifty pounds?"

"Two hundred tons in all."

Sam and Wink looked at each other. "While Europe starves," Wink said softly.

"The Third Reich was nothing more than a very well-organized pack of murderous, unscrupulous, blood-thirsty thieves. But there's more. We have reports that this is not an unusual place. They got loot holed up all over Germany."

Levi led them through a dark tunnel to another stone gallery. A set of tracks ran along one side. Precisely organized sections of paintings, statues, and suitcases stretched as far as Sam could see; he had a feeling that if the next section of lights were switched on this astonishing wealth of European art would continue, and continue, and continue.

A man knelt next to a stack of folios, jotting on a clipboard. He stood and wiped both hands on his pants. "Marsh."

"Dance and Winklemeyer. They're going to figure out how to move all this stuff."

"Know anything about art?" asked Marsh.

"Not much."

"Well, over here I have six Rembrandts." He bent and

flipped large, framed paintings forward. "I can't put a price on them. I mean, I was an art dealer. I've never seen anything this fantastic. Apparently it was Goering's collection."

"His adviser tells us that he paid for every piece," said Levi, with a grim edge to his voice. "Just had to wait till the price was right, I guess. Let's see—a Rubens here, a Dürer there. It adds up. Probably took ten train cars to cart this stuff up here so it could rot."

"That's a Kandinsky," said Wink. Marsh looked at him with respect. "Saw it in a book. It's huge!"

"Yes, well, it's a great surprise to me that they have this so-called decadent art here, but it does have a monetary value. Kandinsky was at the Bauhaus for ten years, and the whole liberal lot of them had to decide either to toe the party line or get the hell out of the country. Kandinsky is still alive, you know. At least, I think he is. He's Russian, but he moved to Germany when Russia threw him out, and then he moved to Paris."

In the dim light, Sam drank in the strange juxtapositions of lines and shapes, the sheer motion of the piece. "He has some interesting thoughts."

"Indeed." Marsh rubbed moisture from the braided coronet of an exquisite marble nude with a rag he held. "Salt water can't be good for this. I guess Goering was thinking he'd be back soon."

They stood in silence for a moment.

"Well," said Levi briskly, "I think we're almost done counting it. I'll get the lists to you tomorrow. One thing," he was leading them back toward the head of the tunnel, the brightly lit office and stopped at another doorway. "I haven't found anyone to catalog this yet."

Inside yet another gallery, three-foot hoops strung solidly with gold rings hung on metal rods ten feet long, rows and rows of them. Sam lifted his hand to touch one of the hoops, then dropped it. He tried to estimate the weight of what he saw. Levi gestured hopelessly toward

what looked like hundreds of barrels, opposite the rings. "Go on," he said, his voice hoarse.

Wink lifted the lid of one of the barrels.

"What is it?"

"Teeth," Wink finally said. "With gold fillings." He set the lid down gently and stood with his head bowed for a long moment.

Levi was gone. Without speaking, they returned to the elevator and held their silence as it clanked to the top.

Night had come to the mountains.

"I don't want to stay here," said Wink.

"Me neither." Sam put the jeep in gear and drove back down the road, on the lookout for craters.

Near the Rhur, where the air was river-damp, they found an empty house and set up camp, carrying candles, food, and wine into the house in silence.

Finally, as they ate bread and cheese and washed it down with Rhine wine, Sam spoke.

"I think we need to make that damned Device work."

"Seconded."

But as Sam lay awake in the darkness, he knew it would be much more difficult than just deciding. He wasn't sure why.

Maybe it was only because it seemed like much work, and that it could drain his soul.

Brian snapped back into the present, nauseated. The experience of his father had flown off the old, fragile paper directly into his brain, as if he was *there* with Sam, *feeling* the horrific revelation.

One's normal reading of the discovery of the Merkers salt mines, which held gold, art, and some of the first evidence of the depth of Nazi atrocities, did not give the full import of *being* there. He mopped his forehead with his T-shirt, and got to his feet, shaken. Yes, of course: After that experience, anyone would want to stop war—and that was far from the worst of it. Compared to the

discovery of conditions at Bergen-Belsen a few weeks
later, compared to a day of combat in which soldiers saw
their buddies blown to bits, or parents their children killed,
this was nothing. Brian didn't know if he could stand
reading Sam's next entry while in this new, strange state
of mind.

But he had heard about the war all his life, at second-
and third-hand; these atrocities were common knowledge. New genocides occurred constantly, worldwide, a
steady, somber note beneath humanity's bustling,
forward-leaning gloss of civilization.

Was he inured, somehow, to the outrage and astonishment that stunned Sam in that salt mine? Was that why
he lacked—even mocked—Jill's antiwar fervor?

Jill was always talking about ending war for all time,
but then, she was a bleeding-heart liberal, who deeply
believed in the goodness of humanity. In fact, before he'd
come up to the attic, they'd had quite a discussion about
the Q-Schools, which would grow from artificial DNA
and cure the world of war, never mind those who didn't
want them.

Brian was a cynic. It had always seemed so easy to
defeat her arguments, to ridicule her utopias, although
while she was working on her doctorate, it had become
more of a challenge. She had studies and statistics at her
fingertips, a great and unfair lot of them. History, however, was squarely on his side.

Brian reread the last few lines. Wink and Sam had to
make *what* work? The question sprang a lock deep inside of him, one of those things from childhood, when
he'd overheard his parents arguing. . . .

Closing the notebook, he placed it back in the box.
There were several boxes of material, and he carried
them all to the top of the stairs, his sweat making little
plops onto the dusty cardboard. Each drop spread out in
the dust like a tiny bomb crater landing, the dirt land-
scapes where his beloved little green Army men had
attacked, rallied, and moved strategically across the

creek. He'd carried them around most of his childhood, setting them up and knocking them down with incoming rocks. Spacies had taken over that mental space in most kids' psyches years ago. They battled not one another but ignorance, greed, and oppression.

He went back and got the instruments, turned off the lights, and stepped onto the landing. The air, a mere ninety degrees, washed over him with marvelous coolness. He remembered to turn around and close the attic door.

After assembling his finds at the bottom of the stairs, he pushed open the kitchen door just a crack. Nobody was in the kitchen. Good. He hoped to smuggle the saxophone out the back door, and then somehow get it into his truck, without Jill noticing it, and then the boxes.

Whens galloped into the kitchen. "Uncle Brian! Come and play with us! What's that?"

"What's what?" asked Jill, as she approached down the hallway.

Brian shoved the saxophone under the table. He held one finger over his mouth. "Shhh."

As Jill came into the room, Brian opened the other case. "Look, Jill. It's your old trombone!"

She looked at him suspiciously. "You know I never liked playing the trombone. I really liked playing the saxophone." She bent down, looked under the table, and pulled out the saxophone case. She sat on a chair and opened it, picked up the tarnished instrument. "Look, Whens. This belonged to Grandpa."

"Oh." He frowned. "How do you play it?"

"Well . . ." She took the mouthpiece from its separate compartment, then searched the entire case. "You can't, without a reed."

"That's right," said Brian. "I'm going to get it spiffed up and working again."

"And then you'll bring it back." It was a command.

"I played this saxophone too."

"I played it better."

"Maybe. Maybe not." His own kids were in the kitchen now, with Cindy and Abbie. He really wanted to say "Finders, keepers," but it would be such a bad example for the children.

He smiled. "Jill, why don't you show them how to play the trombone? I'm sure it still works." The kids dragged Jill and the trombone out of the kitchen; soon he heard the blatting, sliding notes of "She'll Be Coming 'Round the Mountain" issue from a thankfully distant part of the house.

Fortified with iced tea, Brian began to clean up the sax, polishing the nickel until it shone. In some places, the metal was pitted. The pads were in bad repair; many of them were missing felt and the leather had been eaten by some strong-jawed insect.

As he worked, he recalled sitting on the stairs one night in the wee hours, watching his father play. The radio, records, and live music of his father were a hard-wired part of his nocturnal life as a child.

His father would put a record by Lester Young, Coleman Hawkins, or Ben Webster on the turntable and play along about ten times. Then he'd try to play it without the record until he faltered. Maddeningly, he'd put the needle on the part he was trying to master again and again, until it was perfect, and then he'd try to play the whole thing again. Even though it looked and sounded tedious, it fascinated Brian so much that he'd taken saxophone in band.

Over the years, the sound of distant jazz at night became as familiar, as soothing, as the sound of wind combing the trees. Now, when he found it hard to sleep, he'd switch the twenty-four-hour jazz station on low and lie on the living room couch. It always worked.

He hadn't mentioned his other recurring nightmare to Megan. In that one, he was flying a bomber over, improbably, Cambodia, one of the most peaceful countries

in the world, bombing the daylights out of it. Until he himself went down in flames while on his way back to his base in Vietnam.

It was horrifyingly real. As real, actually, as being at the Merkers salt mines in April 1945.

Cindy stood in front of him. "Head in the clouds again? Time to get to work. Do you even know how to play it?"

"Kind of. I played it in high school band. I never told you?"

"Jill said you were awful and would drive us out of the apartment and the neighbors would call the police."

"Just an underhanded ploy to try and get me to leave it here. Pretty unfair, if you ask me."

Brian put the saxophone back into the case and carried it out to the truck. Then he went back to the kitchen and opened the door to the attic stairs and picked up the first box of his father's journals. He paused for a moment, struggling. Jill would want to hoard this too, if she saw it. He'd bring it back as soon as he'd read everything. How long could it take to read this stuff?

The coast was clear. He went outside with his haul and slipped it into the backseat of the truck. As he slammed the door, he sighed. He had to tell her.

He went back to the kitchen, where Jill stood on a stepstool, rummaging through a cupboard. "Where would the paper cups be?"

"Jill, remember Dad's journals?"

"Yes. Why?"

"I just put them in my truck. I'm going to read them."

"What? *I'm* going to read them." She slammed the cupboard door, climbed down, and leaned back against the counter, a wild, lost look on her face.

Even afraid? wondered Brian. "When?"

"Soon. Any day now. Maybe tonight."

"That would be great. Come over to the apartment. We'll order a pizza and read them together."

"I don't—" She shook her head.

"What's wrong?"

"I— Oh, I really don't have time to read them right away. Take good care of them, okay?"

"Are you kidding?" Once again, there was something she was not telling him. "Jill, do you remember—" He was going to mention the weirdly haunting space under the loose attic floorboard.

"Mommy! Help!" Whens had suspended himself upside down by the knees from a crossbar on the swing set.

"Be right there," she yelled out the window.

"Jill—"

"Look, don't worry about it."

"But—"

She snarled—Brian could only think of it as a snarl, flung over her shoulder as she ran down the back stairs— "I said, *never mind*!"

With Jill, that was that. He and Megan planned to sit down and try to hash things out with her, but this certainly was not a good time to mention it.

Zoe, upstairs, was hard at work.

It had been a day of awakening when Zoe realized that she could hear her mother even when she couldn't see her. Using her markers, she could write her mother's sound when she was in another room, when she was at work. Sometimes she was baroque, sometimes she was rock 'n' roll, sometimes she was a cello concerto or a funny cartoon piece, rushing fast toward a roaring conclusion.

She could hear her father too, and write him, but sometimes she didn't want to listen, because her father was complicated to listen to. His music was strange and sometimes even unpleasant, so that it might make Zoe sick to her stomach. She guessed she couldn't really hear everyone, at least not all of them.

Bitsy was just too simple. Happy, all primary colors, the sound of water burbling over smooth rocks in a creek, an unending roar of good stuff.

Whens?

Whens was distant, like a star. His explosions of color were symmetrical and so intense that they sometimes gave Zoe a headache. But he was always there, there, there, like daylight, the sun-star come close, like he was bathing everyone in light but he didn't know it. One Christmas Eve her Crazy Aunts, which was what she and the other cousins called them, had taken everyone to midnight Mass at their old Episcopal church on Connecticut, even though they never went there any other time. Aunt Jill handed her Whens, and Whens was six months old and kind of heavy but not too.

The service was most soothing to Zoe, and deeply beautiful. Candles flickered in wall sconces and the organ music was so magnificent that tears rolled down her face.

Whens was just as deeply happy. Zoe had been afraid that the baby would wail, or squirm, and disturb her enjoyment of the music, but he just stared in wonder at everything around him and Zoe could hear him absorbing everything, like a reverse kind of music. That was when Zoe fell in love with Whens, who before that had just been another boring baby. And after that night, Whens started giving off that music, like a switch had been flipped inside of him, like he was suddenly himself and knew it.

It was really, really cool when the change came to all the kids in the world.

Zoe would always remember it. It happened on a Tuesday night, at least for her, but for other kids it was Wednesday morning, or Tuesday afternoon.

She was lying in bed, almost asleep, when she saw a light on the ceiling, and heard a brilliant music, so brilliant that toes and fingers and even her hair ached with it, brilliant beyond beautiful.

She got up to see what the light was, moving through skeins of color and sound, and saw that it was her classbook, all lit up.

Picking it up and holding it in front of her face, she

was profoundly transformed. The voices were all singing, and she sang with them, adding her own notes now and then, listening for a few seconds, then joining in.

She didn't know how long this happened. But the next day, kids started talking to one another and they talked so much in their own languages and worked so hard that words started meaning the same thing to them as they did to other kids. It was kind of like swimming in the ocean, being pushed here and there with words and meaning and sense, and the words were ground down to sand and re-formed into new words that meant the same thing to everyone, until one morning you understood what everybody was saying, you could stand up, you were on land and could walk where you wanted to go. It was like that. But those were the simple early times and then the words got so you could say more complicated things. They called their talk Zozo. Whenever someone started talking in their own language, lots of kids would shout "Zozo!"

One day when she was much younger, just six, and missed her mother, she had walked out of school and listened for her. She had a kids' pass for the Metro and just went on this bus and that and sometimes Mom got faint but then Zoe would find a bus going the right way. And she walked into her mother's meeting, just opened the door where her sound boomed and soared and Mom saw her and stopped talking. She stared at Zoe. She said, "Excuse me, that's my little girl," which made Zoe mad, because she was not little, and then Mom took her out to lunch and asked how she knew where she was and why she was not in school and there was a big flurry of unpleasant stuff and she found out that it was not good to just go wherever you were hearing said you ought to go. So she found out when it was okay and when it was not.

She had only been two when she last saw Grandpa Dance. They told her she was too little to remember, but she did. He used to grab her up, in the living room downstairs, while he played those jazz records, and swing her

around the room as she shrieked and laughed. He took her out in the garden and taught her names: peony, tulip, hollyhock, lily-of-the-valley, which were poisonous. He told her about Ohio, and riding on the *Queen Elizabeth,* and played any song she wanted on his saxophone for her, and the songs were always stretched with lots of notes and more interesting than hearing "The Erie Canal" on her record player. He'd play "Twinkle, Twinkle Little Star" and it never sounded the same twice, yet she always recognized it somehow.

She remembered running out the door screaming when her daddy told her that Grandpa Sam might not come back, and his big footsteps behind her as he ran and caught her before she could run across the street in front of a car.

Now that she was older, she could see him more strongly, more clearly, in music. He was half a rainbow. The other half was missing. She could still feel him somewhere looking for the rest of the rainbow. She dreamed of him as a walking rainbow with legs and arms and a hat and a saxophone, like a cartoon, but the rainbow had eyes and they were his.

Now the other half of the rainbow was here: Grandma Dance. She and Abbie and Whens were big enough to keep the secret, probably. Maybe. Bitsy was definitely a blabber. So little that nobody would believe her, though. Zoe knew what that was like.

Now that Zoe was older, a whole new stream flowed through her, especially when she came here to Crazy Aunt Jill's house. There were a million sounds and colors here, things she just could not write down no matter how hard she tried, because it radiated from everything, from vases and furniture and walls, and most strongly from the attic. The ballroom was the quietest place, really, like a sunlit meadow in the middle of a forest, and its music was more focused, and older, and clearer. Her aunts were nuts, of course, although it was more than that. Crazy Aunt Megan was crazy in a different way

from Crazy Aunt Jill. Crazy Aunt Jill was like a lot of beautiful marbles all rolling around on the floor, sometimes clacking together with glassy sounds, and there were different levels, and the marbles could roll upward, defying gravity, and then back down. Crazy Aunt Megan was a smooth sheet of glass that you could see things through, things like the circuit board of a computer, brightly colored and precise and organized, but that you worried about what would happen to it all if the glass broke. There were an awful lot of colors and sounds at Crazy Aunt Jill's house that could break the glass of Crazy Aunt Megan, which was why, Zoe supposed, she wasn't there often. Her dad was kind of like that too, but he was more like melting glass, and the colors of the glass were melting together and swirling around and then they would stop and he would just be in one pattern for a while. Dad didn't seem to mind all that. He wanted more melting, more swirling. But sometimes Dad was way too swirly. That's what made Zoe sick, like being on a roller coaster. She tried to throw up in very, very private, otherwise they kept taking her to doctors, and they wanted her blood and she was forced to scream about the needles, at least when she'd been little, and they wanted to take pictures of her brain. There was nothing wrong with her, she knew. It was just everybody else.

The other kids called her mom Crazy Aunt Cindy, but that was because she was just so much fun and so funny and made them all laugh. There was nothing crazy about Mom. She was like a long walk through a beautiful garden and she was always working in the garden too, like she was the garden and the worker in the garden, planting new flowers, planting herself, and dusting off her hands.

There were frightening musics too, that came from other kids, from other people in the world, and then sometimes too from people she saw downtown, maybe in a nice restaurant where she had to really behave her-

self (though that had become easy years ago). She'd heard a lot of scary music in those places, from men and women wearing really nice clothes, and the times when that happened she actually threw up, which was pretty boring for her, it happened so often, and upsetting to everyone around her, so they didn't take her to restaurants much anymore. They just said that she was nervous and had a reflux problem, but it wasn't that at all.

Zoe and the new friends she found on Q talked in notes and colors. Some of them, like Indians, and Arabs, thought in colors more naturally than they did in Western music, and had different forms of notation, which Zoe learned readily. They used cool words like *jins,* and *maqam,* and although there were musics she could not play on the instruments around her, she could at least hear them, and now she could write them down and share them. So she was very glad to find that the complexity she longed for when composing had been thought of before, by other people, and that she was not alone.

It was very important not to be alone, and she had been alone since Grandpa left. Finding other kids like her was the happiest thing that had ever happened to her, other than playing her beloved instruments.

So all day, while the adults did their boring things, Zoe was enthralled to be able to play violin in the ballroom.

Fallen bits of the plaster ceiling lay on the herringbone floor, which needed sanding and waxing, and it needed a new metal beam underneath to hold it up. According to her parents, there was so much work to fixing up the ballroom further that they had no idea if they'd ever do it.

The windows were tall and had half-circles over them with thin pieces of wood like the rays of the sun holding the glass. Old furniture covered with sheets had been pushed over to the walls, spoiling the acoustics. She had tried moving some pieces to different places, but it didn't help.

She had, though, discovered a spot at what she had

decided was the front of the ballroom; Jill had even mentioned that they'd found an old photo in the attic and that was where a small stage had raised the musicians a few feet higher. She dragged a chair and stood on it as she played; then the sounds echoed back, absolutely beautiful.

She especially liked Vivaldi, and was right now playing *Summer*. She played her part very slowly, because it was quite complicated, but heard all the other parts as she played. She wanted the whole world to hear how beautiful it was. So much was wasted. Hardly anyone else could hear it. Sometimes this made her so deeply sad that she cried. At the same time, she cried because she was deeply happy that at least she could hear it.

Zoe was often distressed that other children did not feel the same joy about music. And that they could not hear the music of other humans, not to mention the music of a tulip, or were even unable to meld the perfect with the imperfect musically, for that wide view of everything in one great music, which filled her with light.

She never told anybody else about the filled-with-light feelings. She could show them, with music, and yet her control of her instruments, the violin and the piano, was imperfect, as far as she was concerned, despite how adults raved. That was only because of her age; she knew that she had a long way to go to reach her own goals. Presently, writing her music was the only way to actually transmit that light.

Unfortunately, no one else knew how to read her music in its entirety.

On her classbook, though, she'd met a girl in China who was the same as her. The classbook translated their spoken language, and they also spoke in Zozo. They both understood that people were music and that the parts of them they tried to hide, even the parts of them that they didn't know about themselves, were music. But each used a different method to write their music. The Chinese girl, Dawei, sometimes used equations hyperlinked to her no-

tations. When she tried to explain them, Zoe realized the equation's similarities to her colors, with their infinite hues.

There was also Adam, twelve, in a small town in Cameroon. He too had colors for sounds, but they had a different correlation than Zoe's. He spoke French and some other African language, and again the translator helped, along with their new language. Adam used a lot of drums. The drums themselves, in all their varieties, often comprised an entire piece in Adam's repertoire. Zoe imported many of Adam's sounds into pieces she composed on her classbook.

These, and other kids like them were Zoe's friends, much more than the kids around her in school. Her schoolmates made fun of her, and called her a snob. She minded at first, a long time ago, but now she didn't care. Since she was little, she'd had an imaginary older brother, Paul, who was very kind. She often heard other kids complain about their brothers, so she was glad Paul was kind, and fun too.

She wanted, someday, to be able to teach other kids about music. She wrote her heart out for them and put her pieces out there, on Q, the writing that had no physical manifestation except perhaps in people. She could make music out of people.

As she thought all these things, she was playing, and playing, and playing whatever came into her mind, Vivaldi having been left far behind.

When her father stuck his head in the door and told her it was time to go home, Zoe protested, "I just got started."

Her dad got a funny look on his face. "It's almost six, sweetie. You've been playing since eleven. Did you get yourself anything to eat?"

Zoe shook her head. She carefully put her violin away. "My fingers do hurt, I guess."

Bette, up in the attic, had heard someone stumbling around earlier in the day. Listening in, later, she discovered

that Brian had taken Sam's notebooks, his saxophone, and the trombone.

Without any eavesdropping equipment, she had also felt, as much as heard, otherworldly violin music so sweet it almost made her weep. For some reason, it reminded her of Sam.

But she had been weeping a lot, anyway. She wandered the house when it was empty, and at night, trying to recover her own lost past, her own lost life, wondering if what she had been a part of had been worth the sacrifice.

The threat that had sent her timestream-hopping was still here, although now its origin was not her former employer, the CIA. It seemed as if the CIA had forgotten about the Dances completely. Perhaps in this timestream, the Dances had never been the subject of intense, crippling scrutiny. Bette, at overwhelming cost to herself, had sacrificed those growing-up years for their safety, so perhaps it had been worth it.

But this threat was from a source more mysterious, and thus more unsettling.

She nudged the little window a few inches higher, but with trepidation. Someone might notice the open window, although it was mostly hidden by an ornate gable. It crossed her mind that maybe she wanted to be discovered.

She turned on her vent fan, closed the window, and recalled the discussion Brian and Jill had had about her Q-Schools earlier in the day while she had somewhat guiltily eavesdropped. What right did anyone have to distribute such schools—that is, if the design even worked?

Jill had asked Brian, with some heat, what gave old men the right to mire nations and all their treasure and lives in horrific, endless war?

Not a new question. The answer had always been, because they had the power. Bette tapped a cigarette out of her pack and lit it.

War was just a biological tradition, according to Hadntz, one that could be broken, a terrible dream that humanity could wake from, if properly inoculated, via education. Inoculation could be many layered as well. It might consist of even deeper biological agents, akin, say, to vaccines for polio and smallpox, or any other world-changing drug. Disease, like war, was a natural biological occurrence, but that didn't mean that people had to suffer from curable disease. These Q-Schools, like the Device, were a product of the human mind, as were war, commerce, medicine, and literacy.

She and Sam had endlessly questioned the rightness of the self-reproducing Device, but had never found an exit from the problem—or the promise—its mere existence posed. Unlike its cousin, nuclear energy, it worked directly on the functioning of the mind, of collective consciousness as reflected by the constant feedback of news, education, and communication in all forms. The stuff that informed cultural-racial constructs, the roots of power, the biological evolution of the human brain, and its inherent plasticity were all laid bare by the Device, like rock strata revealed by a receding river.

What would true, radical democracy, put in place virtually overnight, look like? For instance, if girls in certain countries attended these Q-Schools, who would defend them? Armies of other children, perhaps? Child Soldiers for Education? Mothers and Fathers for Education? Would their former oppressors change, overnight? Who knew what might happen?

Bette was indeed in a world that was different, and, in myriad ways, better, than many spun from the timestream in which JFK been shot, despite its problems. Without the Cold War, with which politicians and manufacturers could justify staggering expenses, the wealth of this world was more equally distributed. The marvelous rail system was just one tiny facet of the differences. But one of the roots of war—extreme religious persuasion, which

by definition bypassed reason and conferred great power on some—still existed here.

Bette let her imagination run wild. These Q-Schools could, conceivably, lure fundamentalists of all kinds—those who used religion to control others—strip them down to childhood, and give them the gift of neuroplasticity. Help them—Bette grinned and closed her eyes, hearing herself and Sam, arguing again through long summer evenings down by the creek—understand that true religion was a matter of personal choice and conscience, an experience of natural transcendence, rather than a tool, like totalitarianism, just more subtle, with which to hijack the unwary.

Perhaps just as important, these environments might provide a cure from strokes, a reorganization of the brain, neurogenesis. People might even take month-long neuroplasticity vacations to rediscover the joy of learning and pursue new, enriching paths of study.

It didn't really matter. It was out of her hands, and, probably, had never been in her hands. It was out of Hadntz's hands too. The Device had been born, survived infancy, and was entering another of its own developmental stages. It was human, and was taking humanity with it.

Jill stood on the porch and waved as Brian and his family left, then dropped into the rocking chair and crossed her arms. She probably couldn't keep this up much longer. Brian had the notebooks, which probably had something about what their parents had been up to. Maybe all the information about the Game Board was there—if, as she suspected, the Game Board was actually the Device that that caller had demanded. She was curious, herself. What *did* Megan and Brian think? What *had* happened to them, to their memories. What had lately given them this bug? They'd gone for years—decades—without mentioning that anything strange had happened.

She recalled the menace in the caller's voice the other

night. Maybe she *should* tell them. Maybe together they could figure something out, do something.

Like what?

Whens ran in through the screen door, which slammed behind him. "I'm hungry. What are you frowning about?"

She grabbed him and put him on her lap. "I'm thinking that I have work to do. But I'm hungry. Do you want to walk over to Bazanno's and have a pizza?"

"Yeah! They have Slingers there."

"But not for you. Ready?"

Later that night, when Jill opened her school-planning folder, she noticed that some of her tabs—half-inch, flexible, translucent squares that one pressed to the Q-screen to transfer information—were missing. She'd planned to properly integrate the Q-School plan into the Future Possibilities section tonight.

That was the problem with tabs—they were too small; easy to lose. Manfred could have licked them up. Surely someone without dogs, children, or a portable office had designed them. She searched the carpet, went through all her papers, folders, the top of the desk—and after a few hours, finally fell into bed, too tired to look any longer.

In her garret, her fortress, Bette went over the plans for the school seed many, many times, wondering what it might truly do.

She Q'd it to Hadntz, not expecting a response—or, if any, just feedback. Advice. She had no idea where the woman was. Then she returned it to Jill's rather haphazard notebook.

To her surprise, she got a very quick reply:

Good work. Manufacture in Kyoto set up.
Estimated time of manufacture: ten days.
Immediate worldwide release and distribution
    scheduled.

For the life of her, though, Bette couldn't raise another damned word from Hadntz.

The minute Jill got up the next morning—well, after some very strong coffee—she resumed her search for the tabs. When she opened her notebook, they were there in their little slots.

"I could have sworn," Jill said, then shrugged.

Relieved, she quickly transferred the information to her International Schools presentation.

Brian

THE PLANS

[*May 18*]

BRIAN LUGGED his father's boxes into their cramped apartment.

Every room was stacked with boxes. Most were still taped shut, but some were open, the contents rummaged through. He sighed as he set Sam's boxes next to the coffee table.

"Problem?" asked Cindy, from the kitchen area, ten feet away.

"These are Dad's papers, but I have no idea when I'll get a chance to read them."

"Is two hours from now soon enough?"

Brian gave her an enthusiastic hug and kiss. "Easy to please," she said. "I like that in a guy."

She put Bitsy to bed right after dinner, claiming that she was exhausted, ergo, Bitsy must be too. Zoe lingered, opening the saxophone case. "Grandpa's?" she asked. Brian nodded.

She fell asleep on the couch, holding the saxophone on her lap, smiling. Brian gently removed it and carried Zoe to bed. He was alone.

It was a miracle.

Brian began to unload the dusty contents of the boxes onto the cleared-off coffee table.

He found a sizable collection of notebooks. Twenty? They were all neatly labeled by date in his father's hand. The first one was in December 1941. The last was dated 1967. He glanced inside each of them, briefly, as he stacked them on the table. Each was full of his father's fine engineering print.

Beneath these, Brian found a brown cardboard folder. He untied it and went through memorabilia. Tickets to a show in London. A folded poster that, when unfolded, fell apart at the creases. The Perham Downs, his father's band, would be appearing in the village of Ludgershall on the night of April 12, 1944; a photo of the band was at the top of the poster. He set it aside, to be framed, and put the folder aside too. He'd explore it in detail later. Next: a bundle of papers held between two sheets of corrugated cardboard by rubber bands, which disintegrated when he pulled on them.

He lifted off the top piece of cardboard, and fell into the world of someone very different from his father—a typed treatise. By someone named Dr. Eliani Hadntz. Footnotes referenced scientific papers published in the 1930s, 1920s, and earlier.

He plunged into it.

The process was disorienting. A lot of the speculation in the paper, which proposed a huge project to change humanity from warlike to peace-loving, was based on information he had always assumed was discovered later in the century. But then, he didn't know a whole lot about the history of science; not much more than any reasonably well-educated person.

The paper referenced Schrödinger. Perhaps, he speculated as he read, the author even knew Schrödinger. He realized, as he turned the pages, she definitely knew Lise Meitner, the physicist who had resolved the issue of the possibility of nuclear fission.

And yet, the ideas the author had were more . . .

188 | KATHLEEN ANN GOONAN

organic than Brian thought of physics as being, even though he was familiar with Schrödinger's thin volume *What Is Life?*, which was in the Halcyon library.

Schrödinger had been a physicist. Physics, for Brian, was abstract, a model of forces and their interaction on one another, not alive, as biological processes were. However, it made sense that one's bodily interior, one's brain, one's genes, were also subject to the laws of physics.

How had Hadntz found so much information about neurology? He looked back to the title page. Yes, this *Doktor Doktor* Hadntz was a medical doctor, and also had a doctorate in physics. That might explain her focus, and her linking of such disparate subjects.

He became lost in the strange, inspiring manuscript, which was interrupted, from time to time, with diagrams and equations.

The night waxed. Existence narrowed to this tiny opening into another universe of thought and perception. Yet, when he stepped through the passageway of the paper, the view widened in a dizzying fashion, encompassing time and space and consciousness, entwining them in a way he'd never thought possible. Exhilaration burned in him, paired with a mysterious, nagging undertone of fear.

He came to a set of folded mechanical drawings. He unfolded them, one by one, carefully, on the floor. As he handled them, pieces of paper flaked away. Several had been folded and unfolded so many times that he had to piece together sections that had separated. He opened one of four small canisters and shook out a roll of microfilm, a hallmark of the spy thrillers he'd loved when he was a kid. A thrill ran through him. This was his father's. Or maybe . . . his mother's? That was Megan's theory.

Of Jill's theories, if she had any, he knew absolutely nothing. She had remarkable powers of withdrawal and stonewalling.

He examined the drawings, which were numbered. They were views of a "Device," powered by a top-secret invention, the cavity magnetron. He had to smile. A cavity magnetron powered his microwave. It was interesting that yesterday's top-secret war-winning development, which made possible shortwave radar, was now used in such a ubiquitous and mundane fashion.

Later papers were more speculative. A theory of postulated neural plasticity, accompanied by equations. He worked through a theory of the kinds of forces, and pharmacological interactions—separate, as if they were two different avenues to the same end—that might create a situation of relatively extreme neuroplasticity.

The documents explicated ideas about the nature of time heavily linked to theories of quantum reality and to a theory of consciousness.

The night wore on. His eyes burned. He wished for a quaff of this postulated neuroplasticity so that he could continue. He rummaged through high-up bottles in a cabinet over the top of the refrigerator and poured himself some quite marvelous Scotch. Neuroplasticity, straight up.

At about five in the morning, it struck him: He was looking at the plans for the . . . Infinite Game Board. He remembered it now; it hove into memory like those vaunted memories of childhood abuse he'd heard about: something buried, inaccessible until it sprang into mind with all its ferocious original energy.

The Infinite Game Board was metal, or metal-seeming, cool and hard, with upturned edges, like a cafeteria tray. Beneath it was a platform about two inches high, which held small drawers, like storage drawers beneath a bed, and short metal legs unfolded from each side so an invalid could use it in bed. The drawers held gamelike tools: dice, round, colored chips, decks of cards with faces that varied from numbers to shapes to colors to questions. He and his sisters called it "Infinite" because

it seemed that the number of games one could play were never-ending.

Whenever they got it out, it manifested a different game—unless they called for an old favorite, or a particularly compelling game. Avid game players, they eagerly began each game the board suggested, never wondering at its odd capabilities. It was the golden age of board games, and this game was many in one, not advertised on TV because it was another mysterious thing from the attic, so old that no one else knew about it anymore. It might show them a race, a game of chance, a game of getting the most chips, or a game of strategy. The rules seemed evident from the face of the board, or the pieces they found in the drawers, but if they fell to arguing about the rules, a pleasant teacher's voice emanated from the board, or a printed rulebook might be found in one of the drawers. It was a child's delight. They didn't question it and naturally they didn't reveal it to their parents, perhaps sensing that it might be dangerous and would be taken away. As they grew older, the games grew more serious, and less fun. The board had a mind of its own. The Nuclear Winter game scared the pants off them, for instance, because it was imminent. Brian began to fear playing with it.

Now, he marked that as a true tipping point, the first time he became aware that the game corresponded to realities in the grown-ups' newspapers or the magazines his parents read.

And yet, he had forgotten all that, as if it had been a dream. The possibility of a nuclear winter was, after all, extremely remote. In 1964, Khrushchev and Kennedy had disarmed their entire nuclear arsenals, and all information about the development of nuclear arms had been sealed. Off the table, completely. Too terrible to contemplate.

What if, these papers asked, the idea of any war became obsolete? How? Through neuroplasticity combined with education, cultural and historical literacy,

even shots of live horror from victims of war, making the consequences direct, impressing upon people the necessity for change.

"Game Board," was just one whimsical form that the . . . Device . . . took, according to this paper. Its essence could be embedded in any physical form. It predicted and passed the development of weak and strong nanotech.

But what did it *do*?

He recalled that was what Jill had told him, so long ago, when she'd hidden it, pretending that it had gotten lost. *"Stories come from it."*

And yes, it did seem to link with consciousness, and could instill ideas or feelings, just like books could, except it had the power to bypass literacy and go deeply into the mind, and somehow even control action or engender thought or reflection, the way a timely interjection from an adult might optimally work.

He often wished he had his father's effectiveness in picking these moments. On the shore of Lake Huron, when he was five, he and his father had taken an evening stroll. Seeing an intricate sand castle on the shining wet shore, he rushed to demolish it. After his first kick, his father quietly said, "How did you feel yesterday when somebody did that to your racetrack?" He stopped mid-kick, torn between his joy in destruction and the memory of his own feelings just a day earlier—his racetracks and pit stops and painstakingly constructed driftwood seats and stacked stone spectators so disappointingly smashed.

Someone just like him had built this. Someone just like him would feel angry and sad.

He still badly wanted to destroy the castle. Yet he felt ashamed, and did not. He still recalled that strong, direct conflict of emotions: *Should I do the wrong thing, hurt someone else, and have fun, or do the right thing, and be disappointed?*

It was good to have experienced that. It changed his behavior immediately, and the lesson had lasted the rest of his life. But not every child was as fortunate as he had been. If more children could experience the gist of that, at just the right teaching moment; if they could put themselves in the place of others, and imagine their feelings . . .

How could one give the essence of this realization, the neurobiological event, translated to neural connections both specific and open, to parents and children everywhere, as practical a bit of information as "This is the wheel," or "This letter represents this thought, or this sound." Could it be like a new form of reading, or might it prove to be something more invasive, harder to shake, something that could be used by many people for many purposes?

They came across the strange stuff in the attic less than a year after moving into Halcyon House. It was in an empty space in the attic floor, beneath a board, with a trunk over the top of it. It took all three of them, pushing hard, to move the trunk. They had only moved the trunk to reconfigure an imaginary space, a pirate ship or a castle tower, and then the board was loose, so naturally they pulled it up. Inside was the squishy substance, colorful and seductive, with the firmness of Silly Putty, malleable and fun.

Megan had carelessly pitched a squeezed pinch of it into the attic jumble.

And then he had found a bit of that same stuff, and put it in his pocket. Just today.

He stood, turned his pockets inside out, then remembered emptying them in the truck to search for some change for a parking meter. Great chance of finding it there, with all that trash—unless this bit, small as a kernel of corn, was it . . .

At that, he flipped into his other life, the one he'd tried to hide from for so long, almost as if being in the old

house, being in the attic, just the act of handling these papers, had activated something that had become blessedly dormant, the edges of which he had vanquished by drinking. The life in which he enlisted in the Navy, learned to fly fighter jets, trained in Libya at Tripoli Air Force Base, screaming out over the desert. The one in which he'd dropped napalm over Cambodia.

The one in which his own plane had erupted in flames.

Cindy was shaking him. "Brian! Wake up!"

"You were screaming," she told him as she led him to bed. "Might it have something to do with that Scotch you were drinking?"

"Don't let the kids touch those papers."

When he woke up around noon, she'd folded the plans and put everything back in the box. "Did you read that paper?" she asked him. "Dr. Hadntz writes a lot about Montessori education."

"I didn't get that far."

"I skipped over the physics parts, I confess." She poured what Brian figured was her fourth or fifth cup of coffee of the day; she was a caffeine hound. She handed Brian a cup, along with a little glass bowl of pills, his vitamins. Megan, Cindy, and Jill were huge believers in the power of vitamins, and bought them mail-order from the same company. They always came with samples of protein powders or supplements the company was pushing.

"Take them. You'll need extra today."

"I'm fine, Cindy."

"*Take* them."

He did. "What's this new white one?"

Cindy looked at it. "Came in the new box yesterday. The latest super-duper freebie, you know, like they throw in sometimes. H-something, probably stands for health, some new synergizing additive. Oh, I remember. This is good for your memory."

"Right." Brian choked them all down, as he did every

morning; Cindy seemed to think they "balanced" him and lessened his need for alcohol. He didn't believe that, but he did think they helped him feel better in general. "Bleah." He made himself a peanut butter and jelly sandwich and grabbed his coffee cup.

They stepped out onto the cramped balcony, at treetop height, with a view of the neighborhood playground, where the kids were. Zoe pushed Bitsy on a swing, playing Nice Big Sister, at least for the moment. They settled into the aluminum lawn chairs that took up most of the balcony. "So what do you think?" Cindy asked.

"Jill is hiding something. We knew that, I guess, but I just didn't realize how weird it all was, or how important it might be. It's probably why she cracked up. All the more reason, I guess, for us to tread carefully. I think she knows what Mom and Dad did during the war, and what they did after the war. In fact, I believe they were custodians of the Device that the paper talks about."

Cindy looked startled. "This thing was actually made?"

"After last night, I'm sure of it. It explains . . . everything. Mom's disappearance, for instance. I have a feeling that Mom and Hadntz knew each other. Megan's been saying that Mom was CIA for years. Before last night, I thought Megan was being kind of grandiose."

"What does Jill think?"

"Jill won't say what Jill thinks. It's her trademark. She was extremely nervous about me taking these papers. She knows a lot more than she's saying. She might even know where Mom and Dad went."

"You need to press her on it."

"I'm going to. But I want to have everything in order first."

"Brian. I mean, before next year."

"I don't want to give her any way to slither out of telling us everything she knows. If I ask her anything now, she'll just clam up. Guaranteed. What can I do—threaten to break her kneecaps? I don't understand all of this yet. And I don't understand what it has to do with us, not

really. I'm just starting to get a distant theory. I need to be like a lawyer. Present the hard evidence. Anticipate her evasions. And with all the work we have piled up, that might take a while."

Cindy sighed. "You Dances are all alike. 'Oh, let's not talk about anything important. Maybe next year. After all, we have a lot of urgent work to do and that takes up all of our time.' Have you ever heard the word 'introspection'? How about 'family dynamics'? No wonder you're all so messed up—" She looked away.

"Great place to stop talking, Cindy. I admire your tact, your extraordinary reserve."

"I'm sorry. You're doing fine, now, honey, and I know it's hard. Anyway, there are a lot of strange connections in the paper. Physics and Montessori in the same sentence?"

"I didn't notice."

"That's the reason I read it. Or tried to. It's up front, in the intro. She postulates that physics combined with Montessori education could change the human brain. She indicates that she actually *met* the Montessori. When? How? Anyway, her ideas are full of optimism and the hope of peace. Peace was Montessori's dream too—peace through education. It's a zeitgeist thing, I guess. I'd sure like to get my hands on this gizmo. Make all that optimism *real*. See where it leads."

"You and a lot of other people, probably."

"Fat chance. No one ever made this. Otherwise, we'd know, don't you think?"

Brian stared out at the ineffable there-ness of everything around him. He felt the smooth porcelain of the coffee cup between his hands, the hard web of the lawn chair beneath him, heard the susurration of leaves in the breeze.

Cindy said, "You think it *was* built."

"Yes. The Device was built. By my dad and the guy he talks about in his journal—'W.' For Wink. Winklemeyer. I never met him. And—"

Cindy looked at him sidelong, eyebrows raised. "There's more?"

Brian shifted in his chair; listened to the shouts of his children as they played. He took a sip of cold coffee.

"It was built in a different world."

Cindy smiled, rolled her eyes, and patted Brian on the shoulder.

Jill

REINHABITING THE PAST

[*May 22*]

JILL GOT off the Metro at the Georgetown Park stop. An escalator lifted her toward a light-filled arch, and she stepped out onto Wisconsin Avenue. Whens was with his father and the Lavender Lady. Grumpy, but he had his phone and could complain to her if he felt like it, which seemed to help a lot.

To her left was a sign for the Metro. She had a moment's flash: In the world she now called the original timestream, there had not been a Metro stop in Georgetown. It certainly came in handy. Before, she would have had to wait for a mile-long bus ride from the Foggy Bottom/GWU stop.

To her right was the C & O Canal, an overhead freeway, the Potomac River, and across the river, Virginia.

It was twilight. Cars nosed down the steep hill toward the river and streamed into the mall's underground parking garage. When the light changed, Jill headed uphill half a block to M Street, and turned left.

This block had once been a druggie hangout, heavy with the scent of marijuana smoke, where psychedelic music blared from narrow black-light illuminated clubs. The windows of upstairs apartments were always open in the summer heat, wafting exotic incenses into the street.

Jill had often visited friends in those ragtag apartments full of furniture from Goodwill, huge houseplants, twining cats, and out-of-town crashers. The Cellar Door, on the next block, hosted many a fine performer. Jill missed all that with a feeling that verged on the visceral.

In this world, the psychedelic scene had been much more muted. Without a war to protest against, the former Air Force parachutist Jimi Hendrix, who had been a Screaming Eagle, had not composed his chilling "Star Spangled Banner" interrupted by machine gun fire and the explosions of death missiles. He was, however, alive, and a respected jazz musician.

No, in this world, this particular block of M Street rapidly went upscale after 1970. These mannered town houses, beautifully restored, were sealed against street sounds and smells. Open drapes revealed opulent rooms Jill had visited on Elmore's arm—the homes of tenured professors, lawyers, and lobbyists with spouses in high government positions. The women, and probably some of the men, spent hundreds of dollars—or even thousands, monthly—on upkeep for their bodies, faces, and hair.

Her bookstore was at the end of the block, opposite the end of Key Bridge. Everyone crossing the bridge into Georgetown saw it. She stocked fine literature, the latest political science books, philosophy, poetry.

And science fiction. She longed for a comic section to exude the wonderful smell she recalled from childhood, but Elmore had pitched a fit about that.

She was instantly soothed as she walked through the door, which stood open. The golden oak floor shone softly. Classical music, which she would switch to some quiet Coltrane or the Strayhorn piano solos she'd just gotten her hands on. She counted seven browsers downstairs and three in the loft. Zane, one of the college kids who worked for them, was ringing up a sale. When he saw her, his mouth opened in pleased astonishment.

She smiled at him, said, "Be back in a minute," and went to the office. She locked her backpack in a desk drawer, sorted through the mail while standing at the desk, and poured herself some coffee. Evidently Elmore had taken care of everything in his efficient way. Left to her, it would all be in a tangle. And, she supposed, with a wry sigh, it soon would be.

On her way to the counter, she asked a young woman if she could help her and showed her the biography section.

"How's everything?" she asked Zane.

"Just fine. School's out; sales are so-so. How are you?"

She gave him a quick hug. "Oh, I'm fine."

"Good. We were worried about you."

She wondered what they'd been told, but just said, "Did Elmore pay you?"

"Of course. Right on the dot."

"Good. Okay."

After Zane left, Jill settled onto her stool and surveyed her store. Everything looked exceedingly clean and clear, the books with their bright covers square and neat on the shelves. An hour earlier the usual evening thunderstorm had ended, and cool, still-damp air eddied through the front door. She realized that she hadn't been here since the day before she'd . . . gone nuts.

Well, that was a good thing to not think about. God just had to give her grace to know what she couldn't change.

The main problem was that it might be that she could change just about anything.

But, no. That couldn't be possible. The therapist was right. She was a roiling inferno of insanity.

She could change some things. For instance . . . she slid off the stool and walked across the store to a shelf she'd focused on. There was a book in the history section that needed to be moved to the poli-sci section. There. It was all right to change little things. But how to know what was little and what was world-changingly big?

She smelled cigarette smoke. Someone tapped her on the shoulder and she jumped.

"Sorry," said Koslov. "I didn't mean to startle you."

She saw that he wasn't smoking, but, as usual, his tie had flecks of ash on it. He was too close to her. She stepped back. "That's okay."

"We've all been concerned about you. You left the minute the committee congratulated you as a new doctor."

She certainly had. That day, so soon after getting out of St. E's, she was in no shape for anything beyond the scope of her presentation, and especially did not want to tangle with Koslov.

"I'm glad to see that you're back at work. The store has been . . . haphazard, without you." He usually came by once or twice a month, as did many professors. "So, everything is all right now?"

"Yes, I'm fine. Fine."

"You left very quickly that other day too, after your last class. I'm afraid that I upset you."

"Oh, no, not a bit. I was just doing too much. Not eating right. That kind of thing."

"That's a relief to hear. We were talking about your alternate history, if you recall."

"Like I said, I was pretty tired."

"Sorry you missed graduation."

"Oh, those ceremonies are so boring." She bent down and straightened some books.

"Indeed." He reached into a shirt pocket and pulled out a piece of paper, which he handed to her.

She brightened, despite her interest in sweeping Dr. Nosy out of the store. "A list. Good." All the professors had their lists, and she often stocked their suggestions. Koslov's lists were always of foreign, translated books, many of which she had never heard of. They generally turned out to be interesting.

"Your husband refused to order these."

"He was afraid they wouldn't sell."

"I explained to him that I suggest them to my students, and that they aren't carried by the university bookstore."

She smoothed the list on the countertop. "Yes, I've seen some reviews of this . . . Oh, good, I'd like to read this one myself. We should have them in ten days or so. The Fleiger will take longer."

Koslov pointed at one title. "This is a book of poetry. I translated it. The translation has won an award, by the way."

"Congratulations. The original was Russian?"

"Yes. The author's name is Rosa Hadntz. Have you ever heard of her?"

He was watching her face very closely. She was puzzled. "No. Ought I have?"

"Oh, no. She died long ago, in a German concentration camp, and her poems were only found lately, in Stalingrad. She had been sending them to her relatives there."

Jill sighed. "That's a sad story. I will certainly order a copy."

"Maybe two?" he suggested.

She smiled. "By the way, I'm having a party at my home for the Fourth of July. I sent the invitations yesterday, so you and a few other people in the department will be getting them soon."

He tilted his big, shaggy head. "I hear you've moved. You're getting a divorce?"

Nosy old fart. Well, they probably all knew. "Yes. It's the house I grew up in."

"Very good," he said, and nodded thoughtfully.

Five or six people walked in. The after-dinner rush was starting.

"I'm getting busy," she said.

"Let me just pay for this, then." He did so, and walked out onto M Street. Good riddance. She'd only invited him to the party because she'd asked everyone else in the department, practically. He made her nervous, and he'd

never done so before. Before, it had been invigorating to spar with him. Something had changed, but she wasn't sure what. Her, probably.

She turned her attention back to her domain.

It was good to be back in the store. Orienting. Like breathing. Nothing new, and that was comforting. Elmore was right; he hadn't ordered a damn thing, and not a single sales lunch was on the calendar. He complained that she was too old-fashioned and that she ought to do everything by computer. He was probably right.

She started yet another list, and tried to keep an eye on the man wearing an old, shapeless fedora, pulled low, and a long raincoat, browsing in the mystery section. Students, and street people, had a way of walking out with those little paperbacks. But she was soon too busy to pay close attention, and when the rush was over, and she got back to her stool behind the counter and her cold cup of coffee, he was gone.

When she locked up, though, she felt marvelously successful. A whole evening back at the store.

She was Jill again.

Wilhelm Anderson

THE WEREWOLVES

[*May 22*]

WILHELM—BILL—Anderson sat in the Bank cafeteria sipping coffee and eating meatloaf and boiled potatoes, alone, while around him congenial chatter filled the air. Most colleagues expressed incredulity at his affection for this meal (with boiled green beans on the side) but it reminded him of home. He ate it whenever it was offered, and kept away from their teasing. After all, they didn't know the meal meant something important to him.

His mother would cook such a dinner on cold Ohio evenings, as snow lay heavy on the flat streets of the small town and on the flat land surrounding it, and the 5:00 P.M. gloom outside the kitchen held a just-lit streetlight. By the time they lived in Ohio, his mother's blond hair no longer fell in graceful, 1940s-style waves around her face, but was pulled back in a severe, colorless bun, and her steps, as she endlessly cleaned their plain frame house and dark furniture, were much heavier than those of the lithe Alpine hiker he had doggedly followed on Sunday afternoon family outings when he was small, and visiting her parents in Bavaria. He was sometimes embarrassed by the black, plain shoes she wore, by her German accent (his father, also from Germany, had none, which did not seem odd until Wilhelm got a little older) and by the way she did not fit in with the other mothers—even though, she often said, their neighbor's own parents were from Germany and they had German names, so why could they not treat her with more respect? Still, Wilhelm, who was now, always and only, Bill, understood that his father had preferred that she keep to herself. She attended Mass several times a week, and seemed to return refreshed.

Wilhelm was completely forbidden to ever mention that his older brother had died bravely in the Battle of Berlin. And he had not even told his parents that he, Wilhelm, had taken over firing Hans's machine gun, propped behind sandbags, after his brother died.

It would have been impossible to speak of.

Hans's death was his fault.

On that day in 1945, Wilhelm had slipped from the apartment cellar where he, his mother, and countless neighbors were hiding as Russian missiles shook plaster and debris onto their heads.

When he emerged from the celler, he stared at the empty crater where the corner butcher shop had stood for his entire life. His breath steamed the cold, smoky air,

and then he bent over, coughing and wiping tears from his burning eyes.

He scrambled over a mountain of bricks to see, down the street, fleeing German soldiers raked by machine gun fire fall in their tracks. The apartment where his best friend lived exploded.

Wilhelm crouched, turned, and fled.

He never knew how long it took him to find Hans's company. It seemed a miracle to spot his brother, from an alley, in the ever-shifting nightmare of broken streets where the dead lay still and injured soldiers cried out. He ran toward Hans, yelling.

Hans turned, shook his head at him, and opened his mouth. That clear, timeless image was Wilhelm's permanent nightmare. His brother's head exploded, showering Wilhelm with blood and driving him sideways into the hard sandbags.

His next memory was of his body shaking as he crouched where Hans had been, hugging the machine gun as he had been taught in his brief lesson. Wilhelm fired at men on horses on the cross-street ahead, tanks, and Russians dashing from building to building as they advanced. *Burst! Burst! Burst!* When the soldiers neared him he escaped through roofless buildings, the disintegrating world curiously soundless save for a ringing in his ears, lit by fireworks overhead and blazing buildings before and behind him. After running for a long time, he realized that he held Hans's heavy knife in his hand and thrust it into his pocket. Thinking to hide in a church, he paused at the doorway after seeing pews full of injured men, but a skinny fräulein, her face streaked with blood and greasy hair straggling from the scarf tied around her head, grabbed him and put him to work changing bandages. At three in the morning, as missiles streaked the sky, he flattened himself into crevices as Soviet tanks passed and made his way back to his mother's apartment with half a loaf of bread and some cheese. She wept at

the news of Hans's death, and instead of praising him like a good German mother, screamed as his hearing returned.

He had another memory, of his mother being raped by Russian soldiers the next day as he hid beneath the bed, as she had told him to. As he lay still beneath the creaking bed, he almost grabbed the butt of the American gun that one Russian soldier had dropped to the floor with his pants, so that he could kill the soldier. He was still ashamed, so very ashamed, that he had not. Afterward, his mother asked him to never tell his father what had happened, though she did not explain exactly what that was.

And so, there were many things he had grown up not talking about.

He watched Jill Dance across the room, also sitting alone, her back to him, reading as she ate a salad. There were a lot of similarities between them, connections, so many that he sometimes yearned to tell her everything. He knew she would understand. Their parents, for instance—his father, and her mother—had both been spies. And they were both dead. He was not sure if she was like him in other ways. Did she remember a past in which Berlin had been taken by the Russians, rather than the Allies? But that was just one of the many things he longed to discuss with her.

As a child, Wilhelm was only allowed to play alone, in his yard, but once a week the family would drive to another town where a family with a farm held a German club meeting, and while the adults talked in the living room, in their native tongue, their collective children roamed outside. They swung from the barn's hayloft on a heavy, knotted rope, rode around cornfields on an old knack, or swam in the creek. In the winter, after they tired of playing in the snow, they were sent to the basement, where they could watch *Sky King* and *Fury* and *Rin Tin Tin*. There was one boy he really liked, because he could play chess. Christmases were wonderful, with

the enchanting scents of butter cookies, pork roasts, and stollen filling the house. Sinister Krampus—really (he knew by that time) a man dressed up like a demon—came and handed out sticks and coal to bad children; they chased him, screaming in glee, from the doorway into the cold, snowy night. Krampus was always followed by Weihnachtsman—they were supposed to call him Santa Claus—who brought games like Mr. Potato Head and metal cars and, one fine year, a train set.

Having no friends was hard, but he knew he was different. So did the other boys in school, but they had no idea how different he really was. His father always called him Bill, and mildly remonstrated his mother for continuing to call him Wilhelm, but Wilhelm was already fixed in his mind as his true name, anyway.

His father was often gone on long trips, and during those trips Wilhelm slipped into his father's study. This was strictly forbidden, so it was always when his mother had taken the bus to the butcher shop or the market. The room was full of locked file cabinets, and despite intense and creative searches, he never could find the keys to the cabinets. Sometimes he just sat in his father's big wooden tilting chair and swirled around, or paged through books that were too hard for him to read, or just stared out the window into his lonely backyard with its single elm. There was an odd, melted artifact his father kept on his desk as a paperweight. He'd always thought of it as a war scrap, something picked up in the street after a bombing raid.

Its weirdness had always fascinated Wilhelm, and by this particular day, November 22, 1963, he had grown into a singularly handsome blond young man, much sought after by girls, though his mother refused to let him date. He sat in the office wondering what to do.

He was home "sick," his usual stomachache. If his father had been home, he never would have been allowed to stay out of school, but his mother was much more indulgent. She had gone to Schmidt's for bratwurst, tying

on her black headscarf and shrugging on her black over-coat, telling him that if he felt up to it he ought to practice his piano. Before leaving, she said, "Do you want me to turn off the television set?" She kept it on as she ironed to help improve her English.

"It's okay," he said.

It was not as much fun in his father's office as it had been when he was younger. There were no pictures of Hans in the house, as if he had never existed, and he longed for his brother often. He had only one scrap of paper to remember him by, and this he had kept in his shoe when they got on the U.S. military plane in Berlin. It had fallen apart on the creases long ago because of his ceaseless folding and unfolding, and even the tape was old and cracking now. But he remembered it well.

Hans was only seventeen when he died. For weeks, they had prepared for the Russians after a dreary, snow-filled winter of hardship. Wilhelm and his mother waited with fear and nervousness in their once-fine Berlin apart-ment, now depleted of furniture, which had been burned for firewood, but Wilhelm practiced and drilled with other boys his age in a nearby square every day, led by an elderly farmer who had fought in the Great War, though they had few weapons. They were told to use their wits and to seize weapons. The farmer had man-aged to find weapons with which to train them from time to time—an old hunting rifle, a hand pistol, and once, to Wilhelm's pride and delight, his own big brother Hans appeared and let each of them use his machine gun. It was empty of ammunition; for that was too valu-able to waste, but Wilhelm learned how to manipulate the gun, theoretically at least.

When the cannons began to boom, low and far off, and they knew that the Russians were almost upon them, Hans was still able to stop in every few days for perhaps an hour, dropping off canned food and usually falling asleep in a chair.

The last time he came home, he handed an envelope

to Wilhelm. He said, "You may soon be the man in the family, since we do not know where Father is or whether he will survive the war. These are my thoughts, some things to remember." When he left, Wilhelm opened it immediately. It was written in his brother's beautiful hand with its flourishes and one or two scratch-outs, and was about his *Lebensfeier*, his life ceremony, which all Hitler Youth celebrated the year they turned fifteen. Some celebrated it in lieu of a religious confirmation, but not Hans—he had had to attend catechism classes his entire life. Their mother was incensed at the very thought that this war ceremony might stand in for the eternal verities, for her own son or for any German youth, so she had attended in a very bad mood.

Wilhelm, sitting between his parents, was entranced by its beauty and glory: the drum flourishes and horn fanfares, the special Hitler Youth flag, and the perfect, spotless uniforms worn by all the young men.

But far beyond that was the excitement of Hitler actually attending, which was a great honor. Wilhelm had memorized, along with Hans, who was an indulgent big brother, the oath they swore.

Wilhelm read the missive left by Hans on the evening of May 6, as the cannons grew ever louder and the great city began to crumble. Crowds filled the streets in a great westward exodus, for it was rumored that the Allies would treat them better than the Russians, their ancestral enemy. Wilhelm's mother made no move to leave. "I have lived my entire married life here, and I will not go. If your father lives, and if I live, he will find me here waiting."

Wilhelm went to the front parlor window, settled himself on the floor, and read:

Never forget this wonderful day, my dear brother. I am only sorry you have not been able to have your own *Lebensfeier*. But perhaps, in the future, no matter how dark it looks now, you or a son of yours might

experience the same joy. We must, in these times, hold fast to that thought. The Thousand-Year Reich has just begun. Hitler will never die.

Hitler! Hitler himself came down the row of Hitler Youth and shook all our hands. *He shook my hand.*

As he did so, he placed his own over mine, so that mine was held between his, like a father holding the hand of his child. His kindly eyes smiled into mine, looked deeply into me, and I vowed in my heart to *Lebensfeier*, my life job. My Führer said, in his speech that day, "We want a hard generation that is strong, reliable, loyal, obedient and decent, so that we do not need to be ashamed." This is what I have striven to be, my dear brother, during the long and hard years since.

The vows I spoke that day, and which I saw you, with pride, in the front row, reciting, were these:

We affirm:

The German people have been created by the will of God.
All those who fight for the life of our people, and those who died,
Carried out the will of God.
Their deeds are to us holy obligation. This we believe.
We affirm that God gave us all our strength,
In order to maintain the life of our people
And defend it. It is therefore our holiest
Duty to fight to our last breath
Anything that threatens or endangers the life
Of our people. God will decide
Whether we live or die. This we pledge.
We want to be free from all selfishness.
We want to be fighters for this Reich
Named Germany, our home.
We will never forget that we are German.

And I have not. Wilhelm, I give you this charge: You must continue to fight for the Fatherland.

Remember the Fatherland as I will, if I live: as free, high mountains, as a Nation, working together, as the Hitler Youth book tells us, to rid the world of poisonous blood unworthy of mingling with our pure German blood, our pure German bodies. We are an old, strong people, and our land was glorious. It will be so again. Read your Hitler Youth book daily. It is filled with wisdom.

Work hard, my dear brother, to further the Work given us by our Führer, to use that which I bequeath to you—an idea, a commitment—to move the entire world forward into the bright, glorious sunshine of the timeless ideals of our beloved Führer.

On his brother's special day, Wilhelm had recited the affirmation along with the young men on the stage in a loud, clear voice, while on one side of him his father held his shoulder and squeezed it, and, on the other side, his mother looked down at him in grim disapproval, and dashed away tears. On the first day of the Battle of Berlin, those affirmations had propelled him from the cellar, to which his mother and himself had been dragged by neighbors, into battle.

In America, he and his classmates marched down Main Street on Decoration Day, the day in May when the graves of American soldiers who had killed his kin were decorated. He daily pledged allegiance to the American flag, though at first it took a beating on the part of his father to make him do so, to convince him that this was necessary, and that he had to forget his last name had ever been Konrad, or even Wilhelm; it now was William—except, rebelliously, stubbornly, in his own mind. He had studied government, he had read their history of the war thinking *Lies, all lies, propaganda*, and made *As* on all his tests. There were Jewish children in his school—not many, but they were popular and never

shunned; in fact, most classmates looked surprised when he asked them whether they knew their friends were Jews, and some didn't even know what Jews were. There were no Negro children, and of this he was glad. Sometimes he wondered, *Is it possible that my country might have been wrong, might have done wrong?*, but in the end, that letter, that day in Berlin, the memory of his brother proud in his uniform, were all much stronger than years in an American school, mingled as they were with his brother's sacrifice.

Wilhelm stood, intending to leave the study and turn off the television chatter in the other room. He should not be sitting here in the past; it only made him sad. He heard, "We interrupt this program to announce that President Kennedy has been shot in Dallas. He is being rushed . . ."

In that instant, the odd, burnt artifact on his father's desk glowed and became briefly clear, emitting powerful rainbowed light. He stared, transfixed.

For a moment, his childhood memories became even stronger, and more brilliant, but were infused with something new and unpleasant—the ideas that his mother had often expressed, that Germany had done horrible things during the war and that they were all guilty, all damned, which his father would counter with a mention of Hiroshima. Despite her isolation, she seemed to like the ideals of America, took pains to go through all the preparation for the citizenship tests at home, although Wilhelm's father told her to never do anything so foolish as to actually go out and take the test because *Hear! Hear!* (he would point toward his closed office door) were her birth certificate, which had taken place at home in Lancaster, Pennsylvania, Wilhelm's birth certificate, in Canton, Ohio, and his own, in Pennsylvania as well, and that they were all supposed to forget about Germany entirely, as if their lives before coming here had never happened. Then he would sit stonily quiet in the dark parlor for an hour, drinking schnapps, and finally come out,

apologize, hug them both, and tell them he knew it was hard.

As the paperweight surged with light, Wilhelm saw the world as his brother had described it in that sacred letter, but instead of its populace being of pure German blood and genes, the colors of their faces ranged from pale to dark. Many voices poured from them, a Babel of languages that refuted everything his brother had stood for. All were equal in rights and in education. The human brain grew and changed, shed its ancestral darkness, became a species not of male brother-warriors and aggressors, but a species of women and men who instead used other means to solve conflicts. Ideas flowed through him in waves, as if to wash from him the blood-memories, the ancient feuds, the ideas of racial superiority and inferiority, even the wars fought in the name of his mother's religion, the religion of others . . .

The light dimmed. Shaken, Wilhelm continued to watch it, breathing hard, clenching his hands in tight fists.

Nothing more happened. Finally, he ventured to touch the thing. Its coolness surprised him.

He had taken chemistry courses in high school and since then had wondered how it had been formed, what it was made of. Perhaps it was a meteor? He thought several times about breaking off a piece and trying to melt it in a crucible and see if it gave off an identifying gas, or color, but he did not even dare think about tampering with anything belonging to his father.

Now, he wondered whether or not there might be other reasons not to play with it.

Wilhelm left the office. He closed the door behind him and went into the living room, with its drawn drapes, the ironing board set up in front of the television set, and the heavy dark furniture. It was lit by a single lamp, the base of which was a lovely young blond woman in a meadow of porcelain flowers, sitting beneath crystals that dangled from the silk shade, spangling her face with light.

He turned up the television set. What had he heard? The President had been shot?

But no. The usual soap opera was playing. He watched a commercial for Ipana toothpaste. He turned to the other two channels, adjusted the rabbit ears. Nothing, nothing, about an assassination attempt. Had he been dreaming? Had the glow in the artifact anything to do with what he had heard?

Two days later, he returned from school to find his mother in her immaculate kitchen, leaning on both arms against the table, her head bowed. When she raised it, her face was streaked with tears. "Your father is dead," she said.

He was stunned. "Why? What happened?"

"Two men came today, from his company. He— caught pneumonia and died of it." She pulled out a chair and sat down heavily, folding her hands on the table.

He put his hand on her back. He was the man now. He had to be strong. He shouldn't cry. "Where did this happen? Why didn't he call and tell us he was sick?"

"He probably—he didn't think he was so sick. He just collapsed at a meeting."

His father's funeral was held in the little German farming town they had gone to so often when Wilhelm was a child. His father's casket was closed. Wilhelm beat against it with his fists. "I want to see him!" Two strong men, friends of his family, took him from the church. A few other men came out with him, tried to comfort him. One offered him a cigarette, which he accepted. He was dull and dazed at the funeral, with its incense and Latin, and watched the casket lowered into the ground with a sense of unreality. Something was not right.

A few weeks later, there occurred an afternoon when he felt as though his mother was going to tell him important things. He had felt some tension for several days after the man in a black suit came and talked to her behind the closed, curtained French doors to the living room. When she invited him into the little-used parlor,

always darkened, the furniture always covered with sheets, and they both sat in the dim light on facing chairs, he had hoped. Her lips had been tight when she had begun talking, on that long-ago afternoon, as the other neighborhood children played outside. "Wilhelm, I feel as if I must tell you . . ." But then, suddenly, she stopped talking, got up, and left the room.

Their years in the American town were probably more lonely than they ought to have been, and as he was going away to Ohio State—the United States government paid for his college, which he took for granted then but soon realized was unusual—and his mother lay in the hospital dying of cancer, in what he later realized was a rare private room, also paid for by the U.S. government, she finally talked.

His father, she said ("And I know I can trust you to tell no one, ever, but you deserve to know; I am so very tired of lying") was a spy during the war. He worked for Germany, but also for the Americans. He had been a brave man to do so. She, herself, had not known this until she questioned him severely about why they were able to move to America when everyone else in Germany—her mother, her sisters, her one surviving brother, and his old father—had to stay behind and starve. He said that in exchange for scientific secrets from Germany as well as from Russia, he had bought them all a better life—college for Wilhelm, a lifetime pension for her should he die. He had warned her his being killed was not unlikely, because of his past. Many people were after him—in particular, former Nazis who were angered at his defection. The United States government could only protect him so much. He had things to do, dangerous missions to carry out.

Furthermore, Wilhelm's mother said, his father had told her that he realized American ideals were much better than those of the Nazis. Wilhelm's mother fixed him with a strong, steady gaze. "Remember that that is what your father thought. I am sorry he never told you,

because you probably will never believe me. He was never a Nazi himself, not in his heart or mind. It made him sick to pretend, sick to seem to support his oldest son in joining the Nazi Youth. You cannot imagine those times, Wilhelm, how hard and dangerous they were. Your brother's death broke him. I see how you worship the past, how you hoard those swastika magazines under your bed, when you should instead, if anything, God forbid, be hiding pictures of women! It is our fault, your father's and mine, for not talking frankly to you, but you were so young. We hoped you would forget, and we didn't want to burden you with more than you could understand, with more responsibility than you could handle. And we were afraid . . . you might let something slip."

She fixed her eyes on him, still the young blue of cornflowers, still the eyes that could see right into him, see what he was thinking. "Your brother died for the wrong reasons. It is a tragedy. But we were all caught up in . . . all kinds of wrong ideas, wrong actions, and by the time some of us wanted to stop, there was too much momentum. Hitler made it all sound so glorious, and once he had power, he murdered all who opposed him."

Wilhelm started to protest, and she held up a hand. "I am tired. Do not argue. Your father left you a locked metal box containing something so secret that I was never to open it. It was to be yours after you finished university."

After his father died, she continued, her voice hoarse from medicines and faint from weakness, she opened it anyway. If they were no longer German, why did she have to be an obedient German wife? And that went for Wilhelm too. His wonderful brother had died for no reason, had been made to fight when just a boy, and since she had come here she had taught herself to read English, and she watched American shows, and she learned of how the Jews had been slaughtered in the camps, and none of it was what she believed Germany was, and

certainly not one that anyone with an ounce of religion in them should have stood for. She even revealed, as she lay there, withered, her hair white, with two pink spots from anger on her cheeks, that her sister had hidden a Jew in the attic, and no one ever found out, and now she was ashamed that she had not had the courage to do the same.

Wilhelm became angry at his mother then, and said that she was lying, that their father would have been ashamed of her, and that his brother had died for the Führer, and that he had promised to live for the Fatherland and knew of others who wanted to bring it back.

She threw her glass of water at him and said, "Get out!"

He had. He never saw her alive again. Now he regretted that, since he had so much to ask her, but she died a few days later. He didn't even know, for instance, if she knew that she now lived in a world that believed that the past, beginning in April 1945, was different, and that the change had occurred the day his father supposedly had died. But he never could have asked her directly if she had been raped by an American soldier rather than a Russian.

He had opened the box as soon as she died, and found strange papers he did not understand, but he had known they were related to the melted-looking electronic object, because a photograph of it was paper-clipped to the notes. He still kept the object with him in his Washington condominium as one of his most cherished treasures. He thought that this was why he could see two pasts, and he was pretty sure that Jill Dance could too, because her mother's name before she was married—Bette Elegante—was in a list he found in the box, along with many other names. He had tracked down some of those people. They were spies, every last one of them, he was sure. Not one of them revealed anything to him.

He knew now that the notes were about a Device that could change time, if only because, for a moment, he had

seen another epoch taking place, one in which, after
Kennedy's death, the Russians and Americans might
have annihilated each other and Germany would have
been able to rise again. And yet, he remembered the
other Germany, divided, as if it were a piece of fabric to
be torn in half by housewives arguing at the market.
Here, it had never been divided. No one but himself
seemed to know that. Even the books had changed, overnight, it seemed. Everything had changed but him, and
he was certain it was because of that glowing thing.

There was something else too, in those notes—
nonsense about it being able to change the human mind,
to end war, but he discarded that. His own short war in
Berlin had been glorious, a mad chaos of resistance, a
brave last stand, and he had avenged his brother's death.
That felt good, not bad. It was the one good thing he had
ever done.

Over the years, under the tutelage of a friend, he mi-
grated to D.C., joined the Foreign Service, and found
that any information about his father was sealed for all
time. He learned a little science, wondered more and
more about the strange sounds and the light in the piece
of junk, the coincidence of his father dying the same day
he heard the television say—he was still sure of it—that
President Kennedy had been shot. He also stubbornly
changed his first name, legally, back to Wilhelm. Why
should he be ashamed of it? He didn't go so far, though,
as to change Anderson back to Konrad.

At various times in his twenties, he had belonged to
several clandestine organizations. One was a simple,
straightforward, Hitler-worship club. Wilhelm had seen
the man; his brother had touched him, so Wilhelm was
a minor star. What magnificent power Hitler had, and
that same deep, sacrificial love for Germany. He kept a
small replica of the 1940 German flag on his desk, next
to his Q station, hanging from a cheap plastic stand, and
he had a real *Arbeiterjugend* pennant, which the Hitler
Youth had used in the 1930s, given him as a gift, framed.

He never allowed anyone in his study, and always kept it locked.

He had also, long ago, belonged to groups that believed that a Nazi future was still possible. He had resigned from those groups years ago and had completely expunged his name and records from any of their accounts—not because he no longer believed in National Socialism, or in white supremacy. He did so because, otherwise, he could not have the job he had now. His present job was an avenue to power.

He watched the back of Jill's neck as she read—long, with tendrils of her carelessly swept-up hair curling down against the tan skin he sometimes wished to caress.

He was not that much older than she was—twelve years. They had so much in common. He had contrived to take courses with her, attended the same workshops, yet she seemed to hardly notice him. Which was proper; she was married. But beyond that was a strange reserve he imagined was feigned. She must feel the same as him, that they were fated to be together, eventually. Now, she was getting a divorce—more evidence that his dream of marrying her was true. She knew more than she said. She had some connection with that light-thing.

And he knew more about it than she could possibly imagine. He wanted to share that knowledge with her. Together, they could change the world. Her strange liberal ideas had to be a cover. She had to be more intelligent than that.

The fuller plans for it, possibly, were in the house she lived in now. Together, they could pool what they knew, bring about a new future.

No, it was not coincidence that he worked with her. It was fate. He probably would not have made that connection unless fate had led him here, to the Bank, to this very section of the Bank.

It was true that her ideas were tragically skewed. He could see that. Yet, he knew that he could fix her. Repair

what had gone wrong. She was working on plans that directly opposed everything he believed. Those wonder-schools that supposedly would teach everyone to read. Nonsense, desecration. Some people—some races, and this was a scientific fact—were dumb as dirt. The Chinese, African, Japanese, Jewish, and Indian people he met at the Bank were anomalies.

He couldn't blame everyone else for agreeing with her—they had been indoctrinated since birth to believe that all races were equal, that everyone deserved equal rights. He even caught himself thinking this, sometimes, because he had undergone the same indoctrination—but, happily, too late. He knew how he was supposed to think, and he had to seem to think these things right down to his core. He couldn't let himself get so stirred up like this. It was just that Jill was so—so innocent, so goody-goody, so seemingly unaware that one day you could get up in the morning in an intact, ancient capital city and by night your city could be a pile of rubble filled with bloody, stinking corpses, one of them your brother. He had a "friend" who was Russian, part of another plan he was working on. He knew how useful people could be, how to cultivate them. He'd managed to stay out of the clutches of mental health people; he knew how to lie on an application, on the batteries of person-ality tests he'd undergone. He had a mission given to him when he was five, by Hitler himself, and by his brother, the day before he died.

Women were drawn to him. He was quite good-looking, and debonair. At first, this made him happy, but inevitably, relationships deepened. One fiancée had rec-ommended therapy, evaluation, drugs, and the next one did too, after a year, and in much stronger terms, won-dering aloud if he might be schizophrenic, or worse. It was better, he had decided, and easier, to live alone than to have a relationship with someone to whom he might reveal his most intimate thoughts, and who might then turn on him, even before they knew the whole truth,

only distant fragments. He dated sporadically, picked up women in bars, satisfied his needs without ever getting involved.

Which made Jill's aloof behavior somewhat puzzling, almost insulting. He kept in shape; his hair was still a nice shade of blond, though paling a bit—maybe he should think about some color. He had a doctorate. He was a smart man. He made good money. He had a nice condo, played the piano quite well, had a subscription to the Kennedy Center, and went to all the operas.

Jill finished eating. She dropped her book into the heavy bag she always carted around, hoisted the bag to her shoulder, and picked up her tray. He stood, leaving his own tray on the table, and hurried around a dozen tables to intercept her. "Let me help you with that."

She held on to the tray with both hands—rather tightly, so there was a short battle before he let go—and laughed. "Bill, thank you, but I'm completely capable of disposing of my own trash." She did so.

He stayed close, hoping to ride the elevator up with her, but she said, "See you later," and ducked into a bathroom.

Jill

THE NEW SCHOOLS

[*May 29*]

JILL ENTERED the conference room on her floor. She pulled out a chair at the end of the long, gleaming hardwood table and linked her Q presentation to the projector.

Soon the participants began to show up.

Clarissa, skeleton thin, wore her trademark arm bangles, dangling earrings, and a tight, plain black business dress and jacket. She nodded to Jill and took a seat next to the Nepalese woman they had brought to Washington.

Clarissa had been most vocal, within the Bank, about trying to stop Jill's project. Jill had discovered that while she had been in the hospital, Clarissa had worked hard to weaken the project. She was still trying, mostly in covert ways, like slowing down the loan process. But Jill now had the power to add more loan processors.

At the last meeting, before Jill had gone into the hospital, she had said, "Local populations will regard these schools as propaganda tools." This was only one of her many objections, most of which Jill found useful in strengthening her own position.

"Some people will," Jill had responded. "Even though communities have to request the schools, not every community is a democracy. Let's discuss possible strategies to deal with that and enable children to attend." Those strategies were now incorporated into the vast documentation that all such projects amassed.

There was no question, now. This would be an almost celebratory meeting. The Children's Houses were greenlighted, with the Bank's full support. The United Nations, in their most recent Convention on the Rights of the Child, had included an International Right of Every Child to Literacy. Classbooks and libraries accessible via Q, after one learned to read, contained a world of information—science, literature, anything ever in print. Although licensing fees and payments to content providers were expensive, those fees, and all fees, no matter what was accessed, were presently funded via huge philanthropic institutions. In this world—*this world,* Jill thought, so slightly, yet so potently different from *that world,* her old world, keeping a child illiterate was almost universally regarded as child abuse. Increasingly, technology was available and in development that would cheaply and easily diagnose reading disabilities, and these technologies were embedded in classbooks. If a child was having difficulty, Q diagnosed it and brought forth a new strategy.

The main thing that classbooks could not do was pro-

vide the concrete materials that young children needed to manipulate in order to move information about the physical world into their developing minds. Hence, the Children's Houses, with their full array of materials.

Clarissa had lately sent a paper to everyone on the committee implicating the questionable content of many of their supporters' movies and games in promoting violent behavior because of mirror neurons, recently discovered.

Jill had been pleased. It may have offended or cooled some of their supporters, but it probably made some of them reexamine what they were doing. And it certainly hadn't quelled any of their support. All the research in the mirror neuron paper was solid; it was true, and simply strengthened the scientific underpinnings of the venture. Part of the outstanding success of Montessori was attributable to the activation of mirror neurons; their function in learning was a vital component in the school's pedagogy. Holographic children manifesting local race, language, and culture activated whenever a child touched a particular material, showing each child, nonverbally, how the exercise was done. They could not always count on having a trained teacher in the environment, but the directress had always been only a small, but cohering, part of a successful classroom. A new child in a mature classroom always saw the wide variety of what the other children were doing, independently, and imitated them. The holographic children provided this link in a school that might be full, in a single day, of children ranging in age from two-and-a-half to five, with no teacher. The school might have a few module-trained aides who were also learning about the materials, child development, and conflict resolution strategies. The most important thing the first children to encounter the environment had to learn was respect for the materials, and for each other. Clarissa's objection made a very good teaching point.

The room was filling up. Hank, a middle-aged man with a jolly laugh that belied his critical eye and attention

to the bottom line, hurried into the room. Jill greeted her international team—two Montessori experts she'd flown in, one from Holland and one from the University of Dar es Salaam in Tanzania. The engineer-architect team from China, the computer engineers specializing in virtual environments from Los Angeles, and an Indian physician from the World Health Organization also arrived. Her boss, Farid Lahaoud, who was Lebanese, schmoozed and smiled.

The ubiquitous Bill Anderson—though on what departmental pretense he'd invited himself, she couldn't imagine—stepped into the room and took a seat. He smiled at Jill and she responded with a brief nod, turning to greet representatives from several large philanthropic foundations.

With everyone seated, she thanked them for coming. "This project has required extraordinary cooperation among all of you, as well as years of hard work. You have united unique contributions from many disciplines. The learning environments you have created will bring cheap, effective, science-based education to many underserved children of the world.

"We have already processed loans for five thousand schools, worldwide. Many more are in the queue, and Ms. Danvers"—she nodded toward Clarissa—"is supervising that process. Her department is streamlining the process, due to the huge demand. Once more schools are up and running, we anticipate many more requests. I wish to thank Pacifico Akbay, from Manila, for his work in developing an excellent network to get this information out. We've had articles on Q and in all the major newspapers, worldwide, for over six months, as well as a very well-translated pod special."

"What about the private sector?" asked Hoshi Katsu. "If you've seen my memo from last week, you'll see that we are dealing with several different developments. We've had requests from Sydney, Kyoto, Beijing, London,

and so on, for these schools. Generally, they don't fit the parameters for determination of need."

Jill said, "Dr. Lahaoud?"

Dr. Lahaoud stood and said, "The CEO of the non-profit handling detailed coordination of development and distribution was delayed by weather in France, but should be here just as soon as the meeting is over." Laughter. "However, we're developing a sliding scale, so that those who can pay will, for the prefab school, or the plans, if they wish to give work to local manufacturers. The bookkeeping is rather complicated, but I can safely say that it looks as if we may not have to make as many loans as originally projected. Peripheral problems are arising in more urban environments regarding teachers' unions—although there aren't many unions serving preschool teachers—and schools already in business, which aren't pleased about this competition. These are not our problems, but I just wanted to bring them to your attention."

"I have a question about pedagogy," said a slim young woman at one end of the table. "If this holographic technology is so powerful, how can we keep totalitarian, religious fundamentalists, or any party with a political agenda from using these schools for indoctrination?"

Jill responded, "I don't believe we can. This is not a new idea, and no one can regulate the uses of technology. However, the holographic children are simply there to give children nonverbal cues about how the materials are to be used. The materials themselves are the compelling aspect of the environment, and they, by themselves, keep small children occupied and concentrating for hours on end. I'm not sure that most youngsters would sit around and listen to a holographic child talking about religion. But it's an open question, a possibility. Yes?"

A woman from Tasmania said, "Lately there have been studies linking video games containing violence to increased actual violent actions by children and teens,

and some of that income is being used to support the schools. Isn't this a possible public relations problem?"

Jill said, "The Bank has not underwritten nor developed this visual technology. We're merely licensed to use it, and we will use it only as it is laid out in the plans. I'll let our Hollywood representative have a word."

Jan, the holographic developer, wore a simple jacket over a black T-shirt. "We appreciate this latest research." He nodded, and sat down.

The woman said, "Could anyone reprogram this?"

The young man said, "Not just anyone, but there are hackers everywhere. But what's the worst they could do—make the holographic children throw things? Show them hitting other children? Kids see that every day."

The woman frowned.

The man said, "I think what you're worried about is the potency of these visual technologies. It's very true that they carry a lot of import in the developing brain, from what I've learned while working on this project. But this technology is simply not limited to schools. It's in arcades. Possibly, even, training camps for soldiers. This is just an innovative and positive use of it. We appreciate the opportunity to give back to the community in a positive way."

After all the questions were answered, at least for the time being, Jill continued, "Your Q packet includes all the visualizations I will show, evaluation forms concerning performance of your own developmental modules and how well they are, in your opinion, interfacing with the other modules, a mechanism to provide critiques and feedback and discuss incorporation of the feedback into the 1.3 module currently in use, and, just as important, feedback from the thirty communities that have, in the past month, completed setup and have children in the schools. Tomorrow we will have workshops to go over the results and decide where to go from there."

Dr. Lahaoud took the floor. "I want to congratulate all of you on a job well done. We have had an enthusiastic

response to the schools, and very few problems with assembly in any of the communities. In your packet is a list of the questions and problems presented to the remote consultants. I'd like all of you to review your area in detail as to why the problems might have occurred, and propose solutions."

Jill moved on to her favorite part: the visuals of the geodesic schools.

"Our first school was set up in Kathmandu. Already, the country is asking for more. In Nepal, the population is scattered and sparse; a village might consist of only a few families. If we can get our costs down, it would be nice to be able to have smaller versions in these communities.

"You see how easily the foundation is assembled by this crew of ten, in just one day. The rest of the building took another two weeks to finish, but that included all electrical and plumbing connections as well as installation of the holographic projection panels.

"Our team has, in the past six months, trained thirty 'ambassadors,' one of whom flew to Kathmandu and introduced the school, the theory, and how it functions to community leaders, adults who wished to work in the school, and the parents and children. She was there for a week. She evaluated the learning style of each perspective teacher or aide and gave them appropriate orientation and learning modules, which included written material, theory, videos, interactive material, and holographic training situations. Most applicants competently completed self-administered tests and were then able to improve their performance. She spent four days in the classroom with the children and the adults. She introduced them to the concept of the holographic children. The developmental feedback included in every piece of equipment, coded to each individual child in the environment, seemed to work particularly well."

The Montessori consultant from Tanzania asked, "Can the children now turn off the holographic child when they no longer need it?"

Jan said, "Yes, we added a small red square on the shelf in front of each piece of equipment, so the child can do that herself."

The Tanzanian professor said, "We will continue to monitor, through videos, how well the materials record, how long they are used, which children are using them, and how well the materials are doing in helping children refine a particular motor or sensory skill. This will also help pinpoint learning styles and learning problems, such as dyslexia or more subtle problems, including mental health issues and areas of giftedness." She smiled. "Several grad students are doing very well in devising evaluative protocol as they monitor and compare."

The WHO doctor said, "How did the parents and children respond to the vaccinations and the blood and urine tests?"

Jill skipped to the physical exam portion of the video. "There were plenty of technicians and nurses in Kathmandu who volunteered to help, and we gave parents the option of going through the steps themselves with their child. The children didn't seem to mind the blood prick on their finger or the vaccinations; I guess the technology has done away with any pain. Most of the children found the vision and hearing tests quite attractive. The toilets in the schools, of course, collect information constantly and Q remarkable or anomalous results to your centers."

Her molecular engineering expert from India, who had worked on using the latest developments in nanotechnology, impatiently tapped her pen on the table. Jill smiled and invited her to give her Q-School presentation. She hoped it might put a bug in people's minds; it was actually, in her own mind, the next phase of her project, but the most controversial one, because nanotechnology, strictly and exhaustively defined in legal jargon, was a hot-button issue, along with genetic engineering, in most of the world.

"Hello. I am Dr. Singh." Her long black hair reflected the glow of the visual projections.

"Please understand, first, that what may seem a radical vision to you is simply my contribution to a peace think tank I'm currently involved in. While it is respectful of children, who now have an internationally agreed-upon right to education, it is not respectful of the propensity of governments, municipalities, religions, or individuals to control, as they still can and do, the intellectual and emotional growth of their citizens, whether by design, ignorance, unwillingness to fund education, or fear. I think of this as being one component, and perhaps the most powerful, of a campaign against war itself, which feeds on ignorance, poverty, slavery, and individual powerlessness.

"Imagine a seed, about the size of a soybean, stuffed with artificial DNA"— in quick succession she showed slides of the composition of the "seeds," with sidebars about how each stage of growth worked, adding that they were all in the Q—"shipped to any place of need in the world. Where necessary, all applicable property rights will have been procured."

Jill thought that there would be a lot of questions about how the activists who now dropped classbooks all over the world might well get hold of these seeds, but everyone was absorbed by the presentation.

Dr. Singh showed a time-lapse video of the seed actually growing, which, she said with a smile, had been filmed in an undisclosed location. "Once exposed to sun, or rain, or cold, or heat—for it will be equipped to respond and thrive in all kinds of conditions, depending on what it encounters, much like we are—it will begin to grow. It will put down supporting roots, which draw building nutrients from the soil, adhere to solid rock or concrete and grow using solar energy, or elevate the ground floor above an area prone to seasonal flooding.

"Through the conversion of solar energy into sugars, it produces the carbon nanotubes that will, in a matter of weeks, turn into a classroom in Afghanistan, in Darfur, or in any American inner city, small town, or rural community. They are merely an extension of the present international Montessori network, but they will reach into hard-to-serve areas.

"Parents will like them, because they'll keep children occupied. I would like to think that governments will welcome them, for there are no politics involved in learning the correct scientific names of the plants, insects, and animals in your environment, or learning the signs for the phonemes, which make up one's language and using hand-eye coordination exercises to activate the neuronal pathways of memory.

"Certainly, I can imagine armies hacking at such disturbing manifestations. But my schools will be very difficult to destroy. They will grow back quickly. They will know how close other classrooms are, and how many are needed for the local population, so there will not be too many, or too few. They are, actually bulletproof, and their irising doors shut when stimulated by the pheromones of rage or fear, keeping out those who might seek to kidnap or rape the children inside, at which time Q alerts the necessary authorities. At the same time, the community will have access to information about the schools, and the panels are transparent so that no one need fear that anything untoward is happening to their child inside. Each of you has a copy of this presentation in your packet to peruse at your convenience; an open-source forum is also up and running so that we can incorporate innovations. For instance, we've had a lot of questions about toileting, and you can see the present provisions for help and supervision.

"We can also set up inexpensive self-teaching modules that afford literacy, mathematics, and Internet access to vast portions of the world, and help them understand that the possibilities and opportunities that we take for

granted are available. If temporary brain plasticity for adults is eventually developed, so much the better. Mindful evolution seems a far better alternative than mindless conflict."

She sat down to applause, although Jill noticed that some attendees looked pensive.

Jan, the virtual designer, said, "I can think of places in this country that need these schools. For instance, Los Angeles."

Jill said, "Thank you, Dr. Singh. There is an open forum on our website for discussion of issues raised by this concept. There are many hurdles to its creation, if that ever occurs, and many refinements after that, I'm sure."

The meeting ended on a high note, Dr. Lahaoud congratulated her on a job well done, and Bill Anderson slipped from the room like a ghost.

With Several Characters
[*June 1*]

I T WAS Saturday morning, early.

Like a loosed arrow, Whens ran up the stairs, lodging his bare feet in hollows worn in the wood stairs. "Mama," he shouted, when he reached the landing, and shoved open her door, which stuck, with both hands and all his might.

She was a small lump on a huge bed, a distant, flower-covered mountain ridge, and she did not move.

He took off like a rocket—he *was* a rocket—and landed on top of her, clinging, now a small crab, arms and legs clasped tight. "MOM!"

She pushed her arms from beneath the sheet, grabbed him around the waist. "Get in here! Where are your clothes?"

"Downstairs. I took them off," he said proudly. "Are you crying?"

Jill sniffed and wiped her face with her palms. "Yes."

"Are you sad?"

"I was. But I'm better now."

"What were you sad about?"

"My mother and my father."

"They're gone."

"Yes. I miss them."

"I miss them too."

"You do?"

"Yes. I miss Grandma Dance especially." She was surprised at that, but she *had* been showing him some old family pictures.

"Did you eat breakfast?"

"I tried."

"But what happened?"

"I spilled the milk when I opened it."

"It's a whole gallon. It was pretty heavy."

"Yes."

"And then your pajamas were covered with milk and you took them off."

"They were all wet. When is Abbie coming?"

"Pretty soon, I think. Let's get dressed and clean up the milk."

The kitchen, indeed, was a mess. "Tell you what," said Jill. "Let's pick out the Spacies first." She and Whens, down on all fours, began fishing them out of milk and mushy cereal.

Jill had about five in one hand, and she sat back, crossed her legs, and considered them.

"Mommy, you're not helping," said Whens.

"I'm thinking."

She'd never had much to do with Spacies. She had entered this timestream when she was seventeen, a little too old for cereal toys. Brian and Megan, she knew, had loved them in *their* version of the sixties, which was different than Jill's. The entire moon colony collection—complete!—was arranged on the kitchen windowsill, interspersed with other dusty knickknacks. There was even a tiny multinational flag, which fea-

tured the paradigm-changing photo of the Earth taken from the moon. Brian had told Jill that the flag had been included in just a few cereal boxes; it was rare and valuable.

Whens stuck his hand in every new cereal box and grabbed the cellophane pouch as soon as it came from the store. She used to tell him not to do it, but now she picked her battles more carefully, thus saving herself from complete exhaustion and the embarrassment of issuing ineffectual edicts.

The wet Spacies had an imperative feel to them. She had certain needs when they touched her skin. She had to be imagining these sensations—yet, they were quite powerful. For instance, she had to learn to read. She had to become proficient in spatial and mathematical concepts. And, no problem, she could. She was human.

She had a sudden, dizzying vision of a world filled with geniuses of all kinds, a world in which change and progress in improving health, extending life, empowering marginalized people, and in expanding the artistic abilities and possibilities and individuality of everyone moved rapidly. Instead of just fight or flight, there was a new option: define and discuss.

And there were no wars.

Ah, utopia. Her particular silliness.

She stared at the tiny figures in her hand, descendants of those that Brian had kept since he was a kid, grouped around a pot of salmon-colored geraniums on the kitchen windowsill. She went to the sink, pushed aside a china collie, and saw several astronauts, of varying heights, wearing big helmets and puffy suits. A dark woman wearing a white coat—a physician, perhaps, or a scientist, stood next to a short, blond man playing a flute. But there were many more, along with space vehicles and a few things from the Mars Colony set. She leaned over the kitchen sink and studied them. They were quite detailed.

She felt more urges, more necessities.

She had to contribute to the community. If she was not a part of a community, she had to create one. An altruistic one.

She stepped back from the sink. Altruism. What was that, anyway? She remembered endless marijuana-fueled college discussions about it. Did it exist, was it possible? Given that humans were naturally, when pressed, fairly vicious animals with the advantage of forethought and the ability to raise vast sums of money and armies and to invent fearsome weapons? Beat swords into plowshares, indeed. Generally, plows were melted down for bullets.

Not in the world of Spacies.

Spacies, of course, were not just about space, about The Future, anymore. There were teachers, artists, entrepreneurs, scientists. They all came with stories and scenarios. They were, Jill realized, a propaganda tool.

They rather reminded her, she thought with a chill, of the Infinite Game Board.

She remembered throwing a fit when she'd realized that the Game Board had been left in Dallas.

Coupled with the harassing a few weeks ago . . .

She'd thought about calling the police, and then wondered what the hell she would say. She had, of course, put it out of her mind. She was so very good at that.

How would anyone else even know about the Device?

Her parents, she thought, with a brief, happy thrill. But no, it certainly hadn't been them. She recalled the two other men in the hospital—if they really had been there.

She continued to stare at the Spacies in her hand, trying to grab and follow that slippery thread. All those memories were so damned vague, so dreamlike . . .

"Mom!"

She rinsed the milky Spacies and put them on the counter. "Okay, now. You tell me. What's the best way to clean this up, do you think?"

Whens finished sopping up milk and cereal with a rag, which he'd rinsed in the bucket of water he'd asked his

mother to fix for him. The floor was still a little wet. He looked at it while he dried his hands on his T-shirt. Well, a lot wet. Puddles. But it was clean.

"Mom," he yelled. But of course, she didn't answer. You had to go find her. She never answered yells unless you made them sound like you might die if she didn't come.

He took the Spacies from the counter and stuffed them into his pockets. Then he grabbed the handle of the bucket and dragged it to the back door, opened it, and dragged the bucket out on the porch. It spilled when it got caught on the threshold, but at least everything went out onto the wood and drained between the boards. There was some cereal left behind, and he squished it through the cracks.

There. That was done.

He left the bucket out there, tipped over, and looked into the yard. It would be fun to play on the new swing set. He started down the steps, but then remembered.

The attic. She had told him to come back.

He had gone back once or twice, but she hadn't been there.

Maybe she would be there this morning.

He came back inside, and carefully shut the screen door so that it wouldn't slam. He crept over to the door to the attic, which was on the other side of the kitchen.

"Whens? What are you doing?" Her voice came from the library.

"Playing."

"Is the floor clean?"

"Yes."

She fell silent.

He managed to get the attic door open, just a little bit, without it creaking. Then he slipped through into the long, dark, narrow staircase with its haunted stacks of old magazines.

He continued on, his bare feet making no sound.

The second floor landing was sunny; someone had left

the door to the hall open. He stretched past the opening like a cartoon character in case Mom was upstairs now, and passed the other landmarks—the fascinating metal gas station with a car lift you cranked that his mother said might cut him, and a deflated basketball. Mom said Aunt Megan kept it because she used to be on the basketball team.

Finally, he reached the top landing. It was so hot.

He turned the funny oval doorknob and entered the attic, where the heat was even more intense. He had to be careful, now, not to step on something sharp, or anything that might break.

He liked the gloomy light and the dancing dust. He went over to the trunk, which was where he had been when he'd first seen Grandma, and climbed up on it. Then he climbed down and found the old book he kept there, *My Father's Dragon*, got back up, crossed his legs, and opened it. He loved the story, and the pictures. He knew it by heart.

He turned a few pages, then heard, "Hi."

She was sitting on the floor, cross-legged. He thought she was beautiful. She wore shorts and a T-shirt. "Want to play checkers again?"

"Yeah." He jumped off the trunk and got the old checkerboard and checkers, in its ragged, taped box, from the place next to the trunk where he kept his favorite attic stuff so far. He already had a butterfly kite, a rusty gear wheel, and his dragon book.

"I get black," she said.

"I get to go first."

Jim drove, Megan sat next to him, and Abbie was in the backseat. The car was stopped at a light on Fourteenth Street.

"I'm just not comfortable leaving Abbie there," Jim said, as the light turned green.

"Shhh."

"She's got her headphones on."

"I don't care. What's that thing she's playing with?"

"Some classbook thing from school. Which reminds me, we're supposed to have a conference with her teacher about it like last month. Something about its new capabilities."

Megan sighed.

Jim started up again. "Your sister's a nutcase."

"I can't believe that you just said that. It's not like you."

"I'm sorry, but Abbie is my baby. I feel uncomfortable about it. Why can't she stay with Brian and Cindy?"

"I told you. They're coming over to the house too. For the weekend."

"Then it's the *house*! It's just so *kooky* there."

"Jim! Stop it. You don't get out enough."

He smiled. "All right. But what's all this about calling Stevie 'Whens'?"

"He named himself."

"Maybe Abbie will be 'Little Wheres' when we get back."

"Hon, I have to go to this meeting. But if you'd like to stay here with Abbie, you can."

"*Travel* magazine will really pay me well for the Cuba piece. We could use the money. But . . . that weird old house."

"It's a lovely house," Megan declared.

"Sacred."

"You bet."

"Haunted."

"By us. By Mom and Dad."

"I'm just nervous. You know, I'm not sure if I've been away from Abbie this long before. I'll probably cry the day she goes off to kindergarten."

Megan reached over and squeezed Jim's shoulder. "She'll be fine. And Cuba will be fabulous." She snapped her fingers in a Latin rhythm and nodded her head as if to music. "We will drink mojitos and dance the rumba, long into the night. We will be like crazed mating tropical

birds! We will drink strong coffee and it will make us fly!"

"That will be interesting," said Jim. "I've rarely seen you drink anything stronger than a beer. Don't they have San Pellegrino water in Havana?"

"I thought you were flying in a plane," said Abbie from the backseat. "I hope I see some ghosts in that kooky house while you're gone."

Cindy arrived at Halcyon House wearing shorts, a tank top, and work boots.

"Hey!" she said, finding Jill in the kitchen. Cindy's straw-colored hair was hidden beneath a long-billed cap, and she set her work gloves and goggles on one of the stacks of *Washington Post*s on the kitchen table. She pulled out a chair, sat down, and crossed her long, tan legs at the ankles. "Got any decent coffee?"

"Coming right up." Jill ground some Kenya AA and poured it into a press pot, then shoved newspapers aside and set the pot, a green mug, sugar, and cream next to Cindy. "What's Brian doing with the kids?"

"He's taking them all to the zoo." Whens had spent the night at Brian and Cindy's with his cousins.

"Good idea. Did Nate come?" Nate was one of Brian's employees.

"He's in the truck. Smoking a cigarette."

Jill left the room and returned with a notebook. "I made a list."

"The front step, first," said Cindy, pressing the coffee and pouring a fragrant cup. She added two large spoonfuls of sugar and a little more; stirred. "If I have to cut a new center stringer, the step might take all day. I'll have to take the whole thing apart."

"I really appreciate it, Cindy. You don't have to do all this."

"I like construction work. I almost prefer it to my own job, with all the politics and hoops. Plus," she flashed a

wicked grin, "Brian will appreciate what I do a lot more after today."

"Well, thanks. I can't believe the place will be ready for a big party in two weeks."

Cindy finished her coffee and stood up. "That is pushing it. But at least they'll be able to get in the house without breaking a leg. How many did you invite?"

"About a hundred."

Cindy stared at her. "You're kidding."

"Add up people from Georgetown, the Bank, family, neighbors—comes to about a hundred. I hired a caterer."

"God, I hope so."

Jill ran to answer a knock on the front door.

Three women stood on the porch, looking around doubtfully. Their names—Jonquil, Evelyn, and Carol—were embroidered on their shirt pockets. "You must be from Maids-to-Order. I'm Jill. Come on in. I've got a list. You'll mainly be doing the first floor. Don't worry about the windows today. We'll do them tomorrow."

The women looked at each other. Finally, Jonquil said, "This is a pretty big place."

"Tomorrow's Sunday," Evelyn added.

Jill folded her arms. "So, what do you want?"

"Time and a half," said Carol.

"Okay," said Jill, wishing she'd gotten bids on the job instead of calling a number blind.

Soon the house hummed with activity. Jill switched between a chain saw and an electric trimmer to reveal, after many years of shaded obscurity, the handsome, wraparound front porch. She liberated lush yellow climbing roses from strangling vines. She pulled the rotting remains of a fan-shaped trellis from a thicket of brambles. After thinning heavy flower-bearing hydrangeas and ripping more vines from trees, she cultivated the front flower bed with a hoe and a shovel, digging up and dividing big clumps of canna lily bulbs. She carefully spared a patch of fiery red poppies and freed spears of

yellow and violet glads. She discovered a stand of tall, old-fashioned hollyhocks blooming unseen in the jungle. She was deeply glad to find living evidence of her father's labors still thriving.

As she worked, she thought about her Bank plan to propagate schools as if they were plants, letting her mind run wild. Children in the most politically unstable parts of the world, which was where these schools were most needed, would have to be protected from those who might prey on them. She yanked out huge hanks of weeds as she envisioned how pheromone detectors, or cameras using biometrics, might trigger the emission of a chemical that would put the adults to sleep, instantly, yet leave the children awake and able to escape. Then, the pheromones, or whatever, would go to work on those adults, transforming them into paragons of humanity. She laughed out loud now and then as her vision became more and more audacious, impossible, and illegal. But later, she would recruit people to do hard research on the more possible options.

The saw rang throughout the day, and a myriad of power tools roared, popped, hissed, and buzzed. Constantly mopping sweat from her face, Jill worked mulch, fertilizer, and black dirt into the beds around the porch.

By seven, the front porch steps had been repaired and painted, flowers glowed beneath the mist of sprinklers, a haystack-sized pile of tree branches and weeds stood next to the mulcher, and the grand old house, now actually visible from the sidewalk, drew admiring comments from people on their evening stroll.

"The new steps make the rest of the porch look kind of shabby," said Cindy, as she, Jill, and Nate rested on lawn chairs out front, drinking cold beers.

"The whole porch needs to be sanded and painted." Nate lit a cigarette.

"That would be wonderful," said Jill. "Thanks so much for the offer."

"Whoa, wait a minute," Nate said, holding up both hands in front of him.

"I think we have some down time this week," said Cindy. "We'll put you on it. You can at least get going on the porch."

"All that damned gingerbread." Nate flicked ashes on the lawn. "I think there's a law against it now."

Cindy's phone rang. She pulled it out and smiled. "Brian. Maybe the next time I'll answer it." She stood and stretched. "Feels good to do something besides talk to uncaring bureaucrats all day."

"Yeah," said Nate. He lit another cigarette and slouched deeper in the chair. He stared up at the gingerbread. "I feel completely invigorated."

Although Jill's body ached all over from the unaccustomed work of the day, she was mentally alert even at ten o'clock that night. Whens had eagerly chosen to stay all night with his cousins; Elmore and the Lavender Lady had gone on a no-children trip to some kind of fantasy Caribbean place with three-hundred-dollar-an-hour spa treatments that Tracy, thought Jill rather meanly, might benefit from.

Jill was lying on the library couch reading a book about how history can just jump. It examined the genesis of several huge historical conflicts using an unusual lens, that of statistics. The author claimed that many such events were completely unpredictable.

Right, thought Jill. *Like my life jumped.* In 1970 and 1963 at the same time. Like history was playing a dissonant music in her head, two lines, two instruments. Two sets of memories.

And this house was where they converged.

She threw the book on the floor and got up. Walked around restlessly. Went down the hall past the stairway. Flipped on the light.

Here. This large back sunroom. Her mother's Montessori classroom during the sixties.

And, not. That is, her mother hadn't even been here after 1963, a year after they moved here from Germany. She'd opened her school, but soon afterward was gone. Brian and Megan probably didn't even remember it at all. Although . . . Jill closed her eyes; tried to remember what their stories were, for theirs differed so starkly from hers—and perhaps, she realized, even from one another's. She wondered what the results would be if she had Brian and Megan write timelines of their lives. They all shared Hawaii, and part of Germany, but not anything past November 21, 1963. Perhaps the Montessori materials had remained in the sunroom, for a time. Perhaps Sam had quietly closed it and cleared everything away, and this space, which held so many other memories for Jill, had just been Brian and Megan's playroom, their rainy-day room.

That was all it was, now, and an unused playroom at that, with its storybooks, rocking horse, and blocks. Jill darkened the room and went back to the summer-warm kitchen. She hoisted the windows higher, turned on the overhead fan.

The summer night pulsed with sound. A car drove past, then another; their headlights illuminated the culvert briefly. She remembered watching headlights curve across her bedroom ceiling at night, fascinated. Emerge, grow, retreat, vanish. Pattern repeated with each passing car. Funny what kids noticed.

She didn't blame her therapist for thinking she was crazy. Maybe she was. She didn't think so, though. There was another explanation. And the secret was hidden here, in this house. Probably in many forms. She just had to seek them out. Explore.

The thought of exploring made her nauseous. The thought of not exploring made her anxious.

Her restlessness converged in the reality of Whens being away from her. She missed him with every fiber of her being. She took her phone from her pocket; put it back. *No. Don't foist your own weird anxiety on him.*

Let him learn to feel comfortable in his own newly split world. Right now he was dead asleep, or keeping Cindy and Brian awake along with his cousins.

She smiled. Brian had told her that he'd overheard Whens talking to Abbie about a ghost in the house. Whens was fearless. He'd walk right up to a ghost and try to grab hold of it. Shake the stuffing out of it if he could.

Well, then. There was the old Brian, and the new Brian. The old Megan, and the new Megan. The old life, and the new life. Maybe her job was not to try to blend them together, or even to make sense of it all.

Whatever had happened, however it had happened, there was *that world,* and *this world.* The *other world,* and *this world.* Like a lens that the optometrist puts in front of your eyes. Is this better, or (flip) this?

Do it again, she always told the optometrist. Again.

Was the *other world* better? Or *this world*?

And she found that she too, did not really know. Her memories of the *other world* were fading. It was no wonder that her brother and sister, who had been younger, seemed not to recall it at all.

Or maybe double, triple, quadruple time would be common in that place known as The Future. Perhaps time would be woven of a harmony of beings and worlds and times, all playing simultaneously.

The house itself was evocative, a living, breathing being. Her parents had bought it for its spaciousness, its price (cheap, because of its condition), its location, and for the multiracial neighborhood. And right now, she could almost feel it changing, around her. Coming to life again, after being abandoned for so many years. Stirring in the night wind. She heard a sound, outside, and jumped, then laughed. Just night sounds. She thought she smelled cigarette smoke, like the damned Chesterfields her mother used to smoke, and suspected the smell was still being exuded from the couch cushions after all these years.

Her dad loved jazz. Not in the past, but, stubbornly now, in the present. He *was* alive.

And, in fact, his entire jazz collection was right here, from the late 1930s on—here, in the living room, with its comfortable mixture of high modern and chintz. In fact—she squatted down—one record was sticking out of the bottom row, as if it had recently been played. She pulled it out.

A seventy-eight rpm record. Jimmie Lunceford, a big smile on his face, was on the cover, wearing a pencil-thin mustache. She had no idea who he was, but, apparently, he played saxophone.

Jill mused over the stereo setup, which was on an adjoining shelf, for a few minutes, flipped some switches, and moved the turntable control to "78."

She pulled the record from the cardboard cover; it was further encased in a brown paper sleeve. A piece of paper fluttered to the floor. She picked it up and set it on the shelf while she put the needle on the record. While she listened to "White Heat," she unfolded the paper and began to read:

It may be a quaint concept now, but in the olden days when radio was king and television was something that you could read about in the pages of *Popular Mechanics*, dance bands occupied the airwaves after prime time (after the ten o'clock news— fifteen minutes), and occasionally before prime time.

Thus it occurred that casting about on the radio dial for something to listen to about 7:30 P.M. on a warm summer evening, I was electrified by a swing band playing breakneck music in perfect pitch, harmony, and tempo, apparently without effort. At the time I was not a popular music fan; being involved only in high school band and orchestra. In fact, near the end of the school year (eighth grade), the girls' fad was passing around notebooks with numbered pages in which you entered your name on a numbered line on

the first page and each subsequent page would ask you to respond with your favorite color, dessert, teacher, girl (blush, blush), boy, hangout, school subject, dance band, flower and so on to the end of the book. The main objective, I suppose, was to put you on record on the favorite girl/boy question. The question that stumped me, though, was favorite dance band. I had never paid much attention, so I would copy someone else's answer and then forget it the next time.

That was the situation that fateful Sunday evening I happened upon Jimmie Lunceford playing from the Lodgemont Casino. (Much later I realized that the radio announcer, dispatched from his New York studio, was striving to pronounce "Larchmont Casino.") I discovered that the name of the piece was, appropriately, "White Heat." I had another shock when I heard his theme song, "Jazznocracy." Just as fast, just as intricate, just as flawless, just as awesome. I was smitten, never to look back.

I rushed downtown to the Capitol Confectionary (Jimmie the Greek's soda fountain), the school hangout, to bring my friends up to date, and to make sure that we were together, comfortably ensconced the next Sunday at 7:30 to listen and exchange thoughts on what we heard. There was at that time no affordable equipment to record radio broadcasts or live music. A few rich people bought studio recorders, some of whom had luggable versions built to record dance bands live, but just the record blanks would be beyond our resources. We did have shellac records, seventy-five cents and forty-five cents, seventy-eight rpm; Lunceford, fortunately, was forty-five cents, not a deal breaker. A dud on the second side, however, was a deal breaker for a prospective freshman.

Within our group, however, I think that we managed to buy all of Jimmie's output for that critical year or two. Our source, at the time, was Lyons Music in

downtown Dayton. The store manager (and usually the entire staff) was a lovely young lady named Peggy who was a rabid Ellington fan. She was always pushing Ellington's latest on us, while we were pushing Lunceford's latest on her, with no movement in either direction. As an interesting sidelight, the Lyons store was the nearest full-service record store to Dayton's west side, at the time mostly black population. And which band did the black customers favor? Glenn Miller, that's who! AND OVERWHELMINGLY!

As our affinity grew, along with our nascent record collections, we met frequently for the purpose of entertaining one another with our latest "finds," from the likes of Goodman, Shaw, yes, Ellington, Billie Holiday, Claude Thornhill, Raymond Scott Quintet, Wingy Manone, Tommy and Jimmy Dorsey, Jimmy McPartland and the like, culminating in an early winter meeting on a Saturday night in our basement for the purpose of formally organizing the Squounch Club. I had a Wilcox-Gay Recordio player that had no speakers, but it did have an AM transmitter (FM not yet invented), which I could tune to a dead spot on the radio spectrum so I could tune it in on any radio in a city block radius for clear reception. Certainly one of the earliest examples of off-the-shelf open format wireless transmission![1] Refreshments provided by the group assembled consisted of a pony of POC (Known locally as "Pride of Cleveland" or "Piss on Cincinnati") and a roaster pan of my mother's baked beans. The meeting got under way with a playing of both "White Heat" and "Jazznocracy," a brisk invocation by the Lord High Squounch "e saga dah" and equally brisk response "e saga dah" by the assembled multitude (three). The organizing principles were adopted as read:

1. Lord High Squounch for Life: Leonard Gaver
2. Official band: Jimmie Lunceford

3. Official refreshment: POC Beer
4. Guiding principle: No women.

After word got around of our organizing principles, item 4 was changed by acclamation at the next meeting to read, "Closing of official meetings of the Squounch Club shall be conducted by Lord High Squounch Gaver to the strains of Artie Shaw's "Gloomy Sunday." Other than saving a potion of "frumentatious amber nectar of the gods" (POC) for the final "e saga dah," no further ceremonial changes were permitted. Needless to say, the original Prop 4 was never heard from again.

The record ended. The needle bounced back and forth on an ungrooved portion of shellac. Jill turned it over to hear "White Heat," and continued to read:

In the ensuing years, Lord High Leonard became a high lord many times, and inducted many new members, both male and female, without inflicting any apparent damage upon the body Squounch. I can't say that I regret any time I spent with the Squounch Club, at home or on the road.

Jill smiled, intrigued. She played both sides again, several times, straining to hear something that would jog her memory. The tune was very familiar. He must have played it hundreds of times. But what about it had been so important to him? Was it just this memory? Or was there more?

She even had a faint thought of getting the sax back from Brian and trying to learn the intricate phrasings; perhaps that was one way to get into the mind of her dad. She put the record back in its paper sleeve with care, folded her father's words into the cardboard sleeve, and returned it to the shelf, tapping it in firmly to line up with the other records. Sam's World War II memoirs,

which he called "In War Times," were somewhere in the attic.

But no. Brian had taken them home with him too.

She picked up a hinged photo holder that was on the bookshelf. She had seen the facing pictures a thousand times: her father in his Army uniform; her mother in hers. She stared at the pictures for a long minute, and when she closed her eyes the afterimage remained.

She set the picture back on the shelf. Why *hadn't* she read the notebooks, after all these years? Because she was too busy? That had been her excuse. She'd wanted a nice long time in which to sort them out properly.

Right. Such luxuries of time were just a fantasy. She had been afraid to read them.

When her father was still here, it would have seemed like prying. He'd never invited her to delve into his life then. And after he left, the pressure of having been the cause of both parents' disappearance had made her want to forget. Why relive such devastation, such deep heartbreak?

But—and now she was angry, as she strode here and there in the living room, the screened porch, the library, trying to find a flashlight—if her parents had known about the possibility, why had they not explained it? Cautioned her? Cautioned them all? Thrown the damned thing in the fire? She, Megan, and Brian had found the Infinite Game Board under that loose board in the attic floor. And *played* with it when they were kids. Kept it all secret from their parents, as their parents had tried to keep it secret from them. No wonder they were all crazy. Megan had her Perfect Life, where everything was under control, all mapped out; Brian was a recovering alcoholic, and Jill had rushed to get married, have a baby, and work her fingers to the bone, all as if it would make some kind of difference, as if she were paying some kind of weird penance, racking up points in the Game Board world. Her parents themselves had lived two lives—maybe more!

"Who knows!" said Jill, throwing up her hand, then heading for the junk drawer in the kitchen. After all, was it possible for one teenage girl to thwart a planned presidential assassination? Nancy, her therapist, had simply filed that one under "Megalomania, extreme."

And she was right! Jill yanked open a drawer, and it fell to the floor with a crash. There. She reached down and snatched up the old flashlight that rolled across the kitchen floor.

She had been funneled down a path as surely as a marble, in their old Mouse Trap game; was released by a gear after a roll of the dice, rushed through the open bathtub drain, zigzagged down those crazy stairs, and lowered the trap on the opponent's plastic mouse.

No, she had not arrived in Dallas on her own. But how? What was that mysterious gap; why did her memory not function as it should? Damn it all! She decided to try the attic. There might be something there to help her remember.

The damned flashlight was dead. She jettisoned the spent batteries in the trash can and poked around in other drawers for new batteries, increasingly worried about Dad's papers. Sure, Brian had taken some boxes, but maybe there were more. She would call him tomorrow first thing and tell him to bring them all back! They belonged in the house.

She paused. That wasn't what was really bothering her, was it? Mere possession of the past?

The Infinite Game Board, from which all of this trouble, this strangeness, this sense of her life drifting into two separate parts, was safely gone, left in that previous world.

She was worried because those journals might have information about how it had been made.

Why did she think this?

She found a cache of ancient batteries, tried several, and finally found some that worked. She waved the resulting beam across the dining room, yanked open the attic door, and began to climb.

She thought the journals might have classified information because her parents were so very strange. Because Gypsy Myra, in her comic, had created just the sort of history-changing, time-altering Device that had landed Jill, in real life, in the nuthouse, and because the story of Gypsy Myra, the Madwoman of Time, had come from the Game Board.

Mom and Dad had known about the Game Board— the *Device:* the word popped into her mind, from that phone call. The Device. They had all used it, once, played some kind of game that involved an airplane. She thought. It was all so damned *hazy.* And what about their friend—what was his name? Winklemeyer? Wink? Hadn't he been here, that fateful night on the screen porch when they had *all* played The Game, when they had all flown in that airplane? Even Brian, though he was, at that time, stationed in Vietnam?

The attic stairs, narrow to begin with, were further restricted by objects people had placed on them, no doubt intending to carry them up to the top when time permitted. Jill passed a pile of calendars from 1921, showing the phases of the moon, as she had done countless times; they were a part of her childhood, seemingly immovable. The door to the third floor was open again, but it didn't matter; she had neither heat nor air-conditioning on. She was short of breath by the time she reached the attic door and pulled it open.

Jill flipped on the light switch and moved her flashlight beam around to augment the resulting dim light. She stepped forward tentatively, ignoring enticing boxes and strange, old toys that had belonged to a previous generation of owners. They'd had a loose rule that the area at the top of the stairs, inside the door, be kept reasonably clear. Despite that, she had to execute a slow, balanced ballet past and over an astonishing variety of objects that she and her siblings had just tossed in.

She stumbled over a dark object, caught herself on the back of a chair, and headed toward a looming landmark—

the five-foot-high urn. Once, they had dropped Megan into it. Of course, they'd *asked* her if she'd like to be inside it first, so it wasn't exactly a surprise to her. They had to move chairs next to it, and then she and Brian helped Megan climb in. Once inside, Megan decided she did not like it and screamed with incredible shrillness and power; it was a wonder the urn hadn't shattered. They were yelling at her to hold up her arms and they would pull her out when their mother burst into the attic. She and Brian were sentenced to their rooms. Megan got to go to High's for an ice cream cone.

Jill sat down on a rolled-up carpet and laughed at the memory.

After an hour of poking around, her fears had diminished, as if she had awakened from a bad dream—just what she needed, after all. She was acting like an idiot. It was all just an aftermath of her crack-up. She'd call Brian in the morning about the notebooks.

Running her light around, she noticed something odd: a checkerboard, all set up. She went closer, treading on unknown objects, some of which crunched ominously, and saw that it was dust free.

Who had been up here, playing checkers, especially in this heat? Oh, right. Abbie and Whens.

Then she saw a ragged white envelope on the floor, its contents partially spilled out.

She picked it up, squinted, and trained the flashlight on her find, which she fanned out in her hand: black-and-white photographs.

On the back of the pictures, they were identified, in her father's handwriting, in pencil. "Germany, 1945. Biergarten, Gladbach. Soldiers in a jeep."

Motherlode!

There was one photograph of a courtyard—tables set up, empty, waiting chairs, a bar. She heard her father's voice as if he were sitting next to her:

"It turns out that the castle near Mönchengladbach is the mansion of Joseph Goebbels who unwittingly donated

a magnificent couch to our company day-room that I told you about the other day. Reyhdt is the sister-city or suburb to Gladbach, there being no separation between them. I didn't visit either the *Volkspark* or Goebbels's mansion, so I wasn't aware that the 'mansion' is actually an ancient castle. Not surprised, just not aware.

"Neither was I aware that an American general had taken possession and was assigning sleeping accommodations to honored guests; again, not surprised.

"The *Volkspark* also provided picnic tables, picnic benches and the bar and bar foot rail for our C Company *Biergarten* in the brick-walled garden behind our apartment building. The summer house served as the back of the bar, with the cooler, an old-fashioned arrangement of a barrel on the bar lined with beer coils wrapped around the inside perimeter of the barrel and the barrel interior filled with cracked ice. Under the bar was the barrel on tap, open coolers holding Coke, Rhine wine, pink Moselle Champagne, Krefeld cognac, and schnapps, on ice. We lit the garden with fairy lights and provided music with a record player and records (LPs) provided by Army Special Services, through speakers provided by our newfound German friend at that radio station at Koln (Cologne) I told you about.

"We sent a truck to Maastrich every week. The brewery there made wonderful beer. The deal was that we got to buy a liter per week for each guy in our organization as long as we had empty barrels to change for their full barrels. We went around Gladbach liberating glasses and mugs, beer coolers and piping and oh-those-precious barrels from bombed-out *Biergartens*. We kept finding more empties. By the time we left in August we were drawing 2,800 liters per week.

"When we got notice that we were leaving MG, the battalion club got panicky and we picked up their booze rations too. We had about a truckload of beer that we took to the transit camp. We had a guard posted.

Each tent got two bottles of wine and cognac a day; pretty good stock. We still ran out a couple of days before V-E Day and were forced to celebrate by standing in a mile-long line to get two cans of beer, then getting back at the end of the line while we drank them.

"That was the beginning and end of our *Biergarten*. We had $400 in the kitty at closing time and gave it to Dick Behrens to take home and bring to camp where we were supposed to reassemble in Texas after our R & R. We never got there and he used it to get married. He was very apologetic but nobody would have traded the money to go back to camp."

Jill remembered now, the stories he'd told about setting up the *Biergarten*. Finding the speakers, the booze, the bar from the *Volkspark*.

About how her mother had walked in, one evening, in a red dress, changing his world forever.

She turned off the lights, crept down the stairs to the second floor, and set the pictures down on a table in the hallway. Then she trudged into the bathroom, where she ran a cool bath.

Getting into the claw-footed tub, she submerged her head and ran her fingers through her hair. Cobwebs. Long-dead bugs. Ancient dust. She sorted through the shampoo bottles—where was the stuff she usually used?—and heard a noise.

Electrified, she could hear her heart pound. Where was Manfred? Probably asleep. In fact, the noise probably was Manfred. She relaxed.

"Manfred!" Clicking claws hurried down the hallway.

"You scared me, you silly dog!" Jill got out of the tub, sloshing water onto the floor, and grabbed a towel.

Then she thought she heard another sound.

Shit.

She wrapped herself in the towel and peered around the doorway. "Who is it?"

Manfred looked at her as if she were nuts.

Jill dripped her way down the hallway, intending to get her phone, and noticed that the photos she'd left on the table were now scattered on the floor. She could have sworn that she'd put them all back in the envelope.

But now, on top of the envelope, was a picture of her mother, Bette.

She was wearing a long dark coat, and her hair, pale in the black-and-white photo, was mostly covered with a scarf.

She had her arm around another woman. Jill wiped her hand and picked up the picture, squinted. Was that Gypsy Myra?

They were standing, if Jill was not mistaken, in front of the bombed-out Reichstag in Berlin.

"Damn it! If you're here, just come out and frigging TALK TO ME!"

Manfred barked her own invitation, then whined a bit.

"Go get them, girl!" She wagged her big fat tail, which could have brushed the pictures from the table. But why would this one be so oddly displayed? What were the chances of that?

Jill, far from being afraid, was just mad. Like Whens, she seemed to have no fear mode. Brian thought she should be afraid. Well, maybe he was right; maybe she was just crazy, like they all thought, or maybe she just took too many vitamins.

She searched the house for an hour, finding nothing and no one, and finally collapsed, deeply chagrined, on the living room couch.

In her hideaway upstairs, Bette sat on the bed, her legs drawn up to her chin, smoking a cigarette, was also deeply chagrined. She ground out her cigarette with an angry, stubbing movement, and watched the moonlight glaze the treetops below. What had possessed her?

Fish or cut bait, she told herself. The problem was, she had to do both simultaneously, without a crew for the boat, but instead wanted just to dive into the blue, silky depths of her pure love for Jill, and hold her to her heart. *I am here, my love, I am present.*

I love you so.

Megan

CUBA CONFERENCE

THE INTERNATIONAL consciousness symposium had many tracks. Megan sat on a wrought-iron bench in the courtyard of the old hotel and studied the program.

Scientists were investigating consciousness from many different angles, through many different disciplines. There was a physics track, a neurobiology track, an evolutionary biology track, a religion and philosophy track, and a memory research track. Memory as a distributed field: theory and research. That sounded interesting.

Megan had a list of must-meet theorists—some for her own interests, and some assigned so she could bring back the skinny to NIH. She gathered her papers and got up.

The heat-shimmered tropical beauty of Havana stunned Megan. Plants waved and bobbed in the hot, humid breeze. Their leaves, a phantasmagoria of shape, size, and color, cast moving shadows on one another. Plumeria, hibiscus, and bougainvillea festooned the bricked courtyard Megan passed through on her way to the street, where a large marble fountain cascaded, creating a brief, cool zone. The songs of unseen tropical birds mingled with the distant, constant cries of the seagulls massed at the harbor. She strolled downhill to the meeting center, through a mixture of business people, tourists, and shoppers. Everything was so open and friendly that it was hard to believe this had been an apex of terror in 1962.

The Dances had been living in Oberammergau, Germany, at the time; her father was teaching at the NATO school there. But her D.C. friends remembered it clearly: They had been hiding under their desks for years every Wednesday at noon when the air raid signal went off. Just a drill, kids, don't worry.

"It was scary," her friend Karen recalled, sipping her TGIF martini at an outdoor table on K Street while traffic roared by. Karen had grown up in Tall Oaks. "This time, the siren went off on a pretty fall day in October 1962. It wasn't Wednesday. We hid under our desks but then we heard an announcement over the PA system. God, the PA was new too. Anyway, the principal said not to worry, we all were getting out of school early. The teachers were scared; they wanted to get home as fast as they could. Even though we lived just a block away from school, my mom was there in front of the school with the car, with about fifty other moms. The line stretched around the block. She honked the horn and rolled down the window and yelled, 'Come on!' "

Karen swigged the last of her drink and signaled for another. "We didn't go home. She already had my brother in the car, and we went to the Dillons' house on Nutting Lane. They had an air raid shelter. I'll bet it's still there. We even had to bring one canned food a week to school for *their* air raid shelter. I think it was under the gym. Anyway, Mr. Dillon never came, and neither did my dad; they were both part of whatever operations or alert was going on. So we all played in the air raid shelter for three days. It was kind of fun once we were down there. There were lots of games—Cootie, Mouse Trap, Monopoly. Our moms were really strict about food and water. They'd taken all the food in our houses and brought it down and made us eat what would spoil easily first. Fruits and vegetables and meats. There was a ventilation system and a generator. Mr. Dillon had a huge antenna in his backyard for his ham radio. Mrs. Dillon talked to him a few times, and she talked to a lot of other people too."

"How long did you stay there?"

"God! Over a week! We were pretty rowdy by that time. I don't see how anybody could stand it for much longer."

"Didn't they let you out to stretch your legs?"

"Oh, once, but little Jack Dillon ran away and hid in the woods. He thought it was pretty funny, and the moms were frantic. I guess that if the Soviets had fired those missiles we would have been toast in five minutes, shelter or no shelter."

World annihilation. It sounded strange right now; almost impossible to credit, walking down a sunny street in Havana. But Megan's frequent interfaces with other government agencies made her realize that many people believed, even now, after nuclear weapons had been unilaterally dismantled and outlawed, that a "limited nuclear war" was possible.

How could one make nuclear fission impossible? It was a law of nature. And so some advocated evenly distributed nukes, kind of like the idea that if everyone knew that everyone else was carrying a gun, power situations would be equalized. Yes, I am a hundred-and-ten pound woman, but I can kill you. An odd sort of negative solution.

Megan, on the other hand, wanted to fill people's minds with good pictures. Pictures of being loved and cared for. Pictures of being happy, and finding life on earth good, full of opportunities. She wanted to fill them with an appreciation of the very fact that they were alive, which to Megan was absolutely astounding.

The ideas she had for doing so were not very practical, nor were they very respectful. Everyone had false memories. So—what if people had good false memories? What if, instead of the terrible memories that disabled a rape victim, she had a memory of empowerment? What good would that be, if it wasn't true?

It seemed obvious to Megan that the impulses some men had to hurt women and girls simply had to be

expunged from their brain chemistry, from their physiology, much like polio and smallpox had been eliminated. She, for one, was tired from the wariness that just walking down the street in Washington—or, for that matter, here in Havana—entailed. Why should she be constantly afraid of being robbed, raped, kidnapped, or mugged? Why would unknown others—maybe that man there, behind that bland face, approaching on the sidewalk—intend to stab her, or stalk her? Why keep that part of "human nature"? There was a lot of other stuff that had to go too. The idea of women being the property of men, for instance. She understood why chastity had been such a big deal in the past—some men didn't want to spend their lives raising another man's child. But now DNA testing could easily establish paternity. Still, that made it all the more dangerous for women in many societies. It was easy to conclude that the world would be better without, not necessarily, men, but without men who indulged in these murderous urges, for whatever reason. Perhaps they needed to be sorted out? Preempted, reoriented?

She shivered again. Was Abbie safe at Jill's? Maybe Jim was right. That man, roaming around the neighborhood—what was he up to? Anything? Nothing at all? What pathology made her think that all menace was aimed at her, or her family? How could she tell the intent of the Walking Man?

Maybe Jill was not the only nutsy person in their family. There was this lost, drafty place in her too; this feeling that something was not quite right. When—*look around! think!*—it most obviously was right. The perfume of gardenias, the sounds of a healthy, thriving harbor city, the laughter of people drinking *café Cubano* and eating mango pastries at small tables next to the sidewalk; the blue, blue sky and the saltwater tang of the faint, hot breeze—all was fine; all was very fine.

Megan passed shops filled with goods from around the world. Cuba was an international tourist destination,

and her dollars were good here. Castro had relaxed his brand of Socialism after the U.S. recognized Cuba in 1965, after JFK's reelection.

Megan shivered a bit despite the warm sun, and put down her program. Jill seemed obsessed about those times; she had books piled up to the ceiling about it. She insisted that it would have been a much different world if Kennedy had been killed, one in which dark forces of imperialism and the military industrial complex might have combined to produce a series of endless, useless, depleting wars.

But he hadn't been. So why did that possibility constantly shadow her?

Megan's phone rang. Abbie!

"Hi, Mommy. Guess what? There's a ghost at Auntie Jill's house! I love her!"

"You love Auntie Jill?"

"No! I mean, I love Auntie Jill but I love the ghost too."

"Maybe you should go outside and play. Doesn't Stevie have a new swing set?"

"His name is Whens. We're playing games in the attic."

"That's awful hot, isn't it?"

"It's fun. We have a big jug of lemonade."

"Not Slingers?"

"No. Auntie Jill doesn't allow them."

Megan was often baffled about what Jill did and didn't allow. "Well, okay. Have fun, sweetie. Call me anytime."

She supposed Jim had been right about Jill's kooky house. But, after all, it was her house too! And her childhood. And there was nothing too much wrong with that. Except.

Except Mom and Dad weren't there anymore.

She bought a Cuban coffee at a window on the street, and then, with an impulsiveness in which she rarely indulged, bought one more. The world brightened. Tangibly. The mangoes at a street vendor's seemed almost to

send forth the Kirilian tangles of energy that left-field spiritual nuts claimed to be able to photograph. *Wow,* she thought. *This coffee is really something.*

A woman with long, white, curly hair, held behind her neck with a large silver barrette before it cascaded to her waist, fell in next to her. "Hello," she said. "You are going to the meeting, no?" She laughed. "You are dressed like a scientist who is not really on vacation, like me."

Megan looked sideways and saw almost-black eyes, a professional suit, high heels, and sweat on the woman's forehead like her own: This was not a good way to dress in such a hot climate. The woman's face was slightly lined with age, but her skin seemed to glow, like that of a much younger woman.

"Yes, I am. And you?"

"Yes." She held out her hand. "Eliani Hadntz."

"I'm Megan Dance." They shook hands awkwardly as they walked.

"I'm going to the first memory lecture. Want to join me?" asked Megan.

"Certainly. I'm very interested in memory. In fact, I've just published an article." She laughed. "It was hard to place, because it is cross-disciplinary. It's called 'The Physics of Memory.'"

Memory and physics. The words combined for Megan, as powerfully as a neurolinguistic programming anchor: physics, as in atomic bombs; memory, as in, *Why do I seem to worry about a memory that doesn't even exist?* And out of her mouth came, "What if Khrushchev hadn't backed down?" Her mind filled with pictures. *Children running naked down the road, screaming. And then she and Brian and Jill, orphaned, tried to take care of one another as everyone around them died from the vomiting sickness. They walked out on a rise above Washington, on Shirley Highway, that their mother had always loved, that view, and saw fires rage in twisted buildings, and nothing was recognizable. There was no food or water.*

Megan's field of vision swirled, and a flat, transparent plane in her head flipped over. She saw that she was falling; watched her program scatter in the breeze. Dr. Hadntz grabbed Megan around the waist as she fell forward, and pulled her to a low wall next to the sidewalk.

"Sit."

Megan recovered, breathing hard. "Sorry. I got a little dizzy. Maybe I've got a flu. Oh, I know! Too much coffee."

The eyes of Megan's fellow scientist were sympathetic; even sorrowful. Megan continued to gasp for breath, and looked away.

"Is that what you think?" asked the woman. "Really?"

Megan tried to smile. "I've never been to Havana before. It's a lot hotter than I expected. I'm from the U.S. You're not?"

"You're right. I'm Hungarian."

"Well, you've probably heard of the Cuban Missile Crisis."

Hadntz nodded.

"I just . . . suddenly . . . had a vision of what might have happened if things had gone the other way."

"They might have, easily," said Hadntz. "And then the world would have been completely different, would it have not?" She sighed and said so softly that Megan almost didn't hear her, "The nightmare sometimes breaks through."

"Yes." Megan took a deep breath. "It would have been different. It's not, though. Everything is fine, here, now. It's a beautiful day. Isn't it?" The thoughts she often had—that she was just a temporary vessel for identity, an attractor, a pattern that incorporated the molecules of food to maintain the pattern—suddenly seemed not exhilarating, but frightening, as if she were suspended above a raging, infinite sea by just a thread. Maybe, she thought suddenly, it's a familial thing. First Jill cracks up, now me. Oh, shit. If she'd known, she'd never have had Abbie—

"Of course it is," said Hadntz firmly. "It is an absolutely beautiful day." She looked away for a moment, and seemed to be thinking. Finally she said, "Let's go in, shall we? The air-conditioning might be exactly what you need."

It was so. The cool air inside refreshed Megan, and the familiar reality of being in a lecture hall enveloped her. She loved the frisson of intellectual sharing, of thoughts building on one another. And she loved arguing about these ideas as well.

She took the translation headphones offered her by Hadntz, and they took seats near the front of the auditorium.

The first talk was about mirror neurons. Nothing could restore Megan to full power like new information about the brain. It was her language, her deep reality.

She relaxed, and her relaxation swallowed up her morning's visions.

For lunch, Megan and Hadntz found a café a few blocks from the meeting that wasn't overflowing with people from the conference. Hadntz spoke Spanish, and translated for Megan, who ended up having a salad and another cup of *café Cubano*. Hadntz ordered a sandwich, which arrived looking strangely flat. Megan eyed it.

Hadntz laughed. "They press them. It makes them much better."

"Really?"

"What did you think of the talks?"

"This paper was about mirror neurons and violence, of course, but I have wondered if at some point in the future we might be able to distinguish between mirror neurons of empathy for others and mirror neurons that encourage us to imitate violent actions."

"And then?"

"Oh, then, of course, I'd like to do something entirely unprofessional and invasive. I'd like to zap the violence-

causing neurons and enhance the empathic neurons. I'd ratchet those up to intense levels."

"That's one approach," said Hadntz thoughtfully. "There might be a way to do that."

"How?"

"I will send some information that might be applicable," she said. "Keep an eye out for it. I think we need to get back to the meeting right now."

Later in the afternoon, the group went on a tour to the site where the Soviet missiles had been placed, twenty-two years earlier. A museum stood there now. Megan had wanted to ask Eliani Hadntz to go, but hadn't seen her anywhere after lunch.

As Megan walked past a black-and-white diorama showing U.S. spy-plane photos, she wondered what the world would have been like if the Germans had developed a bomb. Hitler had driven many German scientists out of the country before the war, but enough remained so that they could have built one, had resources and will been available. Jill said that was what killed Germany in the end—no more oil.

Megan thought about a recent observation in primatology.

Chimps were notoriously violent. In every chimp group, a hierarchy of dominant males raped, bullied, and murdered at a constant low rumble.

In one recent recorded instance, though, the dominant males all went off to exploit the succulent pickings at a garbage dump, excluding the subordinate males and the females so they could have it all to themselves.

The dominant males, subsequently, all got food poisoning and died.

When the subordinate males consequently moved into dominance, the profile of violence changed. Perhaps it changed because the social parameters had changed so suddenly.

Whatever the reason, a new society was born—one

more civil, with much less aggression and rape, and had remained so through subsequent generations.

It was easy to suppose that if someone could figure out how to wipe out, disable, or change the top, aggressive males, the ones who insisted that war be omnipresent, the future might be breathtakingly different than the past. She'd just read a book about that very thing, *Sex and War*, written by physicians—men, in fact—which painstakingly documented that, in their opinion, several defining characteristics of maleness were responsible for human war.

But could war be eliminated as if it were a virus, like smallpox? Humans weren't just one small isolated tribe, like most chimp groups. They were spread out across the earth, living quite literally atop one another, many-layered and complex. Not only that, they were not chimps; there was that incredibly small, yet powerfully telling, one-percent genetic difference that made humans capable of long-term planning, nuanced language, record-keeping, and complex storytelling. Any characteristic observed in chimps were removed from human characteristics and behavior by millennia and those few crucial genes. The winds of power in humans simply favored those, male or female, who struggled and connived, people convinced of their need to be in control of others. Absolutely the kind of people whose power-managing skills had been sharply honed by competition. Now, if there was some mechanism in place to choose the most peaceful folk to be in power . . . not that they wanted to be in power. They would run and hide from power. They wanted to read the funnies every morning, and enjoy life. So maybe everyone would be forced to take turns at dealing with governmental issues.

Megan was not, at any rate, a primatologist or an anthropologist. It was amazing, though, how many humans believed that the present systems of behavior were set in stone—and, what was worse, that it was "unnatu-

ral" to try to change such behaviors, when evolution was constant and omnipresent in every living system.

She stared into a representative fallout shelter, where a "nuclear family," life-sized plastic figures, lived in a tiny space with their water distiller, dried food, and emergency flashlights—much like, she supposed, the backyard shelter in which her friend Karen, a thousand miles to the north and a few decades ago, had spent a week.

As she tried to imagine what such a life might be like, Megan hoped that the woman she'd met today might truly have the neurological silver bullet that could lead to human altruism. Perhaps some kind of genetic alteration was possible. Slight, but powerful. Or perhaps just a removal of warfare from the human landscape, like smallpox, polio, and, just lately, many cancers had been removed. A few years earlier a truly terrible virus had emerged, called AIDS, but it had been quickly and effectively eliminated via international cutting-edge research. Sometimes human cooperation truly could bring about results that seemed little short of miraculous. HIV/AIDS was a scourge that they would never have to deal with.

Megan emerged from the shaded displays and walked out into the hot sunshine. The brick pathway wound through rows of royal palms back to the bus. She passed gentle waterfalls and pools full of koi, surrounded by formal gardens. *Peace,* breathed big-leaved, white-flowered ginger, elegant heliconia with their bird-like beaks, and lush bird's-nest ferns beneath manicured bougainvillea trees. All manner of lizards zipped and paused; zipped and paused. Beneath the shadow of a tall intercontinental ballistic missile, she read a multi-lingual sign that explained it lacked its former nuclear warhead.

That woman—what was her name? Megan pulled out her card. Dr. Hadntz. She had been talking about adult

brain plasticity. It seemed that if more intense plasticity were available to adults . . . if they could then take some kind of course devoted to understanding peace, to replicating peace . . .

Megan felt a brief jolt of intense intellectual hope, the like of which she had not felt for a while: the power of the new, the unexpected, the expansion of possibilities. That which lay just over the horizon. Perhaps, a whole new world.

She smiled at herself. That was precisely what teenagers felt, because a whole new world *was* just over the horizon, for them.

Maybe Dr. Hadntz had slipped her some certified plasticity, grade A, somehow. A nice fantasy. How wonderful that would be.

She hoped Jim was back at the hotel. She was ready for her mojito. Brian and Jill weren't here to feign astonishment.

She might even have two.

After returning from Cuba, Megan was in her lab just a few mornings later when her Q beeped. She ceased mindlessly watching a centrifuge, which would turn off when programmed to do so.

She opened her mail. It was from Eliani Hadntz.

Her article, published in an obscure French journal, had been translated into English.

It referenced songbird research that showed in painstaking detail the brain changes that took place, seasonally, in songbirds learning the new season's songs.

Gradually, it segued into analogs of this research in humans, most of it confirmed by super-precise FMRI's of learning taking place in real time.

It then showed how various biochemical composites could deliver the same changes—the same openness to change—that took place in active learning. These drugs mimicked and enhanced the learning process. Out of five human subjects who spoke only English, three had

learned to write, read, and speak Japanese, without an accent, in a month. This, however, was in a Hadntz addendum, and to Megan, the research protocol seemed doubtful.

Still, as she read, Megan tried to tamp down her excitement. She grabbed her notebook and added some molecules here and there. A mouse generation, two, ten, stretched out before her.

And yet, she was so sure. Damn another time-consuming, expensive iteration, for which she had no money. Her requests for grant extensions had been denied; a new round would take at least a year to realize.

If she made this, she could take it herself.

Everything she had ever learned and practiced as a scientist shouted "NO!" And added to that "NO!" was Abbie.

Added to what sounded like an "Everlasting Yea" was a powerful urgency the like of which Megan had never felt—as if she stood on the shore of a beautiful world and had only to step off the boat.

Nuts.

Then she was irritated. If this Eliani Hadntz was so sure of herself, why wasn't this drug in tests, in production?

And then, Megan saw her note at the bottom: "It works. See table 7.4."

Megan had rather glossed over that table, and flipped back to it. Perused it.

The studies were actually very, very good; she could find no flaws in their setup, and she peer-reviewed and discarded studies constantly.

The studies had taken place in ten countries, and the volunteers were from all kinds of backgrounds. PhDs from many countries; even a few names she recognized. Volunteers from mental health institutes. Age groups, beginning with twenty-one to one hundred and one. A woman in Kenya who had just begun to write a very remarkable history of the life she had previously forgotten,

corroborated by experts. So why had she not heard of all this earlier?

Further analysis. She Q'd for a country she did not recognize, Seychelles. Okay, okay. It was off the coast of Africa, very tiny. Andalusia: mostly Spanish. This went on for a bit; she realized that nations were fluid, forming and re-forming constantly, and the extent of her geographical knowledge was embarrassingly tiny.

She recognized a name: Paul Wentworth, a British colleague, and Q'd him. He answered instantly, saying that, indeed, he had participated and by the way (slightly irritated in that British manner) had she not noticed that his name was being kited about for the Nobel Prize? Hearty enthusiasm for the drug, no hesitation at all about it, wondering why she had not heard about it earlier, and wasn't Hadntz a rather odd duck? But brilliant, absolutely brilliant, although impossible to find when one had a question or three, a living testimony to the efficacy of the stuff. Seemed to have no proprietary interest, how did she ever expect it to catch on without slick Q advertising, all that.

She realized: Hadntz had taken this herself.

The magic bullet?

She spent an hour schlepping funding sources about, set up the experiment, and green-lighted it for immediate initiation.

But—where in the world had this mysterious Dr. Hadntz come from? Why, wondered Megan, did she slip *me* this information? What was her background, where did she go to school?

And finally, Megan narrowed it down to her universal obsession: her parents.

Hours passed. During those hours, she came to a stunning conclusion.

Hadntz, her new scientist friend, was deeply connected, somehow, with the origins of Q.

Had she ever met Bette Elegante, or Sam Dance?

Brian

[*June 12*]

A FEW days after he'd taken the saxophone from the attic, Brian jumped from his double-parked truck and hustled into Reed & Case on C Street.

Bells jingled as the door closed behind him. S. J. Williamson looked up from behind his glass counter, where he was perched on a stool perusing a catalog. "Hey! It's the Sax Man."

The shop was full of used clarinets, saxophones, oboes, and a few shiny new instruments as well. Brian had come here with his dad when he was a kid a few times, and Sam would sit down with S.J. and talk about the times they'd seen the Prez, Bird, and, later, Trane. They'd talk about technique and about Sam's new infatuation, Paul Desmond, while Brian drifted around the tiny, crowded place, where shelves laden to the ceiling looked like they might pull the walls down on top of everything. He browsed music books, examined amps, picked up the fine gold-plated tenor sax that S.J. kept in the window and fingered its keys, which opened and closed in a marvel of sweet smoothness.

Brian had once aspired to be as good a sax player as his dad.

Or better. Good enough to satisfy his desire to use the saxophone as another voice, one that could say things that his speaking voice could not say. A voice that did not speak in nouns, verbs, and tenses, but which spoke in emotion—warm, cool, and everything in between.

Now, when he opened the refurbished case S.J. brought out from the back, the smells—plush new padding, a new leather lid for the reed and mouthpiece compartment, the smell of polish, wound into his brain and

brought back the days when he'd tried, and tried hard, to emulate Paul Desmond, when his dad kept busting him back to practicing scales, scales, scales, and working on his fingering, and transposing from one key to another.

He'd hated the hard work then, but now he hoped that at least a trace remained in his fingers and in his brain.

"Try it out," S.J. urged. His large, dark face, always topped by a fedora that seemed ancient in the early sixties, held his easy smile. "Go on."

Brian lifted it out. "The case looks new."

"A lot of it is. Nobody took care of it."

"It was in the attic for years." Brian lifted out the saxophone. "You took out some of the dents."

"The big ones, anyway. What'd you do, throw it off the Washington Monument?"

"It got banged around during the war, I think."

"Don't give me that crap—I've worked on this baby since the sixties, remember? Reed's new. I soaked it. So, go."

Brian coaxed a warm, mellow tone from the sax in his first try; rushed up and down a scale and had to redo the second scale he tried.

"All right! Sounds good, doesn't it?"

"Didn't know it would make such a difference. S.J., you're a genius."

"Tell my wife."

"What do I owe you?"

"After your deposit, another $72.48."

When he looked out the window, Brian saw that he was getting another parking ticket to add to the one he'd gotten last week. "What is it—do they just assign one officer to follow me around all day?"

"Good luck, son," said S.J. "Here—take this. I got the names of some cats who want to jam, if you need any. Little place on Fourteenth Street."

"Thanks, man." Brian grabbed the scrap of paper and

rushed out the door for another fruitless argument with a cop.

Cindy proved not to be a fan of his halting work. She disliked it even more than she disliked what he did on his electric guitar—squalling, squealing amped-up pieces that felt like epiphanies to him, and sounded like garbage to her. He didn't know where they came from.

At any rate, he had taken the saxophone to his trailer, and put it in the closet, next to his electric guitar, his amp, and his wah-wah pedal.

Now, in the wake of another visit from the Fire Marshal, he unfolded the flimsy closet door, removed the saxophone case, and opened it up.

He was the first to admit that he was no damned good, but that wasn't the point. The point was moving the fingers in a certain way, faster and faster, until the piece flowed on its own, until it poured out of the horn's broad bell like his own voice. The strange rhythms of bebop emerged from the deep places in his memory. Sometimes he wished that he was good enough to hang out with jazz players, to slide in and out of bluesy piano riffs, to take a solo and expand on a theme. So he practiced, but fitfully, because it seemed as if he didn't really have time to do it. His business kept him busy from dawn till dusk. Like exercise (what—waste time running when there were five job sites to visit?), eating sensibly (his truck floor, full of empty potato chip bags, candy bar wrappers, and soda cans, attested to his eating habits), and keeping his checkbook balanced (wasn't that what the accountant was for?), practicing was something that he had a hard time doing regularly. He was surprised at how well he remembered how to coax a good sound from the beast, and that he could still read music. Sometimes, as he drove around town, a melody would pop into his head and he'd make a voice memo. He stored them all for "later," the time when he would read the infinity of unread books he'd

bought, and watch all the good movies that had ever been made.

This time, he tried "Billie's Bounce," of which he had mastered perhaps eight bars, so there was a promising wilderness of improvement awaiting him. Mimicking the masters was a learning tool, no more, but he was still at the stage of imitation. Laying down pathways in his brain.

And one of them was a pathway to his father.

Not a literal pathway; just a memory path, something to enhance the richness of memories. Because when you got right down to it, what else was there? Megan had told him that everything you thought was reality was a memory, because it all happened earlier. Maybe only a fraction of a second earlier, but earlier nonetheless. And then, the sensory information piggybacked in on earlier-laid memories eliciting reactions that had worked in the past, putting things into familiar categories.

Megan had told him a lot about the biomechanics of how music affected the brain. One thing that was very obvious, she claimed, was that musicians used more of their brains than most people.

"Just think about it," she'd told him. "You're using your language centers—music is a language. You're thinking about intervals, the distance between the tones; you're thinking in a mathematical, spatial way. Musical tones stimulate your emotional centers as well, and, quite often, you are visualizing as you play."

"No wonder I'm not much good," Brian had said. "I haven't learned to use all those parts of my brain."

She'd laughed. "Just keep it up, old man. It's never too late."

Brian did worry about Zoe, despite, or perhaps because of, her musical gifts.

Zoe had perfect pitch. She'd been in a Montessori classroom since he was eighteen months old, but Brian was pretty sure that she would have had it anyway. She had a fascination with sounds when just a baby—the

screech of tires, the *ping!* of the microwave, the wail of a siren—and would imitate them, endlessly and irritatingly. Cindy, early on, surrounded her with many types of music, sang with her, and listened to her compose, precisely hitting only one or two keys at a time, sometimes hideous, sometimes lovely, pieces on the piano. Zoe was a certified violin prodigy; she'd progressed rapidly from scratchy Suzuki to a top private teacher. "As long as she enjoys it," was Cindy's credo.

Now, her music books were filled with dissonance. "Whens and Bitsy Argue." "What the Fenceposts Said," written as she ran a stick along an iron fence. "The Dishwasher, the Dogs, and the Rain" was rather nice, Brian recalled. But sometimes, as his daughter sat frowning, tongue sticking out, grabbing one marker after another to write her music, Brian thought that maybe it was more of an affliction than a pleasure. Once, Brian had made the mistake of asking why, since each color meant a precise note, she needed the lines of a staff.

Zoe just looked at him disdainfully. "Middle C or high C? Half notes, quarter notes? Time? I already ran out of colors. And then, who else could read it?"

"Of course," said Brian, realizing that he'd belittled the complexity of her work. "I'm sorry."

Was this furious attention to sound something she'd grow out of? Was it good, was it bad? Was it a sign of a problem? Megan said that synesthesia in and of itself didn't usually bother those that had it; it just meant that the synaptic connections in their brains were not fully pruned after the brain had dedicated their use to one or another sense. Some remained crosswired, causing people to think of tastes as sounds, or smells as shapes. "I often think," Megan said, "that maybe we could use this dramatic growth of brain cells that occurs in infants and toddlers later in life. After all, brain growth isn't finished until twenty-five or so, and we've only been living as long as we do now, in such numbers, for a relatively short period of time."

Brian soldiered on through his practice time, hoping his own brain was lighting up—it didn't feel like it—and thought about his father, searching for him in the heart of every note.

And suddenly—he loved this part, when it all came together like an uprush of cold wind at a mountaintop—he was, indeed, flying. He did not consciously think about how to play. He just played.

He played "Billie's Bounce" fast, slow, and in between. He made it sob, he made it laugh; he moved out into complete improvisation, a revel, a romp, a deepening of mind and heart.

It was not his father. It was him.

He played for an hour, neglecting work, not answering the phone, hardly knowing where or even when he was. He stopped only because the euphoria was beyond music.

He fell into his office chair, remembering, remembering, his mother, his father, his sisters. All of it.

Finally, when his phone rang, he did come back to earth. Cindy said, "Are you going to make it home for dinner?"

"Um—it's—seven? Wow. I think those new vitamins are really working. Tell you about it when I get home."

A few days later he got a Q from somebody on S.J.'s list, asking him to stop by the Gypsy Cat late Friday night around midnight to sit in.

At first he thought, *Don't be silly.* But Cindy urged him to go, although he suspected that she thought he might be so embarrassed by the experience that he would give it up. But accordingly, on Friday night after everybody else was sound asleep, he left home just before midnight and headed over to the place, which was on U Street.

He'd heard of it—a co-op, basically, in a Hungarian restaurant that rented its space on late weekend nights for extra cash. He paid ten bucks to a man dressed in a

suit and tie, and felt ragged in his jeans and T-shirt. But the guy was friendly enough, nodded at Brian's sax case and said, "Tear 'em up."

The bandstand was permanent, apparently. Three black women were performing: a flutist, about six feet tall and thin, dressed in African garb; a woman playing an odd sort of drum that Brian could not name; and a guitar player, a man, doing some kind of jump slack-key. Their music sounded both jazzy and Middle Eastern.

Brian found an empty table and a kid in an apron actually came by and took his order for a beer and *halászlé*, which turned out to be a spicy, dark soup filled with onions and rockfish, accompanied by good bread.

As time passed, the place filled up, and people were standing. The brick walls sweated, and faded travel posters of Buda and Pest and various ethnic foods were wavy inside their cheap frames. Smoking was apparently not verboten. The air was blue; he smelled some marijuana lingering in the air as well. He ordered another beer. Groups came and went, and finally what Brian thought of as a straight-ahead jazz streak got going, with drums, the hi-hat, and the piano. Brian became a bit more alert; perhaps he could inflict himself on the stage soon and get it over with.

A man came over and asked to share Brian's table. Behind him were his group, a man and a woman. "Sure," Brian said.

The man's fedora was tilted slightly so that it covered one eye. He sat back from the table so he could cross one long leg over another, and Brian was slightly relieved that he was not wearing plaid shorts, or long socks with garters, but plain khaki slacks. Also, he had no beard. He carried a felt drawstring bag that, when he set it on the table, draped over what looked like a cornet. At the same time, Brian noticed that some other men in the club also wore fedoras, in varying styles of pinched crowns and bent brims, so the sudden, paranoid

274 | KATHLEEN ANN GOONAN

thought that this was Megan's Walking Man almost made him laugh. In fact, he also saw a few flat-topped porkpies, and way too many black berets. His own head felt unstylishly naked.

The woman's dramatic black, curly hair, pulled back with a red scarf tied beneath one ear, contributed to her gypsy look, as befit the venue. Bright, gauzy fabric swirled around her, seemingly in motion even though she was sitting, and gold hoop earrings as large as dollars dangled from her ears. She'd ordered grapefruit juice and kept her face turned to the stage, so he saw only her profile. The man, who rested a violin case on his lap, was thin, weathered, tanned, and ancient seeming, with crow-black eyes and narrow lips. Not very tall. He downed glass after small, quick glass of grappa.

The man with the hat ordered Q-Town, a local ale. He and Brian smiled and nodded at each other, but any attempt at conversation was squelched by the music.

The Jay Street Band departed the stage to scattered polite applause; their timing was awful, and timing was everything in jazz. It might be time to head home. Slink home might be more accurate, yet he hadn't really heard anything that he wanted to help out with.

As if to an unseen signal, the other three people at Brian's table rose. Fedora Man looked over at Brian with a broad, open smile and said, "Come on, we could use a sax."

Brian hustled stageward. Stepping into the spotlight, he quickly assembled his sax, and Fedora Man and Violin Man fiddled with mikes. The woman sat down at the piano. No drummer, then. He hoped the woman would set a good rhythm.

"Body and Soul," said Fedora Man, and counted off the beats. Brian was in luck—Coleman Hawkins's version was grooved into his brain from early childhood.

The woman played an intro, and they played eight bars together, establishing the melody. Violin and cornet

began to weave around each other, and Brian added a phrase whenever one came into his head.

It was exhilarating—like what he imagined skydiving might be like. He had flown in small planes . . . hadn't Mom had a plane?

And then came a maelstrom of a bridge; call and response, moving into the key of F, then a few solos, the piano keeping a basslike beat, strong yet sinuous, with odd, jazzy chords reminiscent of Monk's occasional dissonances.

The violin solo was vivid yet smooth; quick phrasings and surprising twists in which Brian lost himself, recalling, indeed, flying in a small plane with his mother piloting, and then a larger plane—but no, that wasn't possible—then coming to when solid applause filled the room. Gypsy Violinist held bow downward with one hand and violin with the other, nodding his head briefly and stepping back.

The cornet solo was much different; haunting, aching, lost. Yet, oddly, the piano accompaniment provided an understatement of surety with a use of notes and rhythm that Brian knew; even as he heard it he would have to spend a week dissecting to ponder how the two could call up such disparate emotions. This was, for Brian, the heart of jazz, and his near-hallucinatory visions changed to a hundred small clubs, the frontier of a new art form, new sciences; huge crowds packed in to see Ellington, a burst of light—

A moment of piano vamp, a restless cough from the audience, while he realized it was his turn, and he was able to come in perfectly on the downbeat, just as if he'd planned it in his head. And as he played, he actually was thinking ahead, in full jazz sentences, phrases pulled out of his gut he didn't know he had, things his dad had shown him, fingerings he had forgotten—

The final, unison chorus brought thunderous applause, and Brian wiped sweat from his forehead with

the back of his hand, closed his eyes against the bright overhead lights for a long moment. Where had that come from? He felt changed—new—like he could go on playing forever—

But no. When he opened his eyes, a man was kneeling on the stage in front of him, removing an electric guitar from its case; a woman vocalist in a short, tight dress adjusted the height of the mike; behind him, a few exploratory splashes of cymbal.

He looked around. His compatriots were gone. He exited, stage left, knelt and returned his father's nickel-plated sax to its refurbished case, wiping it down, removing the mouthpiece, thinking, Shit, *maybe S.J. put some kind of magic into this thing* . . .

A man with slicked-down black hair, wearing a tight black vest over a black T-shirt came over. "Man, that was great. We've got our own jam session in Macon's basement every Thursday night. And Elroy's an old-timer. Come jam with us some time. Here's my card. We've even gotten a few paying gigs here and there."

"Thanks," mumbled Brian, and stuck the card into his reed compartment. The other band was doing "Begin the Beguine," Bossa nova–style, and the woman's cool tones were perfect, understated. They were good. As Brian walked out the door, they swung into some Afro-Cuban piece that followed him down the street to his truck.

He opened the cab door and set the sax inside, then noticed a ticket on his windshield. What the hell? He grabbed it and looked around, saw a metal sign reading: RESIDENTIAL PASS REQUIRED MIDNIGHT TO EIGHT A.M. Where had that sign been when he parked?

It had been over an hour since he finished his last beer. His head was crystal clear.

That was, perhaps, why he noticed that he felt . . . changed. Different. Renewed, recharged. He stuffed the ticket into the glove compartment with the others.

Onboard Breathalyzer test passed, he swung out of his space and trundled down empty streets, windows open,

night air cool, filled with the sounds of frogs and a whip-poor-will as he waited at a traffic light. Cindy had been in a rock band as a teenager. She'd be their drummer. Zoe, jazz violin; some of her pieces sounded jazzy already. She got it. Megan or Jim, piano. Jill—

He laughed. She'd love it. Jill could play trombone.

Megan and Abbie

ZOZO

[*June 20*]

MEGAN GOT off the bus and hurried up the hill. Jim had asked her to come home early. He had a suddenly-yesterday deadline and the babysitter couldn't make it. She had found herself looking up side streets from her bus window, trying to spot Walking Man.

When she let herself in the front door, she was puzzled. No one in the living room. No one in Abbie's room. She poked her head inside Jim's office. "Where is she?"

Jim nodded. "In your room. In the loft."

"But—"

"I put up the ladder. She's fine. She has a grip like a monkey. Close the door when you go out, please." Jim became very short when on deadline.

Megan went down the hall and heard Abbie chattering. She opened the door, thinking that Abbie must be talking to someone on the phone. But no, she was talking some kind of weird baby talk. "*Mareem? Ush gondo maybe.*"

Megan climbed the ladder and poked her head over the ledge's edge. Megan looked up and said, "*Arabwa— mama aqui.*"

"*Arabwa,*" said another child's voice.

"Who are you talking to?" asked Megan. "What is that?" She crawled into the loft and nestled next to Abbie.

"It's, ah, it's a new classbook."

"Oh. Did you get it at school?"

Abbie nodded.

"Turn it back on. I want to see it."

Abbie sighed and touched it.

Megan saw the back of a boy's head. He was black, and his head was close-shaven. She heard jungle birds and monkey calls and padding feet.

"What is this?"

"Shhh," said Abbie. *"En finate?"*

"Na," said a girl's voice. The screen's view moved dizzyingly, and Megan saw a girl's face. Her skin was very black, and her hair was braided in an intricate, beautiful pattern. She was sweating. *"Un garo."*

"What are you saying?" asked Megan.

"I asked her if they were safe and she said no."

"Safe from what?"

"Soldiers are following them."

As Megan watched, the scene veered wildly. The children appeared to be running.

Then the view turned into a map with a blinking red dot and a blinking yellow dot.

"Eh, vega abuente nin oest. Oest! Bey ingo! Now!"

The red dot veered left suddenly, then stopped. *"Oosha,"* whispered another voice. *"Oosh."*

There was no sound. The yellow dot bypassed the red dot, and after a few more minutes turned right.

"Abwe," said three voices at once.

"Thank be," said the girl whose screen it was.

"Welkum thee," said another child's voice.

"Who are you?" asked Megan.

There was no answer.

"She doesn't speak English, Mom."

"Then what?"

"I don't know. Kids' language. Zozo. We make it up."

"Where is that girl?"

Abbie touched the pad a few times and the view enlarged, showed a continent. "Africa," she said. "The Congo. It's really bad there. We help kids get away from soldiers and find food. It's really, really educational."

"I see. What else do you do?"

"When kids need help, like when parents are hitting them, we call police. There was a girl in New York City last week. Her dad locked her in a closet. We saw it all on her classbook. The police came and got her. Look, here's an SOS."

Megan's head reeled. "Have you seen any—really bad things?"

"Lots."

"I mean, like . . ." *Shootings. Sex.*

Abbie shook her head, still looking at the screen. "*Shanwee ib jump.* No. The screen won't let us. It goes blank. It won't show people hurting other people. I think that maybe that information is somewhere. But I'm too young to see it."

Megan was relieved. "How old do you have to be?"

"I don't know. Way old. When you're older, the *system* knows. Then you can see and do more."

"Can I use it?"

"Won't work for you."

"Why not?"

"You're old. The classbook can tell."

"How?"

"I don't know. But you can't even talk like us. Adults aren't allowed. They just want to fight with one another and boss kids around."

"I don't want to fight. I am your mother, though."

"You have your own places to go. Kids have this place. It's our own place."

Megan recalled Jill's garden. She'd planted it when she was ten. She studied a garden book from the library, in her typical Jillish way, and planted bachelor buttons and carnations and snapdragons. Jill would then take a book inside her private kingdom and lean against the tree trunk and read. Sometimes she would just think, or draw. Maddeningly, Jill would not let Megan or Brian inside, or even pay a bit of attention to them or their distracting antics as they tried to annoy her. It was as if she were

protected by an invisible curtain when she was in there. Sam and Bette enforced this. "She needs a private space," Bette said. "You can make your own if you want."

"I don't want my own," Megan said. "I want Jill's!" She hadn't understood her mother's smile, but she did now.

"Does Miss Ginny know?"

Abbie was silent for a moment, watching her screen. She did not raise her eyes as she spoke. "Miss Ginny told us not to use this part in school because she thinks it's distracting."

"Imagine that."

"Some kids said that their parents wanted it blocked, but other parents got mad and said their kids need it for emergencies. I think people have tried to block it but they can't." Her fingers whitened as she gripped her classbook. She all but curled herself into a ball around it, and glared at Megan.

"Listen honey, I need to take your classbook for now and ask some questions about it." Megan felt very predictable.

"No!" Abbie held it close to her chest. "We need it!"

"We?"

"All of us kids. We made it. It's ours!" She shouted at the screen. *Mommy quieras abro!*

The screen was instantly filled with the faces of angry children, of all colors, all kinds of interesting hair, bright and dull clothing, each in their own little window, and all of them were shouting, in their strange new language.

"What are they saying?" asked Megan, although she had a feeling she knew.

"They say . . . not to let you. They say . . . hide it from the grown-ups." She looked up at Megan, tears in her eyes, and Megan knew she was in for a righteous-passion meltdown, level ten. "I was! You came home early!"

Nevertheless, Megan pried it, as gently as possible, finger by tight finger, from Abbie's hands. "Your father and I will talk about this and decide if it's safe for you."

THIS SHARED DREAM | 281

Abbie burst into loud wails and slid down the ladder, releasing her feet so that she bumped against every rung.

"And don't bother your father now!" Megan yelled, as Abbie slammed the door behind her. Megan sighed, climbed down, and went to grab her before she could bother Jim.

Jill

FUGUE

[July 1]

A FEW days before her party, Jill was in her office at the Bank. So far, she kept telling herself, she'd been doing just fine being back at work. Her colleagues were looking forward to her party, curious, of course, about her house. No one but her boss and good friend, Don Robertos, knew about her St. Elizabeth's sojourn, and it seemed he had not told anyone, because there had been no sidelong glances or any change in manner among her fellows—except, perhaps, a wee bit of jealous surprise that she now had her own office, complete with a window and a door, thanks to her doctorate. That was a part of the deal she'd made a while back.

She was only a few blocks away from Serendipity Books, so it was easy for her to take evening shifts, if necessary, and Elmore had no problem with picking up Whens from school on those days.

Six floors below, outside of Jill's unopenable window, a summer morning in Washington slid into afternoon. Busses, cars, and cabs rolled down Pennsylvania Avenue, and pedestrians thronged the street.

Jill tried to concentrate on reading a report on riots in Nairobi. They were worsening.

One school, an earlier project, not one of the new domes, was now occupied by militants. Anyone who could, escaped out the windows, even from the second

floor. All the girls that couldn't get away were raped; all the boys were marched off to join the insurgents.

She was reading the report for the third time because it seemed that when she read it the first two times the words just beaded up like raindrops on a windshield. They didn't penetrate her mind. Where she wanted to see "Reading scores up" and "Fifty percent of graduates find jobs," she saw *rape, murder,* and, even though the words weren't actually there, *propaganda* and *religious ideology.* She saw *Us* and *Them,* words she wanted to see used in less extreme ways.

She closed the screen, picked up her purse, and stepped out of her office into a large room filled with corrals, locking her door behind her.

Bill Anderson—someone who she would just as soon not talk to right now—showed up instantly, meticulously dressed, as usual. She never saw him with rolled-up shirtsleeves, much less scuffed shoes. His ties were beautifully coordinated, and his haircut probably cost him fifty bucks every ten days. He stood in front of her, looked past her, looked at the floor, and finally came out with, "How about lunch?"

She smiled, she hoped. At least, she made her mouth into an approximation of one, and said, "Not today." Everyone knew about her separation and pending divorce, and she knew that he was working himself up to asking her for a date. For some reason he made her uneasy. He liked to stand in her doorway and talk about Germany, which was his specialty. Hers too, but he once or twice dropped in seemingly casual questions about her mother and father. He was not very good at it. Why would he want to know about Sam and Bette? He tried to cover it up by talking about his own parents, and he was clumsy about that too, insisting on some storybook tale of immigrants from Germany in the 1700s farming and living in nice little farmhouses in Pennsylvania. Of course, tens of thousands of people had done just that, but he made it sound like something he'd learned from read-

ing children's primers from the 1950s. She wished she could have uninvited him to the party, but she could hardly have left him out.

That was just a small niggle, left behind as she headed toward the elevator. The real problem was that she felt stiff inside a straightjacket of ineffectiveness. The World Bank was not supposed to distribute classbooks, a powerful learning tool, proscribed by international law from containing "propaganda." Some people believed that language itself was propaganda, that words, inflections, idioms, all contained cultural biases of which the user was often unconscious. Fair enough. But words were all they had, right now, to combat images of violence in video games, in movies, in real life—images that Megan claimed activated something called mirror neurons, which caused people to imitate one another.

Her International Schools Project was garnering kudos from thousands of sources. She ought to be very happy about that, Don had told her just this morning.

Wasn't she?

Jill slid down from the sixth floor of the World Bank in the elevator, which was sleek and like The Future, like the ideas of The Future she'd absorbed in the fifties, and moved into a different state of mind.

Exiting the air-cooled building, she smiled at the security guy who greeted her each morning and biometriced her in.

She paused in the doorway, hot already, but cooled by bursts of cold air as people went in and out of the building, at a loss. What should she do now? She certainly wasn't hungry.

Cars poured down Pennsylvania Avenue when the light changed. A bus stopped in front of her; the doors accordioned open.

For an instant she almost jumped on. It was a number ten bus; she used to know the routes of all the busses, although they surely had changed since she rode

them everywhere as a child. Streets of small, decades-old shops—drugstores, grocery stores, restaurants—opened in her mind like scenes on a splayed fan: the bus could take her there, there, or there. As she mused, the bus pulled away, the fan closed.

Crossing Pennsylvania Avenue, she quickly entered a neighborhood of town houses. She hiked uphill, angling up the small blocks until she came out on Connecticut Avenue north of Dupont Circle.

The maples lining the sidewalk were quiet, alien creatures in the loud city, and yet, she mused, they would be here, and they would multiply, when the city was gone. It was strange to think of the city being gone, but of course, eventually, it would be. Plants had plenty of time to wait.

Everywhere she looked she saw people—not dense, but quite present, walking in the dappled sunlight beneath trees, each of them made of an uncountable number of cells, each cell capable of generating humans; each one of them constantly, waking or sleeping, generating stories, universes, everywhere, everywhere. . . .

She realized, distantly, that she was in a fugue state, like the one that had put her in the hospital, but didn't care. This one was deeply pleasant. She just walked, and walked, among the alien trees and infinite-celled people, and didn't notice the art store until she was right next to it.

The window was full of completely seductive objects that she had to have. Blank notebooks in many formats, including landscape-sized. Banks of brilliant markers. Easels. Brushes. Watercolors, oils, pastels. Fine paper, in all varieties and weights and tooth.

Though it had been years since she'd done anything in an artistic vein, she felt the thrill of a siren's call. Painting Woman had been asleep for a long, long time.

Asleep since her mother had disappeared. Asleep since Dallas, and having nightmares of debilitating guilt.

Jill gazed at the window display, and let Painting Woman awaken, stretch, and take a deep breath. She was voracious with memory, eager for the delicious joy of drawing, painting, representing. Her hands fairly ached to move, to draw all that she saw—in hopes of what? Interpreting? Remembering? Laying down a record that said to those who followed *This this! is what it was, when it was everything, and everything was magnified; intense, demanding*.

She had used pencils, first, and green Morilla Clipper Ship sketchbooks, to bring Gypsy Myra to life. Before that, she had sketched for years, simplified her lines, studied the classics from Harriman to Kelly, acceded when images called her to record them: Megan, asleep on the couch on a summer afternoon; the polished dining room table holding a vase; the intricate frills and leaf veins of a partially shaded rose.

When Underground comix first came out she felt curiously not a part of it. All of the artists were males. They were all males writing about, and drawing, sex. Because her characters were hard-edged and original and wanted to save the world like all good counterculture kids did, she was accepted, but it was kind of as an honorary male, and she was quickly famous—at least in that small, but national, community.

The panels: shorthand. Swiftly drawn lines made emotions clear without the need for fancy verbal descriptions. The character's background, weaknesses, foibles, were constantly expressed, as if each panel came straight from the center of the story, rather than building with the linearity of a novel. It was a new language.

But it was a scary language. Right now, even the thought of speaking it again brought back all that pain, doubt, suffering, depression, the heavy responsibility, everything that had spiraled outward from Gypsy Myra and had led her to Dallas.

Jill, not Painting Woman, pushed open the door and

walked into its cool, waiting realm. Maybe she had learned something in St. E's after all. How to surrender; the importance and power of being oneself, not many.

She roved up and down the aisles in a time-free interlude of gathering in this land of milk and honey. Unlike in her younger days, she could now afford anything—the finest watercolors, the best paper, expensive brushes analogous to a Stradivarius; pastels and oil crayons to point things up. Good tools that would faithfully reflect her thoughts. The cashier's face registered astonishment as she rang up the bill, and a young man helped her carry everything out to a taxi.

The taxi stopped at her mansion of flowers and wicker chairs and Zen poems, of Bette's school and cool stone grotto by the creek coupled with Sam's cool jazz, of Megan and Brian running up and down stairs, letting screen doors slam, of her father loosening his tie as he strode in the door after work and flinging it on the polished cherry table in the foyer and finding Bette, wherever she was, grabbing her around the waist, and kissing her deep and hard, every single afternoon, exclaiming "Doll *baby*!" Yes, the house was alive again.

It took Jill a while to carry everything upstairs to her old room. Then, she passed out in her old bed wearing all her clothes, including her shoes, while delicious, overwhelming, color infused her with paradise, complete.

The honking horn of Whens' school van woke her an hour later.

She was disoriented for a moment, but that didn't stop her from running down the stairs, opening the front door, and waving to the driver.

The evening passed pleasantly, with Whens so obedient and charming that Jill would have suspected something had he been older. After a perfunctory fuss at bedtime, he was soon asleep. Jill was at his side, falling in the space between waking and sleeping into the replenishing nourishment of Beauty.

* * *

Jill awoke to full, lucid, refreshed consciousness.

The only problem was that it was three o'clock in the morning. Crap.

She wondered if a sound had awakened her, someone trying to break into the house. But Manfred was lying on the floor, peacefully asleep. She eased out of bed, careful not to disturb Whens.

Manfred, instantly awake, followed Jill.

As she prowled the house, Jill wasn't sure what to do if she found someone there. Maybe Brian was right. Maybe she was just nervous about being here alone.

But finally, she declared to herself that everything was clear. She was just having a case of her regular old insomnia.

Then she realized that it was more than that. It was work time.

This had always been Painting Woman's favorite time to work. Somehow, in this dark no-time, while stars spiraled overhead, it was easier to access the interstices, to investigate strangeness, to lay down lines of words or pictures, to create these messages from the present to some future.

She made herself a pot of oolong tea and took it up to her old room. The evidence of rough and smooth paper riffling through her fingers convinced her she was awake. Choosing a sheet of medium-slick paper, the paper on which she had pen-and-inked her Madwoman of Time comic, she wondered: Was another installation coming on?

She smiled, recalling Elmore in those days, then frowned. Elmore couldn't even remember them. Denied them, and therefore, that they had ever fallen in love, caught up in the heady times and their shared commitment to social justice.

As she rummaged in the small top drawer for a clean nib, inserted it into the nib-holder, and opened a jar of India ink, she finally felt the ache of loss that the therapist had told her would come at some point. But it was

not just that he'd forgotten their shared past—in this world, he simply hadn't shared it. Maybe she was silly to think that this made him much poorer in spirit than the Elmore she'd known before. She missed him so! Lavender Lady had no right to him!

She laughed at her thought, then broke into sobs and hugged herself; staggered around and leaned against the doorway until it passed.

Then she hurried down the hall, through ghosts of three kids, and her dad shaving before work as the radio sang "Citizen's Bank of Maryland conveniently yours," and yanked the bathroom's chain light. As large as a suburban bedroom, tiled with tiny black-and-white hexagons, it held the old easy chair where Bette had leaned forward as she watched her kids splash in the slipper tub, next to the tall window admitting the drone of cicadas, and Sam's moonlight-drenched garden.

When Jill opened the faucet to splash cold water on her face, the pipes shuddered and moaned. She rubbed her face dry and was ready: but for what? Not Gypsy Myra.

But once she was back in her room, it became immediately clear. Painting Woman had awakened. Jill's walkabout the previous afternoon had been Painting Woman's yawn, stretch, and coffee interlude, and then she had stocked up with the breakfast and vitamin infusion of materials.

She was, of course, not a separate entity within Jill. But she was a part of Jill's persona that she had buried. Doing art—penning the Gypsy Myra comics—had led to the complete disintegration of her world, literally. No wonder she had stopped paying attention to Painting Woman's urges and demands.

Maybe, Jill speculated, she was stronger now, able to bear and allow Painting Woman her rightful place in the physical world, her own means of expression, because of her breakdown. Yes, that sounded like suitable therapy-speak. At any rate, she had tried ignoring her, using the

time-honored method of Getting on with Her Life. That had been ever so successful. Allowing felt much, much better.

Jill moved pots of dead plants from her weathered oak painting table, sent the remaining dry leaves flying with an old T-shirt, and eagerly unpacked her bags of loot.

Dr. Ph. Martin's colorfast dyes, in eyedropper bottles, with seductive names like Gamboge and Rose Madder. Fifteen tubes of Dutch watercolors. Ten fine brushes of Kolinsky sable—rounds, filberts, flats, in many sizes.

Painting Woman had never registered hunger or drop-dead exhaustion. She always ignored them, and always ignored Megan and Brian frolicking around her, or her mother, trying to get her to come down to dinner or go to sleep.

She radiated ideas—mostly images, but sometimes narrative as well. Generally, Painting Woman didn't much care what Jill did with her radiations—sell them, give them away, or toss them in a corner. She was just adamant about the need to record them. Jill imagined poets felt the same imperative urge regarding their poetry, and writers about their stories.

This night, in the old house, in her old room, as creek frogs sang and warm, damp air suffused the paper, was one of those times. She even imagined the comforting, faint scent of Bette's cigarette, wafting up from the grotto by the creek that Sam had built for her. Bette had been an insomniac too.

Jill rummaged in the large junk drawer, found some masking tape, and taped down the edges of a sheet of watercolor paper. Theoretically, you were supposed to soak the paper in water and tape it to a board, and when it dried, it would remain flat and smooth. But Painting Woman was in a big rush, damn her. She was often wasteful. Not only that, she thought everything she suggested was perfect. Jill, on the other hand, had a moment's anxiety about using such expensive paper for something unplanned, something that might turn out

badly. But using expensive paper was always anxiety producing, whether or not she had something planned.

Jill took a moment to rummage for a water container and found an old enamel pot. Walking to the bathroom, she held Painting Woman at bay, rather like an air traffic controller telling a plane that it had to circle the airport, while Painting Woman yelled over the radio that the passengers were becoming so restless that they just might go to another airport.

It was all marvelously familiar, despite the gap of many years, and a sidestep to another world.

Jill filled the pot with water. She did need water in order to paint, she reminded Painting Woman. She couldn't be expected to have everything ready all the time.

She switched on a small art nouveau lamp that Megan had found at a yard sale that featured rows of tiny green fish within parallel copper boundaries, and poured herself a finger of Oban Scotch from an old, dusty bottle she'd hidden from her parents ages ago.

Painting Woman always wore a long dress. Jill wore raggedy shorts and a white T-shirt, perfect for wiping her brushes. She sipped the fine Scotch.

She hated to be bossed around.

Finally, she snapped, "Okay! Okay!"

She considered the blank paper.

It was an odd weight, two-hundred pound, but handmade and cold-pressed. It had a pleasing, wavy deckle edge and was off-white, rather creamy.

A pencil was required; a sketch. All these expensive supplies, and she needed a pencil! The junk drawer had one that was from Hart's Ice Factory on U Street. Teeth marks broke the white paint. A dog's? A child's?

Its line was too hard and faint. Her old pencils were here somewhere, real pencils, from 9H to 9B. Finally, she spotted them, splayed in an old jelly jar on top of her dresser.

The picture took form.

The process was not much different from the comics

she had created. She saw something in her mind and drew it. It was not that she couldn't do the elementary things that most artists did; she had taken life classes, she had set up still-life tableaus, she had painted portraits of both Brian and Megan when they were ten and twelve, and they had laughed at them quite cruelly. Jill wondered, as she drew, if the portraits were in the attic, or if they had, as threatened, used the sturdy canvases as sleds the following winter.

There was a headless statue in the foreground. Greece? A tree in front of a wall; the rear of a garden.

The garden contained chairs and tables. Soon, it contained a bar, in the background, with a roof. She determined a vanishing point, got a ruler from the drawer, and redrew.

Those were the sketchy parts, the background for the main subjects. A woman and a man, embracing.

Red, wrote Jill on the woman's dress.

And finally, with a mixture of dread and love, she sketched out their heads.

It was clear that the woman's hair was blond, and, although Jill could only see the back of her head, she was Jill's mother.

The man rested his head on top of Bette's head, lightly, and of course, he was Sam; the weathered, sad Sam of the 1970s. But in this instant, his features were illuminated with joy. His eyes were closed, and a slight smile played across his lips. His arms held Bette tightly, crushing her dress in radiating shadows.

The flowering tree had a scent, *linden,* but Jill could not paint that. It was night; and a full moon illuminated the garden, and a light from somewhere—perhaps a house window—brightened a skewed rectangle of Bette's dress. The brass rail of the bar had a dull glint; the shadows of the linden branches required Jill's smallest brush. A wash of gold was too strong; she blotted it out with a paper towel, leaving a pale, almost white, yellow, which she glazed with the suggestion of bricks in moonlight.

It was about four in the morning when she realized that the painting was done.

The *Biergarten*. Was Painting Woman trying to tell her something? If so, she would have to shout much louder. Jill knew all about the *Biergarten*.

She rinsed her brushes and set them bristle-up in a glass to dry. She carried the old enamel pot downstairs to the porch and tossed paint-tinted water into the backyard, washed the white plate she had used as a palette and set it in the dish drainer, returned to her room and made sure each tube of paint was tightly capped and returned to its assigned space in her toolbox, untaped the painting, and thought she was done.

But no.

Painting Woman was only warming up.

Cicadas whirred their slow calypso of sound, ceaseless and yet varying, comforting waves of intensities and lulls. A drawing took form in a large-format sketchbook.

The Madwoman of Time.

She still wasn't sure what had happened. She had pressed her father about it again and again, but he just wouldn't talk about what had happened, about the day of the Kent State Massacre when she had hitchhiked into time to try and prevent Kennedy's assassination, based on the blueprint poured into her mind by the Madwoman of Time.

Jill sketched her quickly.

She had a strong face, a large, straight nose, large, dark eyes, a wide mouth, and long, dark, curly hair.

When she'd picked Jill up outside Slapdown, Arkansas, she'd been wearing jeans—faded Levi's 501s, actually—a light cotton, red plaid shortsleeved shirt, and scarred black pointed-toe boots. Her hair was tied back with a red bandana, and she drove a white F100 pickup truck that rattled something terrible. She'd pulled up next to Jill on the hot, narrow road that seemed to stretch to infinity, leaned over, flung open the door, and said, "Get in."

* * *

"Want a beer?"

Jill looked over and saw that the woman had a bottle of beer clamped between her thighs. She shifted into high gear with eye-blurring speed. Eighty-mile-an-hour wind roared past the open wing windows, and they had to shout to be heard. The woman took a long gulp of beer and thrust it toward Jill.

"No, thanks."

"Got some on ice in the back."

"Uh . . . Want me to drive?"

The woman threw back her head and laughed. "Not quite yet, sister. Now, just look around and tell me what the hell there is to run into out here."

"Telephone poles."

"Aaach. What's your name?"

"Jill."

"That's a pretty name."

"Thanks."

"How far you going?"

"Dallas."

The woman nodded, and a strange look came into her eyes. Her voice changed in a subtle way. She was more serious. And she sounded far from drunk. "Aren't you a little young to be hitchhiking? You should go back home."

"I know who you are." The realization was sudden, but Jill knew that she was right.

"And who is that?"

"Gypsy Myra." Jill turned and leaned her back against the truck's door, laid her arm along the back of the truck's bench seat that they shared. "I created a comic book about you. But there's something beneath that."

Jill thought she blinked away tears, but couldn't be sure. "And what might that be?"

"You tell me." Working with a bunch of radicals, yelling at protests, arguing political points, and being thrown in jail multiple times had honed Jill's naturally assertive nature.

"I can't."

"Of course you can. It has something to do with the Game Board, right?"

"The Game Board?"

"The Infinite Game Board. That's what we call it. Brian and Megan and I."

The woman nodded, as if satisfied. "I do know where you are going, Jill, and I knew where to find you. But you do not have to do this."

"I need to save Kennedy. Once he is assassinated—"

"History will take a different turn, to be sure. The history that you will be in."

"What do you mean by that?"

"There are an infinite number of histories, Jill. And I am beginning to believe that when you average them all out, none of them is any better or worse than the other. Each has their share of happiness, misery, prosperity, poverty, inhumanity."

"But it's all local," said Jill. "I've heard this before."

"You have?"

"Not about an infinite amount of histories, no. But you have to work with what's around you. Change that. It's hard work. But once you change things, there's a ripple effect. You go into a poor neighborhood, start with the little kids. Maria Montessori went into Rome's poorest neighborhood. All the kids were little hoodlums, defacing property, dirty, no manners. And just by thinking scientifically about how humans learn and by developing targeted materials that isolated each step to be mastered, she helped them learn to read in just months. Four-year-old Italian children whose parents probably didn't know how to read. And now my own mother has a Montessori school in the United States. It's spreading. That's what I'm talking about. You need a seed amount of people who have an idea of what to do."

"This is just amazing."

"What is?"

"That you've turned out this way."

"What do you mean by that?"

"I know your parents. But I've never met you. It's just amazing that you have thought about these things at your age."

Jill was surprised. "But that's all we talk about, my friends and I. How to make things better. How to change the world."

As she drew these frames, fifteen years later, it all came back. The background was jumpy, like Krazy Kat's Coconino County. And drawing helped her remember what Myra said next: that her name was not Myra.

It was Eliani Hadntz.

Jill bent from side to side to uncrick her back. The sky was growing light; she'd been sitting on her stool for hours. Making words come out of the character's mouths in little balloons. My Othertime Trip to Dallas. In front of her was a pen-and-ink drawing of Hadntz in the truck, complete with red bandana, as if Jill had sketched it while leaning back against the passenger door as wind riffled the paper, washed here and there with color. She looked around her table. As she worked, she had, without paying much attention, spread all her watercolor supplies around once again. It looked as if a tornado had struck.

Jill forced herself to look at the pictures, the narrative, that had emerged. It took up most of the sketchbook. Her heart was pounding hard, as if she had just awakened from a nightmare. She hadn't consciously remembered these details. Maybe this was what it was like to be hypnotized—one suddenly recalled things that the conscious mind had forgotten. Or hidden from itself. Or—hadn't the therapist mentioned post-traumatic stress syndrome? She didn't know if this was what had really happened.

But it felt true.

And now, with a desire that almost made her sick in body and in mind, she wanted the Infinite Game Board back. But she'd left it in Dallas.

She wanted it just as much, if not more than, the joker who had called her, demanding it, or the Device, back.

Whoever the hell he was.

When It Landed
[*July 4*]

NOBODY WAS home when the school began to grow, way, way back on the huge acreage that even Sam had not been able to thoroughly tame.

Bette had placed the seed she'd received at her PO box at the far reaches of the property within a dense screen of oaks and kudzu. The tiny meadow was frequented by urban fox and deer, as well as the occasional neighbor kid. Nobody could see it because there were trees all around it.

Whens reached the embryonic school several days later, by a narrow path about a hundred feet long, lined, his mother often warned him, by poison ivy, though she constantly sprayed and pulled and mowed. She was terribly allergic to it. She often threatened to plow it under, pave it over. Whens seemed immune, and liked to go down to the meadow to think, lying on his back inside the circle of giant oak trees, in a round place of tall grass flattened by a deer. The creek burbled nearby, and the leaves and grasses made whispery sounds in the breeze.

But this time, after dragging his shirt free from blackberry thorns, he rounded a bend in the path and almost stumbled into the school.

He stared at it, wonderstruck. The walls were shimmering and translucent, and it looked like half of a big strange ball. A half-sphere, he thought, a . . . *hemisphere,* a word he'd learned in school. He knew at once that he would not tell his mother about it. She got so worried

about every little thing. And this, he had to admit, was a rather big thing. He would swear Bitsy and Zoe and Abbie to secrecy—with blood, if possible. Sitting cross-legged during the afternoon, he watched the thin skin thicken while Manfred lay panting next to him. It had a round door and a little tunnel that led into the main dome. Kind of like an igloo, maybe.

He heard his mother yell, in her cross voice, "Whens! Time for dinner! Where are you? What did I tell you about—"

He jumped up instantly and ran out onto the lawn behind the house. "I'm right here."

"You weren't back in all that poison ivy, were you? You're probably covered with ticks."

He ran up the steps. "What's for dinner?"

Later on that night, Bette descended her secret stairway, stretched, lit a cigarette, and headed down into the woods to examine the thing she'd seen from her garret window. It was small, but recognizable, a three-dimensional realization of the plans for the Q-School she had sent to Hadntz.

My God, she thought. *It really worked.*

Jill's Party
[July 6]

JILL'S PARTY began when a few neighbors poked their heads in the front door and asked if they could help, and when Jill said no, helped anyway.

Emmie from across the street filled an old copper tub in the kitchen corner with pop bottles and her husband poured bags of ice on top. Brian tapped the beer ponies and started one of their dad's reel-to-reel tapes; this one was titled "1939/4." Cindy pushed Jill out the kitchen door and told her to get ready.

Jill took a shower in the third-floor bathroom, letting

cold water sluice luxuriously through her hair, washing away the sweat of the day. Someone had cleaned out the tub, which was nice. Megan, probably. Her missing shampoo was here too.

The temperature was pushing ninety, but downstairs an array of fans alleviated the heat. A huge industrial-strength fan in the second floor ceiling pulled in cool evening air through wide-open windows. The house had no air-conditioning; it had been designed, with thick plaster walls, high ceilings, and cross-ventilation to remain almost comfortable on even the most sultry of Washington summer days.

She pulled the shower curtain aside and stepped out of the claw-footed tub onto the cool mosaic floor and peered out the window into the backyard. About fifteen out-of-control children chased a ball. Good. Wear them out. Whens was screaming loudest.

Whens was such a funny little boy. A few days ago she'd found the picture of Sam and Bette that she'd painted propped next to his bed.

"Why did you take it?" she had asked.

He looked worried. "Is it okay?"

"Of course, sweetie. I'm glad you like it. I was just wondering why."

"The lady is very pretty," he had said, and smiled.

Grabbing a towel, Jill walked down to the second floor, rubbing her hair. In the dressing room, she donned the white silk pants she had planned to wear and discovered that they were too big. She looked in the mirror, dismayed. The waistband hung on her hips. Well, she hadn't been very hungry lately.

She pushed hangers aside and came to a chic, simple dress that had belonged to her mother. She recalled seeing Bette wear it, along with a pillbox hat. It was a rather Mondrian dress, bisected with heavy black lines which contained hot pink, the color of the spring azaleas in the side yard, bright yellow, and a strong, Greek-sea blue. Might as well try it.

Cindy opened the door just as Jill, with some difficulty, finished zipping it up.

"Ooh, la la!"

"Does it look all right?"

Cindy tilted her head and put one finger next to her mouth. "Madam, it could go from an embassy party to a PTA meeting with only a few changes. Let me show you a new silk scarf that *just* came in that would accessorize it perfectly—"

"Oh, shut up."

"It looks great. Comb your hair and get on downstairs. Guests are arriving. And," she said, glancing at Jill's bare feet, "I know what you're thinking, but no running shoes. I'm serious."

Jill sighed and pointed at a pair of flat shoes that resembled ballet slippers.

"God, no. These." Cindy picked up a pair of white, very high heels, and handed them to her. "Got any pearls?" She ducked when Jill threw one of the shoes at her, and ran down the hall laughing.

When Jill got downstairs, Cindy shoved a glass of ice water into her hand and told her that absolutely the only thing she had to do was walk around and chat. Jill gulped the water on her way to the buffet and poured Scotch over the ice. She examined the bottle, intrigued. She'd never heard of Teacher's.

Everyone raved about Jill's dress, her upswept hair, the magnificent house, and the extraordinary mixture of guests. The house was full of people, and they overflowed onto the porch and into the yard.

By now, the children had been rounded up by their team of two seasoned, negotiation-proof babysitters and were somewhere upstairs, for once not the loudest contingent in the house.

She spent an hour circulating and sat down at a table in a dark corner of the screened-in porch with a glass of dark ale, watching the crowd.

One couple danced to a Benny Goodman tune. Others took advantage of being semi-outdoors to smoke. Most everyone had a glass in their hand. A man in a far corner of the porch, clean-shaven, sat in a wicker chair smoking, a glass of whiskey perched on the arm of a chair, reading a book and nodding along with Glenn Miller. The top of his head had a bald spot.

Something about him seemed familiar. In fact, he put her in mind of Wink, her father's old friend. Excited, she made to stand up and get closer. The lights blinked off, right then, and just as everyone groaned, came back on.

But the lights were dim and few, now, and a British RAF officer sat across the table from her, looking haggard, though he smiled broadly at her. Dark varnish, marred by a veritable collage of carved graffiti, covered the heavy, ancient, table on which their pint glasses sat, both well below the pint line. At the ornate bar across the room about fifteen people, in forties-style dress or military uniforms, perched on tall chairs or stood with one foot on the brass rail. The same couple still danced; the tom-toms of "Sing, Sing, Sing" beat in insistent pulse; the place smelled of centuries of spilled beer.

The same Wink-like man sat in the corner, this time perched on a barstool, wearing some kind of Army hat. A blond WAC, her back to Jill, spoke and gestured to him with urgent intensity. He responded now and then. Finally she bowed her head as if thinking, looked up again, nodded, and turned to leave the pub.

Jill was going to follow her when she heard the ominous buzz of a V-1 rocket, one of thousands of winged bombs launched from skids on the Continent. They had been falling for months.

All conversation stopped as the distinctive reverberations of hell's own power mower, augmented a hundredfold, roared overhead and went suddenly silent. The fuel had cut off; a full ton of explosives was falling. Somewhere nearby. Or directly overhead.

No one spoke for thirty seconds, but the RAF officer

looked into her eyes as what might be the last few seconds of their lives passed. An explosion sounded; pictures on the wall shook. The officer smiled. "Newcastle, I was saying. But if you . . ."

Someone pried her fingers from the glass of ale. Cindy was bending over her. "Yo. Jill. Coffee break."

"Iced, I hope," she managed to say.

Cindy pulled up a chair and sat next to her. "You okay?"

"I don't know. Am I?"

"You had a strange look on your face. How many fingers am I holding up?"

"None. I'm fine."

Cindy patted her on the shoulder. "People have been asking about you."

Jill gulped coffee and stood up. "Nobody said this would be easy. Thanks, Cindy."

The man in the corner, the RAF officer, the blond WAC, and the entire 1940s scene had vanished.

She recalled that her father had been in many such pubs during the Blitz, and it was always the same: The buzz overhead, then complete silence in the pub the instant gas flow to the engine stopped, and everyone waited for death to come or pass overhead. And then it landed. Somewhere else. The explosion sometimes rocked the room, in which case plaster might rain into the ale, or it might land a few blocks off, muffled but still clear. But unless it was a direct hit and set everything ablaze, the patrons instantly resumed their conversations, not discussing the by-now-routine fact that death had skipped them once again.

Well. She would take a cue from that behavior. This was another good thing for a former resident of the loony bin not to mention to anyone. Perhaps a few molecules of the Game Board lingered here on the side porch, where the whole family had once played an epic game on it with Wink, and the Game Board had taken them for a ride in a very unusual airplane.

302 | KATHLEEN ANN GOONAN

She took a deep breath and drained her coffee cup.

She went out and chatted with a few people from Georgetown about her dissertation, which concentrated on postwar Russia.

Bette had closely observed the party preparations from her perch, and through her listening devices. She'd watched as U Street Liquors pushed dollies holding ponies of various beers and cases of wines up the sidewalk and local groceries delivered foodstuffs.

Her own nexus-sensing cues, some kind of new sense developed by proximity to the Device for so many years, gathered, like ozone before a thunderstorm, clear as lightning on a ridgetop or black clouds roiling overhead. But for the life of her she still couldn't pin it down to sounds, like Sam and Wink, or with the seemingly deliberate poise of Hadntz, who seemed to Bette to just walk down a hallway of time, turn a particular doorknob, and pass from one timestream to another.

Instead, it invaded her being like the aura of a migraine zigzagged across vision, like a snake poised to strike, unavoidable, on the rocky path before her. Something was going to change.

While guests arrived downstairs, Bette readied herself. She donned the clothing in which she'd arrived—her WAC uniform, and prepared for the worst with passports, the currency of many countries, cigarettes for herself and for bribes, as well as jewelry.

As the line of inevitable storm clouds cleared the ridgetop, as a series of dots floated across her vision, as the rattlesnake's head descended, she ran down the back stairs.

She slipped into the nexus through the kitchen door, where dozens of people crushed around the table and leaned against the countertops. She heard Benny Goodman's "Sing, Sing, Sing" issue from the screened-in porch, past the dining room, and made her way to the

open French doors, where Wink sat, waiting. No surprise. Just relief. Information at last.

She glimpsed Jill way down the porch, and turned her back to her, tears welling in her eyes. "Where's Sam?"

She felt a crushing weight on her chest when Wink replied, helpless pain in his eyes, "I don't know."

The tears welled over. She turned on her heel, slipped out the screen door, and stumbled blindly downhill to the grotto and curled up on the bench Sam had built for her. Mercifully, no one else was there, and her sobs were drowned by the rush of fast water over stones, and by music.

She jumped at a hand on her shoulder.

Megan was impressed by Jill's party, despite herself. She wouldn't have believed that the place could be brought up to speed so quickly, and decided that Jill really could work wonders—with a lot of help from Cindy and Brian—and felt a twinge of guilt that she'd been too busy to lend a hand. Jill seemed to have come through what could only be called a breakdown with flying colors.

She overheard a tall, bearded blond man who wore shorts, loafers, and talked past a pipe held between his teeth. "It is just a marvelous example of sixties lines. I mean, the color, the shape, everything!" Megan peered over his shoulder. He held the teal Bakelite ashtray Bette had kept next to her reading chair, a bit marred and melted from extreme wear. He caressed it with reverence and set it back down very carefully.

Megan rolled her eyes and moved on.

She glimpsed Jill, who was trying desperately not to be too busy. This meant a lot of glancing around and strange facial expressions as she suppressed her impulse to get someone a drink or direct them to food, all of which the caterers, Cindy, and several of Brian's multipurpose workers, adept at throwing impressive cocktail

parties for the heads of corporations, were doing without breaking a sweat.

The big house throbbed with conversation, and cooler air wafted up from the creek. Megan went out to her car and fetched a sweater. She turned to go back in and saw Halcyon House as it was meant to be seen by the architect who had designed it in 1902: brightly lit, overflowing with guests who sat on the porch or stood on the lawn. She watched through the windows as a couple on the side porch began to foxtrot to a Benny Goodman piece. His lilting, complex clarinet tune perfectly complemented the party's celebratory atmosphere.

Something caught her eye in the library, but she wasn't sure what, at first. She watched through the open window as she walked back to the house. There it was. Over the heads of about ten chatting people, she saw the rolling ladder move from right to left. A blond man wearing a light-colored suit climbed the first three rungs and reached up, removed a book from a high shelf. He riffled through it, replaced it, riffled through another, removed a third, riffled through it, and carried it down the ladder. She walked a little more quickly. Of course, guests such as these would be interested in books. But these were her parents' books, and she didn't want any of them walking out of the house. Besides, how many people would actually be moved to climb a ladder and take one down?

She took the front steps two at a time, smiling at a couple sitting and smoking on the middle step, and opened the front door.

"Megan! It is you, isn't it? How nice to see you!"

Startled, it took Megan a moment to recognize Albert Treemain, a distinguished-looking black gentleman whose beard was now white. He had lived four doors down for—how many decades now?

"Al! You haven't changed a bit!" They hugged, and Megan stepped back. "Really. Except for this." She tugged on his beard and he laughed. "Remember how I

used to do that when I was little? I bet it annoyed the hell out of you. You're retired now, right?"

He snorted. "Pushed out the door, more like it. Gave me a few plaques for teaching our African-American youth for decades."

"Is Eloise here?"

He nodded. "Saw her last in the dining room, talking with Jill. We're so glad to have her back. We do miss your folks."

Megan angled around so that she could see into the library. To her relief, she saw the man climb back up the ladder and replace the book. Another man, his hair gray, reading while sitting in a leather chair, determinedly kept his head down while she stared at him, trying to figure out where she had seen him before.

Then the book-riffling man sauntered from the library, chatting, and passed Megan.

He had a hundred-dollar haircut. His clothes were equally stylish and perfect. His light blue bow tie might seem a bit different, but Megan noticed that they were just on the cutting edge of incoming style, and his light-weight beige linen suit was perfectly pressed, as if he had not sat down in hours. He wore a faint cologne. The light tan on his ruggedly lined face gave him an out-doorsy look. Probably just this side of his sixties. His sharp blue eyes, which seemed expressionless when he glanced at her in passing, let her know that she had just been as fully appraised and categorized as he had been by her.

Another man bumped into her as he headed toward the front door, and apologized. Unkempt gray hair flared from his large, squarish head like an inconvenient after-thought. His wrinkled short-sleeved shirt and the nasty cigarette-smoke trail he left behind were a complete con-trast to the blond man's couture. He lifted high four glasses he held in one hand and jerked his head to indi-cate that the blond man join him on the porch to par-take of the almost-full bottle of whiskey he gripped by

the bottle's neck in his other hand. He had a most unparty-like air of determination as he opened the front door and stepped out onto the porch.

Megan went to the dining room and made herself a gin-and-tonic with just a whisper of gin. With the icy, squat glass in one hand, she made her way back toward the library through knots of people and saw two other people head purposefully onto the porch.

Megan poked her head out the door and saw that the gray-haired man had pulled a large, round table to the very end of the porch and was gathering a few wicker chairs, helped by the blond man. A tall woman with short, dark hair, wearing a shantung-silk gunnysack from which poked extremely long, bony arms and legs walked her clanky-earringed self out the door and joined them.

The library had cleared out. While they gathered more chairs on the porch, Megan shut the pocket doors, dimmed the lights in the library to near-darkness, tipped the blinds a bit, then curled up in a wing chair only a foot away from the table outside on the porch, where she could eavesdrop. She pulled a heavy book about Kandinsky onto her lap from the coffee table so she could pretend to peruse it, and cradled her drink in one hand.

They settled into their chairs with scooting sounds. "Just a bit of that Scotch, if you don't mind"—a glug and a slosh, then another—"Well, a little bit more wouldn't hurt. Anyone else? Another round for us all, sure." After a moment, she realized that her book was unnecessary; they were so completely involved in one another and in their conversation that they did not realize that anyone was listening, and did not seem to notice that their voices were raised, and often, as they argued.

The organizer had a Russian accent, which surprised Megan. "I'm glad you could all make it."

"It's ground zero, Lev," said a woman with a gravelly

voice. "Light?" Megan heard the snap of a cigarette lighter. "Wouldn't miss this opportunity for the world."

Ground zero?

"What's all this about setting up some kind of controls?" This speaker had a lighter, higher voice than Smoking Woman, and was probably Anorexic Woman, whose legion of bangles raced, clinking, up and down her bony arm as she took a drink.

Lev said, "We need to be seriously thinking about what to do, now that we're getting closer."

Closer?

The blond man said, "I'm sure you have ideas about how to set up that kind of system." He sounded completely middle-of-the-road American.

"I'm sure *you* do," rejoined Smoking Woman, in a gravelly voice. "You have a very distinctive—and, I might add, distasteful—philosophy."

Megan gulped her drink to subdue the tickle in her throat, wishing she had made it a tad stronger.

"You are completely mistaken about me," said the blond man.

"Excuse me," said a man whom Megan had not seen. He had a faint French accent. "We all have reasons of our own for participating in this endeavor. No matter what each of us professes, we all must realize that we are a very loose affiliation, and that the ties that have held us together for the past decades may well have changed. I agree that we need to reexamine them at some point, and reassess our goals. But perhaps this is not the time and place? It's very public here, and I was not, even, actually invited to this party. I've never seen this man before."

Blond Man said, "Nor I you."

"Seriously," the Frenchman said, "who is qualified to be a master of history? Isn't that what we're talking about?"

Smoking Woman said, "I think that any sort of power like this needs to be equally distributed."

Blond Man said, "All the illiterate, unintelligent, unfit people in the world have a say?"

"She means among us," said Anorexic Woman.

"I can speak for myself," said Smoking Woman. "That's not at all what I mean."

Blond Man said, "Such power should not be equally distributed. Perhaps it could be according to educational levels?"

"Something like the three-fifths law?" asked Smoking Woman.

Lev said, "Maybe it just doesn't work that way. It's probably more like Q. It makes itself available. Which is why it is so important that we intercept it as soon as possible. That is why all of us are working together. Each of us has a different past, but we agree on the need to find this."

"I agree," said Smoking Woman. "We're the third generation of people working on locating the source. If it exists, it's getting much more embedded."

Anorexic Woman spoke: "I agree with Bill."

Megan surmised that Blond Man's name was Bill.

She continued, "It's much too important to let the wrong people get hold of it. For instance, Jill is taking over a long-term project to electrify large chunks of rural Africa and put running water in about a zillion villages. If she really had *this* kind of power, she'd use it, believe me. She'd pass it out like hotcakes. Ergo, she doesn't. Or if she does, she doesn't know about it, and that's why we need to find it as quickly as possible."

Smoking Woman said, "She can do all that? You've worked at the Bank for years. You haven't done anything of that magnitude, have you?"

"My main function is to observe and keep tabs. I have no idea what you're doing at the State Department, but I'm not questioning that. I'd like the same respect, if you don't mind." She cleared her throat. "Jill has the power. She can get together loans, determine policy. She works hard. Did you notice all those people following her

around like chicks from room to room? She's their boss. They worship her, for some reason. She has a bug about schools, now. More education, less disease, more economic opportunity—pretty soon women will start having less children, because more of the kids will live to grow up, and you'll have a whole new viable educated workforce on your hands—African women. Millions of them."

State-Department Smoking Woman said, "I don't understand. What's wrong with that?"

Blond Man said, "I'm at the Bank as well, as you might recall. As I see it, this is going to cause great economic imbalance, worldwide, an upheaval. It's conceivable that Africa could very quickly move to a position where it could control world markets. Africa has vast, untapped natural resources. A well-fed, disease-free, educated population in Africa will eventually economically endanger Europe and Asia. And us. We need to decisively move on this, as soon as possible."

Smoking Woman said, "I guess I am mistaken about the aims of this group. Or at least about who has been included in it. Are you sure you're just not racist?"

"I beg your pardon?"

Anorexic Woman said, "He has a lot of friends who are black."

"Thank you," he said.

Megan, sitting sideways in her chair so she could hear better, was a bit surprised too. Were there people who actually wanted to obstruct what she thought of as progress? But yes, economically speaking. People in some of the biggest, most well-funded think tanks in Washington, people who had ascended to power for the wealth it brought to themselves and their friends, who kept a firm hand on all kinds of reins. Until now, such people had always remained an abstraction for Megan. Except when they interfered with science funding, which, come to think of it, they did fairly often.

Blond Man continued, "We simply must either quash

310 | KATHLEEN ANN GOONAN

this—this *thing*, or gain complete control of it, with as much fear and care as if it were the plan for the hydrogen bomb. To do that, we have to find it. The U.S. has a lot of secrets—"

"Please do not shout," said Lev.

"Well, it does, and this needs to be one of them. It shouldn't be in the hands of one person." He slammed his fist on the glass-topped wicker table, and Megan heard all the glasses jump and land.

The Frenchman said, "I didn't have much luck. Her library is terribly disorganized. I don't see how we can possibly find what we're looking for. I mean, if anything is actually there."

Megan snorted, rocking with silent laughter. Luckily, they didn't seem to hear her.

"I might have found something," said Blond Man, "but I felt as if I was being closely observed, so I had to put it back. Any other progress?"

"The drawers to the desk are locked," complained Anorexic Woman.

Hmm. Someone had foresight. *Not me,* thought Megan. She had no idea that keys to that old desk were anywhere to be found.

Lev said, "Let's get down to business before we can't see straight anymore. It's in this house somewhere. You've at least been able to make the map?"

The Frenchman said, "This house is very large, and doesn't make sense, architecturally speaking. I did not get far. A man wearing a fedora followed me up the stairs and told me that the party was downstairs, even after I told him I was interested in period architecture. He seemed . . . forceful. After that he shadowed me. Is he somewhere behind me now?"

"No," said Lev. Megan quickly picked up her art book, but no one seemed to think about checking the window.

"I did not want to make a scene. All I saw before he escorted me down the stairs were disorganized rooms

full of what looked like unnecessary things. It's a nightmare."

Megan's stomach ached with silent laughter, but then she was angry and wanted to go out and kick every one of them in the face. How dare they snoop around when Abbie was asleep—well, maybe—right upstairs?

"Don't forget the attic," pointed out Smoking Woman. "For all we know, there are another five thousand books up there. Look, this house sat empty, by all accounts, for years. We could have done anything then. We could have taken it apart and put it back together ten times. Why now?"

"Sometimes it just takes a long time before information connects," said Lev. "We've all been sleepers for years, and now, something happened. That's why I called all of you together, here."

Smoking Woman asked, "What happened? Something that none of us actually know much about. How many of us—here, at that table—have even experienced The Effect?"

The Effect?

Anorexic Woman said, "That's what I thought. It's just a chimera. Handed down to us by, well, by our handlers, if you please. Mrs. Bette-Dowdy-Dance was some kind of superagent who totally manipulated world-changing information for her own ends? Have you seen her dossier? Just a nice, middle-class housewife who ran a nursery school in her house. Of which no one remembers a thing and of which there is no sign in city hall about licenses, inspections, or any of that. So even that small detail—her so-called cover—is unverifiable. If there's more to it, I say, let us know. I think it's all bullshit. Not to mention that she died twenty years ago."

"Maybe."

"But there *is* hard information," said Lev.

"Then share it with us," said Anorexic Woman. "You can't, because it's just rumors. Like the rumors that the U.S. was making an atomic bomb."

"Which they were," the Frenchman pointed out.

"That doesn't prove these particular rumors are true. What I mean is, there's this assumption that this Device is more dangerous, more powerful, for some reason, than atomic fission. Absurd. We're on a wild-goose chase."

"We owe it to our country to make sure that we track down everything we can about the Device. It does exist, it has something to do with history, mind control, and brain science, and it is something that the U.S. needs to control. That's all there is to it. Bow out, if you wish, at any time." Lev's voice, cultured, self-assured.

Megan was puzzled. Lev, in his Russian accent, seemed to be saying that the U.S. was his country.

Blond Man said, sounding a bit worried, "I'm sure none of us want to do that."

"Look who's coming," said Anorexic Woman. "Meeting adjourned. Hey, Jill. Grand party."

"Glad you could come, Dr. Koslov." Jill's voice.

"How many times do I have to tell you—call me Lev. How's your job working out?"

"I love it."

"By the way, I have a new list for you."

"Q it to me and I'll order them. Hey, are you guys leaving?"

"I couldn't get my babysitter to stay after midnight," croaked Smoking Woman.

"Papers to grade," said the Frenchman. "Thank you for your kind invitation. It has been a wonderful party."

"You're welcome," said Jill, sounding puzzled.

Lev and Blond Man took their leave as well.

After a moment, Megan heard more distant good-byes, and a few car doors slammed. She got out of the wing chair, opened the blinds, and leaned on the windowsill. Jill was holding up the empty bottle. "Vultures," she muttered.

"How inhospitable of you," said Megan. "Listen, I have something to tell you."

From the direction of the front door, Cindy yelled,

"Jill? Oh, good. There you are. You've got an old friend over here who wants to talk to you."

"Jill," said Megan.

Jill paused and looked at her. Megan tried to organize her thoughts and realized that it might take a long time to talk about all this.

"Well, for now," Megan said, "watch out for that Koslov guy."

"I already do," said Jill.

"Well, more so, then."

"What is it?" asked Jill.

"Well, evidently, he and all the people at his table are sleepers. As in some kind of secret agents."

"Really."

"Yes. They were talking about the possibility—or impossibility—of Mom being some kind of intelligence agent. They were trying to make a map of the house—evidently they want to search it. They were going through some of the books up there." She waved toward the fireplace wall of books. "And—this is really bizarre—they think you might have something that would transform Africa into an economic powerhouse that will swamp this country."

"Ah," said Jill. "That makes sense, I guess. That woman—the skinny one? Clarissa. She works at the Bank and not only does she not seem to get much done, but she's always nosing into my projects."

"Who's the blond guy?"

"Bill Anderson. He's kind of creepy, actually."

"Jill," yelled Cindy, still standing in the doorway. "She says her name is Zora."

"Zora!" Jill smiled. "She was Mom's old friend the next block over."

"Right," said Megan. She got up. "I'd like to say hi to Zora too."

At about eleven thirty, after most of the neighbors had left and the party was boiling down to hard-core all-nighters,

Brian went out the front door and returned in a few minutes with his sax. Jill, sitting on the stairs chatting with a student, murmured "Save us, dear Lord," when he walked through the foyer carrying the black case—which, although battered, had been recently polished. He had obviously been inspired by the stellar Lester Young compendium they'd been listening to. She wasn't sure who was in control of the music, but it was all great jazz from the forties. She itched to grab the case from him—after all, she was by far the better sax player. In her opinion. But that would be so unseemly. Her fingers, though, twitched in unison with the notes played by the backup pianist. Her dad would know exactly who that was by recognizing his style; she did not.

Lester Young, "The Prez," played recognizable tunes on this tape, unlike Parker and Diz later on. Brian was up and running in the middle of "How High the Moon," and, after a few dissonant honks, actually created some very sweet harmonies.

"He's been practicing," said Jill.

"He's not bad," said the student she was talking to. "Who is he?"

"My brother."

"Who's the drummer?"

"I don't know."

At that point someone began to accompany Brian on the piano, which was out of Jill's sight. However, she recognized Megan's decisive phrasings in a few seconds. Soon, Brian called out "Jill, we need you."

"Sounds like it," she said, which drew a laugh.

Zoe was in the living room, sitting next to Megan at the piano. Cindy sat next to Brian's old drum set, which, come to think of it, Jill had seen sitting in the hallway earlier, presumably exhumed from the attic. Cindy said, "Come on over, Jill, you're our singer. We've been practicing. Lots of stuff."

"Since you've been practicing without me," Jill replied,

"I can't vouch for the results." But she smiled and joined them, setting her drink on the bookcase.

Megan, a very accomplished pianist, played a suitably swinging intro to "Sweet Georgia Brown." Zoe slid onto the bench next to her and played as well. Jill listened to the beat and dove in. Brian wove harmonies about her voice, which was uncertain and hoarse at first, but grew stronger by the second verse. He and Megan played a serviceable break, but then Megan dropped out and Jill was amazed at Zoe's jazzy side, which she'd never heard. Jill had everyone at least trying to sing along by the end. Much laughter and applause; Megan rose from the piano stool and they lined up and bowed together, provoking more of the same.

They tried a request, which went over well, and were on their fourth or fifth tune when another voice chimed in from the direction of the porch, from behind where they were all set up. "If anyone knows 'White Heat' I'm in with a cornet."

Megan, seated at the piano with her back to the man said, "Lunceford, right? I was just looking at the sheet music the other day." She reached to the top of the piano and pulled out a book from the stack there.

Cindy, who sat angled toward him, said, "We've been practicing it at home. Brian really wanted to learn it. Let Zoe do it, Megan, she's pretty good." She began a drum intro and the others joined in. The man with the cornet was fabulous. There was no singing part, so Jill, by now sitting on top of the piano, turned around to see who it was, but he was bending over, and in the shadow of the porch, inside the French doors, looking at something on the floor, his face concealed. She turned forward again, and looked toward the foyer.

An exotic-looking woman stood there.

She was quite beautiful. Dark, curly hair, styled in a fashion current in the 1940s, cascaded down her back. Bright red lipstick accentuated the strong lines of her face. She held a classic martini glass, which Jill realized

must be one of her grandmother's, brought down from an upper cupboard where a tarnished silver martini mixer also resided. A tight, red, V-necked dress shimmered in the faint light of the foyer, showed off her voluptuous figure.

Her eyes were closed and she nodded her head to the beat. She had a faint smile on her face.

Jill stared at her. Brian's family continued to play, lost in their musical world, and Megan, on the bench behind the tall piano, was turning the pages of the music book. The woman opened her eyes, smiled directly at Jill, then turned and walked out the door.

Jill put her splayed hand to her chest, her heart pounding hard. Megan looked up in concern, and nodded to Brian. They brought their piece to a close. Megan stood and smiled at everyone as Jill tried to smile herself. She croaked, "I'm fine—go on!" With surprisingly strong hands, Al Treemain caught her around her waist and helped her slide from the piano. Jill looked around. The man with the cornet was gone too. Everyone applauded and Brian turned up the tape once again. Conversations resumed.

Megan said, "Are you all right?"

"I'm fine," she said. "I just need some air. Who was that man playing the cornet?"

"I didn't see him," said Megan. "I thought he was probably somebody you knew."

"I couldn't see his face," said Jill. "He was wearing an old-fashioned fedora." She rushed toward the door, though she knew that Gypsy Myra, or whoever she was, would be gone by the time she got there.

Megan was right behind her, and grabbed her shoulder. "What do you mean, a fedora?"

"Just what I said," Jill replied impatiently, shaking her off. One of her colleagues was lighting a cigarette and Jill said, as she passed, "Can I have that? Thanks," and grabbed it in passing.

On the table next to the door, beneath a Chinese paint-

ing Bette had adored, was the half-drunk martini in the elegant hand-blown green glass. Next to it was a card on fine, light green linen stock.

Jill clamped her cigarette between her lips, then picked up the martini glass with her left hand and the card with her right.

Stepping out onto the porch, she walked down to a lower step, next to a purple hydrangea washed by the light of a moon so bright that it cast shadows, and, after looking up and down the street and seeing no trace of the woman, she read the card.

The beaux arts font read, simply, ELIANI HADNTZ, PhD.

A small but perfect gift: the name of the woman who had . . . had done what? All this? Changed the world? Made her parents disappear? Given her a template, in the form of a comic book that she knew a young radical of the 1960s could not resist, and that she knew would literally turn her world upside down? Was she a monster? A savior? Where had she come from? What did she want?

But it was a gift because it was information. Freely given, at last. Although, mused Jill, she obviously could have given a hell of a lot more. She could have sat at the kitchen table and just told her in plain English what was going on, and how to find her way to her lost mother and father.

She had used a thick-nibbed fountain pen and a precise hand to write, on the bottom of the card, "The work is never finished."

What work?

She took a thoughtful sip of the martini and then a drag of her cigarette. Brian settled next to her.

"Great party, sis."

"Thanks to you guys."

He put his arm around her and gave her a quick hug. "You okay?"

"Yes," she said, her voice roughened by the cigarette

and singing. She nodded once, decisively. She felt strangely ready.

For what, she had no idea.

But her readiness took the form of lines of light. She would draw it from above.

A small, foreshortened figure in a pink dress, head a mop of dark hair, face unseen. Thin ephemeral lines extend into the night-fragrant yard in front of the woman, behind her, into the many-storied house, and into other dimensions, those she could not see, but which the reader would nevertheless infer because of the way she would draw them: the future.

And the past.

Megan sat on her other side, out of breath. "I couldn't find him."

"Find who?" asked Jill.

"The Walking Man."

"The Walking Man was here?" asked Brian.

"Who the hell is the Walking Man?" asked Jill.

"He's been following me and Abbie around at Tall Oaks," said Megan. "He wears a fedora."

"Oh," said Jill. "What else does he look like?"

"Well . . . he's medium-tall. Solid-looking; not thin, not fat. Reddish beard."

"Cindy said that the cornet man was wearing a fedora," Brian said. "Whoever he was, he was good!"

Megan said, "It's not funny! Who is he? How did he know there would be a party here?"

Jill said, "He wasn't your guy. He only had a bit of stubble."

"A man can shave. What's that in your hand?" Megan took the card from Jill. "Eliani Hadntz? You know her?"

"Do you?" asked Jill, amazed.

"Yes, of course. She works in memory research."

"Like hell," said Brian. "She designed the Game Board. The Device. It's all in Dad's papers."

"She's Gypsy Myra," said Jill.

"Who?" they both asked.

Bitsy yanked at her father's arm. Brian lifted her into his lap, where she writhed. "I'm hot. My tummy hurts."

Megan felt her forehead. "My God, she's burning up."

At the emergency room two hours later, as everyone waited, miserable and anxious and quite tired from the party, Bitsy was wheeled to surgery to have her appendix removed.

And Bette, toward dawn, walked to Union Station through the still-dark, rain-cooled city. It would take her days to get there, but to her, it seemed like an hour.

Jill

THE COLLECTED POEMS OF ROSA HADNTZ

[*July 11, Serendipity Books*]

JILL READ a few of the poems in the book Dr. Koslov had translated. They were evocative; rich; tragic, and joyful. Rosa Hadntz, Eliani Hadntz's mother, had written them.

She closed the slim book thoughtfully, slid it beneath the counter, and made a note to order five more copies; she could easily hand-sell them to some customers she already had in mind.

Brian claimed that Dr. Hadntz had designed the plan for the Device, and thus the Game Board.

Jill had translated *her* Eliani Hadntz, whom she had seen twice—once, in Texas, in her previous timestream, and now, in this one, at her party—into Gypsy Myra.

Megan said she had met Hadntz. In person, in Cuba, with graying hair. They couldn't all be the same person. Could they? Jill had not actually considered Hadntz as someone's daughter before, as someone human. But Rosa was heartbreakingly human.

Jill had just returned from the hospital, where they had all taken shifts at Bitsy's bedside to give Brian and Cindy breaks. They had caught Bitsy's appendicitis in

time, and she was recovering nicely. Whens was with his dad for the week.

Now, they were all playing catch-up. Brian was already juggling three behind-schedule jobs. Megan had gone to California on Monday morning and would not return until Thursday—tonight—and she had to go to New York for another meeting on Saturday. So, by default, Sunday was the day they'd all agreed they could Get Together and Talk.

The prospect of this discussion felt like a forty-pound weight on Jill's chest. She couldn't, simply couldn't. They didn't even suspect what she had done. From their point of view, if it were a business meeting, it would be called "Let's Share Information and Hash This Out." It would not be called, as she thought of it, "The Unfortunate Sequence of Events in Which Your Sister Jill Deprived You of Your Mother."

But she had to do this, now that things seemed to be coming unglued for Brian and Megan too.

Lev Koslov, according to whatever Megan had overheard at the party, was involved in some kind of conspiracy. This conspiracy was probably at the heart of Jill's life. She could ask Koslov about it, but that would probably only put him and his coconspirators on guard.

Jill didn't think that the delicate translations in Rosa's *Collected Poems* could be the work of an evil man. But, on the other hand, perhaps that was precisely what he wanted her to think, so that she would let down her own guard.

Koslov had said that Rosa had died in a concentration camp. So Hadntz had that burden too. According to some of these poems, Hadntz had, evidently, been saving people in Europe when her own mother was murdered.

For all of its immense powers, the Infinite Game Board had its failings, and they too were immense.

Perhaps, if linked to human consciousness, it just reflected human failings.

Sighing, Jill locked the front door, tidied up, turned off

the lights, and found a zip car at the kiosk on the next block that she could use to drive home in immediately. She was too tired to take the Metro, and tomorrow, Friday, was another big day at the Bank. If Bitsy's recovery was on track, they'd planned to have their talk on Sunday, and wind up with a cookout.

Yeah, thought Jill, turning onto her street, as the moon peeked through the treetops. *A nice little chat.*

Brian

BRIAN'S NEW TOY

[July 12]

Brian, UNCOMFORTABLE in his summer-weight linen suit and tie, drove around the block of Connecticut and M Street three times before he found a place to park. As he quickly fed the meter, he noticed that the driver who had been following him in a black sedan tried in vain to squeeze in thirty feet back from the opposite corner, failed, and turned off his engine anyway. Brian was impressed to think that he was important enough for the fellow to risk a pretty sure ticket. His tail wasn't exactly subtle either. Who wore hats anymore? In fact—he looked again—he wore a homburg, not a fedora. Sam hadn't worn hats, but had once explained the fashion difference to Brian. Homburgs were more formal, and their top crease and brim were fixed, unlike the more flexible fedora.

It was Friday afternoon, and it had been an exhausting week, made worse by his desire to glean everything he could from the notes before Sunday's meeting with his sisters.

Brian reached behind the seat for his portfolio of drawings—the rest of the truck was so perpetually heaped with tools and trash that he always kept his portfolio there—slammed the door, and locked it. It was almost

four, and he hated to be late for an appointment. Sweat trickled down the back of his neck, and the roar of traffic and the smog he'd seen building in a gray band on the horizon earlier that day—less than precarbon-watch days, but still extensive—had now expanded and was gathering into a dark cloud, making it a familiar summer afternoon. He saluted in the general direction of the man in the hat and hurried down the street to the building that held the office of this project's architect, J. M. Hamlin, AIA.

Precisely on time, he arrived in her cool, austerely impressive reception room. Jane, a small, trim woman, who wore the same pair of gold earrings every time Brian had seen her, stood, came around her desk, and shook his hand. They laid the plans out on the large table in her office and went over the changes. Brian pointed out that the three new cloister-type windows accompanying a wide, curving staircase would necessitate rather expensive structural changes, and Jane said she would discuss that with her client before finalizing that particular change. She smiled, walked him to the door, and Brian was back on the street precisely twenty minutes after he had gone in.

The short man in the homburg was standing next to the driver's door of his truck, reaching up, pushing something or other into the place between the top of the door and the truck body. His car was no longer double-parked, but was down and across the street, still illegally parked too close to the end of the block. He must have driven around in vain all that time trying to find a parking place.

Brian broke into a run. The man looked up, and briskly walked down the sidewalk. Brian reached his truck and saw a rubber wedge on the pavement next to his door. That's right, wedge the door open, stick in a wire, unlock it. And steal—what? Empty potato chip bags?

Enraged, he was climbing into the cab when a policeman, who had evidently been behind him, grabbed his arm.

"Not so fast."

"What?"

"It's too late."

"That guy was trying to break into my car." Brian shouted, pointing at the man, still walking fast toward the corner. Of course, he couldn't risk running across the street in traffic—that would attract immediate notice, and a heavy fine for jaywalking. Brian knew, he'd gotten a ticket for it.

"Right," said the cop.

"Look—"

"You look," the officer said, getting out a ticket book. "The meter's expired."

"No it's not. I put in enough for two hours."

"Read the fine print on the meter. A twenty-minute limit after three P.M., except on weekends and holidays. I marked your tire."

"Okay, give me the ticket already." The man was crossing the street with a mob of people.

The policeman wrote it up and slapped it in his palm.

Brian jumped into his truck, as the man got into his car. Ha! He couldn't move; the light was red.

From his high vantage point, he followed the car.

He managed to get a little closer at the next light, and decided to hang back.

The car did not follow any kind of circuitous route, which rather disappointed Brian. Instead, he remained steady on M Street through Georgetown, passing Jill's bookshop, and took a right on Foxhall Road. Although Brian still stayed well behind the car, there was not much traffic. The guy certainly must know he was being followed.

The car turned left on Reservoir Road, then hung a sharp right.

Brian found himself, to his great surprise, in the parking lot of the German embassy, a classy steel-and-glass structure, six stories high.

The car disappeared into an underground parking

garage. Brian had no pass with which to open the gate. He backed up, pulled over to one side, jumped from his truck, and ran through the gate.

There was no sign of any activity in the dark, cool garage.

Brian trudged back to his truck. A security guard approached him. "Can I help you?"

"Yes. I was following a car whose driver tried to break into mine. He went into the garage. What can I do?"

"Turn around and leave."

"I guess I can call the police."

"You're technically in Germany. Your police have no jurisdiction here. And frankly, I don't like your attitude."

"Are there surveillance tapes? I'd like to see who just drove in here."

"Forget it," said the guard, and walked away.

Cursing, but quietly, Brian got back into his truck and sat there, brooding. Absently, he reached over to see if he could find the bag of half-eaten potato chips he knew was there, somewhere.

He pushed yesterday's jacket aside and was flabbergasted. That was what the guy was after. But how did it get here?

It was the Infinite Game Board.

He looked at his phone and saw that Jill was calling.

Jill

THE BREAK-IN

[July 12]

IT WAS six-thirty on a hot July Friday. Jill was weary when she stepped off the bus around the corner of her block. She set her mother's old, scuffed leather briefcase on the sidewalk and closed her eyes for a moment to collect herself. She'd had a rough day. A lot of meetings, a lot of details, two important missed phone calls from

Kumasi that she would have to follow up on this evening from home. Maybe the schools were making a difference, and they wanted to let her know?

Fat chance. More likely they were going to cause a civil war or something.

A whisper of air brushed her cheek and rustled the leaves of the oaks that lined the street. It was safe now to breathe in the scent of the Millers' new-mown lawn and Alice Jenkins's full-blooming Eleanor Roosevelt roses.

When she rounded the corner, the sight of a Metro police cruiser parked in front of her house broke her brief tranquility. Five or six neighbors stood on the lawn. Emmie's au pair pointed at the house, then at the street, while the cop took notes.

She loped in awkward, sweaty haste toward her house. Manfred was lying on the front porch in front of the door, which was odd; Jill had left her in a fenced area of the backyard this morning. She jumped up and ran to Jill.

The officer turned when the au pair pointed and said, "That's Jill."

"Oh." He was one of the joggers she'd met the day she moved in. This time he was in uniform, with a name badge. "*Detective* Kandell. Daniel, right?"

"Bad news, I'm afraid. Someone broke into—"

"I called the police," said the au pair. Jill couldn't remember her name. "It was only an hour ago. Really, I couldn't believe it at first. Broad daylight, and—"

Kandell quieted the au pair with a slight, polite movement of his right hand. "I'd like to ask Ms. Dance some questions, in private. Could we sit on the porch?"

Jill said, "Thanks a lot," to the au pair. She led the officer up the stairs. Manfred followed. Jill asked, "Do you mind coming in? I need something to drink."

"That's fine." Detective Kandell's voice was professional and even, and had a calming effect on Jill. His eyes held a hint of humor, which she supposed he was

trying to hide, since she could see nothing funny about this. As she got out her keys, she asked, "How did he get in?"

"The front door's open."

It was, just slightly, as if it had been closed in a hurry behind someone and the latch had not caught. "I'm sure I locked it this morning."

"He came in through the front door. He left, quite rapidly, out the back, through a window that he broke. A shredded bit of his suit indicates that your dog bit him when he dropped into the yard."

"Good girl!" Manfred wagged her tail.

"Would it be possible for your dog to stay on the porch while we go inside? I don't want her to disturb anything."

Jill told Manfred to sit, lie down, and to stay with quick hand signals. Kandell raised his eyebrows. "I'm impressed." He pushed the door gently with his foot. It swung open, creaking, and revealed the wide foyer, the long staircase to the right, and the hallway to the kitchen straight ahead.

"Please just stand here for a moment. Can I take your briefcase?" His fingers brushed hers as he lifted it from her hand. "Take your time. Do you see anything different?"

"No," she said slowly, drawing out the word. "Not yet . . . Wait a minute." She pushed the door back to full open with her foot, so that it doubled back against the wall, affording her a full view of the library. She took a few quick steps and stopped. "The ladder."

The room smelled of beeswax and the peculiar smell that old books, when they reach a certain density, exude—a mixture of dust, cracked bindings, and inexorably mildewing paper. "The rolling ladder has been moved since this morning."

"You're sure?"

She nodded.

The large partner's desk, which had come from her grandparents' house, looked as it had when she had left

this morning—strewn with papers. It sat catercorner, facing the glassed double doors and the front window at an angle with its back to the bookshelves and a window. The old wooden venetian blinds that covered the side window were tilted upward, throwing stripes of light onto the ceiling. She saw that she had left the blinds to the front windows, behind the couch, open to the porch and the street.

"Did he rifle the desk?" asked Kandell.

She laughed. "No."

The gently sagging, once-elegant couch, upholstered with soft but indestructible moss-green fabric, was surrounded by stacks of books she had been reading. A coffee cup sat on top of one pile. Untidy towers of books hid the top of the coffee table. After the party, she'd wasted no time in creating a comfortable mess.

"Did the intruder do that?" he asked, nodding toward the couch, covered with crumpled papers discarded from a report she'd been working on.

"No," she said, almost certain that he was making fun of her housekeeping rather than detecting. "But he did remove three books from the shelves."

Hands on his hips, he raised his eyebrows slightly and gave her a look that she interpreted as skeptical.

"There." She walked over to the shelf-lined wall and pointed to a tiny gap just above her head, left of the desk. "And up there—he used the ladder. He did move the ladder. I left it on the right side of the fireplace."

"Can you think of any particular reason he would want those books?"

"No. They were some of my dad's old engineering books from college. I've never actually read them. My brother and sister might have at some point."

"Are your parents still alive?"

She hesitated for the slightest bit of time. "Yes."

"Are you sure?" he asked, without a trace of sarcasm.

She blinked, and sighed. "Not really. Officially, they are both missing."

"Are they in the military?"

She looked at him. "Does it matter?"

"I need to make a list of everyone that has access to the house. For instance, do your brother, sister, and parents, if still alive, have keys?"

"Yes."

"Might one of them have just dropped in to borrow a book?"

"It's possible, but unlikely. You can put the briefcase down. Right there is fine. Can we move into the kitchen? I'm dying of thirst."

"Sure." He followed her down the hallway. She kept an eye out for further signs the intruder might have left but saw none. Over her shoulder she said, "I'm not positive that someone took those books after they removed them from the shelves. They could still be in the room somewhere."

"You mean you couldn't tell?" This time she was sure she heard a note that her mother would have called smart-alecky, but when she glanced at his face it was impassive.

"It's been a long day." She slipped out of her suit jacket, a cream-colored, cool silk from Hong Kong, and hung it on the back of a chair.

"Tailor-made." It wasn't a question.

She turned to her left, saw the broken window the thief had left behind, and sighed. "Damn. Another repair. Just when I thought I was getting ahead. Have a seat. Iced tea?"

"Sounds good." He moved past her, opened a glass-fronted cupboard to the right of the sink, and took down two large glasses. Just before setting them on the countertop his hands stopped abruptly. "Spacies."

He set the glasses down, and continued to stare, an odd, yearning look on his face. He glanced at Jill. "Do you mind?"

"Knock yourself out."

With gentle reverence he picked up a black astronaut holding a little radio receiver in one fluffy-gloved hand. "Estrella." He removed her helmet and revealed a wild Afro.

"You know their names?"

"Oh, yeah. This is a real one."

"Real?"

"You know what I mean, right?" He gave Jill a keen glance.

She was ever so afraid that she did. "No."

His deep, pleasant voice had a reasonable timbre that she suspected infused everything he said. She wondered if he ever got angry. "The original Spacies are much more refined. No little plastic tags sticking out of the seams; actually, no visible seams at all. The colors inside are realistically human"—he grinned—"although I don't suppose you ever sliced one up in order to find out, like I did."

"Why did you?"

"I had to find out if they were black all the way through. You know what I found?"

"I have no idea."

"They regenerate." Now his voice sounded a wee bit strained. A tiny, V-shaped frown appeared between his eyebrows.

"What do you mean?"

"If you cut one in half, two perfect Estrellas will grow back."

"How? I mean, they seem pretty tough. How in the world did you even cut it?"

"With a vise and a circular saw."

"Oh. A real professional. Kind of like Snidely Whiplash tying Little Nell to the train tracks?"

"I thought of it more in the vein of scientific inquiry. And they grow back by nanotechnology, of course."

"Really? Self-replication like that is incredibly controlled. I mean, it's possible, of course, but it's so highly

regulated that . . ." She thought of the Game Board. She thought of a lot of other things, like the fact that self-reproducing, self-regulating nanotech was actually a deep national security issue, the very discussion of which the government had repressed completely ten years earlier when the issue first burst into national awareness. Now, the term "nano" mainly referred to harmless commercial products that actually had nothing to do with nanotechnology, or was invoked in kids' cartoons. Her Q-Schools couldn't self-replicate; at least, that's what her designer had told her. But they did, of course, repair themselves. At any rate, they would probably never exist.

Detective Kandell was not, perhaps, exactly what he seemed, yet he didn't seem to care if she knew that. Wanted her to know it, in fact.

Or maybe he was just being a friendly neighbor.

"Will it grow into anything else?"

"Not that I know of."

"And was she black all the way through?"

"No, she was strangely real, kind of a whitish-beige, like you or me, under the skin. So actually, I was satisfied."

"These Spacies all belong to my younger brother and sister. I guess I was a little too old for them."

"The original ones are hard to find. It's as if someone collected as many as they could and sequestered them somewhere."

"So I guess we could make a fortune by putting these in the blender and keep making more."

"That's a thought. Ever wonder why, when you really like something, it disappears? Like brands, for instance?"

"I just always thought I had such esoteric tastes that no one else liked what I did."

He startled her by joining her laugh, then set Estrella back on the windowsill, picked up the glasses, and turned to what they'd always called the icebox. "I know that you're probably trying to do a historically accurate

renovation, but don't you think it might be time to invest in a new refrigerator?"

"This one works fine."

He pulled down the lever of the old Crosley, small by present standards, with rounded, somewhat slouching corners, and the freezer door opened. "Nice big ice bin. Good idea." He shoveled ice into the glasses with the metal scoop that Sam had always kept in his ice bin.

"I get bag ice at the store. I hate ice cube trays. The tea is in that jug."

"Some people are shocked when their house is broken into," he observed, after he filled both glasses with tea and took a seat across from her. The newspapers were rather low today, so they could see each other tolerably well. She was surprised that he didn't ask if the intruder had stacked them there.

"I probably am. Mainly, I'm just tired. It's been a long week. So you think he got in using a key?"

"The doors have deadbolts."

"I might have forgotten to lock it when I left," she admitted.

"Then he could have picked the lock. These old houses are easy. He was in a hurry to leave, though."

He scribbled in his notebook. "Can you call your brother and sister and ask them if they were here today?"

She called Brian. When he picked up, she said, "Quick question. Were you at the house today?"

"No."

"Megan, do you think?"

"No. Why?"

"There was a break-in. I'm talking to a detective right now."

"I'll be right over."

Jill hung up and told Kandell that Brian hadn't been there.

"Okay, here's what we know. He arrived on foot, but someone probably dropped him off around the corner so

he could walk down the street and make sure he was safe. He wore a gray suit and tie, and he was white. He also wore a homburg. He was of medium weight, wore glasses, and was about five foot ten. This is all from your neighbor's description. She was watching from her living room. He appeared to knock and ring the bell and then hunched over the doorknob for a few minutes. He then opened the door and closed it behind him. She said that she knew that you weren't home from work yet because—"

"Because she's nosy as hell."

"Because you always take the dog in. She went out on her porch with the phone and called 911."

"Why did she go out on the porch?"

"To keep a better eye on things, she said. A minute or two later she heard barking and yelling. He shot out of the side yard with your dog biting at his legs. She saw him get into a car that was waiting at the end of the street. A light-colored late-model car, she didn't know what kind. It was too far to see the license plate. I pulled up about two minutes later. We're looking for that car."

"You got here fast."

"I live two blocks away. I was just pulling out of the driveway for work when I heard the call, so I took it. Normally they'd send an officer rather than a detective." He looked quite official, sitting there at the table, yet she felt at ease with him. "I have a little boy, and I want the neighborhood to be safe."

"How old is he?"

"Seven."

"Mine is five."

"A nice age."

"Sometimes."

Kandell said, "I wonder if he got what he came for. He seems to have known what books he wanted, and exactly where they were. Who else, besides your family, have you had over here?"

"I just moved back in two months ago. Before that no

one had lived here for quite some time. I had a party here a week ago."

"I'll need a list of names."

"They were from the World Bank, where I work, and Georgetown—some professors and students—and neighbors. Sort of a moving-in-housewarming-change-of-life-circumstances party."

"I see. Did you go to Georgetown?"

"I finished my poli-sci doctorate at Georgetown a couple months ago."

"Was the house empty before you moved in?"

"Empty of people. Otherwise, all the same stuff was here."

"So he could have come in at any time before you moved in."

"Yes. And he could have taken whatever he wanted then. All of us—my brother and sister and I—used to come by at least once a month or so just to check on the place, make sure that the boy down the street was really cutting the grass, things like that. But no one lived here."

"Okay." He stood up. "Let's just check around and see if anything else is missing. Or if he left anything."

"Such as?"

"Anything. Evidence, or something placed here deliberately."

She kicked her shoes off under the table and stood up. It seemed to her that Detective Kandell was taking this quite seriously. Which was good, but it seemed odd, somehow. Except, perhaps, that he lived nearby.

"What would they leave except maybe a bug or a bomb?"

"Exactly. Is there anything sensitive about your job?"

"No."

He followed her as they walked through the dining room, which was also at the back of the house, with a bank of double-hung windows opening onto the overgrown backyard. This was the one room where everything was always pretty much the same, and after the

party, it had reverted to form. Knickknacks on the buffet had a new coat of dust, just a few days later, which wasn't quite fair.

They'd made a full circuit and were at the bottom of the stairs when Brian came in.

"Hello," he said, and held out his hand. "Brian Dance."

"Detective Daniel Kandell."

They shook hands. "You from around here?" asked Brian.

"Couple of blocks away."

"The reason I ask, you know Truman Kandell? He was my classmate."

Detective Kandell had a very nice smile. "He's my brother. You went to Dunbar?"

"Yeah. In fact—"

"This is marvelous and all," interrupted Jill, "but I'm getting tired and we still need to look through the upstairs."

"What happened?" asked Brian.

Jill and Kandell went through the events of the day. Jill said to Brian, "He took three books."

"Which ones?"

Jill closed her eyes. "*Electronic and Radio Engineering, The Theory of Groups and Quantum Mechanics,* and *The Nature of the Chemical Bond.*"

Kandell said, "I can't believe that."

"Believe it," Brian said.

Jill headed upstairs. Manfred had decided she'd waited long enough and rushed up ahead of them and Jill was too tired to send her back down to stay until released, which she ought to have done. "It might be harder up here, except most of the rooms are pretty dusty, except for Whens' and mine, so that might help."

"Whens?"

"Stevie," she corrected. "He's five and opinionated about his name."

"Did you go to Dunbar?"

"Yes," she said shortly. Just in another timeline, when

the whole country and especially D.C. were torn by riots.

He didn't ask any more questions about that, for which she was thankful, and they glanced through the mess of the upstairs room without him saying a single snarky thing, which rather impressed Jill.

"I don't think he had time to come up here," he said.

Back downstairs, Jill walked down the hall to the sunroom. Detective Kandell was behind her. His footsteps faltered for a moment and she turned around.

He was looking at a picture on the wall, a print.

"Monet," said Jill.

"A rather obscure Monet. *The Magpie.*" He pointed at the black bird that sat on a broad ladder leaning against a snow-laden hedgerow. All the elements of the painting—the long house on the right, the twisted, heavy branches with their burden of snow, leaned toward the magpie.

Jill had always liked the painting. She stepped closer. "It looks like late afternoon, doesn't it?"

"Cold, but with a bit of life. A sunny winter day, just ending. Long shadows." He paused at the next print. "Ah! Matisse." After studying it for a moment, he turned to her and said, "I found a puzzle lately, a wooden puzzle of an elephant that I had as a child. It has, oh, I don't know, ten or fifteen pieces. I was pleased that all the pieces were there—surprised, actually. But my mother had kept it. I thought about giving it to my son, but he's too old for it. I dumped it out and put it back together. It was very strange. I felt the thrill of realizing that the elephant's trunk fit into the arc of a circus tent behind it. I felt . . . it was a kinetic memory, but magical, almost, the way that movement felt . . ." He shrugged. "Anyway, these paintings give me that same feeling."

Then he stepped back from her. Stared at her, tilted his head. Then brushed past her in the hallway and went into the sunroom.

She followed. "What is it?"

He had taken a few steps into the room and was turning in a slow circle, looking at the banks of windows, the mahogany wainscoting. The tiny V between his eyebrows reappeared. Jill watched his expressions, which changed rapidly; she thought she saw fear, wonder, and then, resolution—the look Whens got just before he planned to do something scary, like jump off a high rock. She'd learned to recognize it so she could grab him first.

Kandell nodded once, then walked briskly to the back of the room, with its view of the gullied backyard and the woods. The windows were open, and a breeze stirred the long green drapes.

He squatted and pushed aside one of the drapes. "There," he said. He ran his index finger over something that Jill couldn't see.

"What?"

"I . . . did this. I'm sorry to admit."

Jill bent down and saw a rough capital "D," carved into the wood. The wainscoting had since been stained, so it wasn't very visible.

"I knew that it was here." He stood up and spoke very slowly. He said, "My little brother went to school here. And I stayed here after school some days. I was in public school. I was, maybe, ten."

Jill walked to the nearest chair, an old rocking chair, and sat down hard. Her heart was beating fast.

He kept walking around, delight in his face and in his voice. "It's like the puzzle. I remember Truman learning to write, how excited he was. Tracing the letters. The teacher, Miss . . ."

"Bette," Jill filled in, her voice dull.

"Yes. Miss Bette! Truman adored her. My mother made us call her 'Miss.' She wanted us to just call her 'Bette.' She had me work with the little kids. She did something she called organic reading."

So. Jill had probably seen him, way back when. Even though it seemed impossible. "Sylvia Ashton-Warner's method," said Jill, her mother's lecture, which she had

heard many times, kicking in. "Warner's insight was that the Maori children she taught weren't stupid, as the British believed, just because they couldn't learn to read using English primers. She developed a method to link their own lives, their own words and stories, with the act of writing. Children can write phonetic words about six months before they can read them, decode them. Writing and reading are two different processes. Warner had them dictate their own stories to her, and then writing and reading suddenly made sense—it was about them, their feelings, their own lives. Emotion is kind of the missing link between learning to read phonetically, mechanically, and not really caring, and realizing that it is a tool you can use to say things that are important to you, and no one else."

"Yes!" Kendall paced the room in a fit of reverie, excited. "She'd get all the kids to tell her their own word, and then their own stories. It was all phonetic. I'd sound out each letter as I wrote it for the kids on . . ."

"Computer punch cards," said Jill, her voice still flat. Bette got them from American University, where she was working on her doctorate. Jill remembered how the Magic Markers used to stick in the little rectangular holes when she was writing out the kids' words for them, and how Bette's little recycling economy was so irritating because of that.

"Yes! And they'd trace over them with Magic Markers, and then they *knew* them. They *owned* them. They could pick their word out of a big pile of all the kids' words. We'd dump them out every day, hold one up, and whoever wrote it would call out the word. God! It was like the world just came alive for Truman, overnight. Suddenly he could read! After tracing the letters with his fingers and learning their sounds and writing them . . . what's wrong?"

Jill began to rock furiously in the rocking chair. "So, when you came over here this afternoon, did you remember that this had been your brother's schoolhouse?"

"No." He flattened his lips together and shook his head. "That is strange, isn't it?" His laugh was a sharp single bark.

"My brother and sister don't remember that either."

"But *you* do." His keen look pulled assent from her, inch by inch. She had freely told the therapist because, after all, the therapist just thought she was crazy.

This was different. Detective Kandell believed her.

"Yes." Her throat was tight and the word came out as a whisper.

He chose a straight chair from a side table, straddled it, rested his arms on the top of its back, and perched his chin on top of his hands. "My not remembering it isn't all that strange. It was a long time ago. I didn't come here often, maybe once a week for a few months. We moved to Massachusetts when I was ten. My wife and I moved back here about eight years ago and we just didn't get over this way. She worked at the Justice Department and my beat was always in Southwest, and we lived in Georgetown. Our divorce was just final, and I decided to buy in the old neighborhood. Easier to take care of the old folks here, anyway. It's just in the past few weeks that I've started jogging in this direction. I felt a sense of recognition, but I feel that way about the whole neighborhood. Why don't your brother and sister remember it? Were they too young?"

Although shaken, Jill stood briskly. "Yes. Well, no clues here? Anything else?" As she followed him, she wondered, *Does he have the same memories I do? About history?* She tried to think of some casual question that would reveal the answer to her, but she was, finally, deeply disturbed and too tired to think—for the rest of the evening, she supposed, aggravated at her state of mind, at her sheer exhaustion.

They went back to the foyer. Kandell gave Brian and Jill his card and told them to call him if they thought of anything. Jill thanked him and shut the door behind him.

Then she went into the library and flopped down on the couch.

"Wine," said Brian.

"Right."

He returned with a beer for himself and a glass of wine for her, settled into the desk chair, and leaned back. "Where's your son?"

"With his dad."

"Who probably won't let him stay here now."

"The hell he won't!"

"I'm just saying. So who did this?"

"A man wearing a now-bitten suit and, rather improbably, a hat."

"Like, a homburg?"

"That was the impression the girl across the street gave Detective Kandell. She saw the book thief at the front door."

"Nothing more low-down than a book thief," Brian said.

She ignored him. "Either he had a key or picked the lock. He came in, went right to the books, took what he wanted, then jumped out the back window."

"Ouch. Because the cops came?"

"He saw the au pair on her porch using her phone."

Brian said, "But why did he take *those* books?"

"Maybe they're rare and valuable and he can sell them for a ton of money?"

"They were Dad's. Maybe there were notes in them."

"Probably, but so what?"

"I think Dad was working on something really important."

"Yes, like protecting the Declaration of Independence and—"

"More important."

"Like what?"

"You tell me."

Jill was silent.

"Fine," he replied, with cutting sarcasm. "I thought we were all ready to talk." After a moment he said, "Sorry. That guy might be back. You need to stay with us tonight."

"No. I have a nice evening planned. I'm going to go over some work and then I'm going to watch a PBS show. And first I'm taking a nice, cool bath. If he does come back, I want to be here."

"Are you nuts?"

"Manfred bit him. He'll be afraid to come back."

"Right."

"Unless he can tell I'm gone."

"I called Megan to tell her, but Jim answered her phone and said she's out like a light, going to New York early tomorrow morning. He'll tell her tomorrow." He paused. "I guess I'll stay here tonight, then."

"Don't be silly."

"Don't you. I'll call Cindy and tell her what happened. She's at the hospital with Bitsy, and she's spending the night. I'll pick up the kids from the sitter's and bring them over here. Right now, I'm going to call Jimmy and have him change the locks and put in a deadbolt."

"But what if—"

"If what?"

"What if Mom and Dad come back? They won't be able to get in!" Jill's glass of wine slid from her hand and spilled on the scarred wood floor. Her face crumpled and she gasped for breath.

Brian came over, pushed some books off the corner of the coffee table, and sat down in front of her. "Jill." He handed her the paper napkin he'd brought with her wine and she blew her nose.

"What?"

"I don't think they're coming back."

Jill sat stone-silent for a while. Finally Brian said, "Sis, I have something to show you."

He went out to the truck and came back in, carrying

his portfolio bag. He sat down on the couch and un-zipped it.

And pulled out the Infinite Game Board.

Jill picked it up.

And remembered Truman.

The board is full of stories.

Megan

MEGAN'S MEMORIES AND THE WALKING MAN

[*July 12*]

MEGAN'S MEETING got out late, and everyone was snappish, anxious to begin their weekends. There had been the usual, disquieting rumble about funding cuts. It was beginning to seem to her that only privately funded research institutions could recognize the importance of memory research. She didn't want to look for a new job, not right now, but maybe it was time to get out of government.

She strode out into five-thirty downtown, joining throngs of just-released office workers. Humidity and heat enhanced the smell of concrete and asphalt, and she was soothed.

Megan generally loved everything about these after-noons, particularly Friday afternoons, when everyone was in a comparatively good mood. She loved crossing the street with twenty-five other determined people; enjoyed the green plunge of temperature as she walked diagonally through a park. Jim made fun of her enthusi-asm. She told him it was because she took vitamins. Now, she wondered if perhaps that Hadntz drug was finally taking hold. Her anxieties were soothed too. Jill had fi-nally agreed to discuss everything, just two days from now, the soonest they could all get together.

She'd tried to put Jill's talk about Gypsy Myra and

Eliani Hadntz out of her mind during the week, and she'd been pretty successful, as usual, at compartmentalizing. Taking an evening shift at the hospital to spell Brian and Cindy had made that fairly easy, though she did use Q during that time to do some research on Jill's underground comic. Her inability to find anything could mean several things. Maybe Jill was imagining it. Maybe Q was fallible and didn't know everything. Maybe it was real, and Q chose to hide it. The third possibility was the most intriguing one. At any rate, Megan knew when she was reaching her exhaustion threshold, and she was close. After her New York trip tomorrow for a Saturday morning conference, she could turn her attention to family problems.

At the Metro entrance she stopped and bought a bouquet of frilly pink carnations speared by austere purple irises from a street vendor, as was her weekly custom, and held the crinkly cellophane wrapper on her lap as she sped underground. She tried to relax into the bright colors, but she could not. Neither was she soothed by the Metro ride, as she usually was. Once in Tall Oaks, she peered out the bus window, trying to spot Walking Man.

By the time she climbed the hill to her house, her shoulder ached from her briefcase strap. She went inside, a mixture of heel-clacks (she kicked off her shoes immediately), cellophane crinkles, and a cheerful "Hi!" She put the cone of flowers on the counter, promising them that she would get them a vase and water as soon as she changed.

"Mommy!" Abbie, her face slightly grimy, pounded down the stairs and smashed into her. Abbie lifted her up, licked a finger, and wiped dirt from her daughter's cheek.

"What's up?"

"Come and play a game with me." She tugged at Megan's hand and led her down the hall. Jim, in his office, was on the phone. He smiled and waved as she

passed. Abbie's bedroom was a phantasmagoria of toys, a spoiled child's utopia.

"Okay. But just let me—" Then Megan forgot that she was sweltering in panty hose, that her skirt waistband was too tight. "Where did you get that?"

Abbie yanked at Megan's hand. "Sit down! Show me how to play!"

Megan shucked her skirt and panty hose and tossed them onto a chair, leaving her in cool cotton underpants and a bedraggled silk shirt. She pushed back her hair, which was wet with sweat, and sank cross-legged to the floor. Very quietly, she said to Abbie, "Where did you find this?"

Abbie smiled. "I don't know."

Megan tentatively touched the upturned edge of the Infinite Game Board.

Abbie had unfolded the metal legs, so it sat about a foot off the floor.

About the size and shape of a cafeteria tray, the board had intriguing patterns on its aluminum surface, all of them diminutive, so there was room for many, many games, or suggestions of games, even games that opened outward from other games. A chess- or checkerboard— and indeed, Megan recalled that tiny checkers and chessmen had come with it, sealed into a plastic bag. There had also been colored markers to use with games that required the spinner, in one corner, which pointed toward numbers on colored backgrounds. There had also been a deck of playing cards, and other cards for playing other games. There was a hexagon divided into triangles, each of which held a number; a pair of dice; interlocking squares with a colored dot in each of their grids, a baseball game.

The instruction booklet was long lost. But it had been, Megan recalled, rather thick, printed on thin paper with a font too small for, at least, her own childish eyes to read.

She touched the board again, and remembered the day they bought it. In fact, Megan suddenly realized, the entire

day still stood out for her as if it were a set piece she could enter again and again, a day that would never lose its odd numinosity.

Jill had been sick, and the doctor prescribed cough syrup. Their mother drove down the street to Peoples Drug and said, "Must be my lucky day," as she zipped into a vacant parking spot right in front of the store.

Jill, as usual, stopped for a second and took a deep breath when she went into the store, then headed for the comic book rack, where she put her nose right up next to them and inhaled more deeply.

"That's gross," said Brian.

"They smell *wonderful*," she said, and held the most recent *Superboy* issue to her face, sniffing it before opening it.

"That's enough, Jill," said their mother. "You're spreading germs."

"She doesn't act sick," said Brian, as their mother, ignoring him, receded to the back of the store.

"You're just jealous because you had to go to school," Jill said, piling up her sickbed dues: just about every comic on the rack.

Then Megan saw it.

The Game Board was in a dusty cardboard box with a cellophane front, which displayed its mesmeric diversity. Megan said, "What's that?"

No one paid any attention to her. She couldn't reach it, and she couldn't get Jill to help. Her mother was talking to the pharmacist. She saw a stepstool down the aisle and dragged it over to the shelf.

She climbed onto the stool and could just barely reach the bottom with her outstretched fingers. She teased at the bottom and finally it fell off the shelf, taking down several boxes of tissues along with it.

Megan climbed down. She ignored the tissues, picked up the box, and gazed through the cellophane in a state of complete rapture. It was dusty. She sneezed.

"What's going on here?" Her mother stood over Megan. "Did you make this mess?"

Megan glanced at the boxes on the floor. "Um, I guess."

"Well, pick them up this minute. Hand them to me." She replaced the tissue boxes. "Now where did this box come from?"

Megan embraced the large box as best she could. "I want it."

"What is it?"

"Games," she said. "See? Lots of games we could play with Jill while she's sick."

"How nice of you to think of your sister." She lifted the box from Megan's arms.

Brian showed up with a plastic truck. Jill held about ten comic books.

Their mother looked at Jill's stack. "You're just sick. You're not dying."

"Mo-om."

"Don't whine."

"I need these."

"Put half of them back, please."

"When do I get my allowance?"

"I said—"

"Okay, okay." Jill slouched back over to the rack and began smashing some of the comic books back in.

"Those are the ones you will get, young lady."

"But they're bent."

"Exactly."

Megan recalled her sense of deep triumph as her mother asked the pharmacist, "How much is this?"

He frowned. "Don't recall seeing it." He turned it over and over, searching for a price tag. "Whew. It's dirty. Sorry about that. It's probably been here for years." He put it on the counter, wiped his hands with his handkerchief, and then ran it over the box. "Well . . . How about two dollars."

And then—

"Mom!" Abbie was shoving her on the shoulder. "Play!"

And then, Megan didn't remember anything else about it.

She frowned. "Be quiet, Abbie. I'm trying to think. About the games," she added in haste.

Abbie pouted and flung herself on the bed.

It was true. She really couldn't remember. She couldn't remember playing any of these enticing games, this infinite-seeming phantasmagoria . . .

Infinite . . .

"Hey." Jim stuck his head in the door.

"Hi, sweetie. Do you know where Abbie found this?"

"It was up in your loft. The top of the closet. Next to a stack of old photographs."

"Oh. They were from the attic. I haven't even had a chance to look at them."

"She made me go up and get it. She said you'd be mad."

"I don't remember putting it there."

"Well, that's where it was."

"I got some flowers. They're on the counter. Could you put them in a vase? Please?"

"Sure."

"Let's play now," said Abbie.

Megan stood, picked up the Game Board, and grabbed her clothes from Abbie's chair. Abbie followed her into her bedroom and sat on the bed while Megan changed into shorts, a T-shirt, and zoris. Megan thought while she changed.

Finally she said, "Tell you what. I need to find the game pieces first, okay? We can't play anything without the pieces." As casually as she could, she slid the board on top of a tall wardrobe. "Want to go for a walk to the lake?"

"Yes!"

Bingo appeared immediately, romping and barking.

* * *

Megan walked toward the lake in somewhat of a daze, the weirdness of the day beginning to tell on her. She resolved to take some extra vitamins when she got home. Maybe she should lay off the memory enhancement stuff for now.

She was almost positive that she had not brought the Game Board along with her when she'd gotten married. She had lived at home during part of college, but moved into an apartment later, and could not recall bringing such a thing to her apartment or to her Tall Oaks home. Her old room in Halcyon House was more or less the same. In fact, it was probably exactly the same as when she had left. The bed had not been made, the pile of clothes she'd dumped out of the dresser, all too small, were probably still there—oh, except, she remembered Jill mentioning that Whens had chosen her room. So it might have been straightened a bit. But knowing Jill, perhaps not.

Bingo ranged on his leash, jerking her here and there, sniffing every tree, rock, and bush while Abbie ran on ahead, a flash of green shorts and yellow hair, brightening and dulling as she passed through shafts of sunlight and patches of shade. Megan resolved for the hundredth time to take Bingo to some kind of training course and immediately forgot the thought.

They arrived at a minuscule sandy beach. Bingo almost pulled her over as he lunged for a stick, but she turned around after Abbie tossed a few rocks into the water.

The path had been widened over the years to accommodate service vehicles, and was fairly busy this time of day with joggers, bikers, and other dog walkers. Megan had always felt perfectly safe here. But for the first time, she was anxious when she lost sight of Abbie for a moment.

"Abbie," she yelled. "Abbie!"

Abbie came around the bend, running toward her. "Look what I found!"

The small plastic soldier crouched on a flat pool of

plastic, his rifle aimed at anything in front of him. He was completely Army green, including his skin, and unremarkable to Megan. "Uncle Brian used to play with these when he was little," she said. "He bought bags of them at the dime store."

"Dime store? Is that like a dollar store?"

Megan smiled. "Kind of." Come to think of it, she hadn't noticed these once-ubiquitous soldiers for years. The much more positive Spacies had replaced them.

"Can I keep it?"

Megan slipped it into her pocket. "After I wash it. We don't know where it's been."

"It's been on the ground."

"Right. Okay, time to go home." Abbie turned around and ran toward home.

Then Megan saw him. The Walking Man. Tiny in the distance, but heading directly toward Abbie. Of course, there was no other way to walk, but still . . .

Megan began to run, yanking Bingo with her. She wanted to yell *Abbie!* But that would give him Abbie's name. She settled on, "Hey!"

Abbie turned around. "Get back here."

Instead, Abbie ran forward. Megan caught a glimpse of the Walking Man disappearing into the trees. Small side paths laced the woods. She continued to run until she caught up with Abbie, and grabbed her tightly by one arm. "Don't get so far ahead of me!"

Abbie held up one of her feet, upon which she wore a sandal with flashing lights. "These make me go fast. I can't help it."

"I can," said Megan. She had the fleeting notion that the Walking Man could perhaps tiptoe from thin tree to thin tree, making himself as skinny as the tree, like a cartoon character.

She grasped Abbie's hand firmly. Maybe she really should return Abbie's classbook. Jim had been keeping it, just giving it to her for school, and supervising her homework time with it.

Megan fell into the maelstrom of dinner, cleanup, and getting ready for tomorrow morning's meeting before falling into bed.

When Megan woke up, the next morning, her luminescent digital clock said 3:17 A.M.

She closed her eyes against the baleful time, but the afterimage insisted that it was an ungodly hour of the morning and that she was fully and absolutely awake. It was, indeed, Saturday, and in just a few hours she was going to make a quick trip to New York to catch a Saturday conference at Columbia.

Ugh. Maybe Jim was right, even though his oft-expressed wish that she would develop a drug to treat workaholism, and take it, was actually a joke.

At least, she thought it was.

Jill's message from yesterday, relayed by Jim when he came to bed, that someone had broken into the house, was unsettling. But not to worry.

Of course. Jill never worried. And Brian was staying there. Poor Cindy. She had to be getting to the end of her tether. But maybe not. Cindy was a teacher, although she claimed that she was never patient in the classroom. "That just confuses the kids," she said.

Slipping out of bed, Megan made her way to the wardrobe. She tripped over a pair of shoes and cursed. Jim's snoring stuttered, then resumed its regular, comforting cadence.

The Game Board was right up . . . there. She grabbed it and tiptoed out of the room.

Bingo jumped up from in front of Abbie's door, huffing and snorting and wagging her tail.

"Shh." They went downstairs. The Game Board winked and glowed in the dark, which irritated her. She wanted it to be just a normal piece of metal with paint on it. Clearly, it was not.

The stove light lit the kitchen, dimly. The window over the sink was open, admitting the smell of new-mown

grass. Megan, thinking about the Walking Man, reached up and pulled it shut and locked it. She set water to boil and sprinkled chamomile tea into a Dumbo-shaped teapot. Come to think of it, that was from the Halcyon House attic. A lot of things here were from that attic. She leaned against the counter and waited for the water to boil and then waited for the tea to steep, hoping that she would become drowsy.

No such luck. Finally there was nothing else to do but take her perfectly brewed tea, perfectly flavored with milk and sugar, into the dining room, along with the Game Board, and sit down to have a good long look.

A green dot winked at the upper right corner. Megan leaned forward and took a swig of tea.

It would appear that the Game Board was somehow infused with Q. If it weren't for the fact that Q did not exist when her mother had bought it for her, this would be no big deal.

The board had not manifested this dot earlier today. A slight shiver ran through Megan. Abbie had handled this. She bit her lower lip, thinking.

Finally she got up, and went downstairs, and rummaged through their collection of backpacks, suitcases, and tote bags, and found a fairly large plastic tote bag that read INTERNATIONAL MEMORY CONFERENCE, MADRID, 1989. Beneath that was printed INHANCEX, which was the name of a drug that claimed to impede the progress of Alzheimer's disease.

Good. The board fit. She zipped it inside and set it by the front door, next to her briefcase. She didn't want to leave it in the house, where Abbie could get to it.

She'd given herself an extra hour so that she could have a proper breakfast at her favorite café in the station. She would call Brian and have him or Jill meet her in front of Union Station in the morning to pick it up.

She lay down on the couch to rest just a minute before getting dressed.

Megan

[*July 13*]

T HE HISS of the Metro doors opening woke Megan. The doors clamped shut and the train gathered speed. It took her about two seconds to realize where she was—three stops past Union Station.

"Crap!" She should have driven, but she never drove downtown. She'd left her car at the Metro station in Virginia.

The woman across the aisle glared at her; she had broken the somnolent silence of the early morning commuters. At the next station, she jumped off, paused below a long escalator she'd never seen before, and realized she hadn't transferred at the Pentagon.

It was Saturday morning. It might be twenty minutes before the next train arrived. She dashed up the escalator and emerged about six blocks from the station. "Taxi!" she yelled. "Taxi!"

Right. There were no taxis on this mostly residential street. She could use her phone, but could probably get to the station before a taxi arrived. No zip kiosks in sight.

She launched into an awkward run, handicapped by her low heels, passing boarded-up town houses and a pit bull who raced her from his side of a wrought-iron fence, telling her, in the unmistakable language of barks, growls, lunges, leaps, and snaps, that he would tear her limb from limb as soon as an opportunity presented itself.

Her throat burned by the time she rounded the corner to the station. Inside, she slipped on the marble floor, grabbed a countertop to keep from falling, and scanned the gate announcements. The Magline, an express bullet

train that went two hundred miles an hour, was usually at Gate 9. It had left. That would have only taken an hour.

"Last call for New York," echoed through the station. She'd missed the express, but at least the local Metroliner was leaving right away.

She grabbed the iron handrail next to the train stairs and clanked up the stairs of the last passenger car as the train inched forward. She flung herself into a seat, thankful for the air-conditioning, and wiped her forehead with a crumpled paper napkin from her purse.

"Ticket?" The conductor stood over her, nervously clicking his puncher.

"I'll have to buy one." She got out her wallet and bought a ticket to Penn Station, and watched the train yard drift past as the train picked up speed.

A man sat next to her. She was startled and annoyed, because there were only about five people in the car. She managed to smile briefly, just the corners of her mouth, and said, "Do you mind finding another seat? Most of them are empty." Ordinarily, she would have just moved, herself, but she was not in the mood.

His face was round and pudgy. Long strands of thin, black hair, combed so meticulously that they formed near-parallel lines, surrounded his bald spot. He stared at her with unfriendly blue eyes for a second, and then he smiled himself. With a nod, he got up and moved one seat back, across the aisle. He carried a homburg. What was this, Megan wondered, some kind of homburg revival? Maybe she'd missed a few Style sections. He wasn't her Walking Man; she could see that in an instant.

When the cart came, she was pleased; she only rode the bullet train and didn't realize the local train had such good service. She bought a Danish and two cups of drab coffee that would do nothing to improve her malaised state. She needed raise-me-from-the-dead espresso.

Her first trip to Europe, so long ago, when they were

trying to find Dad, was when she realized the limitations of American coffee. They'd flown all night and arrived in Frankfurt around five in the morning. After customs, they found themselves out on the street with their backpacks. Jill and Brian wanted to find a hotel. She was agreeable until they stopped at a bakery for breakfast. The strong German coffee and the exquisite pastry ignited a fire in her brain. She dragged them to the train station and they were on the next train to Munich. In fact, when she shook her siblings awake at the Munich station, they didn't even remember going through customs.

It had turned out to be a melancholy trip. The village of Oberammergau, still picturesque and small, reminded them that their parents were no longer with them. They had visited their parents' friends, mostly German, and found that Sam had indeed been there on his last known trip. Dr. Schmidt, a historian and one of their mother's best friends, was quite surprised to see them. She invited them inside and served them thin dark bread, gelbwurst with mustard, and cold beer, exclaiming how much they had grown. Megan still had a very strong feeling that there was something Schmidt held back, but they left with nothing more than an invitation to come back anytime. Brian took them up to the caves and insisted that they winnow their way inside the damp, inky-black plane factory of the Third Reich, but they found nothing that would help them in their quest, although Brian claimed that the fact one of the tracks that had carried the rocket planes decades ago showed signs of more recent use was important. He couldn't say why, though. They checked old newspaper records to find out if any unsolved deaths had been recorded. And then they went on to Mönchengladbach, where their father had been stationed, in still-enemy territory, at the end of World War II. Nothing there except paved-over metropolis.

Of the three of them, Megan felt that she was the most clearheaded and objective. Jill had the sometimes silly (in

Megan's opinion) temperament of an artist. Brian was much better, but he sometimes formed opinions too soon and could be stubborn about changing them. She always had to go about giving him new information in a careful, sideways fashion so that he didn't dig in his heels, and let him think that a different point of view was his own idea. The fact that he was older than her, and a boy, clouded his vision sometimes, even though their childhood was long past.

Her phone buzzed. It was Jim. "Did you make the train?"

"Barely. I missed the bullet train; I'm on a local."

"Well, Abbie's still asleep. I'm working. Keeping an eye out for Rover."

"Rover?"

"Our mystery man. I'm a little nervous after Jill's break-in."

"Right. Good." She hung up thinking, time to get to work; but everything was so topsy-turvy. Carrying the damned board around made her nervous too, and when she opened her briefcase, she felt as if the annoying man behind her was looking at the contents. She looked back: he was.

She quickly removed her conference program, then snapped the briefcase shut and set it on the floor between her feet and the window. Some impulse made her fold the program back on itself so that he wouldn't see the cover. She wasn't a presenter at this one, but she wanted to see Dr. Elizabeth Nickolassi, whose work on the biochemistry of intent and will fascinated her.

Damn the man! She really *did* have work to do. Outside, a summer shower fell for about ten minutes; then steam rose from the streets of Baltimore. She fought off the urge to nap, picked up her briefcase, and headed toward the club car.

Once there, she got a double espresso, got out her Q, and wedged her briefcase between herself and the window. Not that she held the secrets of the universe in

it, only the secrets of NIH. Opening the paper she wanted to read, this one about memory storage in sea snails, she gulped the coffee with faint hope.

Her brief spell of concentration ended when the club door slid open and the man she now thought of as her stalker walked in. He hoisted his short self onto a bar stool and ordered a . . . what? A Rolling Rock? He grabbed the unmistakable squat green bottle and took a gulp.

Maybe he was just a random businessman. She watched him as he got out his phone and spoke for a moment, glanced directly at her, then closed it and slipped it back into his pocket.

The train slowed, then stopped at a small station. The man chugged the rest of his beer, grabbed his sandwich and stuffed it in his pocket, and left the train. He didn't go into the station, but disappeared past it, heading toward the end of the train. She turned and watched him until he disappeared from view, feeling rather ridiculous. She was risking a strained neck to spy on a stranger she suspected of spying on her. All this mysterious stuff was driving her around the bend.

But she caught her breath when she saw him picking his way across the tracks a moment later. He climbed onto the opposite platform just before a southbound train pulled in.

She saw him take a window seat in the southbound train just as her train began to move.

Exasperated with herself for the tenth time that morning when she had to pay for a cab to get her to the meeting because she was so late, she missed the talk that she'd wanted to see, but got a Q'd transcript.

Megan stepped into a talk she would not have gone to about objects and memory. It was packed. She found a seat in the back row and watched the video screen.

"Objects are quite clearly nexes of information," the speaker was saying. "But why? We are visual creatures,

and many of us think in images. Images and objects elicit emotion quickly and directly, oftentimes, it seems, more powerfully than if we used words. Not only do we cling to physical objects that are emotionally meaningful to us, but we grieve their loss. Why? Because the object itself is the last real link we have with that past? We are relatively incapable of truly fixing memory and emotion; we want desperately to make it concrete, rather than abstract.

"Many images are universal icons that elicit innumerable emotions. Think of the cross, which can reinforce positive ideas about the nature of God and the Christ for Christians. There! A lot of thoughts flowed through the mind of each and every one of you. What neurons were activated?"

The words "quantum memory" caught her attention. Suddenly, the woman segued into a riff about changing the brains of all humans in such a way that they would value peace, cooperation, aiding the less fortunate, education. Megan had gotten the same message from the numerous papers Hadntz had Q'd her. "I realize that these are just emblems of a liberal point of view. But what if these ideas were truly embedded in action in a widespread manner? What if, for instance, it became apparent not that we all had to pick up weapons and fight other humans for our survival, but that international cooperation was the only way in which we could all survive some specific, looming threat? How would we react?"

What did this have to do with memory? Megan wondered.

"The threats are real. Starvation, subjugation, slave labor, are all real. But they might be abstract to us. What if a 'memory' was released worldwide, piggybacked on a virus, putting each individual, briefly and vividly, into that reality? News reports are ephemeral, and lack a mechanism for specific response, except for those innumerable, ridiculous reader comments. No, no"—she held

up her hand as a low murmur threatened to become an uproar—"I am not proposing that we actually *do* this. But I am saying that it may be possible, and that we need to guard against such occurrences. I am trying to alert all of you to the dangers. This is a new paradigm of thought, behavior, and education that we all need to be aware of. We need to think about the possibilities. How, for instance, can we decide empowerment issues? Whose version of what is best will prevail?"

Megan perked up, tremendously interested. For instance, she thought, you own a factory and make a certain profit. Then a new safety feature comes along and if you buy it, your employees will be less likely to be injured or disabled. But it will cut down on your profits. You will have to raise your prices to implement it. If only you implement it, you may go out of business, and then your employees will have to work in more dangerous places anyway.

What would most business owners choose?

Of course. They would choose more money. But what if everyone had a visceral memory of painful rehab when a saw sliced one's hand? Or, if, perhaps, it was required "reading" if one were to open a factory.

Megan thought about the mice, and their memories, or at least their knowledge of how to run a maze, and about how it could be transplanted from one mouse to another. Memory was, indeed, physical.

Well, Megan thought, let's take this one step further. Let's sublime the memories of mice and think of an easy, nonpainful way to share their memories. Like a pill. HD-50, perhaps. Move a few molecules around . . .

Could we then all be made to share one mass, false memory?

Surely, emotions were shared by a lot of people at once. Love for not the specific person, but for one's country. Or, at least, loyalty to whatever myth of country had arisen over the years or had been planted in the populace's mind.

She stopped listening to the talk and began mulling this over.

All children were socialized—even in the womb, once they could hear the cadences of what would be their native language. They acted like their parents, and were taught to obey social mores and customs of the society into which they were born. Most societies emphasized in thought, if not in deed, kindness, politeness, generosity, and so on. She recalled that Abbie's Montessori school did not emphasize sharing, because if children were concentrating on some piece of material they ought not fear that it might be yanked away from them suddenly in the name of being "nice" to someone else. It was theirs until they put it back on the shelf.

Less fortunate children, like those of Ma Barker, had few options.

Symbols and images definitely had the power to cement large groups of people. Hitler's swastika still evoked something she could only call Evil. Just about every home and certainly every public building in Nazi Germany had had one or more portraits of Hitler. Those images had early on been linked to death, the death of those who disagreed and who said so.

But the memories elicited by objects were usually exclusive to just one family or a small group. Grandma's quilt, valued by her grandchildren because they had known her and because her hands had made it; valued by others only if it had monetary value.

She began thinking about Jill's school project. Jill's interest had spurred her to read more about the situation in central Africa, about child soldiers, civil wars, and wholesale slaughter.

What if soldiers became incapable, mentally, of killing innocents? If she could piggyback some images into this drug . . . use neurolinguistic programming tools . . . after all, much of the media, right now, and much gaming, used images of violence, so none of this would be new. It would just be used for a very different end.

The idea that war could stop war was proven nonsense. There had to be new solutions. Maybe this could be part of one, eventually. Of course there was Nobel, and dynamite. There was Gatling, and his gun. But one couldn't stop hoping, stop trying.

After the talk, Megan tried to get to the front of the auditorium to speak with the presenter. But she was mobbed, and soon hurried offstage.

Jill

JILL GOES TO MARKET

[*July 13*]

JILL, YOU always do this." Brian stood at the kitchen table with a cup of coffee in one hand and a plate of fried eggs in the other. Piles of books and magazines covered the table. There was a small clearing at one end of the table, which was where Jill ate. It was about 9:00 A.M., Saturday morning.

"I'm usually alone." Jill did not say what immediately popped into her head, which was *So clear out a place for yourself*. Instead, she picked up a stack of books and plunked them on a chair. "How about this?"

"But there's all this . . . stuff around me." Brian set his food down and Jill turned her face away so he would not see her smile. He looked like a gopher; his head just cleared a healthy stack of *Washington Posts*.

"If there's not enough to read here, I can fetch something else." She sat down with her bowl of cereal and grabbed a half-read *Atlantic*. She had periodicals and books everywhere in the house where she might sit down. She was a firm believer in the power of serendipitous reading. Things had a way of coming together and augmenting one another; things you never would have related to one another before. Scientific articles mingled with literary reviews. She imagined that Cindy ran a

tight ship. There wasn't any reading matter on her kitchen table. Of course, there probably was room for children to eat.

Brian had spelled Cindy so she could get a nap until midnight, then Cindy returned to the hospital. Jill and Brian had sat up as late as Jill could, even with coffee, but Jill wanted to wait until Megan was there to tell the whole tale. Brian did tell her what he had learned about the Hadntz material and the Device, then Jill suggested that they all be there at the same time to avoid the confusion they seemed to generate when only two siblings knew about something. Her actions would always be soul-shattering to her, and she really did not want to go through the confession, and all the questions, twice.

Jill's phone rang. It was Cindy.

"Jill. I have a big favor to ask."

"Whatever it is, the answer is yes."

"Wait till you hear what it is. Our lease is up next week. It was short term; we thought we'd have the house done by now. So—"

"I hope," said Jill, speaking quickly before the other part of her brain could pile on the objections, "that you guys will move in here for the time being."

Brian looked at Jill with a startled expression on his face. "Is that Cindy?"

Cindy said, "I can't tell you how much that will help us out."

"Now, you're sure? Even after the break-in?"

Cindy laughed. "Especially after the break-in! The more people over there, the better. They're discharging Bitsy later today. She's doing great. She's a little pistol, bless her heart. I'll ask the crew to pick up what we need from the apartment for tonight, and I'll call Brian and let him know."

"Well—good." Jill hung up. "You're moving in."

"It wasn't my idea."

"It will be great. I appreciate it."

"You're okay with it then?"

"Definitely. At first, I wanted to be alone here, but now . . . it's fine. But how about you?"

Brian shrugged. "Better than camping out. Seems like a good plan for everyone."

"But it bothers you."

"Always has."

"I'll try to get that straightened out tomorrow, Brian. I promise."

He called Cindy. "How's Bitsy? Oh, honey, that's great. That's wonderful. I'm so happy. I'll come over and— Oh, all right, if that's what you want. See you guys in a few hours."

He closed the phone. "She's bringing Bitsy. Said we didn't both need to be there. Zoe's there to help. Cindy ordered—I mean, asked—me to cut the grass."

"Did you tell her about finding the Game Board?"

"Yes, but I'm not sure it means anything to her. She knows as much as I know about all of it, but you know Cindy. Nothing fazes her."

"Okay, then. It's settled. Pizza tomorrow." She started her vitamin regimen. There were a lot of pills, a few enticing new supplements from the vitamin company that promised eternal life, or something close to that, as usual, and some even-keel pills prescribed by the therapist. "We can bake it in the woodstove outside." Sam's Folly Number Four, as their mother had called it, was clearly visible from the window, now that the crew had chainsawed away the kudzu. It was a huge brick structure with two ovens, two chimneys, a slate countertop, a stone sink, and even a space for a refrigerator.

"Is the water hooked up?"

"It just needs to be turned on."

"Well, good idea then."

"I'll go to the market in a little while. That will be nice. I don't go that often just for myself."

"Aren't you tired?"

Jill considered. "Yeah. But it won't hit until bedtime tonight."

"I tried to get that Game Board to do something."

"So what happened?"

Brian said, "Nothing, that I could see. I mean, it told me nothing. Didn't you always say that it was full of stories? Not for me. But the damnedest thing happened to me, while I was reading the notebooks—kind of the same thing. It was as if my mind flipped. I would suddenly *be* with Dad and his pal Wink. But the Game Board pretty much stayed blank for me, just a metal surface with embossed pictures on it. Hey, what's that you're taking?"

Jill handed him the jar. "HD-50? Came in the mail. This month's free stuff."

"We got it too. I love it."

"Doesn't do much for me. So, when you use the board, does it . . . seem to become three-dimensional, or move around, or change other scenarios? Like it did when we were kids?"

"I kind of remember that. Vaguely. But, no. That still happens to you?"

"Oh, yes!"

"That would definitely bother me, Jill. I can see why you—"

"Went crazy?"

"Yeah. I did have vivid dreams last night. I dreamed about playing the saxophone with Dad in a jazz band. And the great part was that I could actually hold my own."

Brian's phone rang. "Jim? What's up? No, didn't see Megan this morning. She left you a note saying she'd call me? No. She didn't. Why?" A moment of silence. "Okay, well, maybe we'll find out what's upsetting her when she gets back tonight. Yeah, everyone's invited to Sunday dinner tomorrow. Hah! Yeah, you're right, when else would we have Sunday dinner? Okay, just let her know. Come over early, around ten. We have some family issues to talk about first. Sure, you're welcome to participate, if you can stand it. Cindy plans to hang with the kids.

Bitsy is fine, thanks. Coming home today." He hung up. "Megan was upset about something and left Jim a note saying she'd call me this morning. She didn't. Did she call you?"

"If she did, I didn't hear it. All she does is go to meetings." Memory research meetings. Of course. It was her fault that Megan's memories were screwed up, that she was even interested in memory. Jill sighed.

Brian said, "What's wrong now?"

"Besides the break-in, the divorce, and my recent internment in a mental institution? Nothing. I'm happy as a lark."

"Good." Brian went back to the Outlook page. Jill went into the study, started a long-running reel-to-reel jazz compilation that Sam had made, and promptly fell asleep on the couch.

But it wasn't really sleep. It was more like a deep trance, induced by the first direct notes of "Ko-Ko." Pictures came alive in her mind, but they didn't seem random. It was more like she was in some kind of plane, cued for takeoff, and then the runway lights flashed past, and her mind was put through some kind of paces, some kind of reasoned argument, some kind of carefully calibrated change.

At first she struggled to wake up. But she could not. And it didn't really seem like sleep, more as if she were captured in a dream. It seemed more real than most waking moments, more true than any love she'd ever felt. Her mother was flying them all somewhere in a huge plane. . . .

When Jill woke, it was a little after one in the afternoon. She sat up, marvelously refreshed, as if she'd been swimming in a clear mountain stream.

The lawn mower droned in the side yard, and the delicious smell of new-cut grass infiltrated the room. Brian passed the window as he turned to cut another row.

The tape recorder had turned itself off. Probably just now. Maybe that's what woke her up.

Someone knocked on the screen door. "Come in," she yelled, thinking it was the woman across the street, or one of Whens' friends.

It was Detective Kandell.

He was wearing shorts, a Bob Marley T-shirt, and Converse sneakers. He stood in a pool of sunlight by the door. "Hello?"

"Oh. Hi. Come in and sit down. Or get yourself a beer from the kitchen if you want."

"No, thanks." He hesitated for a moment.

"Well, then, sit down."

"You're busy."

"I'm always busy."

Daniel chose the battered leather chair in the corner next to the open French door. "Anything happen last night?"

"No. Brian stayed here. His family is moving in. We talked till two, then something woke me up around three, and I couldn't get back to sleep. But it was nothing."

"You should have called."

"For a sound? It was just a branch scraping the roof, something like that. I have to have the trees pruned before one of them falls on the house. I think that oak tree is rotten."

"Did Brian find anything?"

"I didn't wake him up. Manfred and I made the rounds."

"Manfred?" Detective Kandell looked at Manfred, asleep on her side and drooling onto the floor, with some doubt.

"Oh, she's much more vicious than she appears to be."

"Right. She did bite the intruder yesterday. Actually, I came to see if you'd gotten that party list together."

"You do work hard."

"It's my neighborhood too. It just seems to me that a

party would have given anyone ample time to browse through the library."

"Definitely. A lot of people did. In fact, Megan said that someone did act suspiciously. I'm not sure who it was, though. I have the party list here." She went over to her briefcase, which was still where she'd left it before, next to the couch. Opening it, she removed her Q, printed the list, and handed it to Detective Kandell.

"Wow. Addresses, phone numbers, everything."

"Well, yeah. I guess I don't look as if I could be very sharp?"

"No, no, that's not it," he said with some haste.

She laughed. "Gotcha."

He studied the paper. "Would you mind telling me who these people are?"

They sat on the couch next to each other with the paper on the coffee table in front of them. Jill had a fine-point marker in her hand.

"'W' for World Bank. 'U' for University."

"That's Georgetown?"

"Right. 'N' for neighborhood. 'F' for family."

"Who is this Dr. Koslov?"

"World War II expert. He's written several books. Um, there, to the right of the fireplace, fifth shelf up, middle. The red, white, and blue dust jackets."

"Snazzy. He's Russian?"

Jill nodded.

"Any Germans in the mix?"

"That's an odd question."

"Well, they did have something to do with the war."

"So?"

"I've been doing a little research. It seems that your mother was in the OSS, and the CIA."

Jill's poker face went on full alert, mainly because she was incensed. "That seems to be information that we mere mortals have no access to. If that's true, why would that have anything to do with the break-in, anyway?"

"A, the break-in was very strange. You have valuable

objects sitting all over the place, like that Chinese painting in the foyer. Not very portable, true, but the little Tang Dynasty jade Buddha sitting underneath it sure is. And on that end table over there are, if I'm not mistaken, a small heap of—let's see—a gold chain, rather ostentatious diamond earrings, and an emerald ring."

"I guess I'm kind of careless with jewelry. I wore those at the party."

"B, the books the man took all have to do with mid-century science, which is something both of your parents were involved in. Your dad, for instance, learned about the top-secret M-9 Fire Director when he trained at Aberdeen."

"Really." Jill was now definitely irritated.

"You can't think your parents' interests are a secret to anyone who's even glanced at the contents of this library." He watched her a moment, his middle-aged face impassive. "Maybe you don't want this solved."

Jill sighed. "I'm sorry. Yes. I mean no, not really, but there is a guy at the Bank, Bill Anderson, who's a Germany expert, but he's from Ohio. I have run across supposedly de-Nazified Nazis, in various places over the years. Old men, now. There are a lot of them in academic and scientific circles. They were allowed to come to the U.S. in exchange for information—recruited, actually. Our rocket program is based on their info. So is Russia's. They got some of them too. Highest bidder—at least those who thought ahead. If not, it depended on where the war caught up with them. We gained a few defectors in later years, and so did the Russians. Now, of course, that's all over."

"Is it?"

Jill wondered whether or not to tell Kandell about what Megan overheard at the party, and then wondered why she was even thinking about it at all, considering what a can of worms it would open.

The screen door slammed behind Brian. His T-shirt was soaked with sweat. "Ah, summer in Washington.

Cold beer?" Without waiting for an answer, he brought three bottles, three pilsner glasses, and a church key from the kitchen and set them up. "Man, it's hot." He glanced at the paper. "Any leads?"

Detective Kandell shrugged. "Maybe. Seems to me that the people who came to the party—"

"Yeah," said Brian. "That Bill Anderson guy, from the Bank, he was pretty nosy."

"The Germany guy?" asked Daniel.

"Right. He sometimes is," said Jill. "I think he likes me. I didn't know he was asking about me, though."

Brian handed Kandell a beer. "He more than likes you, Jill. He asked a lot of questions about Mom and Dad. Who they worked for. What they did. Maybe he's going to ask me for your hand in marriage."

"If he does, say no."

Kandell sipped his beer. "Why do you suppose he was asking these questions?"

Brian and Jill looked at each other for a long moment.

"Daniel claims Mom was in the OSS and the CIA."

"Dad was in fire protection," said Brian. "He worked for GSA. Mom was kind of eclectic. She was going to school, and had the Montessori school, of course. She never actually went to any job, though, at least not when we were kids."

Jill could feel a flush rising on her face. She took another gulp of beer, got up, and turned on an old GE floor fan from the forties. It rotated back and forth like an implacable eye.

"What?" Daniel was looking at her.

"Nothing. It's awful hot." She picked up the party list and fanned herself. "Why don't you come to dinner tomorrow afternoon? The whole family will be here. You can ask them questions if you think it's relevant."

Brian shot her a look. "Jill—"

"We'll be done by that time, Brian."

Brian just raised his eyebrows.

"Thanks," said Daniel. "Since your father's books

were stolen, I think that would be helpful, but we're having a family dinner ourselves, Dad, Grandma Arabelle, and my son."

"Bring all of them. It will be fun." And maybe muddy the waters, she hoped, not so happy about the direction this investigation was taking. Especially considering that Daniel remembered Bette, remembered the school. That seemed way too personal. But then, she thought, *Aren't you trying to open up? Isn't that what the therapist says? Isn't that what your brother and sister want? Sure, let's just tell the whole world that maybe Mom was a spy, and Dad was in charge of the most dangerous weapon since the atom bomb. Let's just—*

Daniel said, "You say that your sister—"

"Megan," she said, returning suddenly to the room, Daniel, and Brian.

"Might know something about them."

"Megan might have a stalker too," said Brian.

"What? She didn't tell me," said Jill.

"Oh. I thought she had. Don't you two ever talk? Right. None of us do. Anyway—this was before the party—Megan mentioned a guy who constantly walks around her neighborhood."

"What makes him noticeable?" asked Daniel.

"The fact that he wears plaid shorts and a fedora," said Brian. "According to Megan. But her husband, Jim, thought he was strange too."

"She live downtown?"

"No. Springfield."

Daniel rested his elbows on his knees, clasped his hands, and leaned forward. He stared at the laden bookshelf. Finally he said, "Do either of you have any idea what this is all about?"

Brian opened his mouth. Jill made him shut it with a sharp glare. "No," he finally said.

"I can't help if you don't tell me," said Daniel.

"I've got to go to the market," said Jill.

"Eastern Market? Can I drive you?"

Jill was slightly taken aback, and she was sure that he noticed. Being a detective, and all. But after an instant's hesitation, she said, "Okay."

Daniel's '64 Pontiac was a faded gold. It took corners wide. The right dashboard was heat-cracked with a small crazed line running from the corner of the glove compartment to the window.

"Was this new when you got it?" asked Jill.

"It was my dad's."

"Is he still alive?"

"Retired."

"Policeman?"

Daniel looked at her with amusement. "Contrary to your belief, not all black professional men in Washington work for the police department."

"It's just that—"

"He's an architect. Actually, he still takes jobs. Just no museums or anything. He'd love to see your house."

"Aha. An ulterior motive. Bring him tomorrow. I'd love to know more about the house. Your mom?"

"She died about five years ago."

"I'm sorry. And your wife? I mean, ex-wife?"

"She moved back to Boston."

"But your boy is here."

"Just for a few weeks in the summer. He's with his cousins today."

"Bring him too."

"I, um, gathered that your brother wasn't too keen about the idea. If you want to change your mind, I won't feel in the least insulted."

"Oh, no." There'd be no talking during dinner, what with all the kids running around. And the Kandells would be gone if they needed to get back down to business later. Jill realized that she rather liked Daniel. He was easygoing, comfortable to be around.

"Okay." They were silent as he pursued a slow, side-street route to the market. Jill got the feeling that he

simply enjoyed driving through different neighborhoods, through the cathedral-like avenues of old trees. She relaxed into the cadence.

"We're being followed, by the way."

She unrelaxed immediately.

"Don't turn around. He's in a blue recent-model Volkswagen. He's not there right now; he's dropped back."

"Can you see what he looks like?"

"I can only see that he's wearing a hat. Like he's on his way to the office forty years ago."

Jill got her phone out of her pocket and called Brian. "What kind of hat did the man wear?"

"A black homburg."

"Tell him to keep an eye on things," said Daniel.

"I heard him," said Brian. "That's what I'm here for." He hung up.

"He said a black homburg."

"Odd bird, eh?"

Daniel pulled into the market's wandering old parking lot.

The market had been ongoing for over a hundred years, long enough for the stalls to relax into friendly dilapidation, long enough to become large and complex.

"Is he still—"

"No," said Daniel. "I lost him with all that fancy high-speed maneuvering."

"I thought so."

"He'll be here. Don't worry. So what are we looking for?"

"Whatever's fresh. I'm going to make some pizzas to bake in the wood oven outdoors." Jill got four canvas bags from the backseat and handed him two.

The instant they got inside she said, "Wow. Look at that flounder!" Fish, shrimp, clams, and oysters lay in attractive rows on ice.

"Flounder pizza?"

"Hey, Dave."

"Hey, Jill. Flounder, right?" Without her asking, the

fishmonger put a fillet on his hand and held it out. She sniffed. "Five pounds on ice. I'll pick it up on the way out."

She said to Daniel, "Cornmeal, cast-iron frying pans. There's plenty of room on the grill. Not everybody likes pizza."

"That's news to me."

Jill headed for the cheese. "Hi, Fred. Can you give me a sample of the Parmesan?"

"She only gets the expensive stuff," Fred said to Daniel. To Jill he said, "You know what it tastes like."

"I always like to check. Make sure you're not slacking on quality. What's that German cheese?"

"Just got it. Actually, it's probably more French than German. Right on the border."

Soon their bags were overflowing with fresh and dried tomatoes, basil, beautiful purple and white striped eggplants that she actually wanted to paint, five red peppers, several cheeses, onions, exotic mushrooms, and assorted cold cuts.

Daniel remarked, "This is going to be quite a party."

"It's always bigger than I think it's going to be."

"Where's your pizza sauce?"

Jill pointed to the tomatoes and basil.

"You're a glutton for punishment."

"Just a glutton, thank you." She froze.

"Don't worry, I've been keeping an eye on him. Over there behind the butcher's stall, right? Can't be any taller than five five. He's packing."

"Why in the world would he follow me here?"

"Jill, you're going to have to tell me."

"I haven't told my brother and sister. Why would I tell you?"

"Haven't told them what?" He faced her. "Jill. Told them what?"

She looked directly into his eyes. She did not tell him to remove his hand from her shoulder, as she had thought she was going to.

"Look," she said. "I was committed just a few months ago."

"I know," he said gently.

"Damn." She was silent a moment. "That's not fair. How do you know?"

"Brian told me."

Jill glared at the market in general. She did not look at Daniel.

Finally she said, "What other personal information did he volunteer?"

"Oh, he just said that you're a brilliant workaholic who is also an exceedingly talented artist."

"Bullshit."

"He said that you work too much, you paint to relax, you read a lot, you're getting a divorce, and that he doesn't like you living in that big house alone. So why do you live in that big house alone?"

"That's none of your business. Well, I think I'm finished here."

"Are you sure you have enough food? We may have skipped a booth."

"Oh, be quiet."

"We'll bring dessert. I bake a mean apple pie."

Jill simmered as they walked through the parking lot. "Can't you at least arrest that guy?"

"What for?"

"Carrying a concealed weapon. You could interrogate him."

Daniel unlocked the car and put the flounder in the ice chest.

"He's stalking me. Maybe he's the one who broke into the house."

"I doubt it. He's too short. I could go over and give him a talking-to, but I prefer to let him play his hand."

"So you're not going to do anything, even though he terrifies me?"

"You know, Jill," Daniel said, as they got into the car and rolled down the windows, "you seem singularly

non-terrifiable. Most other women—I mean, people—would be hysterical right about now."

She sighed. "I guess you're right. I'm not sure where I get that from. I'm more annoyed than terrified. I don't feel at all that my life is in danger, I guess. I don't feel . . . menaced."

"You should. I think this is a serious matter."

"I want to get to the bottom of this. Get it over with. But maybe if you arrested him, another one would just take his place."

"A vast conspiracy."

"You think I'm nuts."

"I happen to think you're correct."

"Based on what? You just met me yesterday, right?"

"Yes and no." He swung out of the parking lot and checked the mirror. "Here he comes. By the book."

"Yes and no? What do you mean by that? Have you been stalking me?"

"No. I met you when my little brother was in your mother's school. You were fiery as hell, worked down at the Poor People's Campaign headquarters, which I frequented, and I was quite astonished to see you, the Jill Who Would March into the Gates of Hell, sitting on the floor and playing with my little brother when I came to pick him up one day. You were wearing blue bell bottoms with big silvery buttons on the bells and a white shirt with Mexican embroidery on the yoke."

"Do you remember what the embroidery was?"

"Is this a test?"

"Maybe." Jill cleared her throat, tried to make her voice less shaky, tried to keep her eyes from filling with tears.

"What if I don't recall such a seemingly trivial detail?" She said, "Do you?"

"Something to do with bluebirds, I think, and big red flowers."

And then she was crying, sobbing straight out, her fists clenched on her knees, and he pulled over and put an

arm around her while she leaned on his shoulder and cried until she couldn't cry anymore.

After that, he was the first person she had ever told about everything that had happened. They didn't get back to the house until much later, when they hurried to stuff everything in the refrigerator.

Daniel said, "Jill, we have more to talk about, but I have to go pick up my son."

"Thanks," she said, and gave him a quick hug.

Brian came in from the living room. "Cindy and Bitsy are upstairs napping. Zoe's in the ballroom. I'm off to pick up more things from the apartment. What was that all about?"

"None of your business."

Megan caught the Magline back to Washington and her ride was uneventful, for which she was thankful. At about five thirty, she stood in front of Union Station, her suit jacket over her arm, her shirt pasted to her back by sweat. This summer's heat was astounding—but each summer's heat was declared the worst ever by those experiencing it. She looked at her watch. Jim wasn't expecting her until later that night, but she longed to see Abbie, to pick her up and hug her very, very tightly. But the damned Game Board hung on her shoulder. She'd decided to stash the board at Jill's and then go home, when a woman rushed toward her.

She was blond and wore a WWII uniform. Before Megan could think, or move out of her way, the woman hugged her, crushed her almost. Then she held Megan's shoulders, and looked her up and down. She nodded, then stepped back and said, "I'm sorry. This war is going on for much longer than we thought it would." Then she turned sharply and walked into the vast doors of Union Station.

Megan ran after her, into an older Union Station, filled with soldiers. She stood stock-still for a moment, absolutely astounded. Then she looked for the woman. She'd

lost her!—no, there she was, her blond hair pushed up under her hat, walking toward one of the gates.

"Wait!" Megan yelled. Her plea faded into an acoustical painting, echo upon echo. Above her, the sign changed, clicking in rapid *snaps,* and then cool air hit her.

Cool air-conditioning. Above her, a digital sign silently changed a track number. The soldiers had vanished; the gorgeously renovated station was a great contrast to the shabby World War II station she'd just—what, imagined?—being in.

She walked over to an old bench. It had been kept, as had any salvageable element of the original station had been kept. Sitting down, she carefully looked over the scene in front of her, wondering what had happened.

A memory? No, she hadn't been alive during World War II. Her ideas about it had been formed by movies, photographs, oral stories. She realized that she hadn't eaten since her breakfast of stale Danish. Maybe that was it.

Who was that woman?

And then it came to her.

She dug her phone from her purse and pressed a button. Jill answered.

"Can you pick me up at the train station?"

"Sure. Are you okay? You sound kind of funny."

"I just saw Mom."

Jill, Brian, and Megan

AN EVENING OF FUN AND GAMES

[*July 13*]

JILL RAN out the front door, climbed into Brian's truck, and fished out the keys from under the seat. She tore through the streets and got to the station in five minutes flat.

Megan stood out front. She looked curiously small; uncharacteristically bedraggled. Her lovely black hair, usually precisely combed, flew every which way, and her frown was ferocious. You wanted to give Megan plenty of room when she was mad.

She was carrying not only her briefcase, but another bag. The jacket of her gray pantsuit hung from her hand and dragged on the pavement as she hurried forward and yanked open the truck door.

"God, I'm glad to see you!" She heaved her stuff inside and climbed in.

"What's going on?" Jill did not start the truck. "You saw Mom? Where? Let's go back and look for her!"

"I tried. I didn't recognize her at first, because she was younger, in her WAC uniform. She hugged me tight. Right there! Right on that spot on the sidewalk! She certainly knew me. She said something about the war going on for much longer than they thought it would, then she hurried into the station. I guess I was just in shock and couldn't move, for a minute, but then I ran inside and everything was old. Like the forties. The people, everything. And I think I saw her, but I'm not sure, she walked out through a gate and the train there was pulling out. Then it all changed back to . . . now. She's gone, Jill. Can we go home? To your house?"

A WAC. Right. Jill put the truck in gear and sped off.

Megan continued to chatter. "I was followed this morning. By a short man in a hat. But I think he got off the train early and came back in this direction."

"I was followed at the market today. By a short man in a hat."

"If it's the same one, he's very busy."

"And not particularly interested in anonymity." Jill pulled up to the front of the house. Megan opened the truck door, slid down to the curb, and grabbed her jacket and briefcase. Jill picked up the other bag. "Inhancex? More memory stuff?"

"It's that Game Board I got when we were little."

Jill stared at Megan across the truck seat. "What?"

"Oh, you might not remember. It was a long time ago. Vodka. Straight. On the rocks. Immediately." She slammed the door and headed toward the house.

Jill tossed the keys under the seat, grabbed the bag, got out, and leaned against the truck door, which closed with a reluctant *clunk. My life is ringed with fear,* she thought, angry and struggling against a wave of resignation. She pulled open the zipper of the bag.

Inside was another Infinite Game Board.

God! Not only did they promise infinity; perhaps the damned things were, actually infinite. Jill had a vision of them marching along like the animated mops in an old Disney cartoon about the sorcerer's apprentice . . .

But wait. Daniel had said something. About . . . Estrella, the Spacie. The old ones replicated.

Okay. Another clue. Apparently, so did Game Boards. But from what? What was the *source?*

She quickly rezipped the bag and forced herself to breathe slowly and deliberately, to cycle the image of air through her lungs, up through her head, out the top.

It didn't help. Her heart raced. She pushed off from the truck and was dizzy, so she waited until the spinning stopped, and then walked steadily up the front walk, feeling as if she was battling hurricane-force winds as she carried the bag containing the Game Board. The green, flat lawn seemed fragile and ephemeral, as if it might wink from existence at any time, taking everything else with it. Washington's famous summer haze hovered over the creek that they considered theirs. Her freshly watered hydrangeas weighed down their branches, their purple blooms huge ostentatious jewels. The freshly painted gingerbread proclaimed her home a sparkling specimen of High Victorian. Her little Whens, although he claimed to see ghosts, was her perfect boy. She even had money, a job, and a bookstore where she would now stock comics. All was well, except that it frigging well wasn't.

She wanted to fling the Game Board far away, back to whatever abominable place had spawned it, but she knew:

Their parents had built it.

It was here.

It would not go away.

Stubbornly, it—no, *they!* the prolific, ever-multiplying Game Boards, would surf onto the beach en masse, wherever the Dances happened to rent a beach house, guided by their heavy burden of histories, and glitter and wink on the sand, happy to have reinvaded their lives. They would escape the center-of-the-earth cave where they'd been dumped by gliding down a subterranean river, and pile up just below Sam and Bette's little grotto, and sing entreaties to children to play with them. They would craftily lodge themselves into a single meteor-lump after being shot into space and return in a triumphant streak of light, signal Brian and Megan and tell them not to worry, they would be home soon, and land in a smoking crater in the woods out back, perfect and undamaged, ready to wreak havoc. The Game Boards would arise from the deeps of time, pursuing them with their siren call.

The three of them had to learn how to use the Game Board. Then she paused as she realized: They had to *remember* how to use it. And then they had to decide what to use it *for*.

She stomped up the front stairs and strode into the library.

Brian sprawled on the couch, holding a sweating beer. Megan lay on the floor, on her back, a throw pillow under her head, staring at the ceiling, a glass of vodka on her chest, the bottle ready at hand on the coffee table.

Jill said, "Megan, I'm so sorry that I don't have any San Pellegrino, but—"

"Shut up," said Megan.

Someone had thoughtfully provided Jill with a bottle of pinot grigio and a wineglass, and she poured herself a

nice cold half-glass of straw-colored wine. A plate of cheese and crackers rested atop the papers piled on the coffee table, and Brian had his own giant-sized bag of barbecue potato chips.

Jill considered closing the blinds, but decided that if she left them open they could see anyone who might try to listen in.

She sat on the floor next to the coffee table and pulled the Game Board out of Megan's bag.

"I thought you said you put that upstairs," said Brian.

"I did. Megan has another one."

"You have one too?" asked Megan. "My, my, my. I came home yesterday, and Abbie was playing with it." Megan sat up and glared at Brian and Jill in turn. "PLAYING with it!" She lay down again, held her glass on her chest, and resumed staring at the ceiling.

Jill said, "I have something to tell you."

"Yes, Jill, TELL us," said Megan. "We are all ears."

Jill could tell that Megan was just a wee bit tired and on edge. She turned to Brian. "Have you finished reading Dad's papers?"

"What is this," asked Megan, "an exam?" She lifted her head at an angle that looked quite strenuous, but which enabled her to take a sip of the vodka before she let her head fall back onto the pillow. "Why don't you ANSWER some questions?"

"I've read some of them," said Brian.

"What do you think?"

"I gather that Eliani Hadntz gave Dad the plans—"

Megan was roused enough to sit up while simultaneously holding her vodka so that she did not spill a drop. Jill thought Megan might even jump to her feet, but no, she was too tired and settled for a ramrod-straight back. "You said that last week. I want more."

"Here's more. Gypsy Myra." She ruffled through some papers on the coffee table and pulled out an old mimeographed comic book. "Remember this?"

Megan paged through it. "No. I mean, kind of, I do

380 | KATHLEEN ANN GOONAN

know that you wrote comics for a while. I never read them. But you're right. I do know Eliani Hadntz, and she looks pretty much like this woman. I've only seen her once. But I'm pretty sure this is her."

"Where did you meet her?"

"She's a colleague. I met her at the Cuba conference. And, in fact, she has helped me complete my memory project. I have ninety pills of her memory drug right here in my purse."

"Finally!" asked Brian. "Let's take some."

"I already have," said Megan. "Then the Game Board showed up. Do you think there's a relationship?" She rummaged in her bag and got out the bottle of capsules. "Feel free, my little guinea pigs. What the fucking hell. Good for the mice, good for us, that's my credo."

Brian immediately took two, looked up, then took another one. "HD-50?"

"That's what her literature calls it. All the info is on my Q, if you want it."

Brian got up, left the room, and came back holding a bottle. "Here they are."

Megan said, "What?"

"Yeah. The new supplements that came in the mail. They say 'HD-50' right here on the label."

Megan grabbed the bottle and shook some of them out. "I'd have to analyze it, but my guess is that they're the same. They came with this month's vitamins? I've been too busy to open my box. I'll check these out."

"Cindy's been taking it too. And the kids."

"Do you think—no," said Jill.

"No." Megan shook her head. "She couldn't, she wouldn't."

"She could and I think she would," said Jill.

"Couldn't or wouldn't what?" asked Brian.

"Get this stuff into everyone in the world, somehow." Megan dropped several capsules into a pillbox from her purse and handed Brian the bottle.

Jill said, "You know that she's the one that got us into this mess?"

"No, Jill." Megan lay down on her back again. "Another fact you have neglected to share with us."

"I didn't even know her name until a few weeks ago. I mean, I must have known it, briefly, but I'd forgotten it."

"I'm trying really hard not to act as pissed with you as I really am," said Megan, once again addressing the ceiling fan. "Since you seem to know so much fucking more about everything than we do and haven't had the decency to tell us."

Jill didn't say what immediately came to mind, which was that she was grateful for Megan's restraint, because she did not like standing outside when lightning was shooting to the ground and exploding nearby trees, which was what Megan's anger used to resemble, before she'd gotten so much—Jill sighed—control over it.

"It's no good to sit there and sigh," said Megan. "I am not well-versed in the language of sighs."

Jill noticed that Brian was carefully not opening his own mouth.

"I'm sorry." Jill stood up and paced from the rocking chair in front of one end of the fireplace wall to the edge of the desk and back again as she plunged in. "Okay. It's my fault that you lost Mom when you were so young. I did too, but I was older, and I knew what had happened." She tried her breathing exercise again. This time it seemed to work. Her voice shook only a little, though her lungs felt squeezed; tight.

Brian said, "How—"

Jill held up her hand. "Let me talk. Look at those *Gypsy Myra* comics. Hand Megan a few."

While paging through them, Megan abandoned her prone position. "This is weird stuff, Jill. John F. Kennedy assassinated? In—"

"Wait, Megan," Brian interrupted. "This is even weirder. Martin Luther King assassinated. In—1968?

The inner cities of the whole country torn by riots? Fires? Megan—"

"That's right. Jill, Brian and I have dreams about this. But both of these men are alive." Megan turned her pale, puzzled face toward her sister.

"Robert Kennedy killed too?" asked Brian, in total disbelief. "In '68 too? Damn! That would have been awful. What is this all about?"

Jill grabbed her glass of wine and dropped into the rocking chair and crossed her legs. "It really happened. To me. And to—that other world, that other timestream. It wasn't a dream." She lowered her voice a notch, and fixed her gaze on a handy, neutral windowsill across the room.

"I was working for the Poor People's Campaign that King started, before he was murdered on April fourth, in Memphis." Brian opened his mouth and she said, "Stop interrupting. I'll get off track and I have a lot to say. You'll just have to believe me. Or at least listen.

"In that world, life, timestream, whatever—in which you two, by the way, were definitely present—FDR did *not* sign the Civil Rights Act in the late forties. It was enacted by President Johnson after JFK was assassinated; it had already been proposed by JFK."

Brian watched her face intently. Megan was lying down again, eyes shut, her face as placid as if she were hearing a favorite bedtime story. Jill hoped she hadn't passed out, but she seemed to have a tight grip on her glass. She continued to tell them the history that had never happened. They had to know why she had done what she had done, and without that history, they would never understand.

"The 1964 Civil Rights Act was groundbreaking. It outlawed discrimination by hotels, restaurants, public places, and in employment. It said that schools had to be desegregated, which reinforced a 1954 Supreme Court ruling. It ensured voting rights. It was not well accepted, in the South particularly, but that applied to other locales

as well. Federal funding was denied to schools that refused to desegregate, which gave the act some teeth. Some places in the South simply stopped having public schools. *Negroes with my kids? No way.* Hard to imagine, I know, but that is the way it really was. Before, and after, there was horrible violence. Federal marshals had to escort some little black girls to school in New Orleans in 1960, and after that a lot of whites withdrew their kids. A lot more happened than I have time to go into right now."

Jill rocked back and forth, back and forth, in the old chair as she spoke, soothed by its rhythmic creak.

"King led nonviolent protests that illuminated, on television, how bestial the resistance to desegregation was. Over a quarter of a million people came to the March on Washington for Jobs and Freedom in 1963, during which he spoke at the Lincoln Memorial to a sea of listeners. That speech became famous all over the world; he won the Nobel Peace Prize; he—he—"

Jill wiped tears from her eyes and smiled. "It's kind of strange, isn't it, for me to cry when here, he's alive? And had a slightly different past? But I was there. I heard it. People believed in him."

"What about when King was killed?" asked Megan.

"Assassinated. Shot while he was on a hotel balcony in Memphis. Oh, there was an uprising all over the country. He was a magnificent speaker—as he is today. The reaction was pure rage, for a lot of people. He'd kept the Civil Rights movement nonviolent—"

"Civil Rights?" asked Brian. "As in the Civil Rights Act that Truman signed in 1950?"

Jill sighed. "Yes, but that *did not happen* in the . . . other world. In that timestream, in D.C., peaceful gatherings and vigils turned into riots quite suddenly. Johnson—"

"Who?" asked Megan.

"JFK's vice president his first term. He deployed National Guard tanks; they were everywhere, and you

couldn't go anywhere because of blockades. Brian, you and your friend went on a bike tour to the most dangerous places and when Dad found out he grounded you. The city was on fire. Looting, violence, clashes. Marines guarded the Capitol with machine guns. Several people were killed, but mostly in fires. It lasted for days. And, of course, the destroyed businesses were all black-owned; all this happened, as in most of the cities, in black areas. We heard that people in the suburbs were terrified that blacks would go out into Virginia and Maryland and burn down all the Tall Oaks subdivisions and shopping centers. Detroit was destroyed."

Megan said, "I think Brian and I remember that. Not the big picture, just the local scary stuff. All the neighbors afraid. So there must be some kind of . . . bleed through. Like the memories are there, in our brains, just not accessible."

"Hmm. Interesting," Jill continued, "I was pretty torn up, and it was therapeutic to use that energy to work on the Poor People's Campaign. We got people to contribute plywood for shacks, a sewage system was set up, and about five thousand people were living on the Mall. Not just blacks, but American Indians, Puerto Ricans, poor mountain people. In June, fifty thousand people marched. But by then, Bobby Kennedy had been assassinated too—he was even more liberal than his brother."

"Incredible," said Megan. "Really different. Stunningly different. But things changed. Somehow. You still remember all this. If we were there, why don't we remember it?"

Jill thought for a moment. "I can't tell you that. Maybe because I hogged the Game Board, and touched it, and used it, for years, to get my comics, like an addiction. And when everything . . . changed, it was kind of like a different past slid in, like a slide in a projector, with whole new events and meanings feeding into and out of them. I remembered the last slide, and if you superimpose them, some of the things in the two histories are the

same. This one seems better, I must say, although not as exciting. In 1968, a lot of people were taking LSD—"

"Like today," said Megan.

"Yes, but—well, let me continue. The mayor of Chicago cracked down on protests at the Democratic National Convention. I went to that too. Got clubbed in the head by police." She smiled. "I survived. Nixon was president."

"*Richard* Nixon?" asked Brian. "People voted for him? That's bizarre."

"I thought so too. In 1970, Nixon escalated the Vietnam War and invaded Cambodia. Students protested all over the country. Back then, there was a draft lottery, so all these young, college-age men were in line to fight and die—but for what? It was completely different from WWII, when Dad volunteered."

Brian nodded. "That's my nightmare, Jill. I'm dropping something called napalm on Cambodia, and then—" His breath got sharp; jerky. His face paled, and sweat popped out on his forehead. He wiped it off.

Jill's eyes softened in compassion. She said in a very soft voice, "It wasn't a dream." She got up and rummaged through the pile of comics, pulled one out. "Read this."

Megan sat on the couch next to Brian. Finally, Brian looked up. "So I—died? In a plane crash?" He turned pale.

She said, "Maybe. If that other timestream had continued. I saw from the Game Board that it would. I really don't know the mechanics of all this. I'm not sure anyone does, not even Hadnzt."

"It's Q, of course," said Megan. "I guess if Q is self-aware . . . but how did you know about these alternatives?"

Jill said, "It came in images, from the board. Pictures. That's the way it always was; that's why I did comics. I believed in the pictures the board showed me. They had a certain . . . imperative quality. That's one reason I hid

it from everyone, and I didn't tell anyone about it. But I didn't think, or know, that *I* could do anything.

"That year, 1968, was wild. The Soviets cracked down on Czechoslovakia, sent in tanks; it seemed like repressiveness was spreading. All over the world, student protest escalated. Nixon seemed terrified of the protests here. I don't think he believed in freedom of speech. He believed he could do whatever he wanted to just because he was a president. Then, in early May 1970, four students were shot and killed by the National Guard at Kent State University in Ohio. They were having a peaceful protest about the Cambodia escalations.

"That was a flash point. Students and professors occupied university buildings, just like in 1968; a lot of schools shut down, National Guard everywhere. It seemed unbelievable—unacceptable—to a lot of us that our own country, the Land of the Free, was so repressive. Before, when mostly blacks were killed during protests and riots, it hadn't been so apparent to white America that this might apply to everyone who questioned or opposed the government.

"Kent State was the last straw. As soon as I heard about it, I realized that the only way to change all that, to keep Brian from joining the Navy and getting shot down, to prevent JFK and King and RFK from being assassinated, to prevent the Vietnam War from escalating, was to thwart the first assassination, in Dallas. JFK had been for civil rights; JFK had a plan on his desk to draw down American advisers in Vietnam the very day he was murdered. Mainly, though, I was really, really furious.

"Back then, a lot more students hitchhiked. I guess they didn't all own cars, like they do today. I threw some things in a backpack and headed for Dallas, November 22, 1963. The board turned into a map, kind of, and while I was hitchhiking, time just seemed to turn back from 1970 to 1963. Every time I got a new ride, it was in an older car, and the roads were smaller. The brands were different, the clothes were different, and I stayed

mad, and then Hadntz picked me up in Arkansas. I'd been sitting by the side of the road for about ten hours, eating dust, and listening to men yell nasty things out the window at me when they drove by. I was ready to call Mom and Dad. But by then, I think they'd already started on their own way back, to find me, Mom and Dad and Wink. They'd been involved in however the Game Board came to be—which I don't know anything about—and they knew how to get to Dallas too. I think they came in some kind of plane. One thing Dad told me, before he clammed up, was that the plane had grown from one of the HD versions. So it *does* grow. But— according to what rules?"

"It grew in the Oberammergau Messerschmitt caves," Brian said, nodding. "When we went there—remember?—I thought there had been some recent activity."

"Right," said Jill. "My question is: After all this happened, why didn't Dad tell me?"

"I've wondered about that a lot," said Megan. "I think they were trying to protect us."

"They knew that Hadntz could go from one time to another." Jill looked at Megan. "I guess she still does too."

"I don't think I like her very much."

"Why?"

"Because she plays with people's lives."

Brian said, "She doesn't think of it as playing. I've read her papers. She believes quite strongly that she is improving all of humanity. She talks constantly about the possible causes of war, and how to biologically modify that tendency."

"How?" asked Megan.

"The latest modification papers I've found in her notes implicate males, I'm afraid. I guess history bears this out."

"So what's her solution to that?" asked Jill. "A world of only women?"

"No. Let's see. Behavior modification, emphasis on

education, learning, science, for women as well as men, women equally involved in government, getting to the biological roots of patriarchal control, or reproductive control, removing the profit from war, in particular giving young men another purpose in life besides gangs . . . lots of vectors. I guess Mom and Dad believed in what she was doing, and her methods, at least at one point. Or maybe that was their friend, Wink. His timestream split from Dad's in August 1945, and he lived in a world where everything *had* improved in those ways. He couldn't get to—to that old world, where you lived, Jill, where *we* lived, very often. All that stuff is in the notebooks. They called that time-shift a nexus. So it had happened before, but I don't think Wink could control it. He just knew when it might happen. For instance, the first time it happened—when Dad saw Wink after Wink's parents told Dad that Wink had died—was at a veterans' reunion, and that's when they started to piece together what was going on. There's a lot about quantum splitting, and consciousness, and the Many-World theory—you've both heard of that."

Megan turned to Jill, "What happened when you met Hadntz? What did she look like?"

Jill laughed. "She was dressed like a cowgirl. You would have loved her truck, Brian. She was drinking a beer. I realized who she was, and that's when she told me her name. We talked. She told me to turn around and go home. She said that no matter what happened, she thought that in the long run it would all average out. But she didn't try very hard to discourage me. She gave me a pistol."

"What kind?" Brian asked.

"I have no idea. We stopped and she showed me how to use it, had some target practice with all the beer bottles rattling around in the back of her truck. She dropped me off in Dallas in front of the book depository. Oh, you don't know. John Kennedy was murdered during a motorcade, from the sixth floor of that building, or so

everything that I'd read about it and everyone claimed. After the murder, there was the Warren Commission report, all kinds of studies. I'd read them all before I went to Dallas."

"Who did it?" asked Megan.

"They said that a guy named Lee Harvey Oswald did it. He had some connections with the CIA. He'd been a Marine, officially defected to the Soviet Union, and some people—they were called 'conspiracy theorists,' or just plain nuts—claimed that he'd gone on behalf of the CIA, or else how did he get back into the U.S. so easily with J. Edgar Hoover, a virulent anti-Communist, heading the FBI? Some witnesses also said that they heard shots coming from a nearby rise that they called 'the grassy knoll.' Oswald was arrested in a movie theater in Dallas, and—now this is the weirdest thing—he was being moved from the jail a few days later, all on national TV, and a guy named Jack Ruby, who owned some strip clubs, rushed up and shot him right in the stomach. I saw it. You guys saw it too. Right on the living room TV. It was pretty shocking. And extremely suspicious. Ruby died soon after that from cancer or something."

"We saw *that* on TV?" Megan was incredulous.

"We were living in Germany then, so it wasn't live, but Mom was furious that we saw it; she thought Dad ought to have known it was going to be broadcast. Whoever set it up made damned sure it was on TV, in the middle of the day, when everyone was glued to their sets. When we got back to Washington, everybody was still devastated. Everybody loved Kennedy."

"Not everybody," said Brian. "That certainly isn't true here."

"Lots, though. I remember being in Peoples Drug and a man looking at magazines picked up one with Kennedy on the cover and just exploded, coughing and crying. You guys watched his funeral cortege on TV too. It had a black horse in it, with no rider, and the boots in

the stirrups faced backward. Solemn. Eerie. Dignified. Just hoofbeats, drums, bagpipes. And so sad. The whole country was in mourning. He was so hopeful. He talked about landing on the moon, improving education, all kinds of things."

"He obviously angered someone."

"Well, the Mafia was high on the list of suspects, because his father, a pro-Nazi during the time he was our ambassador to England, made his money in the bootlegging business, and Kennedy didn't get Cuba back for them, which was where they were making a ton of money. Bobby Kennedy was the attorney general and was really cracking down on the Mafia. But, I don't know. Hoover said 'We've got to convince the American public that Oswald killed Kennedy.' Why? People suspected the CIA and even Lyndon Johnson, his vice president.

"So. This is what I did. When Hadntz dropped me off, I went upstairs to the sixth floor of the depository and hid behind some stacked boards they were using for construction. I knew all the details about it, like I said, I'd studied it, it had happened seven years earlier. Then two men showed up, not Oswald, with some old rifle, and they hung out and smoked and joked and waited. When Kennedy came around the corner in his convertible, they were supposed to fire, but I jumped up and shot at the one poking the gun out the window and rather surprisingly wounded him. Dad came out shooting from behind some boxes. I was astonished. The one I'd shot shouted, "Make the decoy shot!" The other guy picked up the rifle, but Dad then—he told me, I don't remember—Dad carried me downstairs and took me to the car." She was talking now as if in a trance. "I had a bullet graze on my forehead.

"We drove out of town to a little airstrip where the plane had been, the plane that brought them there. Mom and the plane were gone." Tears welled in Jill's eyes. "Just . . . gone." She leaned her head back in the rocker

and the tears rolled down her face. She got up, grabbed some tissues, blew her nose.

"Dad and I drove back here, and it was like when I went, only things got newer and newer and we were back here. We came into the kitchen and Brian and his friend were here. But it was ... it was clear that Mom had been gone a long, long time. I think that Mom knew the truth. I didn't do anything that would have stopped the assassination, so it must have been her, or maybe Wink, or even someone else, who took out the real assassin, and after that, Mom ..."

Jill took deep breaths and turned her face away. When she turned back to them again, her lips trembled; her eyes anguished. She howled, "Mom just *disappeared*! My heart ... was broken. Dad's too. We were just so, so sad." She crossed her arms in front of her chest, so that her hands held her opposite shoulder, and she shook her head back and forth, staring at them, her face crumpled in agony while she wept.

Brian and Megan both jumped up and crushed her in hugs. Megan said, "It's all right, Jill, it's all right."

"It's—*not*—all—right," she managed to get out, in jerky words.

"You did what you thought you had to do," Brian said. "You didn't know that would happen." He handed her some tissues. "Please, Jill, it really *is* all right. From my point of view." He rubbed her shoulders, and Megan hugged her until she calmed down to snuffles.

"Have you ever told anyone else?" asked Megan.

Jill blew her nose. "Dad knew, of course. But no. No one. Oh"—she laughed, weakly—"the therapist. Nancy. She thought I was crazy, of course. But she did say that I had to tell you. I guess"—Jill hiccupped a few times—"she was right. But it was always too hard. And ... Daniel."

"Daniel?" asked Megan.

"Detective Kandell," Brian told her. "He's investigating the break-in. But why tell him?"

"When you wouldn't even tell us," Megan said.

"It's very strange, but he remembers coming here when Mom had a school. His little brother went to school here. So there's some weird kind of . . . connection. A bridge between the timestreams that we share. A . . . nexus? I have no idea why he remembers and you guys don't. But he'd forgotten all about it until he saw the *Magpie* picture on the wall."

"A likely story," said Brian.

"Yeah," Jill said. "It's weird. But he did show me where he carved his initial in the sunroom—"

"What?" Megan looked incensed.

"And I do remember his little brother. And Daniel remembers me."

"Kind of crazy," Megan said. "Maybe he's, you know, a creep."

"I don't think so," Jill said, surprised that she was defending him.

"I really don't either," Brian said.

"We'll have a chance to meet him and his family. I invited them for tomorrow."

Megan rolled her eyes. "Great. But it's still all a puzzle, mostly." She picked up the board. "Maybe we can use this to find Mom and Dad."

"No!" Jill jumped from her chair and yanked it from her. "That's what you might *think* you're doing. It's seductive. It has its own agenda. It *used* me. We need to figure out what it really is, how it's really meant to be used. It might be just a vestige of what Hadntz intended. We need to get in touch with her. After all, she showed up at the party." Jill unlocked the desk, which she'd kept locked since the party, and got out Hadntz's card. "There's no contact information on it. Just her name. On the back it says, 'The work never ends.' "

"Mom told me kind of the same thing in the station. I already told Brian. Something about the war lasting a lot longer than they thought it would."

"Yeah," Brian said. "It is a war. This board is obviously Q, maybe an early prototype."

"I think Mom and Dad created Q," Megan said.

"I do too. From Hadntz's plans. Well, Mom just facilitated it. We'll probably never know the whole story." Brian dragged the box of notebooks out from behind a chair. "It's all in here. Sketchy, but if we pool our information we'll have a lot to go on. I'm an engineer, after all; Megan's got a physics degree. And now we have the latest incarnation. Hadntz-dust, the HD-50, the magical memory neuroplasticity drug that will change us all into drooling babies. Can't wait. When will it start to work?"

"Not babies," Megan was focused and professional, on her own turf. "Probably a bit older. Cindy mentioned once that in her Montessori teacher training course, everyone said they were sure that they were still going through sensitive periods, even in their twenties. It's true. Your brain's still growing in your twenties. Evolutionarily speaking, once you'd gotten your kids grown up, that is, through puberty and into childbearing, probably the only next useful task for you was helping raise the grandkids. Provide wisdom. So maybe this is the next way for humans to engineer our own future, our own destiny, by modifying our biology."

"It's just not fair," Brian said. "When I was a kid I thought I'd grow up and be finished. You know, myself. Instead, I keep changing from one person to another, and they're all just kind of thinly connected with these memories and histories that seem continuous. Is that right, Megan? You're the expert."

"That's what I've been saying."

"Every change is worse than before. More painful. Disease. Memory loss. Yuck. And speaking of memory, Megan, where did you say you first got the board?"

"You don't remember? We went to Peoples Drug to get Jill some cough medicine and I found it up on a high shelf and Mom bought it for me."

Brian and Jill looked at each other. Brian said, "I have a different memory. We found it in the attic under some floorboards."

"That's my memory too," said Jill.

"So? Do we vote?"

"You've heard of false memory?"

"I do research on false memory, as you well know, smarty-pants. But this memory is real."

"So is mine," said Jill.

"How do you know?"

Megan roused herself, backed up to the desk and leaned against it. "You're right. We don't know. Not really. It's the oldest philosophical question in the world. It's called phenomenology. We only know because we know. Our senses tell us." She reached over and picked up the board she had brought, unfolded its metal legs so that it was like a foot-tall table, and set her glass of vodka on it. "Maybe we just have different pasts."

"Doesn't everyone?" asked Jill.

"That's a good question. We have events in common, but, of course, even this moment is different for all of us. Depending on birth order, every child experiences a different family too. Whole groups of people can convince themselves of something—or, more usually, politicians can do that. Fascinating stuff."

"Hitler, for example," said Jill.

"Yes, it works best when there is extreme censorship, but trying to shame a group of people for their beliefs or memories can have an accretionary effect." She sighed. "Well. I'm glad it's not blinking."

"Blinking?" asked Brian.

"It was blinking the other night." Suddenly, Megan shook with laughter.

"What?" asked Brian.

"Where I saw Mom. At the station. There were lots of men. They were all wearing hats."

A laughing fit swept through them. Jill's stomach ached. Tears streamed from Brian's eyes. Megan howled

and curled up, knocking over the Game Board but, of course, holding on to her glass, now almost empty.

"Ahhh—haaa," she gasped at last. She caught her breath, blew her nose again, and said, "Even Mom was wearing a hat."

"Look," said Brian. "Tell us about these pills."

So Megan told them about how she'd met Hadntz, about her meticulous research, and about how she'd made the brain plasticity drug. And about Hadntz's note that she had taken it. "I've tried to get in touch with her again, but she never responds."

"Maybe that's why I could play so well when I went to the jazz club a few weeks ago," Brian said.

"Neuroplasticity is powerful stuff."

"I don't know why I didn't make the connection, though. The papers start calling the Device a 'Hadntz Device' pretty early on, and then later iterations are HD, and numbered, and then the vitamins—ha!"

"I don't know what you're talking about," Megan said. "Back up." Her hair was no longer plastered to her head by sweat, but flying out whenever the fan turned her way, making her look like a wild woman, thought Jill. She thoughtfully refreshed Megan's vodka. They'd eaten most of the cheese and crackers.

"Yes, please," said Jill. "I haven't read the papers either."

Brian closed his eyes for a moment, then opened them. "You know Dad's war history."

Jill said, "He trained at Aberdeen on assembling and troubleshooting the M-9 Fire Director, part of the SCR-584. It could track and shoot a missile in flight, and intercepted Hitler's doodlebugs. It had a 99.9 percent success rate and ended the V-1 attacks. He was in England for a year and a half in Ordnance, preparing for Operation Overlord, and in December 1944 was sent to Camp Lucky Strike at Le Havre to follow the Battle of the Bulge mop-up and set up a troop supply station in Mönchengladbach, Germany, in the British Sector. They

were there till August of 'forty-five, and then were sent back to the States, supposedly en route to the Pacific to supply the invasion of Japan."

"Yes," said Brian. "True on the surface. But what he and his pal Wink were really doing, completely on their own, was trying to follow the plans Hadntz kept updating."

Jill templed her fingers and bent her head forward.

"So, Jill, what are you thinking?" asked Brian.

"I'm thinking that every time there was an advance in her prototype, *time changed*. Or—our timestream shifted. Came into being. Whatever. And I think HD-50 is a prototype change, an advance. Wait a minute. I just remembered something." She looked at Brian. "Remember when I told you that Mom and Dad visited me at the hospital?"

"Yes. I even told Megan about it."

"Two other people also dropped in that night. Like, visiting hours for Jill Dance, psychotic, are from midnight to three A.M. One was a medium-tall man. Wearing a fedora, of course, but kind of familiar, and for some reason, comforting. Hmm. I guess he's the Walking Man. He came before Mom and Dad. Didn't say a word, stayed about two minutes. The other one was really scary. He seemed to be some kind of German SS guy. He had those little lightning insignias on his collar, or somewhere. A metal skeleton-head pin in the center of his hat. I screamed, and he left right away."

"Okay," said Megan. "And?"

"Let's say that these crazy Nazis—I know they're still around—know about the Device, and about Mom and Dad, and have been just hanging out, waiting. I'm afraid that I made Koslov suspicious. He's one of the people you overheard at the party, Megan."

"Right."

"Although he is Russian, so theoretically, he should hate the Nazis. But if one of them could get into the hospital, they could also probably get my therapist's

records, in which I talk freely about my various insanities. Which they know are real."

Megan nodded. "That really makes sense, in the context of what I overheard at the party. So people are trying to get the Device."

"The plans, the notes, the Device, whatever. But if it is the Game Board is really Q—"

"It replicates," said Brian, excited. "From what I understand, for a while, it was just a clear chunk of stuff, with colored threads inside. Dad wrote a lot of stuff in some kind of code, but he taught me the code when I was a teenager. It seemed like it was just for fun, but I guess he intended for me to read these notes."

Jill nodded her head. "So let's say it changes into things that are pleasing to the user. The attractive Game Board. Spacies. And it has the capacity to replicate, to spread. So, Megan, maybe—"

Megan frowned. "Maybe the one in my house just . . . I don't know . . . *grew*? Jim said that Abbie found it next to a stack of old photos that I took from the attic."

Brian added, "Right! And the day I found the saxophone in the attic, I found a loose board, and it seemed strangely familiar. I pried it up, and the hole was empty. I felt around and some gooey gunk got stuck to my hand, and I wrapped it up and tossed it in the car. Maybe that's what turned into my Game Board."

"And maybe," said Jill, sitting absolutely still in her rocking chair, electrified, "I don't really need one because probably this whole house has changed into one huge Device."

"Ugh," said Megan, looking around. "I guess the point is that we have to put this all together, try to figure out what's happening, and try to decide what to do about it. For instance, someone, or some group, I guess, is doing its best to make it unpleasant to live in this house. That is bothersome."

Brian said, "Yes, but Detective Kandell is on their trail."

"On Jill's trail, more like," said Megan. "You said he took her to the market? For three hours? That's detective work? Give me a break."

"Daniel was protecting me. Someone *was* following me. A short, dumpy guy. With a hat, of course."

Megan said, "Oh, it's *Daniel* now. Well, the pursuer that Daniel so bravely saved you from sounds like the guy who was spying on me on the train. He got off around eight A.M. and I think he took the train back in this direction. So, maybe Kandell is legit." She shook her head. "I just don't know if I can handle this, Jill. So much is missing. I know that the people on the porch talked about Mom having a nursery school, and I know that she was taking courses at Georgetown, but I don't recall the school."

"I remember you in 1967 too," said Brian. "You were painting with oils. Filling the house with noxious oil fumes."

Jill said, "See, I don't remember that. I can certainly imagine myself doing that, but I've never used oils, not this me."

"You could probably create a very respectable false memory of having done that," said Megan.

"How could I tell if it was real or false?"

"You can't, not without outside corroboration. And young memories, in particular, are often false, because they're constructed communally. Your uncle tells you about the time you fell in the pool when you were two and he rescued you, and pretty soon all the pictures are there. *Voilà!* So with more enhanced Total Recording of Life, as in the proliferation of home movies, home videos, photos, you can certainly think that you're actually remembering when actually, you're reconstructing, imagining."

Jill said, "But the point is that, for both of you and presumably the rest of the people with you in that life, the international political situation was bland and quiet, right? Economy good, no Vietnam War, no split Germany,

no Soviet appropriation of satellite countries, very little Cold War and even that ended after the Bay of Pigs when Kennedy and Khrushchev negotiated the Munich Disarmament Treaty. Those are things I can read about. Remember, after JFK's assassination I have a gap of seven years, because I was in the first timestream. And once I returned here to yours, the whole past was different, starting near the end of WWII. That's the timeframe I studied to get my doctorate. My lost years. I still slipped, and landed in St. Lizzy's Home for Wayward Timestreamers."

"It wasn't bland and quiet," said Brian. "It was really exciting. China, Russia, Europe, and the U.S. were holding the Moon Congress in Paris, and all the countries of the world had representatives, and they were hammering out the legal framework for the colony. I started engineering school so that I could be an astronaut. I was in a frac band."

"Frac band?" asked Jill.

"As in 'fractious.' Or 'fractured.' It was a style of music that incorporated elements of classical, jazz, and rock. I played the guitar. And the sax, of course. We had some success. As in, once we got a job in Roanoke. I guess that's when I started drinking too much and dropped out of school. We thought we'd gotten big. Instead, frac music just kind of went away. Too weird, I guess."

"Yes," said Jill. "Things got dull."

"But things got done," said Brian. "We developed Q . . . or, I guess, it developed itself. It gave itself a chance to blossom."

Megan picked up the board. "You know, there must be a way to make this thing tell us what it's all about."

Jill sidled over to Megan and looked at it, then began tracing some of its patterns. "Mesmerizing, isn't it? Like, when I was little, I'd play on this Oriental rug, and every design seemed to go somewhere, like those steps, there, over in the corner."

"Yeah," said Brian. "I know what you mean."

Jill nodded. "I left the original Game Board in Dallas. Considering everything that's happened, the thought of trying to use it, however we would do that, makes me feel rather sick. Besides, as far as I can remember, I never really *used* it. I was used by it. The board would manifest pictures, or would just be blank and I would get pictures in my mind. But these narratives, and these pictures, came from the Game Board. I realized, at some point, that this narrative that I was cartooning had a strong connection to reality. Each panel, each point of a story, branches. At any point, you can take many directions. The story divides, and you, the artist, pick one of the possible paths. Sometimes it seems a lot easier, but that's because maybe you see a point far off, like a mountaintop, that you head for. But that just means it's easier to ignore all of the possible side paths. It's just like the decisions we make in everyday life, all the time."

"It sounds a lot like quantum mechanics," said Megan. "The Many-Worlds theory, where existence is always splitting. Some astrophysicists are now saying that there are infinite worlds, where people exactly like us are living our lives exactly like we do."

"So what would be the philosophical difference?" asked Jill. "That sounds rather uninteresting. Just slightly different, now, that's interesting, and seems more like what's happening now. I used to read about all this in comic books too, believe it or not. In the fifties and sixties they were absolute purveyors of pure weirdness. Also, one of the big philosophical problems for quantum mechanics is the observer. Does the observer really make a difference? Is Schrödinger's cat alive or dead inside the box before we look at it? One interpretation suggests that our own will and intent influence reality on a very fine, quantum, level."

"Like magic," said Brian, with a certain glumness.

"Not exactly," said Megan. "We can definitely work on our very own lives using the tools of will and intent,

and other tools like neurolinguistic programming, which bypasses the conscious mind; we're still trying to figure out how that works. Because it does."

"I think the only way that we could possibly figure out how this thing works or even what, exactly, it does is to study those plans," said Brian. "Although first we'd have to get advanced degrees in a lot of different disciplines."

"We already have some," said Megan. "We need to find Handtz."

"Will she want to be found? Will she talk?" asked Jill.

"Good question," said Megan.

"I'm beginning to think that Koslov might have been in this other history. Mom and Dad and Hadntz's timestream. Obviously, some people *have* been in both. Hadntz has been; Wink, Dad's pal, was able to move between two of the trajectories. I know because I saw him, at that last reunion, the night before everything— happened. He was in this house. We all used the Game Board. Even you, Megan. Brian was going to Vietnam. And then—the next day was the Kent State Massacre, and I was on the road to Dallas. But before, whenever Dad talked about him, Wink had died in the war. Koslov has some strong connection to Hadntz; he translated a book of poems by Hadntz's mother. They're beautiful, by the way. All these people at the party, the ones out on the porch, have suspected Mom for a long time. A very long time, according to what you told me about what you overheard. And they've kept an eye on us. I'll bet each of you have people watching you too. People in your lives, that you work with."

"Cindy!" Brian said. "I knew it! The ultimate spy. She even married me."

"No need to actually *work* with them." Megan laughed. "There was that little twerp on the train today. I was going to call you, Brian, and hand this board over to you on the way to the station. But I overslept, then fell asleep on the Metro. I had to run for the train." Her

laugh grew more hearty and she wiped tears from her eyes. "Poor fat little guy. He must have about had a heart attack. Now, he might be right outside the window."

Jill got up and looked out both windows. "No, but our children and spouses have just pulled up and I'll bet all of them are expecting dinner. I'll hide the board, and you guys tell them what's for dinner."

"Pizza," said Brian.

"We're having pizza for dinner tomorrow on the woodstove. Daniel and his dad and grandma and little boy are coming."

"Seems like a bit of bad timing," said Megan. "We have a lot to do, a lot to talk about. Can't you uninvite them?"

"I could, but I don't want to. Don't you think we'll all be completely tired of talking about it by then? And all the kids will be there too."

"I'm already exhausted." Megan flopped backward onto the floor. "And I, for one, have no objection to pizza two nights in a row."

After dinner, Zoe sat cross-legged on the old floral rug in the Halcyon House living room, a comfortable, sprawling, square room of deep chairs and couches flanked by an eclectic mix of tables and reading lamps, the upright piano, and a fireplace centered on the back wall. The wall was filled with deep, spacious shelves, and opened, on one side, through French doors, onto the house-long, screened-in porch.

Her father stood next to her, sorting through a vast collection of old 78s. He shook his head now and then, finding one with a chipped edge, which he set in one pile because he could play part of it, and setting those completely cracked, or even in shards, in another pile. He sighed and muttered and sometimes exclaimed happily.

On another shelf were 45 records with large holes in the middle, mostly records that Brian and the Crazy Aunts had amassed when teenagers. Bitsy and Whens re-

ally liked them; they'd put them on a little record player kept on a lower shelf and dance around like maniacs.

Those on another shelf were 33-1/3 records, sorted into two categories: rock and jazz. Zoe searched in vain for classical, and found a quick run of musicals. *My Fair Lady, Oliver!,* and *The Music Man.*

She began to go through the jazz LPs, which her dad assured her had lots of good music on them. Some individual titles triggered music in her head, like "A Tisket, A Tasket"; she heard Ella for a moment, her voice bell-clear. Some artist names were familiar, but she couldn't particularly link the names to any piece of music. She did enjoy some of the piano artists, especially Keith Jarrett.

"Look!"

Brian paused in his sorting.

"Let's play this."

Brian bent down. "Stéphane Grapelli. Jazz violin."

"Jazz *violin*?"

Brian smiled. "Listen."

Zoe listened. And listened, until bedtime, when the adults closed the doors and went back to talking. Talk, talk, talk, that's all that grown-ups ever did. Well, her father, at least, did like to play music.

Zoe

ZOE'S ADVENTURE IN MUSIC

[*July 14*]

THE NEXT morning, she got up very early and listened some more, refusing breakfast. The grown-ups all went into the library and shut the French doors. Of course. She put a Grapelli LP on and set it to play over and over again. Finally, she felt someone approach, stand next to her, and nudge her with a foot.

"Zoe! Are you dead?" It was Whens.

She didn't open her eyes. "Not hardly."

"We're tired of that silly music."

"I'm not. Go away."

"I'm going to change it."

"You'd better not." She felt Whens standing there for a minute. Then he went away.

Zoe got up and hurried upstairs to the ballroom. Fetching her violin, she went back downstairs. Good. No one had touched the record.

She turned the record over, and set her violin on her shoulder. After a short hiss, the first track, "Sweet Lorraine," began to play.

She played along almost perfectly, and frowned when she varied from Grapelli. She played along with both sides, turned off the record player, ran up to the ballroom with her violin, and shut the doors. At the front of the ballroom, she commenced to play.

She duplicated the entire LP perfectly, but the music drew her to try other things as well. It was an intriguing music, beckoning her to become a part of it in a new way, to expand it, to hear many different options echo in her mind at once, each a pathway, and instantaneously choose which one she wanted to try. It opened her up in a way that most classical music did not—maybe because that was all so old and settled? She could add depth, timbre, emotion, to it, yes, she could work hard to master it, but it was not inviting in the same way.

She was completely exhilarated, and did not know how long she had played, or what, really. Yes, she liked gypsy jazz violin! She wondered if Grandpa Sam had any other gypsy jazz downstairs.

Her eyes closed. She imagined a real gypsy sat on the ballroom floor. Her multicolored skirt tented her knees, on which she rested her head. Zoe could not see her face, for a cascade of curly black hair, liberally streaked with pure white, as if she'd been painting, hid her face. A thin, old bald man stood next to her, and he played and the gypsy stood and played along with him, furious swirling music, filled equally with inky blue darkness

and brilliant joy, gold, with spikes of spring green and rose-pink.

She opened her eyes, and they were still there.

They stood, together, the man with a grave, distant smile, and the woman with closed eyes. Zoe was transfixed.

The music spoke of a hard and necessary parting. It spoke of grief, and endings, yet hinted at a beginning, for Zoe. And, perhaps, for them.

But it sounded like the woman's good-bye song. She was leaving forever. Her sadness was so overwhelming that she could not speak it, but the man understood it, could play it. There was great joy in it too, somewhere, like the most poignant hymn Zoe had ever heard.

Zoe took up her own violin and played, absorbing the music with something she knew must be her soul, until she had to burst out in her own contribution, filled with sweetness, regret, and good-bye; and then it was past all speech, and Zoe played, and played, and played, crying with great, mingled joy and sadness—joy at the beauty of the world, sadness at its inevitable loss. She closed her eyes, watching the colors of it, distant and also close, a place she could see in her mind and walk into, and she did. There was fire there. Death. Unspeakable horrors. She cried as she played, and finally all became light once again, and colors, resolved into a shimmering rainbow.

Zoe felt her mother's gentle kiss on her forehead.

She opened her eyes. The man and woman were gone.

"That was beautiful, honey." The door stood open. "Come on. It's late. You didn't have any lunch. Or dinner." Cindy ran her hands down both of her daughter's arms. As if in a dream, Zoe allowed her to take the violin, settle it into the case and snap it shut. That did not stop the music. She allowed her mother to lead her out of the ballroom and downstairs, where some pizza, and some cookies were left.

It was loud here, with different music. But she had to remember!

Zoe stood next to the empty chair at the table, assailed by the gypsy sounds of the old tablecloth, on which apples danced with pears between strong red and yellow stripes, and the distant, dancing gypsy sounds coming from her Crazy Aunts, her father, and the old things from long-ago Russia from Grandma Bette's family in the very top cupboard shelves. And everyone was talking. She half-turned to get her composition book and pens. Cindy gently grabbed her shoulders. "Sit," she said. "Eat."

Amid the strident harmonies, the distracting chatter, hoping the other music would continue until she could write it down, she did as her mother asked.

The rainbow music had to be finished now, anyway, because Whens whispered in her ear, "Zoe! We can't find Grandma!"

She had to write it. Grandma was part of the same music.

Jill, Brian, and Megan

TRANSFORMATIVE PICNIC

[July 14]

ON SUNDAY morning, bleary-eyed, Jill, Brian, and Megan dragged themselves into the library bearing mugs of steaming coffee, bagels with contents ranging from cream cheese and lox to peanut butter and jelly, piles of Sam's notebooks, the two Game Boards, their Q's, Megan's shared information about HD-50, and a huge determination to bull their way through to understanding of their situation, and a plan of action.

Megan started, after swallowing a mouthful of breakfast. "I've been Q'ing Hadntz, but she doesn't respond. She never has; it's all one-way."

Brian said, "I've come across several photos of the original incarnations of the Device." He shared them on

Q. "The first one is just kind of a metallic-looking blob, but Dad writes:

> Power sent through solution made via Hadntz's plan. After several hours, hear faint music. Radio? Can't be. Some jellylike substance forming in solution. A spark, pure oxygen present, explosion, during which mind ranged through intense musical revelations, seemingly embedded but now forgotten. Brilliance, a sense of altered time, a sense of other paths, other avenues of probabilities. Wink reports same in that instant.
>
> Following small fire provoked search of premises, resulting material passed through several hands and made to disappear by Company Magician Kocab. Returned later for bottle of Scotch from Mountbatten's private stock, though says a few beers would have been sufficient to work his magic of remanifestation. Hidden in good place, along with precious cavity magnetron magnanimously provided via unknown source.
>
> Surprise trip to Bletchley Park, via limo (Wink disappointed, no booze on board), for low-key questioning about radar event observed during time of fire. Shown plans of a Device, but different from one we built with Hadntz's additional microfilm from London. Disavow any knowledge. Saw little of place but looks like great place to work. Wink and I mum.

"Skip to six months later," Brian continued.

> Caravan of three hundred command cars en route through frigid France. Avoid St. Lo, not worth rooting out Germans holed up there. Stop for the night, actually find abandoned house! Even lumber for fire! Heaven! Out of blue a woman arrives: Major Elegante. I remember her, quiet in corner, on December 8, 1941, while questioned about the disappearance of Hadntz after Pearl Harbor. She has provender: wine, cheese, bread! Trade stories about Fifty-second Street. Next A.M.,

abrupt change of demeanor: Pulls rank, orders Wink to drive her Deisenberg, she interrogates me about visit with Hadntz, to underground missile factory where Hadntz found daughter, and V-2 assembly plant at Nordhausen. Wants details of interiors, etcetera. Has order allowing Wink to hear. Records with steno. Finds plans and Device in duffle, drives off, leaving us with command car in snowy field. Nearby ghastly swollen bodies of men, and cows, back of head or arm poking out from snow, remaining carnage of Battle of the Bulge.

Brian flipped pages.

"Next mention of the Device is about a month later. He and Wink are setting up a lab in an abandoned warehouse in Gladbach. A German engineer, Perler, shows them a Device, German-made, and says that he has surmised they are trying to make one from what they have been saving as they salvage equipment from Dusseldorf to fix the German telephone system in Gladbach:

Perler says plans came from blond woman with Berlin accent who said there needs to be a network of Devices for it to work. Wants to trade for sarin gas to kill Hitler; claims Hitler is in Berlin bunker. We cannot procure sarin nor anthrax, but keep his Device. After seeing Bergen-Belsen, begin work on new incarnation. Calls for organic material this time, something to do with H's DNA speculations. We add blood from ceremonially nicked fingers: Wink's idea. Add power to solution. Light, heat, no explosion: visions, like a new brain, feel rearranged, changed, after several hours, which pass like seconds. Left with clear, oblong object. Perler breaks in, steals back his Device. Major Elegante shows up in *Biergarten,* has orders for me to drive her to Berlin. Weird scene, Russians everywhere, at big jazz show Elegante buys HD plans from some Russian, has me photograph them. Afterward, I take her to Ravens-

brück to look for her cousin. No luck. Eventually end up at some manor house, some high command guy she knows, she has to leave suddenly, leaves me book of Chinese poetry. And, not coincidentally, I think, the Russian plans. Miss her.

"So there," said Megan.
"Yeah," said Brian. "They collaborated on that Device for years. There's more important stuff, though":

We leave Mönchengladbach having repaired Olympic pool from 1936, damaged by bombs. En route, Wink and I taken from caravan, put on a plane, eventually shipped to Tinian, on observation plane behind *Enola Gay*. Both of us sickened: just a stunt, killing innocent Japanese. However, Device changes during atomic explosion: I see time as a foam, infinite worlds of consciousness, as I hold Device to window (we surmise we are there via Hadntz's manipulations; she added a note in own handwriting to "bring it with you"). On return over Asia, Wink and I surmise that proximity to subatomic particles released during bomb detonation changed Device—but how?

On return to States, we exchange addresses, phone numbers, promise to meet on Easter next, I keep Device, store in parents' attic. Men in black visit my Cleveland apartment, question me, leave. They know I have something. What, or where, though, they do not know.

Brian said, "Then later, while we lived in Hawaii, he apparently met Wink on Midway. Wink gave him a new incarnation of the Device from another timeline. He decides to distribute the Device across the Pacific. It is apparently malleable, and grows."
"So then," said Jill, "we moved to Germany, and then here, and they hid the 'malleable Device.'"
"The HD-10," Brian interrupted.

"In the attic. Where we found it, it bonded with our kiddy minds, and turned into this super-attractive Game Board, which changed our brains. Maybe it made me into more of an activist than I would have been."

"Perhaps," said Megan. "But I doubt it."

"She talks about altruism a lot in her papers," Brian said.

"Right," said Megan. "And when we talked in Cuba, that was exactly her slant. Maybe her increasingly refined versions of the Device enhance whatever helps humans enlarge their vision of who, exactly, is in their 'in-group,' people they would help without question, would sacrifice for. And enhances whatever causes us to be empathic. I'm also thinking about the latest studies about the power of screen violence. There is no pain. Depending on how the movie or whatever is engineered, we cheer when the enemy dies, no matter how gruesomely—they usually did something very clearly evil, and need to be punished; revenge is satisfying. Proven: Seeing violence on-screen or participating in it in a game actually does make children more prone to commit real violence. Contrast that with how soldiers who have actually gone through battle feel. They are, essentially, proxies of some government, conditioned by patriotism to defend their country 'right or wrong,' fighting proxies in the same situation. But no matter how they feel about the enemy going into it, and no matter how good they feel about their victories, about having survived, about having eliminated those who are a threat to them, about forming a bond with their 'brothers,' traumatic stress, and inability or unwillingness to talk about their experiences, which sometimes become completely submerged, often results. In fact," she said, looking at Jill, "I think that's what happened to you."

Jill sat back in her chair as waves of revelation washed through her. The therapist's mouthed words had meant nothing until now. Suppression, yes. Unwillingness to talk. Almost as if she had committed some vast geno-

cide, destroyed a world. And now, with Daniel's revelation, and the other things that were happening, yes, relief felt like a weight had been lifted from her chest, she could breathe, she could—

The air she breathed in so deeply came out in a sob, and she lost control, continuing to cry, but she tried to smile as tears welled, as her brother and sister once again leaned over her chair and embraced her, held her as she shook with great, racking breaths that emerged not as words, but just as sounds, as she gradually calmed, washed by vast, deep healing.

By now, the tissue box was almost depleted. She blew her nose, said, "Coffee, anyone?"

She was surprised when she saw it was only ten thirty. It seemed to her that great ages had passed.

When Jill left the library, Cindy looked up from a book she was reading in the living room, across the foyer, and smiled. Bitsy lay next to her on the couch, asleep. Zoe was upstairs, playing something gorgeous.

In the kitchen, Jill washed her face and saw that Cindy had brewed a new pot of coffee. Jim was outside, playing with Abbie and Whens in the new sandbox that Brian's crew had knocked together in an hour. Jim turned to look at her, smiled, and waved.

At least, thought Jill, piling bagels, cream cheese, the pot of coffee, and cream and sugar onto a tray, *some things in this world are going well.*

She'd only been gone five minutes, but Brian and Megan had moved on to Topic B: What to Do Now.

"I'm not sure what Hadntz expects us to do with the HD-50," Megan was saying. "I've talked to a lot of prominent people, people I even know, who went through trials with it, and hear nothing but good things. I've started taking it. I feel . . . I don't know, energized, I guess. Able to look at things differently. And in terms of retrieving memory—I think it's helped us realize what happened."

Jill took her seat, with a fresh cup of coffee. "Insofar

as the HD-10 was supposed to grow and spread its influence wherever it went, I'd say that just being in this house has a definite influence. But one problem with Hadntz's ideas are that she seems to just want to . . . inflict these things on people in general, rather than giving them a choice."

"Dad said something about that somewhere. Ah, notebook number seven." He flipped through the pages he'd flagged with stickies. "They're on the drive from Nordhausen when he asks her about this."

One of the first times I've seen her angry, almost out of control, fierce. She compares war to disease: smallpox, polio, the bubonic plague. So I too begin to wonder: Why not treat war like a disease? If it can be cured through some inoculation, through some agent with no ancillary harm, it does seem a good thing. While various agencies and organizations decry war, they are an impotent minority when the war drums begin to beat. I do not want revenge for Keenan's death, and I don't believe he would either. He was there as a soldier, and as I and a few others know, our own nation failed to protect him. The radar report from Opana Point of approaching planes was dismissed. No, I just want him alive again, alive to live out his promise, to raise his children. Killing others will not bring him back, nor will it prevent future wars. We should know by now that horrific weapons, like gas, machine guns, and explosives, do not deter nations from going to war. They are just new ways to inflict damage on the enemy. After seeing these slave labor camps, I am indeed willing to help Hadntz in her mission in any way that I can.

Perhaps that was her reason for taking me.

"The question," said Jill, "is whether increased intelligence, awareness, whatever you want to call it, actually does decrease violence."

"I think it's a moving target," said Megan. "But coupled with enhancement of empathy—I mean, I remember crying and crying when I was little and watching Shirley Temple play Heidi, when she was taken away from the Alms-Uncle and made to live in Frankfurt. The plight of others, even imaginary others, really moved me. I wanted to keep every child in the world from that pain."

Brian said, "That has to be coupled with a real ability to do something. Which we may have. But I don't know how we actually go about presenting this choice to people. Haven't a clue."

"We have our own strengths," said Jill. "I think that the Montessori pods are a great start."

"Well, if music helps, I'm getting better by the hour," said Brian.

"Thank God," murmured Megan. "That frac stuff gave me a headache."

"Oh, this is pure jazz. Dad jazz. The kind that seems to have synergistically helped his insights into how to make the Device and what it could do. We have another problem to consider, though. A more immediate one. That group of people that Megan overheard during the party think that Q is hidden in the house. And they're right. But what are their goals?"

"The Clarissa person seemed to hate all of Jill's plans for Africa, the schools," Megan said. "I got the distinct impression that they want to use it for their own ends."

"That may simply be impossible," said Jill. "Unlike the atomic bomb, this changes human brains. Human behavior. Maybe if we just give it to them—contrive to make them think it has fallen into their hands, or something, *they* will be changed by it." She grinned. "Clarissa could definitely use some Q-work. She's been trying to throw up roadblocks against the school project since I started it, years ago."

"Our way right, your way wrong," said Brian.

Jill replied, "I just believe that access to education is a

human right, for everyone, men and women. You know, Grandma Elegante's dad took her out of school when she was in eighth grade. Her mother died, and she had to take over the housework. She was bitter about that till she died."

Brian nodded. "Great-grandpa Dance's father told him at that age to quit school or move out. He moved to town and shoveled coal for the city's steam plant so he could get his high school diploma."

"Grandma was a girl," said Megan. "She didn't have that option. It's much worse than that in a lot of the countries today. Girls just aren't allowed to go to school, period."

"So—to get back to the break-in," said Brian. "I surmise that Dad left important notations in those books about the Device. But how did the thief know which ones to take?"

"Some of them were nosing through the books during the party," Megan reminded them.

"Right," said Brian. "Brings us back to the same questions. Whodunit, what are they doing with it, what can we do about it?"

"And where are we going to hide those notebooks now?" asked Megan.

"The attic, of course," said Brian. "Let's say that thief gets up there and starts looking around."

Uproarious laughter.

"Well," said Brian, "that's a unanimous yes. And the Game Boards? Use them, touch them, wrap them in anti-Q cloth?"

Jill was thoughtful, then she spoke. "I kind of used yours on Friday night, and was just swamped with ideas, memories, vignettes of Dad's, actually. But it may be just a very personal thing. I wonder what would happen if we just 'gave' one of them to that crowd. Some man called last month and demanded the Device."

"You never said anything!" said Brian.

Jill just looked at him.

"Okay, okay. But they know about it, they want it."

"I don't think they should have it," said Megan. "What if they went back in time and changed the war? Made Hitler live, or something."

Brian said, "Might it not have some kind of fail-safe? It is, after all, the Device, and it does implant 'good' pathways, 'good' ideas. At least, that's the plan."

"But we don't know if it works. Who decides what's good?"

"It accesses and assesses everyone. All the time. It's pure democracy in action. Read the papers."

Megan stood up. "All I know is that the kids have been playing in the attic a lot. So we need to be smarter than Mom and Dad."

"The board wanted us to have it," said Brian. "That's all there is to it."

"Well, I hope the board does not want Abbie to have it," said Megan, crossing her arms. "I'm sorry," said Megan, "but I'm crashing. That vodka last night . . ."

Brian smiled. "HD-50 can probably cure a hangover."

"Good God! It's two in the afternoon." Jill jumped up. "I have to get dinner started, anyway."

"Dismissed," said Brian, stood, and stretched.

Jill went through her prep work for the picnic with an oddly light heart. Despite all this angst, she realized that she was looking forward to seeing Daniel again.

She planned to set the kids to chopping mushrooms, onions, and other ingredients for the pizzas. All the vegetables were on the kitchen table, along with knives and cutting boards. They would each make their own pizza, since no one could ever agree on toppings. The dough was rising in a huge bowl on the counter; she lifted a red-and-green striped tea towel and punched it down.

It was a lovely, hot day, around four in the afternoon. A slight breeze occasionally stirred the leaves of the oak tree just outside the tall kitchen window. Brian was

416 | KATHLEEN ANN GOONAN

outside, readying the grill, turning on the water, and gathering furniture from hither and yon, including a big comfy wicker chair for Daniel's grandmother.

Everyone, except the kids, had slept pretty late after last night's powwow. When Jill had gotten up at ten thirty, she'd found Bitsy, Whens, and Abbie in the attic—probably looking for that Game Board that Abbie had described to them, along with the great betrayal of her mother confiscating it just like she had confiscated her classbook. Jill shooed them downstairs, saying it was too hot, but they went back up as soon as she got busy again. It was actually hidden in the basement.

Her thoughts turned to Detective Kandell. He was only one of the disturbing events of the past few days, but at least she could focus on him.

He was about five eleven, and seemed fit; at least, fit enough to jog a few miles a day, but muscles didn't bulge out of his shirtsleeves like a bodybuilder's would. His skin was medium-dark, a rich, glowing color, and he wore a short, plain beard; none of that weird fancified facial hair she often saw around town. He kept his graying hair short, but she could imagine him in the sixties with an Afro. He had a marvelous sense of low-key humor. And he was smart. Very smart.

His eyes were quite sharp; no doubt about that. No sleepiness about him, but instead an alert quality; she could almost see him thinking. His voice was soothing, which, she told herself, was a good alarm sign. She thought Megan might be right—he liked her. But, on the other hand, there was obviously a lot he was not telling her. Maybe he just wanted to seem friendly in order to get some answers to whatever his questions might be.

Jill was now deeply unsettled by the break-in—much more so than she had been originally. It took a while for things to register, with her. She was glad that Brian and Cindy were moving in. Right now, they were bringing over a load of boxes from their apartment. Jill and Brian had both decided that Dad's papers should remain at his

apartment, for now. It seemed certain that the thief, who could be any number of people, was looking for them.

And for the Game Board.

She agreed with the theory that the boards had simply grown, but what had activated them to do so, just now?

Obviously, she thought, as she whirled wine-plumped sun-dried tomatoes in the blender along with fresh basil and an unholy number of garlic cloves, some party, or parties, wanted them to use the boards. How did they know about the board? How did they know what they were capable of?

Could it be Q itself, deciding?

She jumped at a touch on her shoulder.

It was Daniel.

"Sorry to startle you," he said. "Zoe let me in. So tell me what to do."

"You can get about fifteen plates from up there." She pointed to a high cupboard. "There's a stepstool."

"Real plates? Are you nuts?" He climbed up the stepstool and began handing down plates.

"Not a polite question. But I'll let it pass. The kids will use paper plates. Where's the rest of your family?"

"Dad will bring Ma Ellington—Arabelle—around five thirty, and Ron, my son. Arabelle tires easily."

"Are you related to the Duke?"

"Actually, yes. Descended from one of Edward Kennedy Ellington's many uncles."

"Impressive."

"Well, any musical talent seems to have passed me by, although I do like jazz. And opera. And Motown. Where do these dishes go?"

"Outside on that big slab of stone."

Daniel glanced out the window. "Now that's what I call impressive."

"Dad rented a crane to get it situated on the base. He just loved it. And his gardens. This was his little paradise, really."

Daniel gave her a look she couldn't read, which wasn't

surprising, considering that she didn't really know him. He took the dishes outside and came back in to pile silverware in a basket, muttering, "No plastic? This is insanity." She heard him opening and closing drawers, then he went back outside, this time with a tablecloth draped over his shoulder, clutching a beer in his right hand.

Megan finally dragged herself into the kitchen; she'd napped after their morning session. She said, "Remind me that I don't drink the next time I request alcohol."

Jill said, "I did, remember?"

"But in such a rude way." She poured herself some orange juice. "Who's that guy?"

"Detective Kandell. Daniel. He lives a few blocks over."

"Ah." She gave Jill a knowing look. "So that's the wonder-man. I gather he kind of likes you."

"Strictly professional," she said. "Although Brian did know his little brother, Truman, in high school."

"Truman Kandell? I remember him too, kind of. Neat. Maybe something's coming back. The HD-50 is stimulating my neurons. At least I have great life insurance."

They watched Daniel out the window. He turned and waved at them, yelled, "Am I doing all right?" He was setting out the silverware in rows on one of her fifties tablecloths. Jill would have dumped them in a pile. But she definitely would have used the tablecloth.

"Superlative!" Jill yelled back.

Megan said, "Jill, you can't deny it. That guy is really trying to impress you."

"Maybe he's just insanely compulsive."

"That impresses *me*."

Megan had the kids outside running through a sprinkler, except for Zoe, who had retired to the ballroom to play her violin. Jim was finishing the salad, and Jill had just slipped the flounder into a half-gallon of milk in a large bowl, a practice that everyone always made fun of as a waste of milk while they scarfed down the final product.

She decided to make a roux-based sauce with the left-over milk, this time.

Then Daniel was in the kitchen. "Where's the salt and pepper? Oh, not these cardboard shakers! I'm simply not used to doing without cut-glass shakers. But I'm flexible." He grabbed them, along with the pizza toppings in their Tupperware containers and said, "My mother always soaked the fish in milk. Delicious."

Jill watched him descend the stairs, a bit vexed. He knew how to say way too many right things.

Arabelle and Gerald Kandell arrived; Jill only knew because she looked out the window and saw Brian wheeling Arabelle's wheelchair over the lawn, getting her down to the party. Ron, Daniel's son, walked next to his grandmother.

Ron was not at all shy; Whens had him putting together a pizza right away. Jill noticed that Whens was drinking one of Zoe's Slingers and decided not to mention it. She descended the stairs with a big bowl of flounder breaded in cornmeal. "Hi!" she shouted. She set the bowl on the table. Daniel introduced them.

A beautiful wild halo of white hair surrounded Arabelle's heart-shaped face. A tiny gold cross on a thin gold chain nestled in the hollow of her throat. Stick-thin, she wore a cool white linen dress with a Chinese scarf that Jill recognized from the Smithsonian catalog, held to the dress with an old-fashioned rhinestone brooch.

"How nice to meet you," said Jill. She shook Arabelle's thin, frail-looking hand, noticing that she had very long, though gnarled, fingers, and a surprisingly strong grip.

"Yes," said Arabelle. "What a lovely place you have. You can't see how beautiful the gardens are from the street."

Brian furnished Gerald with a beer and took him on a tour of the house. Cindy slid the kids' pizzas into the wood-fueled oven. Jill began to fry the fish, Arabelle at her side in the wicker chair, facing the party, clutching a glass of red wine with both arthritis-ravaged hands.

"Who is playing Vivaldi?" she asked.

Jill looked up at the house. "That would be my niece, Zoe. Brian's girl. She should be out getting something to eat."

"She's very accomplished. I'd like to meet her."

"Whens, could you please go get Zoe and tell her it's time to eat?"

"Could she bring her violin?" asked Arabelle.

Zoe emerged in a few minutes, frowning, carrying her violin. She stomped down the stairs and declared, "I am not hungry. I'm busy."

Arabelle said, "Would you mind playing that last passage again?"

Zoe's face lit up. "Well, I'm trying to get it right."

"Could you please hold this?" Arabelle handed her wine to Jill, who set it down and turned the first batch of fish over.

"Let me have your violin," she asked Zoe. It was more along the lines of a command.

Zoe handed it over.

Arabelle astonished Jill by firing off the passage with great verve, despite her crippled hands. "I used to be better," she apologized. "But you must set the bow position before moving it."

Zoe said, "I know. I try, but it seems like I just can't get it right."

"Here's a very simple exercise you can try," Arabelle said, "Set. Up-bow. Set. Up-bow. You must separate the movements. Exercise like that a few minutes during your warm-up. Soon it will be yours."

Zoe tried it. She smiled. "Yes. That's better. Thanks. I'll put this away now. I think I'm getting hungry."

Cindy had been listening. "Do you teach?" she asked Arabelle.

"I used to, but it's more difficult now. Some days I just can't move my hands."

Daniel came over. "Arabelle trained in Europe."

"Seventy years ago. Seventy!"

THIS SHARED DREAM | 421

Cindy said, "Please think about teaching Zoe. I don't think the teacher she has now is doing her much good. She seemed very pleased with your suggestion, and that's really unusual. So—think about it." She frowned a little. "It's about all she does. Besides write music."

"What does she write?"

"I don't know. I don't know much about music, and she says it's mostly too hard for her to play."

Arabelle smiled again. "Interesting. I will think about it."

Jill, all-consumed by the picnic, did see Daniel talking to Brian and Megan now and then, in a serious fashion. She even saw him writing some notes. And then, after dark, as they were all sitting around the fire, although rather far back as it was still hot, Jill felt a pang and realized that she missed him. That was *really* not good. She had no intention of getting romantically involved with anyone. Nothing but trouble.

Gerald was telling stories about the architect who had designed their house, and told them that it most likely contained one or more of his trademark secret passages, listening tubes, and hidden doors with little rooms behind them. The kids got pretty excited about that.

Jill saw the red glow of a cigarette down through the garden, near the creek, in her mother's grotto.

Her heart swelled; for a moment, she could almost imagine that Bette was there, making wisecracks, or just relaxing.

She walked down through the damp grass and found the stone steps.

Inside the grotto was Daniel.

"I was wondering where you were," she said.

"I'm here. Just thinking."

Jill was oddly glad to see him. "Mind if I sit with you?"

He smiled. "That would be just fine."

Jill

JILL AWOKE to a great whooping, and powerful strobe lights—those of the sturdy alarm system Sam had installed when Bette's school was in the house. Manfred barked in her face.

She smelled smoke. Sam had also installed sprinklers in the big wooden house. Why weren't they on?

She ran to Whens' bedroom. The bed was empty.

"Stevie!" she shouted. "Whens!"

She wondered where the fire was as she wildly searched rooms, and was fleetingly and deeply thankful that Brian's family was spending one last night in their apartment, though most of their stuff was here. She smelled smoke, but saw no blaze anywhere as she searched the upstairs. Fire engines pulled up in front, adding to the din.

She heard someone yelling and she said, "Up here!"

In a moment, the fireman, carrying an ax and clad in protective clothing, wearing a mask, had found her. "Anyone else in the house?"

"My little boy. Stevie. I can't find him."

"You'll have to leave. I'll find him."

Manfred appeared in the doorway, barking, then wheeled and went to the second-floor door to the attic. Taking the steps two at a time, Jill dashed upstairs, following Manfred. "Stevie!"

They burst into the attic. The fireman was right behind her. "He's not here."

"Whens!"

Manfred had Whens by the arm, and dragged him from behind a dresser. "Ow! Stop!" he yelled, hitting Manfred on the head with what looked like a board.

The fireman stepped over and grabbed the boy. "Now run," he instructed Jill.

Once they were out on the front lawn, Brian's truck rounded the corner. He jumped out, took one look at the house, ran back to his truck, and dashed inside, gripping a flashlight.

Jill yelled, "Brian!" A fireman held her arm, keeping her from rushing after him.

Flames shot from the sides of the screened-in porch, licking the old lumber of the house, filling the already noisy scene with deep crackling sounds. The firemen aimed their hoses at the base of the fire.

Brian staggered from the house, coughing, and ran around to the side of the house.

Elmore arrived in his Mercedes. Tracy—Lavender Lady—was in the front seat. Elmore slammed the car door and went directly to Jill and grabbed Whens, who still clutched the red board from the attic in both hands. As Whens dangled, Elmore said, "He can't stay here anymore. It's dangerous."

"How in the world did you know there was a fire so quickly?"

"Ambulance-chasing friend." Elmore turned and started walking toward the car. Whens wailed, kicked, bit, and pummeled his father with the board he still clutched with one hand. "No! No! I have to stay here! No!"

"Ow, you little brat." Elmore slapped his son's face. "You will *never* bite me again! You're going with us." He wrestled the board from his son's hands and flung it to one side. As it fell, it opened up to reveal the black and red squares of a checkerboard. Whens' wails were deafening. Elmore shouted at Jill, "This is all your fault!"

"Don't we have enough to worry about?" she yelled at Elmore. "I'm calling the police. Where's a telephone?" She grabbed a neighbor's phone from her hand and dialed 911. "Yes? My husband is illegally taking my child. Yes. I have custody. Thank you."

"See," she said. "You can't just take him."

"Watch me."

Whens sobbed, limp, in his father's arms.

Brian strode across the lawn and said to Jill, "The chief says it's—" Then he noticed Elmore and Whens, and stopped.

"The chief says what?" demanded Elmore.

"Ask him yourself," said Brian, and walked away.

If he hadn't been so nasty, Jill would have been glad to relinquish Whens to Elmore for the night. But now she dug in her heels. Even Tracy got out of the car and tried to convince Elmore to leave him with Jill, citing various child custody cases while he glared at her.

He set Whens none too gently in the backseat, slammed the door, and stalked to the driver's side.

"He needs a car seat," yelled Jill.

Elmore roared off. Jill could see Whens pounding on the rear window, hysterical.

By three in the morning, the fire was completely out. The living room stank of smoke, and the neighbors had all gone back to bed, with promises of help if needed. Brian and Jill sat on the front porch, talking.

"The chief was pretty sure it was arson," said Brian. "They'll start a thorough investigation in the morning."

"Isn't that what you do?"

"It's one of my specialties, and I charge a lot for it, but I can't step on their evidence. I have an interest in this. I mean, a somewhat negative one."

"What do you mean?"

"Well, in arson, the first suspects are the owners, obviously. And we have sprinklers. The instant I got here, I knew they weren't on—that fire should not have gotten out of control. Someone must have shut off the sprinklers and disabled the water-flow alarms. First I went inside and checked the breakers; they were fine. Then I went to the pipe—it's around the side of the house there, and is always on. Period. It had been shut off."

"But how could someone just do that?"

"It's outside. You've seen it, I'm sure. It's on the side of the screened-in porch behind the peony bushes. I had it chained in the on position just to keep the kids from playing with it and accidentally turning it off. I never imagined that someone would come and deliberately cut the chain and turn off the valve. I check out the whole system once a month, breakers, battery backup, and so on, because this house is just a tinderbox. Two weeks ago, the chain was fine."

"Oh." Jill was silent for a moment. "But why would I start a fire with my little boy in the house? And turn off the sprinklers?"

"People do really strange things. So let's think about who else it might have been. Elmore? He got here awful fast—like maybe he was just around the corner."

Jill recoiled from the thought. "Absolutely not."

"Then it must be one of those people from the party. This is getting serious, Jill. At the very least, we need to track down whoever did this and charge them with arson. Maybe they're trying to kill you."

Jill was silent for a moment. "Maybe, but why be so obvious? Why leave such a big loophole—possible rescue? Why not poison, or just a hit-and-run while I'm riding my bike? That would be ridiculously easy. Is the chief sure about arson?"

"Reasonably. They found an empty gas can on the porch. They took it for fingerprints."

"Why would anyone be so clumsy?"

"Maybe they're not technologically inclined. A lot of people think that the evidence will burn up in a roaring fire. The porch was a good place to start it, though—good ventilation. And they knew the house had sprinklers, so my vote is for the conspirators. They've been inside; they've seen the sprinklers."

"We need to call a cleanup company first thing in the morning," said Jill. "Aren't there companies that specialize in cleaning up after fires?"

"Yes—more suspects. Let the insurance company choose one."

Jill sighed. "I guess Elmore is right. This really isn't a very safe place for Whens. He needs to stay with Elmore until we know who did this and why."

"It's not safe for you. I think you need to at least sleep at our place, and just come here in the day? We need to rethink moving in."

"Nope. I've got Manfred."

"Right. Are you a complete knucklehead?"

"Probably, but I'm staying. Remember how we were talking Sunday about how the house may have turned into a huge Hadntz Device?"

"Yes."

"Maybe the person who started the fire knows this and wanted to destroy it. Maybe he hates the Hadntz Device."

"As good a theory as any, except he may just hate you."

"Daniel is investigating all the people who were out on the front porch at the party."

"I wish he'd get a move on. And I hate to be so jumpy, but who is that sinister man walking down the street?"

"That guy? He looks all right to me."

The man paused in front of the house. "Had a fire?"

"Yes," said Brian.

"Everybody all right?"

"Everybody's fine, thanks," said Jill.

"Good," he said, and continued down the block.

"Was that the Walking Man?" asked Brian.

"He was definitely walking. But he wasn't wearing a hat," said Jill.

Jill

[*July 19*]

Two evenings later, Jill was at a World Bank reception at the Four Seasons Hotel in Washington, D.C., after a long day of dealing with insurance agents, repair people, and an arson investigator. She barely got there on time, but she had to attend.

Jill, in the midst of dignitaries wearing suits, black dresses, or exotic garb, said, "I don't believe that" to her immediate companion, and was suddenly, instead, in a London pub, surrounded by hard-drinking servicemen and vivacious women coifed and dressed in the style of the 1940s.

An ominous whistle pierced the air briefly. Everyone stopped talking. Benny Goodman, facile and riveting, played out a break.

I've been here so often, she thought.

In the corner of the pub, a dark-haired woman had clearly been arguing with a serviceman whose face Jill could not see. She opened her red-lipsticked mouth to retort but did not break the silence; the spell of waiting for the fall of the bomb could not, apparently, be broken. The pub smelled pungently of dark ale and whiskey.

A dull explosion; a glass fell from the bar and shattered; the Goodman record skipped. The V-1 had fallen elsewhere, not here; the roar of conversation resumed.

Then Jill was back, her familiar world restored. She staggered as if that persistent vision had a gravity that suddenly let go, and she glimpsed slices of the outdoor garden, rich with opulent flowers and well-dressed people in golden sunlight, a potted tree, the bar. The hubbub of many languages rose around her as she crashed against the UN representative from Nigeria, down from

428 | KATHLEEN ANN GOONAN

New York especially for this reception, especially to talk to her. He staggered sideways. His martini and her glass of wine plummeted to the bricks and smashed.

Then there really was a brief silence as Bill Anderson, conveniently next to her, reached down to help her up. She rose on one knee and tried to shoo him away, but he grabbed both of her hands and pulled her up. Because her eyes were just inches from his chest as she stood up, she noticed his name tag, which said that his name was Wilhelm.

"I'm so sorry," she said, irritated and embarrassed, brushing Mr. Umbobi's martini from her black silk dress. "Mr. Umbobi, are you all right?"

"No, no, *I* am sorry," he said, his voice deep and earnest. "I have ruined your dress."

"Don't believe in what?" asked Wilhelm. He would always be Wilhelm now, she realized.

Jill cast her mind back with great difficulty, then realized that Wilhelm had been seriously eavesdropping on her conversation with Mr. Umbobi. "Nothing."

Wilhelm said, "You've been working too hard. Maybe you've caught a flu or something."

Conversation resumed, the incident forgotten, except that Mr. Umbobi patted her on the shoulder as Wilhelm led her away and said they could lunch together tomorrow.

She pulled away from Wilhelm and set up the lunch date with Umbobi, and a Four Seasons employee moved in to clean up the mess.

Wilhelm had called for his car, despite her protestations that first, she was fine and would stay, and then, that she would take a cab, and then she was in his car, feeling uncharacteristically foggy. One of her knees was bleeding, as if she'd fallen while roller skating. What a fiasco. Maybe she *was* sick. But she was mostly angry. She had had a lot of work to do at this reception.

Wilhelm pulled up in front of the house. Jill opened her door. "Thanks."

He jumped out of his side. When she turned back from gathering her purse, he was next to her, holding out his hand. "I'll help you inside. Is there anyone you want me to call?"

She tried to pull her hand back, but his grasp was strong, and he propelled her from the car in one quick yank. She staggered to catch her balance, and he put an arm around her waist.

Manfred clicked down the walk. "Get away!" said Wilhelm, swinging one hand in Manfred's direction. Manfred looked at the human pest, then sniffed at him. Jill saw her upper lip tremble just a tad, a prelude to baring her teeth. Her growl was a low, long rumble.

"Don't worry," said Wilhelm, reaching inside his jacket. "I've got a—"

Jill wrenched herself free, knelt, and put her arms around Manfred's neck. "She's my dog. What are you doing out, girl?"

Manfred wagged her tail. Jill stood with great determination, rather dizzy, and grasped the fur of Manfred's back to steady herself.

"Will he hurt me?"

"She. She is very protective."

Wilhelm stepped toward her.

"I'm fine." Jill retreated a few steps.

"You're not fine. I just saw you faint. Gosh, what happened to your house?"

"Just a little fire, the other night." Jill started down the walk, concentrating on each step.

Wilhelm followed. "That's terrible. How much damage?"

"Not too much, thankfully."

"Where's your house key?"

Jill smelled mint, roses, and cigarette smoke. "I think I have company." She raised her voice. "Who's there?"

The man sitting in a wicker chair on the porch stood, a dark shape in shadow. All Jill could see was the end of his glowing cigarette.

"I'll call the police," said Wilhelm. He pulled out his phone.

"Hold your horses," said Jill. "Who is it?" she called again.

"It's me." Daniel ambled over to the top of the stairs.

"Hello, is this the police?" said Wilhelm into his phone.

Jill giggled. "This guy is the police."

"What?" He squinted at Daniel. He looked crestfallen. "What is he doing here? He isn't in uniform."

"He's a friend of mine, Wilhelm."

Wilhelm swallowed. "Oh. What's this Wilhelm stuff?"

She pointed to his name tag. He reached up and tore it off. "It's Bill."

Jill said, "Thanks for the ride. I can make it from here." She reached out toward Daniel, who was next to her now. He took her hand firmly.

"Detective Kandell." He offered his hand to Wilhelm.

"I'm Bill Anderson from the World Bank. Jill just passed out. I'll help her inside."

"I don't think I really passed out," said Jill.

"She wouldn't go to the emergency room."

"I don't blame her," said Daniel. "Come on, honey." He put his arm around her waist.

Jill almost resisted. Then she saw his point. "Thanks, babe." She turned to Bill/Wilhelm. "Thanks again."

Wilhelm drove off with what seemed an unnecessary rpm ratio. Jill watched his taillights and started to laugh. "Honey?"

"Babe? I wouldn't have thought you were the fainting type."

"I said, I didn't faint! It's these stupid shoes!"

"He says his name is Anderson? The Anderson from the party?"

"The very same. Bill is mainly German. I used to work with him a lot more, but when I went back to school they put me in Africa. I'm not sure that I'm the best person for the job, mainly because I know a lot more about

European history and World War II. I'm part of a team, of course, but I'm not sure I'm doing Africa much good. And now that I'm missing that reception, not to mention looking so stupid in front of everybody—"

They were on the porch now; Daniel had practically hoisted her up the stairs and settled her in a chair as she chatted. The condensation on a tall glass of something cold sitting on the table next to her, shimmered in the streetlight. The front door was open a bit.

"Did you go in?"

"Nope. I walked over here with my drink. Nice evening for a stroll."

"I assume there's nothing alcoholic in that open drink."

"Of course not."

"Why is the front door open?"

"I don't know. That's why I waited. I knocked, and there was no answer, but Manfred came out and said hi. I called Brian, and he said you'd gone to a party and they were all at the apartment, packing—they're still moving in?"

"We all hashed it over, and they decided that they still want to."

"Well, Brian was surprised about the door, but said that they must have left the door unlocked and that I should lock it. I thought I'd finish my drink on your porch. It's quite pleasant."

"It's odd that the door was unlocked. We're trying to be more careful. Oh, shit—" She staggered to the railing and vomited into the garden. "Ugh." She wiped her mouth with the back of her hand, then was sick again.

Daniel put his drink into her hand. "Rinse."

She rinsed out her mouth and spit. "Wow. That's strong."

"Something you ate?"

She returned to her chair rather shakily and plopped into it. "No. I didn't have time to eat anything. I only had a few sips of wine—" She frowned.

"What?"

"I wonder if someone put something in my drink."

"Like who? Like what?"

"Like Wilhelm. He thoughtfully brought me the wine. Like what? I'm not sure. But I'll tell you something interesting. He didn't ask me the way to the house."

"Major mistake."

"Well, he did come to the party."

"I only retract major."

She took a deep breath. "If you'll excuse me, I'm going to take a bath. Want to wait downstairs?"

Daniel stood at the foot of the stairs while she pulled herself up by the banister. "You seem kind of weak, honey. Holler if you need some help."

"You wish, babe," she said, over her shoulder.

When she got back downstairs, wearing sweatpants and a T-shirt, Daniel was reading one of her mother's Chinese poetry books. He closed it and held it on his lap. "Elegant. And ancient. Huang Po is one of my favorites. Helps put things in perspective. Feeling better?"

"A little. A lot, actually. Wow. That's never happened to me before. Very unpleasant." She lay down on the couch. "So you just came by to visit?"

He looked slightly apologetic. "Yes and no. I have something to tell you."

"What? That you work for some kind of black ops part of the government and know where my parents are?"

His hand went to his mouth. Astonishment filled his eyes, but his voice was mocking. "Jill! How did you know?"

"Well, let's see." She held up both hands and ticked off points with her fingers. "One, you showed up suspiciously quickly when the house was broken into."

"Mistake."

"Major."

"Minor."

"Major. Two, you know way too much about jazz."
He and Brian had talked jazz into the wee hours after
the picnic.

He protested, "It's my heritage."

"Way too much. You've studied it in order to ingratiate yourself."

"Ellington *was* my uncle. Brian wanted to know about
Uncle Ed Ellington. And a lot of people know about—"

"Okay. I'll give you that. But three, you act in ways
that seem unprofessional for a police officer, but fine for
a spy, because they have no morals."

"Excuse me, but aren't you of the opinion that your
mother was—is—a spy?"

"She is not a spy. She works in intelligence, and she is
saving the world."

"That's no excuse. Besides, I have plenty of morals."

"I didn't say that you have no morals."

"Yes, you did."

"I said that you act unprofessionally, for a police officer. It seems to me that they don't generally start personal relationships with the people they're helping. They
especially don't show up at their house all the time not
dressed—"

"I'm dressed!" he objected. He grinned, and then he
couldn't stop laughing. "Jill, you sure can spin a tale!
You're amazing."

"*Not wearing their uniform.*" She frowned, crossed
her arms, and stared at the ceiling. "Now you made me
lose count."

"Wait, Jill, wait." He caught his breath. "I'm pulling
your leg. I am not a spy. I do not report to Langley, then
drive around D.C. in an out-of-date police car. I do have
a confession to make, though. I find you attractive, and
interesting, and I wandered over here to see if I could
help with the moving process and further ingratiate myself. And make sure the arson team came by today; they
should have sent me a report."

"They were here. Excuse me if I get just a wee bit upset,

but it seems to me as if there are a lot of people nosing around here, including you. And another thing: You knew about my mother's school. A very major mistake. To mention it. You're trying to throw me off the track."

"I was . . . surprised," he said. "Truly. That's what opened all this up for me. Like—I don't know—like those buried memories that seem to conveniently surface on the witness stand, I guess. I'm helping you—or rather, I want to. I'm on your side."

"I'm not on a side."

He sighed, sat cross-legged on the floor next to her, but not too close, and took her hand. She didn't object. In fact, it was comforting. "Jill, I'm sorry. I know this must be disappointing." He smiled, but quickly made his face serious again. "I'm really, really, not a spy. I'm not quite that glamorous. But I am a moderately smart guy, if I do say so myself, and I'm afraid you are on a side. It certainly seems that way. At least, there seem to be people on some *other* side who are hatching conspiracies, breaking into your house, tailing you, burning your house down, slipping you drugs, and things like that that you really oughtn't ignore quite so strenuously. But— and excuse once again this untoward talking behind your back—but Brian says that you're very good at ignoring things."

She wanted to jump up and yell at him, but felt a bit weak, and she didn't know what she'd say. "Then tell me what my side is. The side of good, I hope?"

He shoved aside the coffee table, stuffed a handy couch pillow under his head as he stretched out on the floor, crossed his arms, and looked at her appraisingly. "I would imagine, knowing you, and observing the other side's criminal behavior, that you are probably on the side of good. Or, at least, law-abiding. But you tell me. What in the world is going on? I don't want to scare you, but I'm pretty sure that Brian locked the door when he left. So let's put it together. That guy slipped you a drug, and took few pains to hide it. I guess he's never done it

before because he overdosed you and you vomited it all up. Otherwise, you'd probably have forgotten the rest of the night. Just a blank. Someone came over in advance of your friend Wilhelm and made sure the door was open so if he couldn't find your keys he could get in."

"How do I know it wasn't you?"

"It wasn't, but you don't know."

She sighed. "I do know. He keeps trying to ask me out, and I keep avoiding him. Are you saying he gave me a date-rape drug?"

"I think so, but I'm not sure that rape was the object."

"Well, look, he knew I'd be occupied all evening there. If he wanted to rob my house, why not have his cohorts come over while I was busy?"

"Maybe he wanted you here, so he could talk to you. So you could just show him what he was after. Those drugs erase volition. Do you know what they're after?"

She was silent.

"If you want me to leave, just say so. No offense taken. I'd rather stay here until somebody gets back, but you can lock the door and I can sit on the front porch."

"Don't be silly."

"Okay. Then can I get you something to eat? To drink? Some hot tea and crackers?"

"Crackers, cheese, and wine. And water. And peppermint tea. It's in the side cupboard. No drugs, please, or I'll report you."

"This spy stuff is hungry work," she said, finishing off her snack. "Nice wine choice. You've been paying attention."

"Thank you very much, but I got it out of your own pantry. Do you normally buy wines that you don't like?"

"Don't change the subject. Tell me what you've deduced about this grand overarching conspiracy."

"It has something to do with Q."

"I may fall asleep."

"Let me jump forward a bit."

"Do."

"It seems that there are a lot of people—a new kind of people, I suppose, that walk from one timeline, one gestalt, to the other."

Jill set down her wineglass and looked at him. "Just like walking across the room."

"Right."

"What makes you think so?"

"Evidence."

"What evidence?"

He looked at her with his head tilted. "Are you one of them?"

"If I were, why would I tell you? Or, for that matter, why would I not tell you?"

"You might not tell me if you were afraid that I might have you committed."

"Oh. Right. So why would I tell you?"

"To increase the gestalt."

"To what?"

"I have more to tell you, and it's what I intended to tell you tonight, anyway. I'll start with a little story about my dad. It's about when he was in the war."

"But—"

"Just listen. He was recruited to spy on the Nazis in Morocco. I grant you that this was unusual, but he'd had a high school year in Europe studying architecture. Arabelle had connections. She always pushed him, and got him that scholarship—chiefly, she said, to show him that elsewhere in the world, Negroes were treated like people. He spoke French and German. He'd learned them so that he could read novels and philosophy in the original. When he came back, he was an able draftsman, and got a drafting job in a local, prominent, open-minded architectural firm, and started school at Howard. Because of his language skills, his firm took him along to the high-profile parties and diplomatic dinners where they made connections and got jobs—they discovered he could sell the firm to foreigners pretty well. He met Dulles at one

of these parties, and Dulles snapped him up. He was perfect for the OSS; they sent him to Istanbul and then Morocco.

"No one ever suspected he was a spy; he was just an African working the black market, not to make a pun or anything, tending bar, waiting tables, operating as a manservant so he could be in people's rooms and go through their papers and pockets. In Casablanca he met a gypsy violinist. The violinist knew a woman named Eliani Hadntz. My dad heard the most amazing things about what she thought. Now, he was terrifically unuseful in Europe, being black and therefore always a bit too remarkable. But after Berlin fell, there were months of complete chaos, and he was right in there with his cigarettes, dollars, and diamonds—all OSS issue. And he was able to trace something that intelligence was calling the Hadntz Device."

Jill felt weak. "And?"

"He traced it to Germany. To a small city called Gladbach, actually. He was there, ostensibly part of the French Underground that was allowed to retaliate against the Nazis. It was a thin cover, of course, but it was pretty chaotic then. He was there when a certain . . . event occurred. It was an event related to the Device. But then the Device went to Russia. And then the leads all went dead. But I do know one thing."

"What's that?"

"Your mother gave the plans to someone who sold it to the Russians."

"They were our Allies."

"Yes. They were."

"Can you prove this?"

"No. Of course not. And my old man is as close-mouthed as your parents apparently were. He returned, picked up his architecture career, but as you might know, and I know from being in law enforcement, one is never really free of the OSS, or the CIA. At some point, he was alerted about your mom being right here."

"So—Truman was a baby spy?"

"I'm not sure," he admitted. "I imagine that he was behind Truman coming here to school. I imagine he came to any gatherings. But by that time I think he'd sworn off all of that. He didn't want to do it anymore. Happy family man and all of that. Then, with all the assassinations and riots, he might have become a little more serious."

Jill asked, "He remembers? You remember? You know, I've wondered for years what happened to all the people from what I called Before. Now I know. They're everywhere. Except that my therapist isn't one. Or maybe she is. She's a spy, like you."

"Jill, I'm not a spy. I didn't really remember until I saw that Monet. Mom is the one who told me all this about Dad, before she died. Not him. She told me never to tell him that I knew. I think she kind of wanted me to understand his . . . quirks. But I don't think that she knew about the jump, the implications of what he'd told her. She just kept living along, like most everybody else, and was completely in this new reality. And I didn't know—I wasn't sure—till I came here. Just vague dreams, questions, that déjà vu feeling. When I saw that picture, I just suddenly made the connection. That's all."

Jill felt exceedingly dark, and grumpy too. "Now that your dad has been to the picnic and allowed to prowl all over the house, courtesy of me, what does he think?"

"I don't know."

Jill glared at him.

"Really, I don't. He's a philosophical man. Prone to long spells of quiet. I did ask him, believe me, when we got home. What he thought of the house, and all, and he said he was utterly delighted to have the chance to see such an architectural gem, with hardly anything ruined by uninformed renovations."

"That's for sure."

"He and Arabelle had a wonderful time. It was so nice of you to invite them."

"So which side is he on? Did you tell him what you told me? That you remember the time jump?"

"No." He was quiet for a long time. Finally he said, "I want to. I've tried. I will. Because it's important not just to you, but, obviously, to a lot of people. But I know he'll deny everything and be difficult and avoid me for weeks afterward, just like when I used to ask him about Mom. Only worse. Before I met you, I thought I might just be imagining everything, like my past was just a very real dream. I don't think that most people recall their pasts all that clearly. Try it yourself, day by day."

"No thanks. Do you think I could ask him about it?"

"I certainly wouldn't mind if you tried. He might be of some help, but he might not know any more than my mother said he did."

Jill stared into the room, her anger growing. She could not move. Her body was stiff; her mind was stuck. She had trusted this man. Well, kind of.

No, really.

He looked at her steadily, sitting up now, elbows braced on his knees, his hands folded together and his head resting on top of them, like some kind of solid Buddha, as if he knew everything that was going through her mind.

Then her thoughts raced, as though a tiny chink in a dam had grown huge, and a tumult of feelings rushed through her. Her mind did a wild flip, and her anger flowed out of her. "I understand."

The lines of his face loosened, moved from tension to deep relief. He let out a breath and bowed his head. "Thank you. Thank you, Jill."

Whens

FUN WITH TRACY AND ELMORE

[*July 22*]

WHENS DID not like the room he stayed in when he was at his father's. The color of the wall was like a gloomy day. His mother had helped him pick out the colors of his room at Halcyon House. It was bright yellow and bright red, and he had painted part of it himself, so parts were also a very pretty orange color.

Also, at home—what he thought of as home, though his father was saying now that this would be his home—no one cleaned his room. It was his job, his mother said, and sometimes he did and sometimes he didn't. Walking into this room was always kind of depressing, because it was always exactly the same, like no one really lived here. No matter what he did, he couldn't make a dent. The bed was always made, and before he cuddled into it he had to move the fancy pillows and bolsters and pull down a heavy fancy quilt that he was not allowed to do anything on, including color pictures, eat, or drink. By the time he finished with the work of getting his bed ready, he was all woken up.

He was not allowed to leave his room after he was officially put to bed by Lavender Lady, which meant that she came in, pulled the covers up around his neck, kissed him on the cheek, and turned out the light. She had just done all that, and now he was lying here in the big bed with nothing to do but watch the light from car headlights on the street ebb and flow across the ceiling and race across his desk before disappearing.

He wasn't sleepy. But he had to stay in his room. He wasn't allowed to wander around the house or go into the kitchen and get something to eat. His father and Lavender Lady were very strict about this. They kept saying

that his mother was crazy to let him eat whatever he wanted no matter what time it was. In fact, they often talked about how crazy his mother was, which made him mad.

It made him mad right now.

He rolled off his bed and reached for the light switch, but then stopped. When he turned the light on, Lavender Lady always seemed to know it, and came right away.

It wasn't very dark anyway. He knelt beside his pack, which rested against his desk. He opened a zipper pocket on one side and poked around. His phone wasn't there. In the third pocket he opened, his fingers touched the smooth surface of his phone and he pulled it out and called his mother.

She answered right away. "Hi, honey. How are you doing?" She sounded very glad to hear him.

"I hate it here," he said.

"I know, but your father really loves you and he wants you to stay there with him for a while. Tracy said she had the room specially fixed up for you. It looks really nice, doesn't it?"

"No."

"I hope you are being polite about it?"

"I just want to come home."

"You can't, not right now. I wish you could. I really miss you. I'm coming to lunch at your school tomorrow."

"Why can't I come home?"

"Because of the fire," she said, but he knew that it wasn't just that. "There are a lot of people working here now, with saws and things, and it can be kind of dangerous. Are you reading anything fun right now? I'll bring you some new books tomorrow."

"Okay. Can you come over now?"

"No, honey. I'll see you tomorrow. I love you!"

It was not even dark yet and here he was, alone in his room, in his pajamas. He liked to read big books with hardly any pictures, like the grown-ups. Well, *Winnie-the-Pooh* did have some pictures, but not on every page.

He wasn't supposed to read books at night here because it would hurt his eyes—they had taken his flashlight away—and Lavender Lady said that he was too young to read and that it would hurt his brain. He had laughed at that and told them that he couldn't feel his brain; brains didn't have feelings. His father and Lavender Lady had then looked at each other with The Look, and his father just said, "Well."

He went to the window and yanked on the window shade. He was not allowed to open the shade himself because when he did it rolled up all the way to the top, *flap, flap, flap.* This really made Lavender Lady mad. She had to carry his desk chair over and pull it back down perfectly halfway. All the shades in the house had to be that way. Until she went around and pulled them down for the night. There were a lot of strange rules here.

He yanked on the shade, and it went *flap, flap, flap,* and he looked down on the street, with its fat green trees. A few cars drove past, but he couldn't hear their whooshing sound. Some people were out walking their dogs, and there were even children playing across the street in the park. He couldn't yell at them because another rule was that the windows had to always be shut because of the air-conditioning. Also, there were alarms on them.

He went to his dresser and got out his old shorts and his old T-shirt, which he'd put back in a corner after his dad threw them in the trash, saying that his mother was dressing him like a ragamuffin and they were too worn out to wear. He liked them. They were soft and cool. He put them on.

He then opened his pack and considered what to put in it. His treasures were few but essential. A smooth swirly stone he'd found in the creek that most certainly was magic. He could feel it. He just didn't know how to use it yet. He got it out from the bottom of a drawer where it was hidden and plunked it in.

The Hobbit, which his mother had been reading

to him, went in next. It was a bent-up old paperback. He had shiny new books here, all perfect on a shelf, but he had to be very, very careful in handling them and even sit in a special chair and not sprawl on the bed. Lavender Lady had deeply insulted him by telling him not to color in them.

And the checkerboard on which he played with Grandma, which his mother had rescued from the front yard after the fire and given to him.

"Whens, Whens, Whens. My name is Whens," he chanted in a whisper as he packed. Maybe that was the worst thing here. They refused to call him by his name. They didn't even know who he was.

Finally, he was packed.

It was a little bit darker outside now. The streetlights were on.

Lavender Lady and his father were watching television in the special theater room right now. He wasn't allowed to go in because of what might be on the television. The door would be closed.

He put a pillow under the covers to make it look like he was there. He had read about that in a book. He slipped out of his room and went down the hallway, past the closed door of the theater room, where there was a loud noise of machine guns, and went down the steep, long stairs.

At the front door, he pushed the button to turn off the alarm, went out onto the front porch, and closed the door quietly behind him.

Sam Dance
[*July 22*]

SAM HAD wandered the same nexus-shot London underground for what seemed weeks, searching for Bette, surfacing occasionally to a London of half buildings and bomb craters, or dull office buildings in the fifties,

444 | KATHLEEN ANN GOONAN

then trying another dead end. Trying to get back to D.C., 1991, where Jill was in the hospital.

One night, as he slept in the underground on his bed-roll, he awoke to exquisite violin music. Gypsy violin.

He stood and packed his stuff, then tracked the source. Was it a musician in an echoing entrance, one of many who roamed at night, keeping spirits up and playing for food? Maybe.

But it bore a strange resemblance to the music that, for him, had always signaled a nexus—the odd, aural flavor from a distance, or as if he had some kind of neurological disturbance. He walked down the platform, stepping over sleeping Brits, following it as it strengthened and then shifted to—yes!

"White Heat"! But not like any "White Heat" he had ever heard before—which for him, was the stamp of true jazz. Originality. His excitement grew as a train roared down the tunnel.

He got in.

He was just getting settled, and "White Heat" was fill-ing his brain and his entire body, reaching its crescendo, pulling up memories of the Squounch Club, the Perham Downs, the Army reunions during which timestreams merged and he and Wink could meet, when a voice an-nounced that the next stop was Union Station, Washing-ton, D.C.

He picked up a discarded newspaper on the seat next to him. It was 1991. In the blink of an eye, confluent and then congruent with London, 1944, the two timestreams blending then parting, coming in from infinite angles, close enough to touch and step into, from one side and cross to the other, if one knew how, if one's being was infused with enough of Hadntz's blend of quantum physics, neurobiology, and . . . in his case, luck.

He was in an orange, plastic Metro seat. Opposite him, a stylized grid map of the Washington Metro butted against an ad for George Washington University.

Stepping out of the car as soft lights flashed along the platform, he took the up escalator. Ignoring the splendors of Union Station, he headed through it and emerged into the golden light of a late afternoon in full summer, which kindled the impatiens and daylilies in the park across the street to a blaze.

He headed unerringly toward Halcyon House, hoping to find Bette there. When he was only a block away, a familiar figure hurried toward him, waving.

"Sam!"

"Wink?"

He and Wink met, embraced, stepped back. "Well, old man, glad to see you back again," said Wink.

"Old man, eh? You're not looking so hot yourself. Is Bette here? I've been—"

"She's not with you?"

"Do you see her?"

"Calm down. I'm sure—"

"Don't tell me to calm down!"

"She left to look for you last week. But listen to me. Listen! You need to stake out Elmore's town house in Georgetown. Here's the address."

"Elmore's house? Isn't Jill there too?"

"No. They're getting a divorce. She's here. But your grandson, Stevie, is there. I'll call you a cab. I've been keeping an eye on Halcyon House, and I saw you from way, way down the street. Brian and his family are here now, so I'm heading out to Megan's."

"Just tell me what the hell is going on."

"That Perler Device. Remember? He stole it from us in Mönchengladbach, and then the Russians got it. Somebody here in D.C. has it, and we don't know exactly who, or where it is."

"It was no good, though. It didn't work. It was a failure."

"That was way back. In another timestream, even. I believe, and Hadntz believes, that it might activate."

"I got the impression from you that Q was self-healing, incapable of doing wrong, like a new improved God almighty, only better, so if that's true—"

"The Perler is still a prototype of the original, primitive Device. Hadntz has been looking for it too, and can't locate it— Look, Sam, she is just exactly one step ahead of this game, that's all. Even if she's echoed and magnified through a zillion timestreams and even if she isn't blindsided by her own humanity, *she is still human*."

"Okay, so why isn't this goddamned Q-stuff *fixing* everything?" Sam threw his duffle on the ground and glared at Wink.

"I don't know. All I know is this: Someone is targeting your family, and I've been keeping an eye on all of them for months, and it's all going haywire, and you need to get your ass over there and watch your grandson, okay? Here's the cab. Here's the address. Here's my Q. Try to call Bette."

Sam's heart felt like lead. "Is this all I can do?"

"I think so, right now. Grab something to eat on the way. You look like hell. Here's some money. But hurry. Something's going down. I'll call you soon."

Sam didn't stop for food. He watched Washington, a Washington not a whole lot changed from when he'd left, thirteen years earlier, but with the vehicle charging kiosks he'd predicted on every other corner, and tried to forget that he was, after all, seventy-two years old and numbed by everything happening so fast, after so many years of lulling calm.

Sam had just settled himself on a picnic table across from Elmore's town house, a dressed-down renovation that screamed Money and Good Taste from every understated detail, and was examining the Q device Wink had given him, when the door opened, and a little boy slipped out and closed it ever so carefully.

Whens!

The boy looked around, then hurried down the steps.

It was a wonder that the huge pack on his back didn't pull him over backward.

Sam stood, thrusting the device toward his pocket, not noticing when it missed his pocket and fell out, and left his heavy duffle on the ground.

He side-leaped the fence, which was not very high, just meant to keep children from running into the street, and landed with a *clump!* as his scratched combat boots hit the sidewalk, and felt silly because he now had a hell of a pain in his left knee.

He wondered if he should just grab Whens, risking arrest, or follow him. He reached for the Q, so he could ask Wink, then searched every pocket. Gone. Crap.

The boy's blond hair shone beneath a street lamp then darkened as he moved past the light. The boy moved in a determined and fierce short-legged jog. Sam drew closer, deciding: He would simply pick up his grandson and let him scream for help. He didn't want to frighten him with pursuit, though—he could easily get away from an old man. Sam was thirty feet away when a car pulled up next to the boy, then moved in tandem with him.

"Whens!" Sam broke into a run, feeling like a very old man, wheezing and puffing with the sudden effort.

A short, fat man in a suit, wearing a ridiculous homburg, jumped from the car and seized the boy. The hat fell to the sidewalk.

Whens indeed screamed and hollered. And kicked.

Sam punched the fat man in the face. He staggered backward. Whens bit the man's hand, which covered his mouth, and the man let go.

Whens darted down an alleyway, his pack bobbing behind him.

Both men took off after him.

Wilhelm

WILHELM'S EVENING

[July 22]

IN WILHELM'S sanctum, a slight breeze rattled his plastic window blinds as he patiently tried to put together the material he had. He'd thought the books he'd taken from the Dance library would help.

But apparently, he still did not have enough information.

He shoved the books away from him, and took a few swallows of fake German beer. He'd been very disappointed to read, on the label, that Löwenbräu was manufactured in the United States.

Everyone, everything, had failed him.

The only helpful thing had been a very strange note, just a jot on the endpaper of *What Is Life?* The book itself was piffle, of course. Schrödinger was not a Jew, but he'd left Germany because he did not like Hitler's anti-Semitism campaign, so he was obviously not very intelligent.

The jot said, "Game Board?"

His spies—helpmeets and friends he'd cultivated over the years—had been keeping a close watch on the Dance family, and on their house. They understood the import, the majesty, of his quest, and that they would share in the outcome. They also agreed to wear old-fashioned homburgs, but he wasn't sure now that that had been a good idea. The brims could disguise them, somewhat, if they were pulled down low, but the hats made them stand out. The real reason was that he was sentimental about homburgs; his father had worn them; many men at that time wore them, in Germany. Everyone would wear them again, once the right people were in charge.

Setting the house on fire—that was another mistake.

He'd let his anger get the better of him, but he thought the house would go up like tinder. It might have killed Jill. But Jill had gone to the market with that colored man, according to his compatriot, Adler, his Eagle—short though he was, he was far-seeing—and it was then he began to suspect that her respect for coloreds, and all her work for Africa, which he had assumed that some-one as brilliant as Jill could not be sincere about, might be sickeningly real. Maybe he was mistaken about her. But no—later, at the house, she had actually allowed the colored man, Kandell, to touch her . . . his stomach roiled.

Yes, he had been stupid. He might have killed her. Maybe that was what he had wanted, at that moment. But he had endangered the big plan. That was what happened when you let emotion overtake you. Without Jill, he might never know the secrets he must learn. And he might have left clues at the house.

At any rate, Eagle had seen, on the seat of Brian Dance's truck, a metal board, covered with . . . games. Just games. A small checkerboard. A racetrack. Things of that nature. The Game Board of the scrawled note? He had wasted time calling to ask Wilhelm if that might be something he wanted.

Wanted? *Yes!*

But it was too late. Brian had surprised Eagle when he was trying to break into the car, and to escape pursuit, he drove to the German embassy, where he worked as a janitor. He kept an eye on things there too. It was terri-ble, the things he saw and heard; Germans had forgot-ten their great mission altogether. They had lost their soul. Wilhelm knew, though, that he only needed to find out how to empower the Device, or build one himself.

The plans. That was all. He'd broken into the truck himself, later that night; no need to leave it to amateurs, and the board was no longer there.

It didn't matter. The plans were what mattered. And now, he could think of only one way to get them. It was

desperate, yes, but once he had the Device, or the plans, he would have the power—the power that Jill didn't even seem to know she had.

He Q'd Eagle: "Time for Bip." Bip was a useful thug—white, of course—with connections to other thugs. "Yes, that's right. I've made the decision. I know it might take some time. Be alert, though. You never know when an opportunity might arise."

He looked back at his security screen. Now what?

He had hacked into the condo's security system when he moved in, ten years ago, and enjoyed keeping an eye on things. He always knew what his neighbors were up to. Right now several police cars were pulling up in front of the building.

He picked up his poor, twisted Device, then, in a split-second realized that if indeed they were after him, and he had it on him, or if they found it here . . .

Opening the hooks on the window screen, he pushed it out the window, and rehooked the screen. He was only on the fifth floor; there was nothing but a small, unused grassy verge behind the condo.

He locked his office, ran out his front door and down the hallway, toward the emergency exit stairway. Once through the door, he left himself a slice of vision. The police got out of the elevator and knocked on his door.

Gently pulling the door closed, he descended the stairway. They wouldn't realize he had known they were coming until they got into his locked room, so if he was lucky he could get out of the side exit before they surrounded the building.

When he reached the ground floor, he listened. No shouts, no unusual sounds. He opened the door, looked out, saw no one, and walked away, swiftly blending into pedestrian traffic. As usual, there were plenty of strollers and window-shoppers in Georgetown this evening.

He would come back later, after they had left, to retrieve his artifact. No one, walking by casually, would

find it remarkable enough to even pick it up. It looked rather like a rock.

His phone rang. It was Eagle. "What? Excellent news. I will give you a new address. Bip must take him there immediately. There is a key over the doorjamb. No, I won't be there until tomorrow afternoon. I must prepare . . . things."

He increased his pace. Luck was on his side at last.

Lev

KOSLOV'S TALE

[July 22]

JILL WAS at the bookstore. Whens had just called from his father's, sounding forlorn. She gathered some books to take to him when she visited him at school tomorrow during his lunchtime. She agreed with Elmore that he should not be at Halcyon House right now. As she resumed her place at the counter and began looking through the books, Koslov walked in.

She tried not to freeze, and wondered if she should call 911.

The store was full of customers. She tried the *Golden Arrow of Breath*, but still her heartbeat quickened.

He walked quickly to the counter. "Jill, there is something I must tell you."

She looked him in the eye. "What?"

He looked around. "Not here."

"Here. Now." Koslov stepped back while Jill sold a stack of books, and then returned to the counter. His deep-set eyes were worried. *Even concerned?* she wondered.

He pulled his wallet from his back pocket, opened it, pulled a photograph from behind his driver's license, and laid it on the counter in front of her.

It was a black-and-white photo of three people standing

on the wide front steps of a stone house; behind them, the doorway looked regal, and on both sides of the door were potted palms and wicker chairs. On the left was a middle-aged woman, possibly from the 1930s, judging from her clothing. Next to her was a young woman, whom Jill recognized, instantly, as Hadntz. And the third person—

Koslov put a nicotine-stained finger on the young man. "Me. I was twenty. I was a friend of Rosa Hadntz. I also knew her daughter, Eliani, a very talented woman. She had an M.D. like her mother, and a doctorate in physics, like her father. I have been trying to—"

Another customer approached. Koslov whipped his photo from the counter; Jill chatted with the customer and sold a paperback mystery. The customer left.

Koslov said, "I know what happened to you, Jill. The same thing happened to me. I've been tracking down a . . . valuable artifact, for years. I know it is in Washington. I met your mother, long, long ago. I am trying to help you. You are in danger. Please meet me in"—he looked out the window—"that restaurant, there, across the street, when you close. You don't have to be afraid. There are plenty of people there."

Jill watched him jaywalk across the street and enter the C&O Restaurant. The door closed behind him.

Jill called Daniel. There was no answer. She left a message: "Koslov asked me to meet him in the C&O Restaurant when I close. I think I should. Maybe you could sit at the bar and keep an eye on things? Call me."

Only ten minutes until closing time. There was only one customer in the store, browsing. Jill turned off the lights in the back. The customer looked up. "I thought you were open till nine."

"We are. Just getting ready to close. Do you want anything?"

She shelved the book she'd been reading. "No, not tonight." She left.

Jill locked the door behind her, put the cash in the safe

instead of in a deposit bag, which she usually did, grabbed her purse, and locked the door behind her.

Daniel wasn't there. Koslov was in a booth in the back, nursing a drink. Jill ordered chowder and wine on her way over, then slid in opposite him. Koslov lit a cigarette.

"I don't have all night," she said.

"You're a bit like your mother, you know. Businesslike."

Jill absorbed this information with a mental *check*! Aloud, she said, "How did you meet the Hadntz family?"

"Eliani's father is Russian, as is a great-aunt on her mother's side, which is how they met, when they were young. I'd always known their family. I visited whenever I was passing through Vienna. By the time this picture was taken, Eliani had developed many interesting theories about the brain, physics, consciousness, and her thoughts about ending war, which she shared freely with me."

Jill dug into her clam chowder and sipped her wine. She was hungry. "I'm listening."

"Eliani went to colloquiums with the luminaries of the day. Bohr, Dirac, Pauli, Meitner. Meitner got her a job with Rutherford, in England, and she worked briefly with Fermi in Chicago but was disgusted. She wanted nothing to do with the atomic bomb. Instead, she went her own way, invented her own use for the powers of quantum physics."

"Her Device."

Koslov nodded, apparently unsurprised. "During the war, a version of the device fell into Russian hands, through a man named Perler, who sold it to them."

Perler again. "What did you do during the war?"

"I was lucky. I had a heart condition that exempted me from military service. It was fixed by surgery about twenty years ago, but"—he glanced ruefully at his cigarette and shrugged—"I was teaching at what was then

Leningrad University, as a graduate student; history was always my passion. The university was evacuated during the siege, but I stayed there; I had formed a close attachment to Rosa's mother-in-law, who was elderly. I helped her, and many others, survive. There's a story in that, but no time for it now. We managed to get out during one of the evacuations, and spent the rest of the war in Saratov, at the evacuated university. I actually taught; made a little money. During that time I had ties to an anti-Stalin organization. Late in 1944, a packet with Rosa's poems came to us, and several more arrived thereafter. I think that Eliani's father died during the war, either in Germany or Hungary. Eliani's grandmother died too, before him, perhaps; she was quite elderly, weakened from the siege, and I believed that grief from the war was the final cause of her death.

"By the end of the war, everyone knew what Stalin was doing; he was a murderer on a much grander scale than Hitler. My underground ties strengthened, and I lived, quite dangerously, in St. Petersburg, which was renamed Leningrad, and a time of purges began. Kosmopolitanism, of which I had always tried to be guilty, was a crime, for which you could be arrested." He laughed.

"After the war, your mother sought me out. She was trying to track the Perler Device, and also those plans. I was astounded at the breadth of what my childhood acquaintance, Eliani, an older woman whom I admired from afar, had accomplished. Bette recruited me for the OSS, and I agreed readily. I was always sure death was around the next corner, anyway. She worked out my emigration, and procured a teaching post for me. When your parents moved to Washington, I was a frequent guest at their house, and I remember you when you were young, Jill. Ah, I've finally elicited surprise!" He smiled. "One day, you and your brother and sister recruited me to play a game on what you called the 'Infinite Game Board.' I told your mother, afterward, the strange effect it had on me, and I believe she took it away."

"I found it again."

"So I gather. The Perler Device was tracked, solely by your mother, who took pains that the CIA not know the extent of her involvement, to another expatriated Russian, whose name was Mikhel, but by the time she found him, he had passed it to someone else, and he died without revealing who that person was. And so it was left hanging."

"So—why do you suppose you remember both histories?"

"A very good question, Dr. Dance. After—the change, in 1964, both your mother and Eliani Hadntz came, separately, to visit me."

Jill didn't bother to try to hide her astonishment. Tears filled her eyes. "My mother was—*here*? In Washington? And she didn't . . ."

Koslov said gently, "Yes, but not for long, and it was months after the original event." He tilted his head. "Eliani, you see, had visited me fairly often over the years; we could reminisce about her mother, her father. She loved to hear stories about her grandmother. Because I knew so much, she freely confided in me the powers of the Device, her concern about what she had unleashed. She talked about her progress in other timestreams—about how, in one, she had won a Nobel Prize, and how she wished, once and for all, for the change she had envisioned in humankind would sweep through them all, via some kind of physics event that I was not remotely qualified to understand. So I knew that this Device, which changed people on a genetic level, at a . . . quantum level, I suppose, whatever that means, enabled her own ability to exploit what she called the nexes. Your mother took her leave of me most tearfully; she had already met with your father and told him of her decision. She felt that even in this timestream scrutiny would follow her, would attach to her family, and further endanger you and your brother and sister. They made the decision together. He would stay behind

and raise you. But at some point, I think, even he lost track of her, and even your mother could not find her way back. I did not even see Eliani for a number of years."

Jill grabbed a napkin and mopped at her tears.

"But when you began taking my classes, I felt . . . hope, somehow, that this could all be resolved for your family, for Eliani. This hope was enhanced by the fact that I had met the son of the man who had the Device. His father's last name, originally, was Konrad, and he worked for the CIA under the name of Anderson."

Jill stared at him. "So Bill—Wilhelm—"

"Yes. I had, eventually, been able to trace Mikhel's contacts, and Wilhelm's father was one of them. I tracked possibilities down, one after the other, slowly, over the years, discarding one after another, and finally focused on Wilhelm, though his father was dead. It seemed worth a look. I took pains to meet him; I joined one of the anti-American societies he belonged to, briefly, in his late twenties. I convinced him that I was a secret Nazi—he was surprisingly gullible on that matter, considering that I was Russian, but I had no shortage of historic knowledge. Even if he had tried, he couldn't have tricked me into involuntarily admitting that I really belong to no country. He simply couldn't believe that, given his insane devotion to a fable. I cannot give my heart to nationalistic dreams, because they are always, in the end, just so much dust, after much suffering. If I have any religion, it is Eliani's vision." He signaled for another drink; lit another cigarette.

"I convinced him we were brothers, of a sort, and he eventually revealed everything to me. I helped him with his education, helped him come to Washington, where he formed another circle of friends with like goals, and insinuated myself into becoming their old, wise, learned leader. Your sister heard all of that during the night of your party." He smiled. "Oh, yes, of course I knew she was there, listening."

"So where is the Device that he has? Does it have any sort of value at all?"

"He has tried to analyze it, he has wormed his own way into the past, he has his own CIA contacts, thanks to his father. He hinted that he had something extraordinary, early on, but no, I don't think it does work as intended. Without Eliani to verify it, I could not have known, anyway. I don't believe that it does, because he has always been intent upon finding the original plans. But because I have no specialized knowledge, I have no idea of its potential.

"His CIA contacts led him to suspect your mother. He might even know more about you than you know about yourself. In fact, he is obsessed with you. I have broken my silence to warn you: He is a dangerous man."

She shivered, but anger immediately replaced her fear. "I knew there was something weird about him. But I don't know what to do about him."

"I'm not sure either, but this is something you deserved to know."

Daniel, who had slipped into the booth behind Jill without her noticing, joined them, holding a cold beer. Koslov nodded at him.

"Oh," said Jill. "Hello." She slid over to give him room, and he sat next to her. She was comforted by his presence.

Daniel said, "One thing we can do is arrest him for arson. That's why I couldn't answer your message, Jill. I connected the dots this afternoon, finally; all the evidence was at hand, I got a warrant, and we went to arrest him at home."

Koslov exhaled with a long stream of smoke. "Excellent news. Excellent. After all these years. But—arson?"

"Someone set my house on fire a couple of days ago."

Daniel said, "It's not that excellent. We went in, but he wasn't there."

"Damn." Jill put her hand over her heart. "What now?"

"We staked out his condo. If he doesn't come home, I hope he'll show up at work tomorrow."

"No matter how close Wilhelm and I became, he would never admit me to the locked room in his condo, and I suspect he had—" Koslov paused and looked at Jill.

"He knows everything," Jill said. "This is Detective Kandell. My history professor—"

"Lev Koslov," he said, reaching across the table and shook hands with Daniel.

Koslov said, "I suspect that Perler's Device was there. Was it?"

Daniel shook his head. "We're inside, doing a search. We found lots of Nazi memorabilia there, as well as detailed information about Jill on his Q. He was, apparently, totally consumed with knowing everything about you. Wall of photos, the whole stalker thing, textbook. I didn't have time to read much, but he dreamed of creating a new superrace. You'd be the lucky mom."

"I might have nightmares for quite some time."

"When we get him, what with the Nazi stuff, and the threats on his Q to many people in public life, including detailed plans, he's in the pokey anyway. Oh, Jill, I forgot: The books you said were stolen from your library were there too. The exact same ones you thought were taken."

"You sound surprised that I was right."

"Brian has a picture of it," she said. "An early incarnation of it, actually. The catalyst, maybe. It's in the attic."

"Then," said Daniel, "I move we adjourn to your attic."

Whens and Bip
[*July 22*]

WHENS WAS not at all pleased with this development. He had been heading home, and now he was in a stupid apartment with two really stupid people. They wanted him to watch the same dumb television shows that Tracy and his father watched, shootings and sirens and stuff.

There had been little improvement.

However, they did not hesitate to provide him with Slingers.

All in all, though, he would rather have been at his father's. He was a little bit afraid, especially after that punching fight . . . all right, he was a lot afraid. At least that really mean short fat Eagle man was gone. He had spit in the man's face as he struggled to get away in the car, and the man had thrown him against the side of the car, yelling in a strange language.

He had known, in the back of his mind, before he even left the condo, that it was not a good idea to try and get home, especially after dark. But sometimes it wasn't easy to think of everything that might happen.

One of them threw his phone out the window as soon as he took it from his pocket. To his surprise, they gave him his classbook. Before he asked for it, though, he threw a stage-ten meltdown purely on purpose.

After he started screaming, one of the men, the short fat one named Bip—"Bip?" Whens had asked, when he said his name. "Really?"—said, "Shut that kid up, will ya?"

"Shhh," said Bip, putting a finger to his lip.

"No, not like that," said Tall Thin Man, who was trying to talk on the phone. So far he had no name. "Belt him one."

"We're not supposed to. All he wants is something from his pack. Some kinda game."

"Give him the goddamn thing. Just no phone."

So, Bip gave him his pack. Whens took out his classbook, turned it on, and Tall Thin Man kept talking on the phone, saying, "Yeah? Where?"

But just as soon as Whens got to the emergency band of the classbook, Bip came in and said, "Let's move. They're takin' us somewhere."

Tall Thin Man grabbed Whens' hand and yanked him along. Whens looped one arm through his pack strap.

"You can't take that," said Tall Thin Man.

Whens writhed and screamed and tried to bite him, and Tall Thin Man hit him in the face. Then Whens started to scream for real.

He managed to keep hold of the classbook, though, and his pack, as Bip hauled him down the stairs and out into a waiting car.

Bette

BETTE COMES HOME

[*July 22*]

BETTE HAD been gone for four days—or decades, depending on how you looked at it, which she hardly even tried anymore. When she returned, she had the information and equipment she needed, stashed in her bag, taken from a more technologically advanced timestream, no help from Hadntz, thanks. She was terribly upset. Sam was truly not to be found. He had probably tried to follow her, and he was not at all good at it.

She returned as her "real" age: seventy-two, so this time she was clearheaded and prepared—although a bit stiff. None of this had been easy; her emotional as well as her physical self had teetered on the brink of rushing darkness more than once.

She arrived at Union Station unscathed, with her new

tools, and hurried back to the house. Halfway down the block, she paused. It was dark. And it smelled of smoke.

She ran to the house, and studied it, terrified.

The streetlight illuminated a blackened screened-in porch. She recovered some presence of mind and pulled her bags off the sidewalk, into some bushes. Then she walked slowly past the house, surveying it closely. Other than dark licks of burnt wood above the porch, it appeared to be intact. She went up the sidewalk and around the library side of the house. The rest of it seemed intact. Just chillingly empty.

She was surprised that a fire had even gotten started. This house probably had the most sophisticated residential fire protection in the city, thanks to Sam. It must have been arson.

Had anyone been hurt?

A darker fear invaded her. Perhaps she was in the wrong place, had made a mistake—

Then she heard Manfred barking inside and let go of her breath. They were still here.

She knew that all her sensitive equipment in the attic had been particularly protected; steel doors would have slid over it and an inert gas, or whatever the government was using to protect its data when Sam had left, had filled the compartment, protecting it from heat as well as fire. He had designed those systems.

Returning to her bags, she carried them around to the back, and opened her secret door.

Slipping upstairs, she found her room intact. And dry. Puzzling. Why hadn't the sprinklers gone off?

Opening her electronics room, she saw that everything had functioned as Sam had planned; the equipment was sealed beneath a metal cover.

That was Sam, all right. He thought of everything. She sank into her chair, cradled her head in her hands, and blinked back tears, sucking in deep breaths of fire-soured air.

She had failed Sam. She had not found him. She had left, and encountered Megan in the train station, to search for him—again, at the high cost of what Hadntz called "splintering," although she probably called it something else, now, damn her. The "update" she had given Bette at the party, down in the grotto—her neuro-plasticity augmentation substance, which Bette had taken—had done nothing to enhance her search.

Bette stood, flung open the window, and found the switch that opened the electronics bank. Settling down to work—and now she wanted to work very fast—she went through the equipment, testing. Everything worked. Naturally.

Ripping open the zipper on one of her bags, she pushed aside the original Game Board, which she had gotten in Dallas and retrieved from Mönchengladbach on her timestream jaunt. She found the small, cushioned box holding the interface she had brought back from another timestream—one that did not contain Sam, her children, her grandchildren, or, she thought, even Hadntz. In that timestream, war was indeed just a memory. Something had gone right. She hoped that she had adequately described her antique system. If she had, this would interface between it and Q.

First, she slid the interface, which looked like a floppy disk, circa 1991—small, encased in square plastic—into a drive, heard the machine whir, and took the disk when the machine spit it out.

Flipping open a tab on the disk cover, she found another disk the size of a child's fingernail, paper-thin, glowing green. Taking her Q from her pocket, she pasted it onto the Q's screen, where it seemed to melt.

"Not Enough Information," said the screen.

She almost screamed. All that timestreaming—fruitless! She'd returned to a burned house, without Sam—with *nothing*. She was too old. She couldn't do this anymore. She needed help. But where could she

turn? She had always depended on herself. Hadntz was absent, as usual. . . .

She let her mental tantrum play out. She opened the window, breathed fresh, untainted air, sensed, though she could not see, the new dome growing, the new school, the new International Teaching Environment, the Q-School . . .

She extracted the original Infinite Game Board from her bag. *Infinite, my ass,* she thought. *Prove it.*

She went through the pink room and walked out into the attic. From there, she walked down the regular stairs until she got to the ground floor. Manfred ran up to meet her, and she patted the big dog's head.

The lights were off, but the house was not really dark. Streetlights threw shadows across the old wood floors and Oriental rugs. She breathed in memories of all the years she and Sam and her family had lived here, the Thanksgiving when Jill insisted on working in the soup kitchen, Megan splashing to school in oversized galoshes, Brian growing up much too fast—

In the library, she turned on the desk light and ran her fingers over a row of books on a lower shelf behind the desk. Her books of Chinese poetry. Read and reread, it seemed, hundreds of times.

Her fingers touched the ragged cloth spine of the book she had carried through most of the war, and had given to Sam after their first night together, after their foray into Berlin to buy those vagrant plans from the Russian in the wild, terrible days of late May 1945, when the blasted city was filled with bloated bodies, and she had photographed the plans.

She pulled out the volume, turned off the light, and left a disappointed Manfred inside when she closed the back door behind her.

She descended the path to her grotto. She knew it by heart. Sam had placed every stepping-stone.

Curling up on her bench, she watched the creek,

below, flash silver back at the rising moon. The roar enveloped her, isolated her in time and space.

She lit a cigarette. The book fell open to her favorite "On Hearing That His Friend Was Coming Back from the War."

> Yet I never weary of watching for you on the road.
> Each day I go out at the City Gate
> With a flask of wine, lest you should come thirsty.
> Oh, that I could shrink the surface of the World,
> So that suddenly I might find you standing at my side.

She could almost hear Sam's voice speaking the words. She touched the board. It came to life.

After all this time, all these *times,* she still remembered that seminal night. After meeting Hadntz at the Opera House on what later became known as Kristallnacht, Hadntz had taken her through the burning city. In the course of that night, Bette had shot a German officer, for which she was later reprimanded by Dulles, and Hadntz had gone with her back to her Ringstrasse hotel and showed her the embryonic plans for the Device. That was the night when Hadntz had, basically, recruited her from the OSS, on Kristallnacht in Vienna, 1938.

It was as if she were there.

That was what the board did.

The memory, precise and powerful, flowed up from her fingers and flowered in her brain.

Once again she was on the balcony of the Imperial Hotel, in 1938, in the dawn after Kristallnacht. The memories were precise, crystalline. She smelled the smoke, witnessed one planned stage of the destruction of a civilization bound by laws, respect, and decency.

She once again felt the lines of AE's poem ring through her:

> Out of a timeless world, shadows fall upon time.

Then, she was assailed—later, she could think of no better word—by memories. But they were not her own.

She was Hadntz, doctoring in a small German hospital on the front in WWI, realizing that the gassed man dying of pneumonia was her former fiancé; witnessing also the horrific, futile deaths of thousands of men whom she had not the power to help.

She was Hadntz, twelve years old, with her feminist mother in Berlin, at the first International Women's Congress in Berlin in 1896, which seethed with Communists, Utopians, Socialists, radicals of every possible stripe, hearing Maria Montessori's rousing speech declaring that all women had a right to equal work for equal pay, feeling the joyous, fierce, imperative to join the battle for human rights dawn within her.

She was Eliani Hadntz, first mastering the timestreaming capabilities her device had opened within her mind, accessing other quantum possibilities, uniting scientific disciplines, dropping in knowledge from other timestreams, growing infinitely old, infinitely sorrowful, infinitely dedicated to helping humanity, through science, past its self-destructive stage.

She was Eliani Hadntz, shepherding her own chain-release mechanism through World War II and finally, now, finding the strength to relinquish it, to bequeath it to humanity to do with it as it willed, no matter what might unfold.

She was Pandora, Shiva, and Buddha, riven and tattered, surrendering.

I climb by a phantom stair to a whiteness older than
   time.

Each step was laborious, infinitely painful, a struggle against a part of human nature that flooded time with death, blood, and sorrow.

Finally, Bette could stand no more. She threw the board from her, fell to the stone floor of the grotto, and wept.

* * *

When she finally stirred and sat up, she found that the memories had ceased, leaving her cleansed and clear-headed. The stream, below her, moonlight-filled, was the same stream of her other life, yet different. It ran through both timestreams, as did her children and their children.

Other, darker things ran through this timestream as well.

Those children and grandchildren were in danger—the danger she'd tried to draw from them by leaving, with so much heartbreak, decades earlier.

She had climbed the phantom stair. Here was the fruit of her labors, in her lap—the Infinite Game Board, the first, basic, and tremendously effective interface of the Device with humanity. It was one of Q's precursors.

This was what had started it all. There had to be a lot of them in this timestream, except—

Perhaps, when she had retrieved it from Dallas, she had thwarted its continued evolution. Perhaps. This board, this incarnation of the Device, was like a wild horse, a collection of possible futures, constantly averaging the next possibilities. Q, the next incarnation, was more refined and elegant and focused on what most people would believe were positive goals—the cessation of war, the increase of free knowledge and of Hadntz's original vision, wrought through the rapidly advancing sciences foregrounding the central mystery of consciousness in all its manifestations.

But this board—this surely could, thought Bette, find its ancestor with ease, wherever it was.

This time, when she touched it, she seemed inoculated against its deepest horrors. When she touched it, the old stories arose—Sam's war stories, both hidden and secret, including Hadntz's plans. Those plans branched from the original, skipping through timestreams, touching some lightly, sinking deep into others, transforming them.

Lightly, quickly, she touched, touched, touched again,

wrenching herself from the personal stories, coaxing the board to show its own history, where bits of its self were now lodged.

And yes, there was one botched Device, on the trembling verge of coalescence, of transforming into a useful Device, much like the connection between brain and eye might be completed, in Georgetown.

She wondered—what would this timestream, with Q, have to fear from it. Surely Q could absorb and transform any possible negative consequences—

Bette looked up, aware of a presence, and saw Eliani Hadntz standing on the bank of the stream, barefoot, but otherwise dressed as Bette had first seen her—vibrant, her long black hair catching moonlight in its waves, wearing a red dress. It was like the Hadntz of Kristallnacht, of the war, and later—vast, though tiny; brilliant, aware, committed. Not a person, but a force.

Q personified.

She turned toward Bette and walked up the stepping-stones. Gently, she took the board from Bette, without speaking. "Get out your Q," she said. "Set it on the board. It's ready."

Bette took her Q from her pocket, set it on the board.

It became translucent, glowing, shot with colored threads, with universes.

At the same instant, Hadntz—the brilliant, ever-young, Hadntz, a force barely contained her slight body, vanished in front of Bette's eyes.

At first, Bette thought it was a trick of moonlight. "Eliani?"

There was no answer. A blinking light on the board caught her attention.

An address in Georgetown flashed on the small screen of her Q, which was restored to its previous density.

Bette stood. "Eliani! Dr. Hadntz!"

The night was far from still. Cicadas whirred; the moon reappeared as a cloud blew past; coneflowers

ranked before the stream on the low bank bowed before a breeze, then stood upright again.

Flooded with relief, Bette headed through the garden. When she reached the car kiosk on the next block, she slipped in her pass, unlocked a car, and plugged her Q into the dashboard.

It said, "Turn right at the next corner. In twenty-five feet—"

Good grief. She knew where she was going. This would rot her brain. She snatched it from the dashboard and sped toward Georgetown, careening down alleys and little-used side streets.

When she got close to the address, she parked a block away. A few police cars were out front, doors open, blue lights flaring. She left the car, taking her Q.

A good distance from the building, she turned onto dew-damp, neatly mown grass to avoid setting off any motion detecting lights, alert for any other people, following her Q's signal. A guard stood at the building's side door, scanning the street; he didn't notice her.

The signal led her behind the building, a brick wall broken by regularly spaced windows, patios, and, above, a few balconies. The patios were deserted. Most of the windows were dark. A tall fence backed the property about thirty feet back, faced by bushes.

She advanced slowly as the frequency of the flashes increased.

There! She'd almost stepped on it.

She picked it up.

Finally. It had not changed in forty-five years; at least, she couldn't see any changes in her cursory examination by the light of her Q.

What was it doing out here? She'd expected to find it stashed in someone's basement, or locked in a Langley lab. The dad-blasted Perler Device, a loose end that had plagued her for decades, was just lying on the ground for anyone to find.

She dropped it in her bag and returned to her car.

* * *

Back in her room, she turned on the voice-activated tape of what had taken place while she'd been gone.

Many things had happened, but not anything she had expected—discussion of the party, the fire.

Instead, there'd been a break-in, an investigation, something that sounded like a budding romance, multiple Game Boards, and general uproar. The fire seemed like the least of the problems.

When Jill began to cry in the course of her confession, Bette turned off the tape. She'd left her daughter a terrible burden. But of course she'd known she would on that bleak Washington day in early 1964 when she'd met Hadntz at the Peoples Drug store on Connecticut Avenue and realized that staying here might well bring death to her family.

Jill had blamed herself for what seemed, essentially, her mother's death. Bette wept as well, for a long time.

It was always so hard to be a parent, to know what to say or do or tell. It was, simply, hard to be human, to make the right decision.

Cars pulled up, doors slammed. She stumbled to the front window and saw Jill and two men she didn't recognize file past the flowers. She hurried back to her room, hearing footsteps on the stairs.

She heard a commotion in the attic, then whoever it was went back downstairs. A few minutes later, her microphone picked up their exclamations, their discoveries.

Daniel Kandell. She'd investigated and discovered that she knew him, although she remembered his little brother, Truman, better, and their father Gerald. Gerald had been involved in intelligence; he'd been there in Germany, and it was natural that he'd be back in D.C. It was his home, and home base for the agency, and the intelligence world was small. That past was the same in both timelines, except at the very end, when the Americans took Berlin instead of the Russians.

She was surprised to recognize the distinctive voice

and accent of Lev Koslov, who said, "I'll call a mutual friend. Hello? Yes. It's Lev. Have you seen Wilhelm? No? I have an important message for him; have him get in touch with me immediately if you hear from him." Then, to Daniel and Jill, "No luck."

Wilhelm Konrad.

Bette understood everything in a flash. Wilhelm was the son of Anson, whom she'd shot in Dallas; she knew his background well. Anson's other son, who had died in Berlin, had been a Hitler Youth, a Werewolf. Someone an impressionable boy would worship; emulate. A martyr.

Apparently, Wilhelm was the man who had so conveniently left the Perler Device lying on the ground under his window, so she hadn't even had to bother with the elevator. She could see now how it had made its way from Russia—through Anson, who probably kept it as a bargaining chip he had waited too long to use—and how it had languished so long, unfound and undetected.

Wilhelm, she heard, as they discussed the evening, was also the person who had set the house on fire.

It was a wild night of revelations downstairs—among the participants, and for their eavesdropper. As she listened, Bette was deeply thankful that no one had been hurt.

So far.

In the meantime, she considered the problem of Wilhelm. Her first thought was to just shoot him and throw him in the river.

She lit a cigarette and sat back in her chair.

After a while, she again got out the Game Board.

She touched it on and set to work, loosing its energy, fully linking it to Q.

By the time everyone retired, she was ready. She took what she needed and left the house. Picking up another car at the kiosk, she drove to Wilhelm's condominium with the windows open, enjoying the scent of the damp night air.

No police cars, but of course police were there, watch-

ing and waiting. They might not be quite as alert as they had been earlier. She was hoping that Wilhelm would think along the same lines.

She returned to the spot at the back of the condominium where she had picked up the Device, retreated to the inky shadows, sat on the damp grass, leaned against the stockade fence, and waited.

She waited for hours, and would have waited much longer, but at around 5:00 A.M., he arrived like German clockwork, before a new, sharp police shift would come, poking his head around the side of the building.

He zigzagged across the grass. He was the type of person who would be on the condo board; he probably knew where the motion detecting sensors were. Beneath a window she assumed was his, he looked back and forth, then fell to his hands and knees. Bette stood as he inched his way forward, making wide arcs through the grass with his hands. He didn't dare risk a flashlight; Bette supposed he surmised that someone was posted at one of the upstairs windows.

When he got close to Bette, she said, "Is this what you're looking for?"

He jumped to his feet and reached for, surely, his gun.

She stepped forward and before he could move, she cuffed his hands, in front of his waist, in plastic restraints. Then she pulled him at gunpoint past the building's end, past the sleepy guard. His upper arm shook as she held it with a firm grip. "Here's the deal."

He stared at her in the faint light of the coming dawn. "You're not a cop."

"I have what you want. And I'm going to give it to you. First, drink this." She held up a disposable plastic-lidded fast-food cup with a straw sticking out of the top.

He spat at her, which she had anticipated, stepping back before he even tried it. She slapped his face and said, "Now, let's try again. Don't bother to spill it; I have plenty."

"What's in it?"

"Wilhelm, you should rejoice. It's your holy grail, the Hadntz Device, fiftieth incarnation. A powder."

"I don't believe you. Who are you? How do you know about—"

"Drink it."

After a bit of expert persuasion, which Bette assured him would not cause permanent damage, he fully complied.

Jill
[July 23]

JILL WAS getting dressed for work when Elmore called.

She'd had a very late night. They'd found the photograph of the Perler Device. Daniel and Koslov had perused the notebooks all night in the library.

She went upstairs to sleep at four. When she returned at six, Daniel was asleep on the couch. Koslov snored in the rocking chair.

She had awoken Daniel and told him she wasn't going to work. She didn't want to see Wilhelm there. He had convinced her she had to go; he had a man outside the house, dressed in a suit, with a Bank entrance pass, waiting to follow her to work for her safety. He would follow her inside. "Wilhelm might be watching to see if you go into the building," Daniel said. "We could nab him. Depends, I suppose, on how obsessed he is."

Now, as she gathered her briefcase and keys in the foyer with unsteady hands, her phone beeped. Elmore.

"Jill," he said, then said nothing more.

"I'm right here."

"Is . . ."

"Is what?"

"Is Stevie with you?"

"What? No. What do you mean?" Her voice rose. "Isn't he with you?"

"He's run away. He turned off the alarm and left. I don't know when."

"What are you *talking* about? When did this happen?"

"I'm not sure. We put him in bed at seven, and—"

"Seven? *Seven?* He doesn't go to sleep until at least *nine.*"

"Tracy—we think that he should get more sleep. He seems kind of cranky."

"He was there at eight. He called me at eight. He sounded really lonely. I got some books for him—" She made herself stop. *This can't be happening,* she thought. "Did you look everywhere? He likes to hide. Look around outside. Isn't there a park across the street? Maybe he's playing there. Maybe he just left a few minutes ago."

"I looked everywhere." Elmore sounded despairing.

Don't panic, Jill told herself. "So you're saying that he's been gone for *twelve hours,* maybe?"

"We checked on him—"

Now she was screaming. "Twelve *hours,* Elmore?"

"Yes."

"What did the police say?"

"I haven't called them yet. I just found that he was gone. I went to get him up and—I was hoping he was with you."

"Oh, right, it might get in the paper. I'm calling them right now."

"I'll call now. I just wanted to check—" His voice caught. "They'll want to come here."

"Maybe I should wait at home," she said. "Maybe he's on his way here. Or maybe I should call someone to stay here. I'll do that. I'll go out to look for him."

"The police might want to question you."

"I'm going out. Where would he go? Can Tracy check the school? It's not far from you. Maybe he just walked over there."

"Tracy's, ah, in court."

"Right. Court. Okay. I'll let you know." She hung up, furious, afraid, and at her wit's end.

She called the school. An aide was there, setting up, and Jill listened as she combed the school, calling his name. Finally, breathless, she said that he wasn't there.

"Call me immediately if he shows up."

She hung up the phone. *Dread,* she thought. *This feeling is pure dread.*

Daniel was at her side. "Whens is missing?"

"I can't stand it," she whispered. "I just can't stand this anymore."

Zoe

SOMEWHERE THERE'S MUSIC

[*July 23*]

ZOE HAD been working in the ballroom since seven in the morning, when everything got so crazy. She sat on the floor next to a tall window and slanted light blessed her scorebook, propped on her knees. Her markers were scattered around her.

Zoe's Dad and Mom and the Crazy Aunts were in the library when Zoe got finished, around nine. Some of them were talking on phones. There were other people there she didn't know. Crazy Aunt Megan was putting on her running shoes. Her dad picked up his car keys.

Zoe handed Brian her scorebook. "This is where Whens is."

Brian looked down at the familiar-looking manuscript, the interesting spatter of color that Zoe's bits of music always were, as if the colors were as much of a pattern as the tones that were simultaneously represented. Except—

"Okay. You have extra lines down here. Not five staff lines, but seven."

"I put those in when I do people."

"Okay," Brian repeated, as he always did when he was trying to be extra patient with his kids. He continued to study it.

"What do you mean, when you do people?" asked Crazy Aunt Jill. "Can I see that?"

Brian handed it over.

Zoe frowned. "You didn't know that I do people?" She sounded hurt.

"I'm sorry, honey." Jill reached over and hugged Zoe to her. "No, I didn't. What do you mean?"

"All of you have sounds. Can't you hear them?"

"We're not as gifted as you, sweetie."

Zoe stepped away from Jill and looked around at all of them, puzzled. "Well," she said finally. She paged through her book. "Mom sounds like this." She held up the notebook briefly. "And Bitsy looks like this." She held up another, more antic-looking page, with colors and notes scattered wildly.

"Can you play them for us?" asked Jill. "Can you tell us what they *mean*?" She sounded very crazy today, but Zoe understood. She shook her head. "These notes aren't on the piano. The extra ones." She sighed. "The violin is better, but there's just too much space when I play it. I fill it in with my head. It's—kind of behind things, or in front of them." She brightened. "I just need to invent a new instrument, that's all. Anyway, now we can find Whens. I'll just have to show you."

"How?" asked Jill, her hands white and clasped to her chest.

"We can drive there," said Zoe. "Don't you see?"

Her dad and Crazy Aunt Jill looked at each other. Detective Kandell was there too, but looked like he was getting ready to leave. Zoe liked him; he was kind and never acted like he thought she was nutsy.

Then Brian said, "I don't think we can go right now. We're—really busy. How about tomorrow?"

Zoe stared at them, one by one. Then she walked away in silence.

Zoe stood on the front porch, uncertain, for a moment. She thought she might cry, but she didn't.

Instead, she looked at her score. Then she turned left and turned left again at the corner, where the bus stop was.

The bus trundled up just as Aunt Jill's car came around the corner. Jill and her dad were in the front seat. They did not look at the bus as she climbed into it and showed the driver her Metro pass.

The driver nodded and pulled the door shut; the bus lurched forward.

Zoe sat in the front seat, straining forward to see out better. She looked at her score. At one stop she started to get up, and then sank back into the seat.

Finally, when they were at the George Washington University stop, she got off. She waited until the walking light came on, crossed the street, and went into a side entrance of the hospital.

It was getting a little tricky. She was glad the adults weren't with her; she knew they wouldn't follow her through this.

She got on an elevator and went to the fourth floor. A nurse at the station glanced at her when she got out of the elevator, then looked back at her computer screen.

Zoe walked briskly down the hall. She missed Whens so much! She blinked away tears and took the stairway down two floors, walked down another corridor, and took the elevator to the basement, where she went to the cafeteria.

She walked through the kitchen, which smelled like mashed potatoes. She felt like she was in a movie! This was where people always ran to get away from someone who was chasing them. However, she didn't feel quite strong enough to smash over the big chafing dishes on

wheels, or push the shelf of glasses over behind her to slow people down. It was kind of boring when nobody was chasing you. Then a thin woman carrying a stack of napkins said, "What are you doing in here?" and she broke into a run. Much more fun!

She burst through some double doors and was on a big concrete delivery bay. Two men were there, loading boxes onto a dolly. She rushed down the stairs and shot out onto Washington Circle.

A streetcar was coming around the circle. It was connected to a wire up above the street and ran on a track. The cars all looked funny. Zoe closed her eyes and listened. The clanging of the car grew louder, then stopped.

The streetcar door was open in front of her. A woman pushed past her and got on. She was dressed in a different way too. She wore a kind of tight dress and a round, little blue hat that matched her dress.

The woman sounded like the bottom note on her score, which was kind of like a drone note. Everybody here did.

The driver looked at her. "Getting on, girlie?"

Zoe reached into her pocket and the driver said, "Kids ride free."

Zoe stared out the window. Washington looked the same, but different. It was fun, but scary. She knew she wasn't dreaming. The perfume of the woman next to her burned her eyes.

She closed her eyes, listening. Sweeter in this direction . . .

She leaped from the streetcar on a quiet street lined with trees and ran past some picket-fenced yards until she got to the one on the corner.

Whens was in the front yard, playing with a big white dog. The dog fetched a stick and then Whens took one end. They pulled. Whens let go and fell down backward. The dog ran off, tossing his stick in the air and catching

it with great joy, looking at Whens with a laughing sideways glance.

"Whens!" Zoe ran up to him. "Everybody's looking for you!"

"My name is Stevie," said the boy. He stood up.

"I'm Zoe." She was taken aback. This boy looked exactly like Whens. But Whens would never say that. "Don't pretend. We have to get back right now. Come on!" She took the boy's wrist.

The boy yanked it away. "I really don't want to play with you."

A woman came to the door. She looked kind of like Crazy Aunt Jill, but different. She wore a cotton dress with a big wide skirt.

"Hi," she said, wiping her hands on her apron. "What's your name?"

"Zoe," she said. The sounds were so strong. She looked down at his music in the notebook, and the colors glowed and matched. Most of them. This was Whens. But it was a different Whens. "I've got to go."

She walked back down the street, thinking. She wished very hard that she had her colored pens. She realized that she needed to make yet another line on his staff. The music was getting really complicated.

She took the trolley back to the hospital, and went through the various floors, in a bit of a daze. She paused at the gift shop window and looked longingly at a set of markers there, then hurried away. Maybe she could get home before she forgot this new part of the music.

She got on a bus and was home by eleven.

She turned onto the front walk and her mother came running out the door. She grabbed her and hugged her close. "Where were you? We were worried sick! Oh, I'm so glad you're back." Zoe watched her send a message to her dad.

In a moment, Brian pulled up in his truck and jumped from the cab. "Zoe!" He knelt in front of his

daughter. "I'm so sorry. We'll take you to look for Whens now."

Zoe said, "That's okay. I have to work on it a little bit more." Her father looked so upset that Zoe gave him a hug, then walked into the house, thinking.

Across the International Date Line

THE NEW SCHOOL

[July 24, Senegal]

A BAKAR TARAB was five, and on his way to the store to fetch a Fanta for his big brother, Yaccoub.

He passed the small houses of his neighbors and ran down the dirt road, his bare feet making soft plashes of dust. They needed rain. He often heard his mother talking about it, and about how Yaccoub needed to find a job. Yaccoub always laughed at that, his lean face just a little bit mean, in a way that scared Abakar. Sometimes Yaccoub hit their sister, Issa, who was thirteen. Once, when their mother got between Issa and Yaccoub's raised hand, Abakar had been afraid that his brother would strike their mother—a complete, absolute taboo. Abakar had held his breath while their mother stared hard at Yaccoub, a warning like steel in her eyes, and breathed again when Yaccoub lowered his arm and said, "How do you think I get the money to feed us, woman? I have a job. It is not an easy job to feed three other worthless people."

But even Abakar knew Yaccoub was doing something bad. Something he got a lot of money for. He kept a lot of guns under his bed and Issa said that he sold them.

Abakar ran faster, passing people lugging buckets of water for the day back home. A poda-poda passed him,

stuffed with passengers, with a chicken coop tied onto the roof. He dodged the wadded-up paper bag someone tossed out the window right in front of him and coughed in the dust of the van's wake. Sweat ran into his eyes and his mouth was very dry. He pictured the Schweppes Yaccoub had said he could get for himself, imagined the rattle of ice falling into the space his aching-cold bottle would leave when he pulled it from Mr. Hauron's big washtub.

"Abakar!"

He glanced across the street, past two mules carrying baskets, driven by a man with a stick. A motorbike roared past. It was more crowded here; the market was only half a kilometer away. Across the road, a young woman swept the dirt in front of her compound, while some older people sat around a pot of plantains boiling over a fire, talking in the morning sunlight. This road led to other villages.

"Mauka?" Mauka was only a little bit older than him. Her eyes danced and her bright green scarf lifted in the wind.

"Come," she shouted, and waved her hand.

"No!"

"Just for a minute! I have something to show you! Something strange!"

He thought of the Schweppes. He thought of something strange, and veered across the street.

Then he saw it. On the vacant lot in which they often played, and where old man Zbu sometimes kept his cow, was a large white building, shaped like a dome. The door was round, with twisty sections that untwirled into a short, low tunnel. He could see children inside; a lot of the wall was clear.

Mauka said, "You have to crawl inside! Come on! It's fun."

"I'm getting a Fanta for Yaccoub." He felt the big money in his pocket, the money that would get him a soda too.

"Just for a minute!" She bounced up and down in her eager way, grabbed his hand, and pulled him through the door, which twirled shut behind him.

Inside it was cool, and a soft white light fell on everything.

The floor was light-colored planks, like wood, but they had a smoother feel beneath his feet.

"Come and play! *C'est amusement!*"

He walked, slowly, drawn by the colors and shapes he saw before him.

Low shelves held some kinds of toys. Children played with them on small rugs that lay on the floor. He saw tiny Zanir from down the street, wearing his usual bedraggled red shorts, sitting with his own big sister Naufa, who was counting wooden sticks. She could count very high. But Abakar could count high too. He counted fourteen children.

"Come and play with me," Mauka said. She plopped down in front of a pile of blocks and began building a tower. "Find the next big one," she said impatiently.

He heard low, quiet words when he touched one of the blocks. "Cube," the voice breathed.

"Is it all right to play in here?" whispered Abakar.

Mauka laughed. "Yes! I have been here for many days. Look. If you want a snack, you can make it at that table. Ground nuts and biscuits. Oh! And sugar-cane."

Abakar didn't know how long he stayed there. He played with many things. He learned sounds. He learned names. There were many, many things to do, and Mauka showed him how to do things.

"Hey!"

Abakar jumped up. Yaccoub had his head inside the center of the dilating door. It was too low for him; Abakar saw that he was on his knees. "I can see you, you little maggot! So this is where you've been playing around. I'm going to slap you so hard that your head will spin!"

Abakar trembled. He couldn't help it.

"No," said Mauka, putting a calming hand on his calf. She didn't seem worried. "He cannot get in!" She giggled.

"Don't be silly." Abakar yanked his leg from her grasp and tried to see if there was a back door so he could get away from his brother. The places that were clear became white, most of them, but he could still see through some of them to the dusty street outside, and people gathering around Yaccoub's butt, pointing at him and laughing.

Yaccoub struggled, trying to shove his shoulders inside. "This fucking thing is crushing me!" He backed out and the door shut completely. In a moment they saw him beat the walls, very hard with a stick. It was a dull, thudding sound, accompanied by his curses. "I will sell all of you children! You girls! You know what is coming!"

"He will shoot!" whispered Abakar. "He will kill all of us."

"Bullets bounce off. He cannot come in! The building knows if someone is bad."

Abakar didn't believe her. But he found that it was true.

They didn't all die, even after Abakar heard the familiar *pop-pop* of bullets flying. Instead, Mauka got out a small tablet and started talking funny to it. And after a few minutes, soldiers came and dragged his brother, who kicked and cursed, away.

Abakar watched in amazement. "Where are they taking him?"

"I don't know? To jail?"

"Who will feed us?"

"Haven't you been to the New Market?"

"What?"

"Here," she said. She went over to a shelf and pulled out a basket. The basket was full of plastic rings. "Put one on."

"Can I have any color?"

"Yes."

Abakar chose a red ring with a snake on it. "It's nice."

"The New Market is on Saturday mornings, over on Wbab's field. You show them the ring and they touch it with a wand, some kind of computer wand, and then they will give you food. Millet, jackfruit, even lamb."

"No! Why?"

"I don't know. But the ring works."

Suddenly, a lot of children picked up small tablets that they carried with them and started talking that silly talk again. There was urgency in their voices. Mauka pulled one out of her pocket.

"I want one," said Abakar.

Mauka frowned. "Someone is in trouble. One of our friends. In the United States."

"No one is in trouble there."

"His name is Whens. We must tell someone." She jabbered to herself for a moment. "The ambassador. We're telling the ambassador. And then the police. They can find him by his classbook."

"Who is the ambassador?"

Mauka talked into the classbook then held it in front of Abakar. A voice said, "An ambassador is a person from one country who represents the people to another country. He or she lives in the other country. They have special legal rights . . ."

"What is 'represents'?" asked Abakar.

"Aggh! I have to get you your own classbook right away!"

The Ambassador
[*July 23*]

SIR?"

The Senegalese ambassador pushed his speaker button. "Yes?"

"It's those troublesome children again who can't speak English very well. They keep saying 'Senegal.' Maybe they speak your language. If you could please, sir—"

"Just hang up." He glanced at his budget, unknotting his tie. It was getting late, and he had a ceremonial luncheon to attend. Sighing, he left his budget to get ready.

He had just finished changing to Senegal dress for the luncheon when the phone buzzed again.

"Sir?"

"Yes?"

"This time it's a little girl who says she's from Nantes. She does speak English, quite well. She says that children from your country know about a little boy who has been kidnapped in Washington, D.C. His name is Whens."

"What kind of name is that?"

"I don't know, sir."

"What can I do about it? Why doesn't she call the police?"

"I asked her, sir. She said they tried, but that the police wouldn't listen to them because they are children. And also, if I may, sir? I'm not sure that the children from Senegal trust the police."

He sighed. "Put her on the line."

"Hello? Sir ambassador?"

"Yes. To whom am I speaking?"

"Adelie, sir. This is very serious. Please do not hang up. Are you there?"

"Yes."

"This little boy doesn't know where he is, but he has been kidnapped in Washington, D.C. He is talking to us on his classbook. Maybe the police can tell where the classbook is and find him."

"Please hold on." He switched to his secretary. "Could you please get the Metro police on the line?"

In a moment someone said, "Metro police."

"Yes. I have gotten a very strange call about a kidnapped boy—"

"Is his name Whens?"

The ambassador was surprised. "Yes."

"Please stay on the line." In a moment, another man came on the line. "Detective Kandell. To whom am I speaking?"

"The Senegalese ambassador, here in Washington. Is there really a kidnapping?"

"Yes. What do you know?"

"I have been getting calls all morning from some children who say they are in Senegal, and now a girl from France has called and says that he is using his classbook to try and get help. I suppose they have a frequency you can track?"

"Thank you for calling. Thank you very much. I'm going to give you back to the desk sergeant to get some information. Is the girl from France still on the line?"

"I think so."

"Good. Keep her there."

Jill

A TURN OF EVENTS

[*July 23*]

A s soon as Zoe got back, the phone rang. The house phone.

The FBI guy nodded. Jill picked it up, trembling. "Hello?"

"Is this Jill Dance?"

"Yes."

"This is GW Hospital."

"Yes?" She imagined Whens, badly hurt—but they'd called all the hospitals, again and again—

"This is kind of a strange call, but we have a John Doe here that had a bad concussion last night. A blow to the head. He has no ID. He was brought to the emergency room, and he's finally revived. He can barely speak—can't write; his hand is broken. But we think he's asking for you. I'm sorry to bother you; we've called about ten

people whose names sound like yours. We can't quite make out who he's asking for."

"It's not a little boy?"

"No. An elderly man with a beard."

Jill's heart seemed to stop. "An elderly—"

"He does keep saying 'I seem to have lost my wife again.'"

"I'll be right over."

The FBI agent looked up from his console. "Ma'am you can't leave. You have to wait for the ransom call."

Jill called Brian. "Where are you?"

"Driving around with Elmore."

"I think Dad is in the GW emergency room."

"I'll be there in two minutes flat." He hung up.

Jill stood in the silent foyer, searching for the *Golden Arrow of Breath,* but it seemed to have disappeared permanently.

"Jill?"

Jill shut her eyes. She hadn't heard that voice in . . .

Her mother's arms came around her. She pressed her cheek to Jill's. "It's okay, honey. You can open your eyes. It's really me." Jill felt her heart beating hard, and could feel her mother's heartbeat too, soft and comforting and very, very present. After a moment Bette murmured into her ear, "Can you forgive me?"

Before Jill could speak, Zoe came in with her notebook. She dropped it and stared. "Grandma?"

Bette kissed Jill, turned to Zoe, and knelt. "Yes, honey, it's me. Just older." She hugged Zoe, her eyes glistening, a huge smile on her face.

Jill said, "You're the ghost in the attic they've been playing with! You gave me the photos! You—"

The phone rang again. Everyone hushed. The FBI put it on their speakerphone. It was Daniel.

"Whens is in Anacostia. We know the block, from his classbook, but we've lost the signal, and can't get any more precise. I'm sending some men, along with the am-

bassador from Senegal, who has just arrived at the station. I'm hoping we can pick up the signal."

A hundred questions crowded Jill's mind. Zoe interrupted. She held up her notebook, a wild spatter of color. "I know where he is now. Really."

Whens had been in the nasty apartment all night. They made him sleep on a blanket on the floor, in his clothes, and Tall Thin Man took away his classbook and put it on top of a shelf in the kitchen, which was empty and bad-smelling and filled with bugs that scuttled under the cabinets when you went in.

Bip brought them breakfast in a bag and gave him some kind of awful sausage thing and a Slinger, and they drank Slingers with their breakfast too. Maybe his mom was right. Maybe Slingers were bad for you.

He drank all of his, though.

Tall Thin Man went back to watching television. Bip joined him on the couch. Whens went into the kitchen, where they peed in the sink, trying not to breathe. He climbed up on the counter. He could just reach his classbook. He turned it on and found the emergency band and started to talk to some kids who were listening just then, in Africa. He thought of his globe. Wow. Really, really far.

"Hey," said Bip. He was in the front room, looking out the window. The TV was on, loud.

Tall Thin Man didn't pay any attention.

"Hey, there's a lotta kids out front."

"So?" The man turned the volume up.

"It's weird."

Whens ran from the kitchen, carrying his classbook, and ran to the window. He waved, then pounded on the window, and yelled. They were looking at him. They waved back. They talked to their classbooks.

"Hey, kid, stay away." Bip pushed him back. "And stop that crazy smack talk. You retarded or something?"

A sleek black sedan pulled up in front of the apartment building.

"Some African dude getting out," said Bip nervously.

"So? We're in Anacostia."

"I mean, he's wearin' funny African clothes and all."

"Lotta them dealers do."

The regal-looking African peered up at the building. He leaned down and talked to somebody in the car. A white girl stuck her head out the car window and nodded.

"What did I tell you!" Bip smacked Whens across the face and the classbook clattered across the floor. "No more a that talk! Hey! Another man comin' up the walk."

Tall Thin Man finally turned, an angry look on his face. "Look, just get away from the fucking window. Now! Nobody's gonna come lookin' for us here. You're botherin' my show." He turned the volume up to a deafening level.

The door burst open, hitting Bip from behind. "Police!"

Bip staggered and fell. The other man grabbed his gun from the arm of the chair, half-rising.

The policeman fired, and the man with the gun slammed back into the couch, screaming, "You killed me, man, you killed me! Where's your warrant? Man's got a right to defend! I'm gonna sue!"

Whens ran out the open door and down the narrow stairs. As he rushed out the door onto the sidewalk, Zoe leaped from the car and hugged him. "I told them you were here! I could hear you! I showed them the way." A police officer grabbed her and hauled her back inside.

His mother leaped from the car, grabbed him, and smothered him in kisses. He was very glad to see her. His mother was crying. "Don't you ever, ever, do that again!"

About ten children of various ages stood in the street around the sedan, shouting, "*Aqui!* Whens!" into classbooks. A thin, harassed-looking woman hurried around the corner and stopped. She looked relieved. She put her

hands on her hips and shouted, "You kids get back to the center right now!"

A tall black man in beautiful robes stood watching, bemused, as an ambulance pulled up behind them. Some EMTs dashed into the building.

A second ambulance pulled up. Elmore dashed from it, and grabbed Whens, hugging him until Whens thought his back would break. "Ow," he said, surprised. He had never seen his father cry before.

Brian followed Elmore from the ambulance, then turned and helped a woman climb out. Whens saw her over his father's shoulder.

"Grandma?"

Wilhelm

WILHELM'S GAME

[July 23]

A T ABOUT five that afternoon, Wilhelm Anderson staggered into the Metro police station on L Street. From one hand dangled a metal tray with a map of the world on it—green continents, blue oceans, a simple child's map. Parts of the oceans and all the land were almost invisible, peppered with tiny red dots.

Tears seeped down his face, steady as springwater from the ground. Anguish reverberated in his voice as he stepped up to one of the glass reception windows. "I want to turn myself in."

The people in the tiny waiting room looked up with interest. The guard next to the window became alert. The clerk asked, "Name?" Then he took a second look. "Don't move."

Wilhelm didn't move.

The clerk pushed a button. "I've got Anderson, the guy we've got an APB out on, standing in front of me. Wants to turn himself in."

* * *

A few hours later, Wilhelm was in an interview room with his lawyer, Detective Kandell, and another detective, Dabelle Fleck. On the table was the metal tray. Wilhelm had been processed, and looked weary. His reddened eyes had dark circles beneath them; his face seemed thinner, more deeply furrowed, and his hair was noticeably whiter than his Bank ID photo, renewed only a week ago. He had already signed his arson confession, his lawyer arguing with him every step of the way, in the end shaking his head and assuring Wilhelm that he could get it thrown out.

Daniel was asking about the board. Wilhelm's lawyer slouched back in his chair, looking resigned.

"Like I said, this woman behind my condo put cuffs on me and made me drink HD-50. The Hadntz Device."

The lawyer had a bit of life left in him. But not much; he didn't even change his posture as he said, "I would like to again state for the record that my client is undoubtedly mentally deranged—obviously, he was drugged."

"He's no stranger to drugging others, and without their knowledge," replied Kandell. "Mr. Anderson, did you or did you not slip Rohypnol, the 'date-rape' drug, into the drink of Jill Dance, one of your colleagues, at a World Bank reception at the Four Seasons Hotel on Pennsylvania Avenue on July nineteenth, after which she collapsed in view of at least a hundred witnesses?"

"Yes, I did," said Wilhelm. His lawyer sighed.

"Why?"

"So I could drive her home and get into her house."

"What for?"

"To find this." Wilhelm nodded at the board. His weariness was palpable, a thousandfold worse than that of his lawyer.

"Not to sexually accost her?"

"I hoped that she might agree to have sex with me. I even hoped she might marry me. But that was not why I wanted to get into her house."

"Why did you want this metal tray?"

"It's the Hadntz Device. One incarnation of it."

"Look," said the lawyer. "I demand that a psychiatrist be present and that my client be immediately committed."

"I don't need a psychiatrist," said Wilhelm. "I'm perfectly sane. But if you want one, I don't object."

The lawyer opened his Q, typed something, and closed it.

Daniel asked, "What is the Hadntz Device?"

"It is a tool for promoting the end of war throughout the world."

"Why did you want it?"

"I misunderstood its capacity, its purpose. I thought it would give me power."

"Power to do what?"

Tears gathered in Wilhelm's eyes once again. "To impose a Nazi regime on the world. To bring back Hitler's vision and make it a reality, this time."

"And what happened instead?"

"Try it yourself and see."

"Just describe what happened."

Wilhelm stood and paced the room. "Visions of horror filled my brain. It was as if I were a Jewish businessman in Treblinka, watching smoke rise from the crematorium, which I had been forced to fill with dead Jews. I was a child, hiding in terror in an attic. I was a Prussian officer, about to be hanged for treason. I was Goebbels, I was . . . but that's not all! Touch it! See for yourselves! I was an American soldier on a death march in the Philippines. I was a Chinese woman a thousand years ago, watching as raiders raped my mother and sisters. I was—"

He seized the board and flung it against the wall. "I was a billion horrors, one after the other, and they all ran through me like a fire, and I couldn't stop seeing them, couldn't stop touching the goddamned board, sitting on a bench in Dupont Circle, even though that woman cut the cuffs and walked away hours ago. I—"

He looked up, suddenly calm, his eyes quite clear. "I have been changed. This Device, which I thought was about power, is actually quite the opposite." He sat down, put his elbows on the table, and clasped his hands. "It's about empowerment, but for everyone. It's about equality, freedom, education; it's about the evolution of the human mind; it is about leaving behind our legacy, our habit, of war." He looked at them for a moment, his eyes lucid, his face relaxed, a bit of his handsomeness reappearing as a thatch of hair fell across his forehead. "It's much simpler for me now. My mind was imprinted with the rightness of my task—my old task, to defend the Thousand Year Reich, when I was a child, in Germany, when I saw Hitler at my brother's swearing-in as a Hitler Youth. He really did seem to me the epitome of fatherly love, of the essential goodness of his bizarre strange fantasy of German dominance. Do you know that because of his love of animals, it became illegal, or at least frowned upon, to manufacture using leather? And yet—" He shook his head. "Incarcerate me, please. I deserve punishment for the crimes I've committed. I need much more time to heal. Perhaps ages. I only ask that I be allowed a writing device—pen and paper, if necessary—and an outlet for my thoughts. I believe, now, that I can help. I may not be able to help much. I realize, now, that I'm only one man, capable of evil and of good. It's . . . very complex. I'm just at the beginning."

At a knock on the door, Kandell said, "Come in."

"This is Dr. Bernstein."

"Hello," she said. "I'm the on-call psychiatrist." She handed all of them a card.

The lawyer rose and stretched. "I foresee a long and complicated case." He did not look unhappy at the prospect.

A Marvelous Evening
[*July 23*]

THE EMTS pulled Sam's stretcher from the back of the ambulance, put down the legs, and rolled him up the walk. He was beaming; Zoe could almost see light coming out of him. Bette, walking alongside, squeezed his hand.

The doctor at GW had been reluctant to release him, but Elmore quickly filled out a power of attorney for Brian. Sam was released to his son. At Elmore's frantic, unyielding insistence the ambulance detoured to the scene of the kidnapper's arrest.

When Bette climbed into the back of the ambulance, his confusion cleared, somewhat. His smile suffused his entire face. "I've been looking all over for you!"

"And I've been looking all over for *you*." She kissed him tenderly, and they headed home.

He had a broken rib, which had been taped, and the brain swelling was going down. The doctor emphasized round-the-clock observation, and told them that he wanted to see Sam back in two days even if everything seemed fine. His assailant had slashed him with a knife, which cut his forearm deeply. Then the man had apparently knocked him out with a punch and grabbed Whens. The right side of Sam's face looked like a bad watercolor, purple and reddish, yellowing around the edges.

Jill and Megan were strongly for taking him back to the hospital, but, as he was shifted from the stretcher to the bed in the living room, he heard them, and was able to reply, in a clear and forceful voice, "I want to be home. I'm fine."

Bette nodded at them. "We'll leave him here, for now. I'll stay with him."

"Oh, we'll *all* stay with him!" Jill leaned over and

hugged her father. He hugged her back with one surprisingly strong arm.

Daniel called soon thereafter, saying that Wilhelm had turned himself in. "Apparently," he said, "he had an encounter with a woman who administered HD-50, then gave him a Game Board and left him in Dupont Circle. He says he spent most of the day reexperiencing World War Two—from the point of view of other people."

"What a relief! I was imagining him still roaming around, filled with evil intent. Regarding the woman, I can only think of two possibilities."

"Well, don't mention them to me. His lawyer is here, and he looks hungry. I will be over later this evening. Is Whens okay?"

Jill looked over at Whens, asleep on a couch. "He's pretty worn out. Not hurt physically. We'll have to wait and see. Thank you so much, Daniel."

"Just doin' my job, ma'am."

Jill hung up and looked at her mother. "Did you, by any chance, meet a man named Wilhelm today?"

She grinned. "I am a teacher, remember? I showed him some of the latest advances in education."

That evening, she and Sam filled their children in on how those advances had happened, and what they had been doing since they disappeared.

Kind of, anyway.

Before he went to bed, Brian asked, "Dad, do you play the cornet?"

Sam smiled. "No. But Wink does."

The Reading
[*July 31*]

JILL WAS setting up folding chairs in the bookstore for Koslov's reading of Rosa's poems.

The trees in front of her store, between the sidewalk and the curb, rustled in the wind. Their leaves turned up silver. The darkening sky over Rosslyn presaged a storm, which, depending on when it happened, might be in time to cool off the store. Her patrons knew of her hatred of air-conditioning, and apparently didn't mind sweltering a bit for the privilege of perusing her latest choices. She had big ceiling fans, and if she kept the back door open, there was a nice breeze. She set a large copper umbrella holder next to the front door with one umbrella in it to suggest its use.

She pushed back some wheeled shelves to make more room, and asked Zane to open the first bottles of wine.

She'd gathered that Wink had probably been the mysterious man who had visited her hospital room. She and her father had both assumed he had died during the JFK assassination attempt, so Sam was infused with hope, thinking he was the man who accompanied Brian at the Gypsy Cat. They hadn't heard from him, though.

Zoe, Brian, Abbie, and Cindy arrived, and pitched in to help. Zoe had brought her violin. After reading Rosa's poems, and talking to Lev, she had written some music to back up the poems. She had been practicing, with Arabelle's help, in the ballroom. Brian's family was all moved in now, and it was working out very nicely. Sam had recovered well, and was enlarging his memoirs for Brian. Megan was gathering support for a start-up company that would produce HD-50 and preparing to submit it to the FDA, which would be a long process. When it cleared the FDA, she planned to sell it at just above cost, and was arranging to distribute it for free in many places.

The pod school in the woods clearing had grown quite unnoticed by any of the adults until lately, and was now mature, a neighborhood attraction for kids. Jill and Cindy visited it daily, just to bask in the wonder of it, to explore new additions, and to note any improvements they thought necessary. Q-Schools were appearing all over the world, to much enthusiasm, and in increasing number.

A week ago, Jill had invited Clarissa and, with Lev's help, the other people who had been a part of the clandestine circle, and many of their friends, to an open house night at the school. There, she dosed their drinks liberally with HD-50, left them to explore some interesting-looking metal boards, and did not feel one whit bad about it. There were more and more stories in the *Post* about schools opening in parts of the world where women and girls had been denied an education, or where children had been denied a full education, and of officials welcoming them with major policy changes. Jill strongly suspected an underground dissemination of HD-50.

She looked around. Everything was ready.

Lev arrived, with a fresh haircut, exuding the smell of Wolf cigarettes. He stood at the lectern going over his marked poems while greeting students, colleagues, and members of the poetry-reading public. Soon, there was only standing room. Jill sent Zane to the bar next door to try and borrow some chairs.

Zoe leaned over her violin case and removed her violin and bow, beginning her preparations as people wandered around with glasses of wine, chatting. Jill was surprised to see Zoe set up a music stand; she was sure she had the piece memorized. Arabelle, Daniel, Gerald, and Ron appeared; Arabelle sat next to Zoe while Daniel gave Jill a quick kiss and asked what needed to be done next.

She looked around. "Oh, I think everything's under control. Go ahead and sit down; I saved you the front row."

A sheet of newspaper skittered down M Street as the wind picked up. Distant thunder rumbled from the west. Jill stepped to the podium to introduce Lev.

"Most of you know Lev Koslov, who has translated the poems of Rosa Hadntz. Rosa, a medical doctor, perished in a concentration camp in early 1945. Dr. Koslov has also written a short biography, which appears at the back—" She stopped.

Eliani Hadntz and a wizened old man carrying a violin walked in the door. And—was that—

"Wink!" Bette and Sam rushed to embrace him as Lev said, "I would like to introduce you to Eliani Hadntz, Rosa's daughter, who has honored us with a surprise visit. I hope you will do this reading for us, Eliani."

Zoe's eyes were wide, and widened farther when Eliani winked at her.

Her long, curly hair was white, and she had not worn her red lipstick. She wore a long, multicolored skirt and a white blouse and was spare, almost thin. She looked around for a second, and then moved a low stepstool from behind the counter, stepped onto it, and smiled. "I need a little extra height." The audience laughed lightly with her; the ice was broken.

"My mother was, like myself, a medical doctor, but wrote poetry all her life. During her last year, she lived in Budapest, before an unanticipated Nazi crackdown captured her in its net. I, unfortunately, was not there at the time." Her voice was somber. "I was unable to help."

Zoe and the old man stationed themselves a few feet from Eliani. Wink, in full fedora regalia, extracted a cornet from the duffle bag he'd dropped by the door, and stood on the other side of Eliani. Jill had a glimpse of the wild spatter of colors on the sheet music Zoe set on the stand. Arabelle rose unobtrusively, stood behind and between Zoe and the old violinist, and the music commenced, low and haunting.

Eliani began to read, her deep, rich voice filled with pain and love:

ELIANI, 1944

i

my daughter, visiting me in Budapest,
brought a gypsy violinist
she rescued from the Nazis.

his music flowed
fluid as her long black hair
fluid as her mind in childhood.

she told me of her thoughts:
how the brain is a series of tree and root
linked in quantum chorus

singing with light and thought: how the roots of trees
    themselves
mirror their sunlit branches
partaking of dark minerals—

crystals, like our own memories—
while their leaves
devour the sun; how each of us

are mirrored
in some elsewhere,
still growing

while we, here in Pest, are changed to
sudden spears of light
that pierce the night sky

as bombs explode,
or when we fall in droves
like the Ukrainians,

twenty-four thousand in one day
into

one
large
grave

whose name is Europe.

ii

I bind wounds.
Set bones.
Cut skin in thin red lines.
Yank an arm and set the shoulder free;
Make them live;
Pronounce them dead.

My daughter draws; thinks; writes
in a back room
away from the surgery.

She seems younger now that her father has died
of a broken heart
when his own mother ceased writing from besieged
    St. Petersburg.

She helps sometimes
when I can't find a nurse
and says things like

"Mother, don't worry.
I am fixing everything.
there will be a better world."

To have her here,
In this world,
while war rages,
is like a light surrounding me.
She cuts gauze,
removes a bullet,
comforts a child without a leg, and without parents,

Her hands as practiced as mine
while the gypsy down the hallway plays unceasingly
driving me mad.

When she leaves,
I live only
for her return.

Jill was surprised at how Wink's cornet could wind so
solemnly through and punctuate so perfectly the war-
time milieu. Apparently, he could read Zoe's music. Arabelle turned a page.

Eliani continued. She read poems that pulsed with
deep happiness; poems of impatience; poems of depth
and intensity, poems which Jill regarded as the work of
a genius. Zoe's music skirled, gypsylike; gardens and
tranquil city streets, piney mountains, a clear pellucid
lake and a child: all were induced in their turn, floating
through Jill as if she were there, herself. The storm loosed
suddenly in a great silver burst. Rain bounced from the
pavement; thunder echoed long-ago, distant canons.
Eliani raised her voice a bit, and the spell was fully woven when she finally finished, half an hour later, to great
applause.

She nodded. The musicians stood still, their instruments at their sides.

Eliani Hadntz concluded, "I have been working for the
cessation of war my entire life, along with a wide circle of
colleagues, close friends, and my beloved husband, long
dead. I believe that we can move from the terrible waste,
pain, and tragedy of war, which I hope will someday be
seen as only a stage in the growth of humanity. I have let
go of many parts of myself in the process. And now I
have done the final letting go.

"Some of us have opened a peace center, on P Street,
and all of you are welcome to visit; I will leave information. Please thank our musicians, thank Dr. Koslov for
his masterful, perfect translation, which is a work of

love, and Jill Dance, for offering us this opportunity to be here tonight."

After a standing ovation, Hadntz and Koslov signed books, all of which sold immediately. After a few skirmishes among customers, Jill raised her hand and shouted, "I can have more by Thursday for whoever wants to order one."

"I will sign the others when they arrive," Hadntz promised. Jill looked at her, surprised. Hadntz smiled. "I am thinking of staying, at least for a while. I think your parents are too. We all need to catch our breath. It has been a long, long war."

The rain was over. Steam rose from the street, water dripped from the trees, and the sun emerged in one bright beam, turning street, trees, cars, and unheeding pedestrians, on their way to a restaurant or heading home from work, into moving, living gold.

Chapter the Last

THE GIRL was, perhaps, fourteen. She was tall and thin and almost purple, the color of a glowing, beautiful aubergine.

Her hair was cropped short, and zigzagged in a pattern that caught the soldier's eye, as he stood there in the center of the village with his machine gun trained upon the girl, her parents, her aunts and uncles and brothers and sisters—indeed, the whole village was before him and his cohorts, shaking, sobbing, and pleading.

Her movement, as she reached into the large, baggy pocket of her dress, was slow, almost dreamlike, and yet it was so swift that his eye could not really follow, nor could his finger pull the trigger nor his mouth open to utter the rote words of terror he had so often used before and which would make them fall down begging while he smiled.

He did not see what was in her hand when she pulled

it from her pocket. He supposed, in those very long seconds, that it would be a small pistol, useless in her situation. As they stood there, poised for the usual drill of rape the women, kill the men, subjugate the children—the same thing that had happened to him and his family three years ago, when he had begun his training as a killer—he did not have a very long time to remember what happened next.

It seemed to him that she drew forth moving pictures, which moved very swiftly indeed. And then as in the pictures, the entire village let forth a scream and rushed him and the other soldiers that were part of his band.

Instead of pulling the trigger, as he had done thousands of times before (although very few villagers had ever challenged them, believing to the last that they would be killed if they did so, which was true—but it was also true that most would die anyway), he felt in brief amazement his hands drop, as if he had been inflicted with a fast-working virus that rendered his muscles uncooperative. But no, it was his very mind that refused to fire, as he was rushed, pummeled, beaten with sticks and shovels, and very nearly killed.

As he lay on the ground in deep pain in front of the small concrete-block school, he saw children gather around him. They stared down with curiosity on their faces.

"Is he dead?" asked a boy. The soldier felt a vicious, hearty kick in his left side, and pain shot through him.

"Na," said the girl with the dress that had the deadly pocket. She knelt and looked into his eyes. "You want to know what happened, soldier boy?"

He made a strangled sound; he decided that blood must be pooling in his throat. It tasted like blood, thick and iron-tinged.

"When you were training, eh? With those video games? There was a fast sequence slipped in. A subliminal image. You saw it a thousand times. It is in the opening sequence. Too fast for you to realize you even saw it, eh? It is called

neural linguistic programming, a new and powerful kind of it, precise. It works on your brain, on your mirror neurons. Your mirror neurons cause you to imitate what you see others doing. At first, the imaging was not precise. Now it is. We can do things with it. Eh? You understand, boy-man?"

He tried to shake his head, no, but could not. She continued in her soft, inexorable voice, that voice that sounded like the voice of his dead sister, whom he had so loved. He had not heard a soft woman's voice in years. The only sounds women made now were pleading wails, sobs, whimpers, shrieks.

This girl's voice might be soft, yet it was somehow sharp and hard as a razor, drawing tracks of oozing pain through his brain. Maybe that, he thought, was what his mirror neurons were. Pain places, places that had locked down and shut, a series of doors closing, closing, closing, releasing him, he had thought, into manhood, which meant killing with no pity.

"So when we resist, you cannot kill us." Her dark eyes held very little. No contempt, no fear, no anger, no sense of vindication or revenge; not even satisfaction. They were pure, dark pools observing him. But she did speak a few words of hope. "You are lucky. You are still alive. These very angry people have killed all of your soldier brothers. If you survive, you will be sent to the UN rehabilitation center. Maybe you, like myself, can come back here as a teacher."

He looked a last question at her. She nodded. "Yes. I was like you. A child soldier. The UN saved me. And maybe they can save you. I don't know."

She paused for a moment, then said, "But I hope so."

Grace Note

ZOE STEPPED OUT of the door of Halcyon House, one hand in Grandpa Sam's, on her way to Arabelle's for a violin lesson, and stood on the porch looking out at the bright garden.

Things had changed. It was like she had had wings before, but they had been curled inside her. She had not even known about them.

Now, she was held aloft by colors, which were sounds. The thoughts and dreams of others had colors, and their colors tinged her wings and gave them strength. Her wings were even strong enough to hold aloft her parents, Bitsy, Abbie, and Whens, and even her Grandpa and Grandma. Even her new friend, Aunt Eliani. She felt their heavy past, but it supported her instead of pulling her down. It w̶̶̶̶̶̶̶̶̶̶̶̶̶̶̶̶̶̶̶̶̶̶̶̶̶̶̶̶w music that she could v̶̶̶̶̶̶̶̶̶̶̶̶̶̶̶̶̶̶̶̶̶̶̶̶̶̶ a few seconds, a few no̶̶̶̶̶̶̶̶̶̶̶̶̶̶̶̶̶̶

"Ready?" asked Sa̶̶̶̶̶̶̶̶̶̶̶̶

"I think everything̶̶̶̶̶̶̶̶̶̶̶̶̶̶̶̶̶̶̶̶̶̶̶̶̶̶

"I think you're righ̶̶̶̶̶̶̶̶̶̶̶̶̶̶̶̶

Also by Kathleen Ann Goonan

In War Times

THE NANOTECH QUARTET
Queen City Jazz
Mississippi Blues
Crescent City Rhapsody
Light Music

The Bones of Time

Praise for *This Shared Dream*

"A richly imagined tale of gypsies and jazz, Nazis and nanotechnology, war and assassination, and the Summer of Love. As elegant and complicated as the ever-changing timestreams that wind through it, *This Shared Dream* is a must-read in this or any world."
—Connie Willis

"A great adventure story, an engaging alternate history, characters the reader can really care about, and jazz. What more can you ask?" —*Analog*

"There are some beautiful turns of phrase and on more than one occasion the novel achieves that holy grail of utopian writing: it makes you stop and think about issues that you might otherwise have taken for granted. . . . *This Shared Dream* is an accomplished novel." —*Foundation: The International Review of Science Fiction*

"The urgent necessity for our species to master its worst impulses and take charge of its own destiny—a core tenet of the SF genre—has seldom been conveyed with such emotional and intellectual force." —*Barnes and Noble Review*

"A time-travel adventure novel with neurochemistry, quantum physics, and Maria Montessori at its heart. How cool is that? Pretty darn cool. This book is a compelling read for thinking people, and I totally recommend it." —*Eileen Gunn*

"A rare novel that combines a darkly realistic vision of history with a ⬚⬚⬚⬚⬚⬚ SF optimism about the flexibility of th⬚⬚⬚⬚⬚ —*Locus*

"*This Shared D⬚⬚⬚⬚⬚⬚⬚⬚⬚⬚⬚⬚⬚al, and provocative n⬚⬚⬚⬚⬚⬚⬚ —*...terzone*

D0818464